The Soldier's Wife

Married with a large family, Rachel Moore has spent all her life in the West Country. *The Soldier's Wife* is her first novel.

The Soldier's Wife

Rachel Moore

POCKET
BOOKS

LONDON • SYDNEY • NEW YORK • TORONTO

First published in Great Britain by Simon & Schuster, 2004
This edition first published by Pocket Books, 2004
An imprint of Simon & Schuster UK
A Viacom Company

1 3 5 7 9 10 8 6 4 2

Simon & Schuster UK Ltd
Africa House
64–78 Kingsway
London WC2B 6AH

www.simonsays.co.uk

Simon & Schuster Australia
Sydney

A CIP catalogue record for this book is available from
the British Library

ISBN 0 7434 8373 1

Typeset by SX Composing DTP, Rayleigh, Essex
Printed and bound in Great Britain by
Cox & Wyman Ltd, Reading, Berkshire

For good friends, old and new

Chapter 1

Saturday was as golden as only a Cornish day in summer could be. Over in Penzance the sun would be glinting and sparkling on the bluest of blue seas, and Carrie Pollard had to remind herself that she was a married woman as she resisted the urge to hop and skip along the village street, where the local children had chalked out hopscotch squares.

'Heard your man's coming home today, Carrie,' old Tom, the cobbler, called from his seat in front of his shop where he was working on his bootmaker's last.

The piquant smells of leather and heel ball teased her nostrils, homely and comforting and familiar, in contrast with the jittery feelings inside her.

'That's right, Mr Tom, we're expecting him home on the afternoon train from Bristol, all being well.'

She automatically crossed her fingers as she said it, even though there was no need anymore. The war was over, the troops were gradually coming home, the POWs had been liberated. For a moment she spared a thought for her friend Gwen, whose husband had been torpedoed, then listed as missing, presumed dead. In the end it had all turned out all right, though, and David had turned up like a bad penny. Only by then Gwen had had what some called a complete change of personality.

But for Carrie, nothing could dim this day, and two sets of parents had already planned the party for when Archie came marching home, as they kept saying. Just as if he had won the war single-handed . . .

She brushed aside her annoyance at knowing that she had to share this homecoming with her parents, and with Archie's too. It was natural for them all to want to welcome him and to put out the bunting and the big 'Welcome Home Archie' banner, but it would have been so wonderful to have had him all to herself.

If she'd had the gumption she would have done what Velma Gould had done, and arranged a special night for them both in an hotel as Velma had when Stan came home from the Front. Velma had had her own reasons for seeing Stan alone until she had told him her news, but she didn't have a family to be concerned with anyway.

Carrie shivered, glad that she didn't have the kind of secrets that other girls had. Glad that she had kept herself nice for when Archie came home. Even Shirley, with her chapel upbringing, had reacted in a way that had shocked them all when the Yanks came into town with their chocolates and their nylons and their sweet-talking ways.

But she wasn't going to think of any of them now. Later in the year there was going to be a big town dance for all their returning warriors, as the local newspaper called them, and they would all get together then and compare notes. Or not, as the case might be. Right now, all Carrie was going to think about was Archie coming home at last, and just how soon they could look for a place of their own.

They'd hardly had time to get to know one another properly as man and wife before he had joined up, and she dearly wanted them to begin married life properly in a prefab. The walls might be thin in those places, but at least they wouldn't have the thought of her mum and dad listening to every squeak of the bedsprings . . .

'I'm home, Mum,' she called out as she went indoors, hoping her mother would think her face was flushed on account of her running down Kellaway Terrace, and not through remembering how Archie could almost crush her to death with his powerfully muscled body and his vigorous lovemaking.

Her friends often joked that they wondered how she survived being married to such a he-man, her with her delicate bones, her big blue eyes and her smooth brown hair, so fragile-looking she could have passed for a ballet dancer, no mistake.

'Did you get the fish?' her mum asked, pushing such thoughts out of Carrie's mind at once. 'Mrs Thorley down the lane said there was a queue for it at the fishmonger's, and of course Archie's dad will frown on it, him and Archie being butchers, but I know Archie likes a nice bit of fish for his tea. We want to put on a bit of a spread for his folks tonight, and then decide who we're asking to the party next weekend. The weather's nice enough for folk to spill out into the garden, and we'll need to borrow some deck chairs from Archie's as well. Good thing he's so hefty. Your dad wouldn't want to carry them from round the Pollards' house.'

'I got the fish,' Carrie said once her mother had paused, while wondering, as always, how she could manage to go on for so long without drawing breath.

Anyone would think it was *her* husband coming home, she thought resentfully. Or *her* son. She wondered just what plans Archie's mum might be cooking up right now to celebrate Archie coming home. No doubt his dad would already have his job lined up at the butcher's shop again. She shuddered, having forgotten those nights when Archie came home still with the smell of blood about him, no matter how often he bathed and scrubbed his nails and changed his clothes.

'What's up with you now, girl? You should be over the moon and you look about as thrilled as ninepence.'

'How thrilled is that?' Carrie muttered, wishing she wouldn't talk so daft.

Edna Penney cocked her head on one side. 'You're not worried about the – well – the other side of things, are you, girl? I know Archie's been away for a long time, but he'll expect you to do your duty.'

Carrie felt a wild urge to laugh out loud. As befitted a butcher's boy, his duty was what Archie had been doing these past few years in the Royal Catering Corps, wasn't it? It was hardly the most heroic of jobs, and how he had come to be a POW from an army kitchen she still couldn't fathom. Anyway, she wasn't talking to her mother about 'the other side of things', which Edna would never refer to in words. What she meant was making love, and doing her duty seemed such a sad description of it.

Once tonight was over, Carrie thought mischievously, perhaps they should wave the Union Jack out of the bedroom window to prove that they had *done* it, which of course they would after all this time apart! With the thought came the unbidden image of every house in the town with a returning warrior in it having a flag hanging out the bedroom window, and she couldn't contain her laughter a minute longer.

'Well, I'm sure I don't remember saying anything to amuse you, miss,' her mother said crossly. 'I thought you took your wedding vows seriously, unlike some others in this town that I could mention, and why you still insist on being friends with them I can't think.'

'It's called loyalty, Mum, but please don't start that again,' Carrie pleaded. 'Let's just be glad the war's over at last and that things are looking up for all of us.'

Though perhaps not for Velma Gould, when Stan got to know what she intended . . . and as for Shirley and her blessed conscience, well, everybody said that what people didn't know couldn't hurt them . . . and Shirley was behaving like the blooming Virgin Mary, that's what, she thought piously, which started her giggling again. Anyway, perhaps Shirley should have been a Catholic, then she could have gone and confessed and forgotten all about it.

'I'm going upstairs to have a wash,' she went on, still thinking about her group of friends and not wanting to imagine the scene in that hotel room when Velma finally got up the courage to tell Stan she didn't want to be married to him anymore. Everybody would think her wicked for doing such a thing to a returning hero, but it was better to face him than to have sent him a Dear John letter. So she had no choice now, unless she was planning some great escape and never returning home at all – but it was a bit late for that. Velma swore she no longer loved Stan, so she had to tell him she wanted a divorce and that was that.

Carrie's mother always said that war broke people's hearts in more ways than one. She went even more moral when the suspicions broke about Gwen and her affairs, saying that you made your bed and you had to lie in it. Gwen had done that all right, and even though she had been away in Penzance most of the time, there wasn't much about their own that Penhallow folk didn't know, or suspect.

Once she had had a good strip-down in the tiny bathroom her dad had installed, and liberally splashed cologne under her armpits, Carrie went into the bedroom that had been hers since she was born. Since her wedding day two years ago when she was just twenty years old, she had slept alone in it almost all that time, but from tonight she would be sharing it with Archie again.

She glanced at the old-fashioned double bed with the squeaky springs, and shivered. She loved him, of course she did, and her letters had been full of hope and optimism and longing for the day they would be together again. But two years was a long time, and they would be meeting almost as strangers. She hoped Archie would be considerate and not rush things. She hoped his eagerness wouldn't turn him into an animal . . .

She retracted such bad thoughts at once. Archie would naturally want to show her how much he loved her and missed her, just as she did him. It was just that sometimes, without the wedding photos to remind her, she couldn't always remember his face too clearly. And that was so disloyal she had never dared mention it to anyone, not even her closest friends. It was weird how the four of them had become so close, considering the difference in their ages, but meeting once a week at the knitting circle for soldiers', sailors' and airmen's comforts that all the young wives were encouraged to go to had firmly established their friendship.

Carrie dressed quickly in a summer frock of blues and greens in readiness for meeting Archie at Penzance railway station – he liked her in fresh colours – and she brushed her brown hair until it hung straight and gleaming on her shoulders. As a final gesture to his homecoming, she laid her broderie anglaise nightie on her pillow, and on the other she put a pair of his striped pyjamas that she had freshly washed and ironed. It symbolised the fact that two people shared this bedroom from now on.

Her heart was thumping as she went back to where

her mother was buttering bread, though it was still hours until tea-time. Edna was a stickler for getting things ready in advance, especially when Archie's parents were coming round. And how they were all going to fit into this cramped house for a party next weekend heaven knew, but when her mother got an idea in her head her dad always said it was wisest not to argue with her.

'That bread will go dry,' Carrie observed, for want of something to say. Her hands felt clammy inside her cotton gloves as her mother looked her over.

'No it won't. I'll put my casserole dish over the top of it. I must say you look a picture, Carrie, and Archie will be proud to have you to come home to.'

If there was the slightest sniff as she said it, Carrie ignored it. The fact was that Edna had never thought a butcher's boy was a good enough match for Carrie, the daughter of a town councillor, with brains enough for working in a library before the war, and book-keeping for the council and organizing the comings and goings of the evacuee kids in the surrounding area ever since.

Not that it made any odds, of course. Delicate though Carrie might look, she had a core of steel running through her, and what she wanted she usually got. And she had wanted Archie Pollard the minute she'd set eyes on him when they were catching tiddlers in a stream and he'd hauled her out of a mud pool. She was six and he was ten, and that evening she had solemnly told her parents that she was going to marry him. They had laughed at her nonsense, but as her blue eyes had widened into that unblinking and determined gaze they knew so well, they should have realized that one day she had every intention of doing exactly that.

Despite her excitement at the thought of this special day, Carrie couldn't help wondering how much his experiences would have changed Archie. He had been such a cheeky, happy-go-lucky boy when they were children, but then there had been that awful incident with a gang of older boys, who had taken his cheek for insults.

Archie hadn't meant anything by it, and anyone who knew him would have known that. But the others didn't know him well, and they had waited for him one afternoon after school and marched him off to one of the old tin mines on the moors. They had tied his hands behind his back, blindfolded him and lowered him down inside the mine until he had begged for mercy, but, in the silence and darkness, he had finally realized he was alone. They'd left him for a long while before they returned and hauled him up, choking and crying and in a state of total panic.

They had taunted him then for being a big baby and a coward, but it hadn't been cowardice. It had been a genuine and logical fear of being left alone in the dark, with no means of getting out if they had left him to rot. The experience had changed an impressionable and imaginative child, and Carrie knew that being in a POW camp for two years must have changed him even more, his having always been haunted by thoughts of being incarcerated.

It wasn't something Archie was proud of, and nor had he told many people of his ordeal at the time. But Carrie, who was practically his shadow by then, knew by instinct what was troubling him, and eventually he had blurted it all out to her.

'You're not to tell anyone else,' he had said fiercely, his eyes dark with the painful memories. 'Promise me now, Carrie.'

'Of course I won't,' she had said, childishly honoured that he had trusted her with his secret fears. 'You know I won't. It's a bond between us, Archie.'

That's all right then,' he had said roughly, and, young as she was, she had known how much it had cost him to tell her. She had also known then just how special she was to him.

The train steamed and snorted into the station at Penzance, finally giving up its momentum in a hiss of smoke, and as the doors opened it began to disgorge its passengers. Some were ordinary shoppers, a few were daytrippers, taking advantage of this late-summer day, and some, like Archie, were soldiers returning home from the war, finally released from captivity as he was, but whole and alive. She was thankful for that. There were many who had returned without limbs, blinded or burned, or scarred beyond belief.

He had been spared that, thank God, for she knew he couldn't have borne it. Despite the fact that he could hack a carcass of meat in half with one blow, and never minded the sight of blood, he wasn't good with weakness in himself.

She couldn't see him at first, even though he was tall and dark-haired, and brawny as befitted his butcher's trade. Yet those same arms could be tender when they held her, and it was that sweet memory she had kept in her heart all this time.

'Carrie. Carrie, love.'

Hearing his voice right behind her, she whirled around, having been searching the platform in the wrong direction. She registered instantly that he looked older and harder, and a good deal thinner – which she should have expected when he had been incarcerated for so long. But before she could register anything else, she was swept up in his arms, and he was crushing her to him in the old familiar way, his mouth finding hers in a kiss that took her breath away.

Her straw hat fell off her head, and she grabbed it wildly, laughing and crying as a flurry of wind caught it and sent it dancing down the platform. Someone rescued it and brought it back to her while she was still trying to familiarize herself with this stranger who was her husband.

'You could have left the damn thing,' he said accusingly, not even thanking the man who had rescued it.

'What, when I wore it especially for you!' she teased, her heart thumping.

'I don't care about a blooming hat. All I care about is you. I want to look at you, and never stop looking at you.'

He grabbed her to him again, forcing her head back and kissing her so hard it bruised her lips, and she twisted her head slightly away from him, still clutching at the ribbons on her hat.

'Archie! Everybody's watching!'

She was embarrassed at such a show of passion on a public railway station. People did it all the time in wartime, and would certainly continue to do so when their boys came home, but this was a little too much ... too soon ... didn't he realize, as she did, that they had to get to know one another all over again? They couldn't just pick up the pieces after being apart for almost all of the two years they had been married. Apart from the honeymoon, they had hardly been married at all.

'You're right. Let's get home where we can be alone. I want you all to myself so I hope your parents have done the decent thing and arranged to go to the flicks or something this evening.'

'Oh, Archie, no they haven't.'

She saw his face darken. 'Christ, don't tell me there's a reception waiting for me, because I can't stand all that. We've got a lot of catching up to do, Carrie, and I've been thinking about this day for long enough, and especially this night.'

His fingers dug into her arm as they hurried out of the station. The smell of his khaki uniform was slightly off-putting, a mixture of damp wool and sweat, but he had been travelling for a long time, she reminded herself, and he clearly hadn't wanted to wear his demob suit. People gave more respect to men in uniform than those in ordinary civvies. It was a strange old world now.

She spoke quickly, before she lost her nerve, knowing that his face would darken even more as soon as she told him what was planned.

'My mother's preparing a special fish tea for you, and your parents have been invited. We all want to welcome you home, Archie, and it really doesn't matter that we have to wait a little while longer to be properly alone. We've got the rest of our lives to be together now, haven't we?'

The shiver than ran through her then caught her by surprise. It was excitement, of course, but it was something else too. It was nerves and apprehension, and the hope that Archie was going to take his time and not overpower her as he had done on their honeymoon, bruising her and hurting her. She was surprised to have forgotten that aspect of his love-making until that very minute. She knew it was because he loved her so much, but it was a bit scary too.

'Come on, or we'll miss the afternoon bus,' she added quickly.

'I think a returning hero needs better transport than a ruddy bus,' Archie snapped. 'We'll take a taxi and hang the expense.'

Carrie gaped. His father had laughingly suggested meeting him in the butcher's van, but she wasn't having any of that. There was nothing wrong with the bus, but it evidently wasn't good enough for Archie, and she meekly agreed, even though being meek wasn't one of her strong points. She had a fiery enough temper when she was roused, which Archie had always found endearingly funny in the past. He stamped his feet impatiently outside the station as a taxi crawled to a stop beside them, and she began to wonder if he would find it quite so funny now.

She knew the adjusting would take time. You couldn't expect any of them to come home after months or years away and be exactly the same as before. Even these last few months had been frustrating for him, waiting to be sent home when the war had finished in Europe and the POWs had been freed. Even then there had been weeks in some kind of hospital that he never mentioned, for what was called a recuperation period. Not that he'd been ill, he'd written to her in frustration, but it was meant to get the POWs to readjust to civvy life, as if getting home wouldn't have done that. But now that it was all over in Japan too, thanks to Hiroshima and that terrible atom bomb, they could all settle down again.

Carrie knew it was inevitable that people would have changed through being apart. She wasn't the same young girl that Archie had married in St Jude's, the little stone church in the centre of Penhallow. She was two years older than the last time she had seen Archie, and even if the war hadn't touched Cornwall in the way it had touched other places, they had still done their bit in various ways.

They had had no air raids, no bombs, no scuttling to the shelters or having to sleep in the underground like the people in London and other cities had done, all herded together like sheep – and stinking like them too, her dad had often remarked. Just as if it mattered when the alternative was being blown to bits by a Jerry bomb!

'Cat got your tongue now, then?' Archie said, when she had been silent for several minutes.

'No. I was just thinking, that's all.'

He laughed shortly. 'You don't want to do too much of that. It's bad for the brain. Anyway, now I'm back, you don't have to think anymore. You can give up that job of yours now I'm here to look after you. The evacuee kids will all be going home anyway, if they haven't gone already.'

'They have, at least those who've still got homes to go to,' Carrie began, but her words were lost as Archie bundled her inside the taxi and threw himself down beside her after giving the address to the driver.

He sat back with a satisfied smile on his face. 'This is the life. And it'll be even better to get between proper sheets again tonight, I can tell you.'

Carrie blushed, seeing the driver's eyes in the mirror ahead of them. It wasn't hard to see what he was thinking.

'Just demobbed, mate?' he said chattily. 'How was it?'

Carrie felt Archie stiffen beside her. She leaned forward, forestalling the blistering words she guessed would be welling up. Archie had never had much patience for answering the obvious.

'We don't really want to talk about it, thanks,' she said firmly.

'You're right there,' Archie snapped. 'And the sooner I get out of this damn uniform, the better. I knew the folks would like to see me in it one more time, but right now it's making me itch like the devil, as if it was riddled with fleas. It has been from time to time, mind,' he added, almost lasciviously.

This was not the kind of conversation Carrie had dreamed about when he came home. All this talk of fleas was hardly romantic . . .

As the taxi trundled on, Carrie remembered the times when Archie had been as romantic as any girl could want. The glorious summer morning he had proposed to her for the first time was all that Hollywood could ever have dreamed up. They were up on the moors looking for mushrooms, and he was on his knees, ignoring the dew on his trousers, and trying to tie a ring of grass around her finger. She had laughed into his face, her eyes dancing with happiness because he looked so absurd.

'Get up, you idiot,' she teased him. 'What do you think you're doing?'

'I'm proposing to you,' he said, frowning, 'Or I would be if this blessed grass didn't keep on breaking.'

'What? Proposing like asking me to marry you?' she said, still teasing, because she didn't think he could be serious when she was still only twelve years old, and he was then a lofty sixteen.

'What else do chaps mean when they propose to a girl? Oh, I know we're far too young, and you're hardly out of nappies—'

'Charming!' she said, finding it hard to breathe now, because he suddenly looked *really* serious.

'But I have to ask you now, before you become so

beautiful that some other chap will come along and steal you away from me,' he said awkwardly, taking her completely by surprise, because she'd never thought of him as so poetic, and the special understanding between them had never been put into words before.

To Carrie it was just magical. Magical words, said in a magical way, in their own magical place . . .

'Nobody will ever steal me away, Archie, not from you.'

He laughed then, breaking the spell. 'So the next time I ask you, with a proper ring, you'll think about saying yes, will you? When you're all grown up, I mean.'

'I'm all grown up now, inside,' she said softly. 'And of course I'll say yes.'

'You'd better keep this daft old ring then, to remind you of your promise,' he said, kissing the piece of grass wrapped around her finger, and making her go all soft and giggly inside.

She'd kept it until it crumpled and fell apart, but on the morning after their wedding, long after he had put the real thing on her finger and they had made love for the very first time, he did something that touched her beyond words.

He produced a new piece of grass from his wallet and tied it around the brand new gold ring, showing that he remembered too. It was silly and sweet, but oh yes, Archie was an old romantic inside, even if he didn't always show it, and she knew he had always loved her as much as she loved him.

*

She groaned, remembering the welcoming committee as the taxi turned into Kellaway Terrace. Pollard's butcher's van was parked outside their house. Archie's parents were already there.

'This the one with all the bunting and flags outside?' the taxi driver asked.

'Ten out of ten, chap,' Archie said sarcastically.

The front door of number 19 burst open before he and Carrie could reach it. In seconds Archie was swamped by hugs and kisses and handshakes, but instead of resenting it all as Carrie had feared, he suddenly seemed to enjoy the attention. However, as soon as they were inside he announced that he was going to have a wash and change his clothes, and then he'd be down for tea.

'I need my wife to remind me where everything is,' he commented. 'We'll see you all in a little while.'

Carrie smothered a nervous giggle, unsure if there was a double meaning in his words. And even more unsure how she was going to stop her heart from hammering in her chest as he grabbed her hand and pulled her towards the stairs.

Her mother's face was a mixture of outrage and embarrassment, but then she went off into the kitchen fussing about putting the kettle on, as if to say that whatever went on upstairs it was a married couple's business, and nothing to do with her. Mrs Pollard joined her with offers of help and the men started talking loudly about the downfall of the Japanese and debating whether Clement Attlee was going to make a better job of running the country than old Winston had done.

In their bedroom Archie swung Carrie round and round before bouncing up and down on the double bed and pulling her down beside him.

'That'll teach them to think I just came home for my tea, won't it?'

'You're wicked,' she said, laughing. 'But we can't stay up here for long, Archie, we really can't. They've gone to a lot of trouble, and they all want to see you. They're so glad that you've come home safe.'

He was suddenly serious. 'I know that, but I needed these few minutes alone with you in our bedroom, knowing I no longer have to pinch myself to know that it's really over, or wake up in a cold sweat, wondering what tomorrow will bring. I can hardly believe that I shall be sleeping in my own bed tonight with my wife beside me instead of a raving mass of strangers all going out of their minds.'

Carrie caught her breath. There was a note in his voice that she had never heard before. It was as intense and resonant as ever, but there was an underlying fearfulness too. He might be here beside her, but the nightmare of the past two years still wasn't over. She folded her arms around him.

'Tonight and always,' she said softly, kissing the roughness of his unshaven face, and feeling the passion rise in him immediately. She pushed him away.

'Archie, go and have that wash and change your clothes and then let's go downstairs. The sooner we do so, the sooner the welcome party will be over.'

'Sensible as always,' he said. 'All right, leave me to it. I shan't be long.'

One last kiss, and then she fled back downstairs, her cheeks flaming, but knowing their relatives would acknowledge that they hadn't been away long enough for any shenanigans.

The real reunion would be later, she thought, the shivering excitement returning, and she prayed that her parents in the adjoining bedroom would be discreet enough to close their ears to it.

By the time Archie reappeared downstairs the tea was ready. Rations permitting, Carrie knew her mum had made a real effort, and even the finicky Mrs Pollard wouldn't be able to find fault with anything. Carrie smiled at Archie as she took her seat beside him at the table. He was newly shaved and wearing a comfortable pair of old flannel trousers, a tidy white shirt and tie and the Fair Isle pullover Carrie had knitted for him. He looked more like his old self again, even though the clothes were looser-fitting now than they had been.

Even more now, she was looking forward eagerly to the time when they would be able to rent one of the little prefabs that were being built on the edge of the town, and for which she had already put their names down on the housing list in Penzance. It was to be her big surprise for Archie.

Chapter 2

Velma Gould gazed out of the hotel lounge window overlooking the wide expanse of St Ives Bay. As a child, she had come here every summer with her parents and two younger brothers. People never ventured far from home for holidays, and although it was only a few miles from Penhallow, for Velma's family it was like entering an enchanted world of narrow, maze-like streets and breathtaking beaches.

They were idyllic days, with the smell of the sea in their nostrils, the frantic games of dodging the swooping seagulls, and listening to the old fishermen lounging by the quay and spinning wild yarns about their day's catch. Days when finding a pearly shell or an oddly shaped pebble, or taking a screaming dash, hand-in-hand into the waves, could cause such excitement. Childish days that seemed destined to go on for ever, and were so long ago now. Their parents had wanted to give them the best childhood, and so they had, the best of everything.

And now she was no longer a child, the parents had gone, and the little brothers had both been killed in

France. At thirty-five, there were already a few white hairs in Velma's abundant curls that Stan had once loved to ruffle. Still might, if she gave him half a chance.

She turned away from the window with a sigh, not wanting to see any new families enjoying themselves the way hers had once done. She was what generous people called a handsome woman, which to her honest assessment meant that she had an angular jaw and a square, determined chin.

She was mature enough now to know what she wanted out of life – and unfortunately it was no longer Stan. Sometimes she wondered sadly if it ever had been Stan.

For a moment she thought of the close friendships she had made during the last few years. Especially Carrie Pollard, poised on the brink of her wonderful new life with her returning POW husband, and full of the same kind of hopes and dreams as she herself had once had. She thought of fluffy Shirley, still trying to find a way to deal with her conscience before her young man came home. And Gwen . . . oh well, Gwen would be all right, she thought with certainty, providing the town gossips didn't drop their little bits of poison.

They all had new lives to sort out, and hers was the most pressing. She couldn't let her farce of a marriage go on a moment longer than it had to, and before Stan got the mistaken idea that she wanted to settle down into the boredom of being an army wife, he had to know.

He had promised to be here by six o'clock, and the orange glow of the sun was already low in the sky now, throwing a translucent sheen over the incoming waves of the sea. It was so beautiful here, so perfect for a romantic reunion . . .

She saw him then, striding through the gardens of the hotel, handsome, prematurely greying at forty, which only made him look more distinguished, his soldierly upright stance in his uniform giving him an air of authority. She had loved that once. Loved walking beside him, knowing that heads turned whenever he entered a room.

He caught sight of her and raised his hand in greeting. He looked far too elegant to have been driving tanks in the desert, she thought incongruously.

'Velma, it's good to see you,' he said when he entered the hotel lounge, with its sprinkling of other guests glancing his way, as she had known they would. He was always formal in public, and now he merely pressed her hands and gave her the briefest kiss on the cheek, just as if this was a business meeting, and not one of the most important meetings of their lives. But he didn't know that yet, of course.

'Where's your luggage?' she said inanely. 'Haven't you come straight from the station?'

While here she was, with her small suitcase beside her, feeling like a refugee, still flustered from the bus journey to this anonymous meeting place – which she now knew she was mad to have chosen, and which was not anonymous at all! This seaside haven held too many lovely memories of days past, when what she was about to do would ruin any chance of their future. And Stan would almost certainly have got the wrong idea about it. Why on earth hadn't she thought of that!

'I managed to get an earlier train from Portsmouth and got here last night,' Stan said easily. 'Thought I'd take the chance to look around the old place before you got here.'

'I see. Good idea.' God, this conversation was so inane!

He could have come straight home, she thought indignantly, surprising her as he would have done in the early days of their marriage. Sweeping her off her feet and delighting her by a rare spontaneity . . . but as she realized she was being totally dog-in-the manger now, she tried to be reasonable.

They didn't have a telephone so he couldn't have let her know he had arrived at the hotel early. Even now, nobody relished the sight of a telegraph boy on his red bicycle stopping outside the house. But this was going all wrong. Velma had intended to take the initiative, and now she supposed Stan had already put his luggage in the double bedroom she had booked for them. It would have looked very odd if she hadn't, even though she'd had the foresight to ask for single beds, and had already planned to tell him it was the only room the hotel had available.

'Do you want some tea or shall we get you unpacked?' Stan was saying.

She had forgotten how masterful he could be. Taking over, when she had been doing just that for the last four years when she became a bus conductress.

From being rather repressed and introverted after the deaths of her parents and then her brothers, and clinging to this man for love and support, she had gradually discovered she had an easy repartee with passengers, and she had also welcomed the companionship of the wartime knitting circle with open arms.

'I don't want tea,' she said abruptly. 'I want to talk to you, Stan.'

They hadn't even kissed properly. There was none of the rapture that other husbands and wives would have found on being reunited after so long. In their case, there had been a few home leaves, so it hadn't been a war-long parting, but those brief visits had been more traumatic than happy, with her juggling her hours on the buses, and Stan practically looking over his shoulder and clearly wishing he was back in the desert being a hero. Velma bit her lip knowing she was being unfair. He *was* a hero in the town's eyes, serving with Monty as a Desert Rat. They were all heroes.

'Did I tell you there's going to be a big dance in Penzance at the end of October for all the returning servicemen and their families?' she said, as they walked up the stairs together, Stan carrying her small suitcase. 'I want you to meet my friends, Stan, my very good friends. I've mentioned them to you in my letters; we've all supported one another in so many ways.'

She spoke quickly, nervously, almost exaggerating the part that Carrie and Gwen and Shirley had played in her life for the past few years. But would Stan even be there at the end of October? Would he want to stay once she had told him her news? Wasn't the whole idea of being divorced to part company immediately? But you couldn't wipe out ten years of marriage just like that.

There were things to be discussed, to be shared and divided . . . and she knew, with a rush of pain that had been absent for years, that if there had been children this situation would never have arisen at all.

She thought particularly of Shirley then, and thanked God on her friend's account that the affair with her GI hadn't resulted in something she simply wouldn't have been able to handle. Hank was a charmer, the way all the Yanks were, so polite with their 'sirs' and 'ma'ams' whenever they spoke to you, and their promises of a new life in America as a war bride and the tantalizing thoughts of visiting Hollywood and meeting all those glamorous film stars.

It seemed like a different planet, all milk and honey, and Shirley was no different from lots of other girls who had believed it all.

'You're very quiet, darling,' Stan said.

She jerked her thoughts back to today. He was smiling that half-smile that said he knew she had something on her mind, and was prepared to wait patiently until she told him what it was. That was his trouble, she thought in sudden frustration, his nature was always to be patient, which made him a good soldier, and his occasional spontaneous gesture had been like a breath of fresh air to be cherished. So different from herself, who had wanted everything tomorrow. She had wanted children. She was only thirty-five, and she could have them now, providing she stayed married to Stan. And providing he thought this brave new world was the right one in which to bring them up.

She hardened her heart. Let Carrie Pollard and her butcher's boy do the procreating. They were the ones who were madly in love, while all that was left for her and Stan was fondness and tolerance, and it wasn't enough. It definitely wasn't enough.

When they reached the hotel bedroom her eyes widened at the sight of the double bed. This wasn't what she had arranged . . .

'They'd given us a room with single beds until I persuaded them to change it for this one. It's surprising what a uniform will do these days,' Stan said.

He held out his arms, and she went into them numbly.

'So!' Archie said, when his parents had finally gone home. Edna was in the kitchen doing the washing-up, and Walter, Carrie's dad, was reading the evening paper with half an ear on the news bulletin on the wireless. And she and Archie had at last gone upstairs and closed the bedroom door.

'So?' Carrie repeated, resisting the urge to giggle as Archie discarded his grey flannels and pranced around the bedroom in his shirt and Fair Isle pullover, trying to tear off his socks without actually falling over.

By now she was sitting up in bed, as pure as an angel in her virginal white broderie anglaise nightie, trying not to notice how rapidly her heart was beating. They were married, so it was right and proper for them to share a bedroom, but they had only done *it* so few times, and she had once heard some coarse factory girls say that if you didn't use it enough, it would heal up.

Not having much idea of the workings of her own body, because nice girls didn't investigate what went on down below, Carrie hadn't even wanted to think about such a thing. But she was thinking about it now. Supposing it didn't work, after all this time? Supposing she really had healed up . . .

Archie pulled the Fair Isle pullover and shirt off in one go, and then his vest. She didn't look. She was too modest to look. It wasn't what you did, anyway. You turned out the light and you fumbled about a bit . . .

'You can take that thing off for a start, sweetheart,' she heard him say, a grin in his voice, and the next minute he was in bed beside her, tugging the cotton fabric over her head so that she was briefly enveloped in it.

She could hardly breathe as she felt his hands roaming over her breasts, and then she was aware of the nightie being tossed to the floor, and of his impatient hands moving lower. She closed her eyes, praying that everything would be all right. It was a husband's right to do this, and hers to enjoy it, regardless of the old-fashioned idea that women just had to lie back and think of England.

At the thought, she unconsciously relaxed her tense muscles, and Archie's fingers found their goal at once. And it was all right, she thought jubilantly! She felt the dampness there, and she knew she hadn't healed up at all. She was going to be a proper wife to Archie. While she was still relishing the fact, he was inside her, without waiting to know if she was ready or not, thrusting and gasping as if his life depended on it, spurting into her in moments, until he lay panting alongside her.

He finally spoke. 'Well, that was worth coming home for, wasn't it, girl? There'll be plenty more from now on while we make up for lost time. Here, put this on before you catch cold, while I find my cigarettes.'

He was out of bed at once, throwing her nightie back at her, and struggling into the striped pyjamas that she had carefully washed and ironed, which now resembled dishrags. When she had recovered her nightie she snapped off the light quickly, her face even hotter as she realized they hadn't even done it in the dark.

Archie was standing by the window now, the red glow of his cigarette the only light in the room. Her mother forbade smoking in bedrooms, she thought incongruously, and for a perverse moment she hoped Edna would smell the evidence and berate Archie soundly in the morning.

She was totally bewildered. She had wanted this night to be so loving, so romantic, a revival and gentle reinforcement of the love she had had for Archie for all these years, and instead it had all been over so quickly, the way it had on her honeymoon. Then, she had put it down to Archie's eagerness, and perhaps she should give him the benefit of the doubt now, since they had been apart for so long.

But supposing it was always going to be like this, leaving her sore, her inner thighs bruised where he had dug his fingers into them, leaving her feeling so unfulfilled? Carrie felt like weeping.

She awoke with a start, wondering what the noise was; wondering why the bed was shaking as if some demon had got hold of it and was thrashing it to pieces. Then she realized it was Archie thrashing about, and she was in danger of being caught a blow from those flailing arms. His body was bathed in sweat inside the striped pyjamas, so much so that she was dampened by it too. He was half muttering, half shouting, caught up in whatever nightmare gripped him, and she had a horror of him not only waking up the whole house, but the whole of Kellaway Terrace too.

She shook his arm, whispering his name in a low, urgent voice, and he was awake in a second, jerking away from her.

'Get away from me, you bastard,' he snarled. 'Come any nearer and you'll get a knife in your ribs.'

'Archie, it's me!' Carrie went on more urgently, terrified at such fury. 'It's me, Archie. It's Carrie, your wife. You're home, darling. You're home with me.'

Snapping on the bedside lamp that had been one of their wedding presents, she leaned up on one elbow and looked down at him. He was still lying there, his body stiff and taut, his eyes unfocused and seemingly somewhere else. He *was* somewhere else, Carrie thought, in spirit anyway. He may have returned physically, but a part of him was still back there in that POW camp, reliving whatever horrors he had endured. He seemed oblivious to her right now.

She slipped out of bed and hurriedly changed her nightie for a dry one. She knew she had to get him out of bed and make him change too. He would catch his death of cold if he lay in those damp pyjamas for the rest of the night.

She crept out of the room to fetch a damp flannel and towel from the bathroom, meaning to sponge him down in an effort to bring him back to sanity. She felt desperately sorry for him. Then she groaned as her mother's portly figure emerged from the other bedroom, swathed in a voluminous dressing-gown, her hair a tortured mass of metal curlers.

'What on earth's going on, Carrie? Is Archie having some kind of fit? If he had too much to drink last night, then it's your duty to curb him in future. Your father needs his rest and we can't be putting up with all this noise.'

The thoughtlessness of her words took Carrie's breath away, and her temper flared in an instant.

'Mum, he's sick,' she hissed. 'He's been through a horrible time, and he can't get over it in a moment. It might even have been that bit of fish you cooked for him that's given him nightmares,' she added.

'Well, if that's all the thanks I get I'm sure I shan't

bother again!' Edna turned on her heel and flounced back into her bedroom, banging the door shut.

Carrie's anger died just as quickly as it had come, and she was aware that she was trembling. She had been goaded into saying that bit about the fish, and now she was ashamed of it, knowing she would have to apologize in the morning.

But that was unimportant for the moment. She went into the bathroom for the flannel and towel and returned to where Archie was sitting up in bed now, resting his head on his knees with his arms tightly clasped around them. He looked young and vulnerable, like a small boy who'd had one of those bad dreams that small boys have, like being caught pinching apples from a neighbour's orchard, or catching his new trousers on a nail and knowing he'd get a cuff around the ear from his father because of it.

He looked the way he had looked when she fell in love with him, when she was six and he was ten. And she rushed across the bedroom and put her arms around him.

'Oh, Archie, was it an awful dream?' she whispered.

He didn't respond for a moment, and when he did, it was to push her away.

'It was nothing. It comes and goes so you'll have to get used to it. But I don't want to talk about it, do you hear? I don't want anybody to talk about it.'

His voice was full of frustrated rage and a sense of shame. For all his self-confidence and his brawny physique, which was not quite so brawny now, he hated anyone to see weakness in him. In particular he had never wanted Carrie to witness the result of the recurring dreams. He had thought they were over. It was the reason he had spent all those weeks in that bloody hospital, to have the treatments that were supposed to wipe the slate clean – for his mind to be wiped clean – but there was no medicine to eradicate the memories of the brutality meted out by their captors – or the way that even trusted comrades could turn into animals for the sake of an extra ration or two, or to ingratiate themselves with their warders.

He never intended Carrie to know about any of it, and the fact that she was now aware of the weakness that he couldn't hide made him lash out at her. She reeled back in shock at his vicious words.

'I only want to help you, Archie. I've brought you a flannel and towel, and I'll find you some clean pyjamas,' she said, turning away in distress, and wondering how often this was going to happen. It surely wouldn't be a nightly occurrence. If it was, she just couldn't bear it.

'Let's forget it, then,' he said, slightly less aggressive. 'Find me those pyjamas and let's get back to sleep or it'll be morning before we know it.'

He didn't bother drying himself. He quickly changed his pyjamas and turned his back on her in the bed. The sheets were uncomfortably damp, but she didn't dare suggest remaking the bed. She merely edged as far away from him as possible, torn between wanting to put her arms around him and snuggle into him, and keeping as much distance between them as she could until he was his normal self again. It wasn't the homecoming she had expected, and as well as her pity for the strong lover Archie used to be, she felt a huge sense of let-down for herself.

In the morning Edna was frosty as she slapped the teapot on the table, poured out four cups of tea and put a plate of toast in the middle with a jar of her homemade plum jam. Carrie's father hadn't yet come downstairs and neither had Archie, but that didn't stop the morning ritual of the tea being poured out until people deigned to come to the table.

'I hope we're not going to get a repeat of that nonsense in the middle of the night, Carrie,' she said sharply.

Carrie was tempted to ask which nonsense she meant – the nonsense when she and Archie had made love and got the bed-springs creaking joyfully, however briefly, or the other nonsense, when the bed had shaken fit to break the springs altogether. Maybe her mother thought they had repeated the first exercise, and the thought was embarrassing enough to make Carrie blush.

'I told you, Mum, Archie was sick. He had an awful nightmare, and you're not to mention it to him. Dad wouldn't have heard it anyway. You always say it would take an earthquake to wake him.'

She glared at her mother, daring her to say otherwise as she heard Archie coming downstairs.

''Morning all,' he said cheerfully, just as if nothing untoward had ever happened.

34

'Good morning, Archie,' Edna replied. 'Are you coming to church with us?'

He shook his head. 'I'm going to see my folks. I'm sure Dad will want me back at the shop tomorrow, so I need to make arrangements.'

Carrie looked at him in shock. 'You surely don't need to start so soon, and you always came to church with us before.'

'That was before I was taken prisoner and when I believed in all that stuff,' he said, with an edge to his voice that told her it would be wise not to argue with him. Edna wasn't so reticent.

'That's blasphemy, Archie, and I'll not have such talk in this house, returning hero or not. You'll apologize to the Lord at once.'

He went on calmly putting a scrape of margarine on his toast before being generous with the jam. 'I can't apologize to the Lord because I don't believe anybody's listening. But I'll keep my thoughts to myself in future, if it upsets you.'

'I should just think it does!' Edna said, outraged. 'I never heard of such a thing, and I'm sure your mother would be horrified to hear such talk.'

'Well, she doesn't have to, and neither do you, Edna.'

Carrie felt her heart begin to pound. These two had often had friendly spats, and it hadn't meant a thing, but this was different. Edna's faith was the one area where she wouldn't compromise, and Archie had done just about the worst thing he could. Thankfully, Walter came downstairs then, unaware of the small fracas, and everyone began talking at once to cover the moment.

'I thought we could go for a walk this afternoon, Archie,' Carrie said quickly. 'You'll appreciate the fresh air, I'm sure.'

She hoped her words wouldn't remind him of how long he had been incarcerated. Or how it had all come about. She wondered if she would ever know, and in his present uneven mood she was certainly not going to ask him.

'Suits me all right,' he said. 'So I'll be off now, and I'll be back for my dinner about one o'clock. Is that all right, Edna?'

'On the dot. But don't you even want another cup of tea?'

'No thanks. Mum will be filling me up with all sorts when I get home.'

Carrie managed to resist saying that this was his home now, instead of his parents' house, guessing that it would only result in another black look. Besides, if all went well, they would be able to move into a home of their own just as soon as they reached the top of the housing list for one of the prefabs on the edge of town. That would surely cheer him up.

He bent down and kissed her briefly on the forehead before he went out of the house, whistling, and she looked dumbly at his half-eaten breakfast. Her mum wouldn't like that. Nobody wasted food these days, she thought dismally, and rationing was probably going to go on for years and years . . . the war might be over, but the peace they had once had wasn't truly won yet.

'Give him time, love,' her father said, unexpectedly gentle. 'He'll need a few days to find his feet again. Once he's back at his old job, and things are back to normal, it'll be as if he'd never been away, you'll see.'

Maybe. But Carrie had a feeling it was going to take more than a few days, and she had wanted so much for them to be doing everything together from now on. It was how a marriage was meant to be. She admitted to herself that she had wanted to flaunt being with him at church that morning, her brave husband, back from the war unscathed, despite being a prisoner of the Germans.

But she was quickly acknowledging that he wasn't unscathed after all. He didn't have physical injuries, no lost limbs or battle wounds, but there were still unseen demons inside him that might take even longer to heal. She panicked again. She was only twenty-two years old, and she wasn't equipped to help in such matters. A husband was supposed to be the strong one, the one who took care of her, and she felt horribly out of her depth with this new person she didn't understand, whose mental problems were keeping her at arms' length.

Carrie flinched even as she thought it. Archie didn't have mental problems, and she wished the words had never entered her head. She was no nurse or pro-fessional person, but she resolved to do all she could to make him happy, even if it meant walking on eggshells for a while, until he was restored to her as the old, loving Archie she knew.

Chapter 3

Penhallow, once a sleepy little village, was gradually growing into a small town. The groups of miners' cottages from the heyday of tin mining mingled with several rows of pre-war council houses and now the small new colony of prefabricated dwellings that were being built.

Those who lived in Penhallow said it had the best of both worlds, being about midway between both coasts of Cornwall, just before the county narrowed right down to a slim finger at Land's End. On the south coast was the market town of Penzance with all its amenities for those who wanted them, and on the north was the beautiful seaside town of St Ives. The towns were linked by an intermittent bus service that ran right through Penhallow.

It had the church of St Jude and a Wesleyan chapel, each with an adjacent hall for community use, as well as the occasional dance; two pubs; a village green where the old men sat and gossiped on the benches under the gnarled oak trees; a war memorial from the Great War; an infant school; a library; a cluster of shops, and a surprising number of small businesses and offices for a village-cum-town of its size. A narrow stream meandered through, crossed by tiny stone bridges.

The narrow lanes leading in and out of the town were overhung with a profusion of colour in the hedgerows from early spring until late autumn. The foliage was sometimes so thick that it threatened to obscure the lanes themselves, making a glorious and fragrant backdrop to the blue of the sky above and the sea beyond, and the distant, gaunt chimneys of the old tin mine workings.

When the GIs were in the area during the war, they often wondered, on their various explorations of the countryside from their nearby barracks, just what kind of an insular backwater they were coming to. Such comments never bothered the locals. It was 'keeping Cornwall for the Cornish', as the old wags were heard to say.

'One of these days,' the sages added, 'we'll probably find ourselves overrun with them upcountry tykes wanting to take a look at we quaint folk down here. When the war's over and they can get the petrol, they'll be coming down here in their posh motor cars, and then let's see how they can get through the lanes.'

It was always a case of 'when the war's over . . .'

And now it was, and most God-fearing Penhallow folk turned out for the church of their choice on Sunday morning.

Carrie Pollard walked the short distance to St Jude's

with her parents, wishing all the time that she had Archie by her side to show him off. In the distance she saw her friend Gwen Trewint, hugging the arm of her husband. David still walked with his rolling sailor's gait, despite having been wounded twice in the leg. He had nearly drowned when his ship had been torpedoed in the Atlantic.

He must have a charmed life, being posted as missing, believed killed, and then turning up a long while later when all hope for him was gone. Gwen had certainly thought so. She was heartbroken and inconsolable for months, and then, in a bizarre way of burying her grief, she had gone to work in a Services canteen in Penzance and thrown herself into a series of wild, quick affairs to forget.

Unfortunately, there were other people from Penhallow who worked in the same area, and those who watched the metamorphosis of the ex-fisherman's widow didn't forget. On the surface, she appeared to have forgotten her marriage vows, and to be brazen and shallow. Only her close group of women friends knew how badly she had grieved for her adored David, and of the nights she sobbed herself to sleep clutching his pillow to her heart.

And then, three months before the war ended, the miracle had happened and a second telegram arrived at the cottage where they lived, to say he was alive and well, give or take a few bullet wounds, and was coming home.

'Is that Gwen Trewint, Carrie?' Edna Penney said with a sniff.

'You know it is.' Carrie hid a sigh, wishing as always that Edna wasn't quite so narrow-minded, and so obvious about it too.

'I thought you'd have finished with the likes of her now that the knitting circle has disbanded. When that poor husband of hers was presumed dead, she behaved disgracefully by all accounts, and just look at her now, hanging on to his arm as if butter wouldn't melt in her mouth.'

'What would you expect her to do? She's thrilled to have him home again. Anyway, you know that most of it was just rumours.'

But she crossed her fingers as she said it, since it was hardly the right time to tell little white lies when she was on her way to church. Gwen looked amazingly happy now, and David had recovered remarkably well from his ordeals. It came from being a tough fisherman, Gwen had told her, being out in all weathers coping with the tremendous seas that occurred off the Cornish coast, and letting it hold no terrors for him. All fishermen had a great respect for the sea, though David must have felt differently about it when it nearly drowned him. But he was back at the fishing nets in St Ives now, doing the job he loved best, and he and Gwen certainly looked cosy together.

For a moment Carrie felt a pang of envy, remembering the disappointment of last night in her own reunion with Archie, and hoping it would get better – and then she remembered his nightmare and was instantly forgiving.

'I'm going to say hello to them,' Carrie said,

breaking away from her parents, and not bothering to listen to her mother's objections. Her dad was always more understanding, and believed in standing by your friends, no matter what they did.

She joined Gwen and David, marvelling as she always did how physically alike they were, both tall and willowy with amazingly blue eyes and crisp dark hair and the widest of smiles. If there was any truth in the saying that happily married couples grew to look like one another, it was personified in these two, thought Carrie.

'It's lovely to see you, Carrie,' Gwen said in her warm voice. 'Did the wanderer return all right?'

'He certainly did,' Carrie said, smiling, and not prepared to let on that all was not as it should be – yet.

'Where is he then?'

'He wanted to spend some time with his parents, and to talk to his dad about returning to work tomorrow.'

'Already? He must be mad,' David put in. 'The first thing I wanted to do when I was demobbed was to spend as much time as possible with Gwen. I didn't want to think about work or anything else until we had got to know each other all over again. There's only one good thing you can say about this war – apart from the victory, of course – and that's the chance to have a prolonged second honeymoon once it's all over. Right, Gwen?'

'Right,' she said, her smile never wavering. 'But you'd better stop talking like that or you'll have me blushing.'

'There's no need to blush in front of Carrie. She'll be having her own second honeymoon by now,' he said, with a chuckle and a wink. 'I'll bet you girls told each other a lot of secrets while we were away winning the war, didn't you?'

'You couldn't guess the half of it,' Carrie said airily. She looked directly at Gwen. 'See you on Thursday evening as usual?'

'Of course, if Archie's letting you out.'

She glanced back at Carrie for a moment as they parted company, and Carrie didn't miss the message in her eyes. As always, it was a silent prayer that Gwen's secret never came out. But that was the trouble with secrets. They so often did.

Carrie found it hard to concentrate on the morning service. She wished Archie was sitting beside her. He *should* be sitting beside her. Plenty of people had asked after him before they entered the church, including the vicar. She could feel her mother's disapproval, remembering how Archie had said he didn't believe in the Lord anymore. She became more and more resentful that he wasn't here, especially seeing the dark heads of Gwen and David as they knelt in prayer in the pew in front of her, so close, so very much a complete unit, and obviously thankful to have finally come through the dark years and still be together.

For a moment Carrie wondered what David's reaction would be if he ever knew the truth; he was a jokey kind of man and he had been teasing about the secrets that women friends shared . . . but he couldn't begin to know the terrible days through which she and Velma and Shirley had comforted Gwen, almost out of her mind with grief when she thought she would never see David again.

The local doctor had suggested she find something outside the house to do to take her mind off things, even away from Penhallow itself. Such a stupid remark, when her mind was totally suffused with the enormity of her loss and she could think of nothing else. Until then she had been doing a postal round in the town, which wasn't exactly essential war work, but relieved the men who had joined up.

But, to everyone's surprise, Gwen agreed that she had to get away from the pitying looks and sympathy from everyone who knew the circumstances of David Trewint's presumed death. For a long while there were many servicemen stationed in the south-west of England, preparing for what was eventually known as D-Day. So Gwen volunteered to work at the Services canteen in Penzance, where at least she could give a cheery word and a smile to lonely servicemen far from home.

In the end, she gave far more than that.

'Carrie,' her mother hissed. 'Show some respect, please.'

She realized she had been gazing into space. The vicar was already intoning the Lord's Prayer to mark the end of the service, and everyone else was joining in.

She paid full attention then, and by the time they

got home from church, the house was filled with a welcome smell of the small joint of slow-roasting beef in Archie's honour and the vegetables that Walter grew in the back garden were boiling away. Carrie determined to tell Archie that afternoon about her plans for the prefab. They could walk around their favourite haunts, and she would make sure they returned by way of the brand new estate of half-finished buildings.

For a moment she visualized herself there as the perfect housewife, cooking and cleaning and keeping the place as bright as a new penny. She didn't want to give up her job though, and that was something else Archie needed to know. It wasn't only the house that was going to be bright and shining. Carrie was bright too. She had a brain, and she wanted to continue using it.

Although there wasn't any real work for her to do at the council since the evacuees had all gone home, and she was only doing token office work now, her local library job was always open to her, and she did enjoy helping the elderly ladies choose their romances and advising the men on their war books. There was a bigger branch in Penzance, but she doubted that Archie would want her away there all day.

He came breezing in just as her mother was dishing up the dinner. Good thing too, or there would have been words at best or a chilly silence at worst. Carrie always preferred her mother's snappy retorts because then it was over and done with. Silences could go on for days.

'I'm going back to work tomorrow,' Archie announced at once. 'So there'll be a few under-the-counter extras every week, Edna,' he told her with a wink. 'No more half a slice of beef for Sunday dinner, eh, Walter?'

Walter Penney cleared his throat noisily. Edna was at the kitchen sink straining the vegetables, and Carrie saw her back stiffen. This was a dodgy area.

'Mum's always done wonders with the rations, Archie. You wouldn't know what miracles she's created with dried eggs and turnips and such like.'

'Oh, I'm sure, but when a chap's been eating little more than fresh air for two years the chance of getting a bit of proper food's not to be sneezed at, is it? My mother says I need fattening up again, and you and I can go there once a week for a good meal if we like.'

Carrie groaned. Couldn't he see how he was slighting her mother with such a tactless remark? Predictably, Edna was quick to take offence as she dumped his plate down in front of him.

'Well, I'm sorry if my cooking don't meet with your approval, Archie, but this is your Sunday dinner, so if you don't like it you can do the other thing.'

'Now, Mother,' Walter began, and she rounded on him at once.

'Don't *Mother* me, Walter, for heaven's sake. I'm not your mother, and I've told you so enough times.'

'*Look*,' Carrie almost shouted, her eyes prickling with angry tears. 'Can't we all just enjoy being together? This is the first Sunday dinner Archie and I have had together for two years, and it would be nice if we could eat it without arguing. You've done us proud, Mum. Hasn't she, Archie?'

She willed him to agree, and she saw him grin as he nodded.

'It looks good enough to eat, Edna.'

They visibly relaxed as he tucked in, and the meal passed off amicably after all. But to Carrie's mind it was one more thing to prove that they shouldn't stay here. They needed a place of their own, and as soon as possible.

'Are you sure you want to go for a walk?' Archie asked her when she had helped her mum with the washing-up.

Edna had gone to her bedroom to fetch the book she was reading, and Walter was snoozing in his arm-chair, his unlit pipe hanging loosely from his mouth.

'Of course I do! Why? Do you want to cycle into St Ives instead?'

'I was thinking of something far more enjoyable,' he whispered in her ear, 'but I suppose that's out of the question.'

Carrie felt the hot colour rush into her face. She hoped her dad was really asleep and not just pretending. She saw the slow, regular rise and fall of his chest and was reassured.

'Don't be daft,' she said quickly. 'It's the afternoon.'

'What's that got to do with anything?'

'It's daylight for one thing, and it's, well, not quite nice, is it? Besides, we couldn't possibly, with them down here.'

'We're married, aren't we?'

She realized he was starting to get belligerent – and there was something else.

'Have you been drinking?' she asked suspiciously.

Archie laughed shortly. 'Are you going to start reining me in already? I had a beer with my dad. Is that all right, miss prim and proper?'

'Of course it is. I just asked, that's all.'

He grabbed her around the waist. 'That's why I thought it might be a good idea to do what your dad does – and mine too. We could have half an hour on the bed, sleeping off the Sunday dinner, and then go out.'

She knew very well they wouldn't be sleeping, and with her mum and dad downstairs knowing exactly what was going on, she wasn't having any of it.

'Archie, I really do want to go for a walk. I didn't think you'd want to be indoors all the time, anyway. You always said how you hated being cooped up in that POW camp. I thought you'd be desperate to breathe some good Cornish air again. Besides, I want to show you something.'

'What's that?' he said, a little surly, but with his interest caught now.

'I'll show you when we get there,' Carrie replied.

He had recovered himself by the time they had been walking for half an hour. People kept stopping them, wanting to shake him by the hand and wish them both good luck. It was a bit like having Christmas and birthdays rolled into one. It took ages for them to get across the village green, where so many Sunday afternoon strollers wanted to chat, but eventually they had walked right through the town and up to the bare stretches of moorland above Penhallow. Here, the old tin mine chimneys stood tall and sentinel-like, abandoned now, but with a wealth of history in their crumbling stones, and in the maze of mineshafts beneath the ground.

'This used to be our favourite spot, didn't it, Archie?' Carrie said softly, when they were exhausted with walking and were sprawled out on the short, springy turf. The late summer air was aromatic and sweet with the scents of clover and yarrow and celandine, and here in this idyllic spot it was difficult to believe that the country had ever been at war at all.

'I used to think of it sometimes, when I was stuck in that miserable cell block with a dozen other chaps, all stinking to high heaven, and even more so when I was stuck in the solitary pit for stirring things up,' he said, lying back at full stretch with his hands linked behind his head.

'Did you?' Carrie said, wishing he hadn't broken her romantic mood quite so effectively. 'Well, you're home now, and the sooner it's all forgotten the better.'

'You think we can switch it off just like that, do you?'

'Of course not, but I think we've got to try, otherwise the bad memories will stay with us for ever. And we've got the chance to make good memories now, haven't we? We've got our whole future together. We can think of a home and starting a family—'

'Only a fool would want to bring children into this rotten world!'

At his harsh words, Carrie sat bolt upright, staring down at him. She hadn't meant that she wanted children today, tomorrow or even next week, but someday.

'You don't mean that! The world isn't rotten, anyway, just some of the people in it, like Hitler and that awful Mussolini, and the Japanese who bombed Pearl Harbour. Dad always said that even they did a weird sort of good in a roundabout way, by bringing America into the war. But they're all gone now, and we have to rebuild our lives, otherwise what was it all for?'

'You have no idea what it was like, so stop being such a bloody saint. You sound just like your mother, and I suppose she's forgiven them all, even when she sees the poor cripples come limping home from the Front.'

Carrie shivered, resisting the urge to lash back at him. He didn't know what went on in the ordinary life he had left behind, either, and as for her mother forgiving everybody, she might do so in the wider sense, but when it came to people like Gwen, who were only human anyway, and Shirley . . .

She couldn't understand why Archie was behaving so oddly. He had never been much of a philosopher, but his moods had never been so unpredictable either. She wasn't sure what to make of it, especially that comment about not bringing children into the world. It was natural for married people to want children.

She and Archie had never particularly talked about it, but it was the right order of things. You fell in love, you got married, you had babies. She didn't want them right now, but she definitely wanted them. Now it seemed that Archie didn't.

'Anyway, you think the Japanese did some good, do you?' he persisted.

She sighed. 'Of course not, not in the way you're implying. I'm just saying that the Americans—'

'Oh yes, the Yanks. I was forgetting them. All you girls had a soft spot for the Yanks with their flash talk and plenty of money, didn't you?'

'Not everybody! I was married to you, and I never looked at anybody else. I never have, Archie, you know that!'

She began to feel increasingly upset. This afternoon had started out so well, with Archie being fêted everywhere they went, and the victory flags and bunting all around the town still cheering everybody up. He had only been home a day and already they were squabbling for no reason at all.

Turning away so that he wouldn't see the shine of tears in her eyes, she heard him curse beneath his breath and the next moment he had pulled her down beside him and was pressing kisses over her eyes and lips and cheeks. His words were muffled against her cheek, his voice contrite.

'I know I can be a bastard, Carrie, and when I get these black moods it can take a while for me to shake myself out of them. Of course I never thought you'd be hanging around with those bloody Yanks. I knew you'd be faithful, not like some of them, finding themselves in the club after their fast-talking fancy men left them high and dry. We all knew what went on. Some of the chaps got letters about it, even in the camps, and it nearly killed them. When they suffered, we all suffered.'

'You didn't have to worry about that as far as I was concerned.'

'I know. That was the one thing I could be sure of, when everything else was falling to pieces all around me. Life was hell, Carrie, but I suppose you've got to have something to believe in. For me, that was you. It still is.'

He held her so tightly that she could hardly breathe. She was overwhelmed with love for him, and for all that he had been through, which she was sure now that she would never hear about in any detail. It didn't matter. She had always loved him, and she always would. She had never betrayed him, nor ever wanted to.

She could excuse Gwen, because finding solace where she could was her one way back from the nightmare of believing that David was dead. She could forgive Shirley for having her head turned the way she had by her glamorous GI, but she wasn't sure she could forgive herself for the part she had played in it all, together with Gwen and Velma.

They hadn't procured Shirley's miscarriage; there had been no steaming hot baths or doses of gin – they had done nothing as wicked as that; but when it had happened naturally they had thankfully covered up the whole affair, blotting it out of their memories. By then the Yanks had already left the area, leaving more than one girl weeping and leaving home on some pretext of staying with relatives well away from insular Penhallow.

Between them they had advised Shirley to say nothing, to let Bernard go on believing in the sweet, bubbly, innocent girl that she was when they became engaged. They had made her swear to do the sensible thing, the way they had all sworn to keep her secret . . .

Archie was talking persuasively now. 'There's nobody around but us, sweetheart, so what do you say? There are no bed-springs to squeak and nobody around to hear us.'

His voice had thickened and his fingers were pushing up the hem of her skirt. There was no doubting his intention.

'Oh, Archie, we can't! It isn't right!' she said in panic.

'Why not? Do you think God will object?' he mocked. 'Didn't the vicar tell us that marriage is supposed to be for the mutual comfort of man and woman, or some such talk?'

And for making babies.

She had forgotten how ardent he could be, how seductively sweet when he wanted to, and how long they had been apart. It was true, there was no one to see or hear. They were in a blissful, secluded world of their own, beneath the shelter of the old mine chimney, the wild flowers forming a fragrant mattress, the sounds of distant seabirds a chorus of celebration in their ears, and love was binding them together, obliterating all sense of shame or modesty.

Later, with their arms entwined, they walked slowly back towards the town, spread out below the moorland where they had lain together. And on its outskirts was the small group of half-built prefabricated houses, as neat and tidy as something out of toytown.

'Look at those damn monstrosities,' Archie said, catching sight of them. 'I'm surprised they were ever given permission to build them in a rural community like ours. They belong in towns upcountry, not in our village.'

Carrie licked her lips. 'People need places to live, Archie, and you should take a look inside before you condemn them. They're really nice, and so compact. Any woman would be happy to live in one and keep house for her husband. They call them labour-saving.'

He looked at her suspiciously. 'I hope you haven't got any ideas about getting me in one of them, then. They're no bigger than rabbit hutches.'

'They're just as big as the old miners' cottages, probably bigger than some.'

'How do you know all this?' he said, removing his arm from around her. The gesture seemed ominous.

'I've seen the plans, and you can't judge them by the outside. You know what they say – you can't judge a book by its cover.'

She spoke nervously, seeing their lovely afternoon disintegrating as the dark frown reappeared between his eyes.

'We're not talking about bloody books,' he snapped.

'I'm not interested in going anywhere near one of those garden sheds and that's the end of it.'

Carrie's temper exploded. She moved away from him, her eyes blazing.

'Well, that's just too bad, because I've already put our name down for one, and the least you can do is agree to take a look, instead of coming over all lordly about it. After being a prisoner of war for two years, I'd have thought you'd want us to have a home of our own.'

'Whatever I want, it's not exchanging one prison cell for another, and you had no right to put our name down for anything without consulting me.'

'And how was I supposed to do that, when you weren't even here!'

'No, I was away serving my country, and if this is how the country rewards us, by building us all garden sheds to live in, it's a pity I ever came back at all.'

Carrie stared at him, appalled at the way they were ranting at one another, and heartbroken by his last words. She caught at his arm again.

'Archie, you don't mean that. You can't. If you knew how I've longed to have you home again, you'd never say such a cruel thing.'

But she could see that he wasn't ready to be reasonable yet, nor even to compromise. Instead, he became unbearably arrogant.

'I'm sure that's what all you women are saying now, but the war's over, and you've got to remember who wears the trousers from now on. A man who can't be boss in his own house is no man at all.'

'Isn't that just what I'm saying? We'd *have* our own house, wouldn't we? What difference does it make which one of us put our name down on the list? It would be our own place, our own dear little place, Archie, where we could come and go as we pleased, with nobody to bother us.'

She held her breath, aware that she sounded coy and girlish, when in fact she was still seething inside. The way he had virtually dismissed women as second-class citizens was an insult to everything they had done during the five years the country had been at war. Women had fought long and hard to have their voices heard, and Carrie was no different. She wasn't asking for the moon, but she wanted this prefab, and come hell or high water she meant to have it.

Chapter 4

Shirley Loe was sorry when the Women's Land Army was disbanded. She had enjoyed working on a farm, loved wearing the uniform of green jersey and brown breeches, and especially the jaunty brown felt hat. There were plenty of farms in the area, and when she had been given a choice of staying in Cornwall or moving upcountry she had been glad to stay near enough to Penhallow to cycle home each night, where she lived with her parents and her sisters. She could also see Bernard whenever he got leave. They had been engaged for a couple of years, and when the war was over and he was home for good they would be able to plan their wedding. And she could forget that other madness.

She was fiercely proud of Bernard in his air-force blue with the brand new wings he had attached to his uniform when he became a pilot, and qualified to fly planes over Germany – though she never cared to think about that too much. Every day you heard about the sorties over Germany, and of the planes limping back over occupied France and the dangers of the

English Channel, and you knew there would be some who never came back. If they did, they might be horribly burned.

It made what she had done all the more shameful. At the time she had unloaded all her panic on to her women friends, since it was something you could never tell your parents without risking their shame and disgust. And her friends hadn't let her down.

All that had come later. In the middle years of the war she was more worried about Bernard and the fact that she hadn't seen him for months, except for the occasional snatched weekend when he could get leave. Even then, travelling to Cornwall took ages from his base in the south-east, so he didn't always make the journey home. And for Shirley there were always the weekly dances in Penzance while the GIs were in town, and a little harmless flirtation to make the Yanks feel less homesick and to cheer everybody up. But it had all gone too far . . .

Without her friends, Shirley didn't know what she would have done when the truth had hit her in a wave of panic and despair. Then the miracle she didn't deserve had happened, and she wasn't going to have a baby after all, and she had thanked God for forgiving her wickedness. She had needed considerable bolstering up afterwards, her nerves shattered, wondering whether to confess to Bernard. But it would surely have killed him to know she had been unfaithful, even for that brief time.

Like the others, Carrie had insisted there was no point in worrying about things you couldn't change, and that she should think positively and leave the past where it belonged. But Shirley had continued to punish herself.

'We can't all think sweet and lovely thoughts, and your Archie may be a POW, but at least you know where he is and what he's doing, don't you? My Bernard could be flying over Germany this very moment, dropping bombs and risking his life,' she had snapped. 'And all you can think about are the stupid prefabs the council has proposed building. What's the point of building them here, anyway? They're supposed to be for bombed-out families, but since we don't have any in Cornwall it'll just encourage grockles to move down here.'

Once she got started she never knew when to stop, and when she got on her high horse she looked about twelve years old. But Carrie was instantly defensive.

'There's only going to be a few and they won't be properly fitted out for months yet. And they'll be for people like Archie and me to start married life on our own, that's what. Returning servicemen will have the first chance of renting them. You and Bernard might even want one.'

'Yes, we might, but I bet your dad put in a word or two for you, didn't he?'

Carrie had snapped back, not prepared to humour her friend after her snide remark about Archie having it easy as a POW. That was the daftest remark she had made yet.

' My dad's not in Housing. He's Parks and Gardens, as you very well know.'

And for all her mother's puffed-up manner about Archie being only a butcher's boy, everyone knew that Parks and Gardens was one of the lowest jobs on the council. But Shirley was younger than the others, and they always forgave her for her moods, knowing they were on account of her guilt over Hank, and her anxiety over Bernard. He was still the love of her life, despite everything.

There had been a terrible time when she'd wondered if Bernard was ever coming back, when several aircraft in his squadron were reported missing. She remembered the awful day when his mother had turned up on Shirley's doorstep with the dreaded telegram in her hand. Shirley wasn't even the first to know, being only a fiancée and not yet a wife. They had kept their ears virtually glued to the wireless then, desperate for the truth and yet dreading what they might hear among the intermittent details of pilots bailing out over France and the few lucky ones who eventually made their way home.

Shirley had prayed so hard that that was what was happening to Bernard. If it was anything worse, she would blame herself for ever for her wickedness with Hank, knowing this was God's way of punishing her. But He didn't have to punish Bernard too, and she bargained with God that if only he would send Bernard home safe and unharmed she would never do anything bad again.

The day she received a tattered letter from somewhere in France, her knees buckled under her and she simply kneeled down in the kitchen at home and wept.

Bernard was safe. Like so many others, his plane had been shot down in France, but before it exploded into flames he had somehow managed to bail out and then had crawled his way to a French farmhouse, where his badly burned leg and side were still being tended by the generous French family who had taken him in at great risk to themselves.

'I didn't know where I was for weeks, and even now I keep getting lapses of memory, so I'm not ready to come home for a while yet. But I'm learning a bit of French while I'm here. Marie, the farmer's daughter, is a nurse, and she's trying to teach me to keep my mind off my troubles,' he had written. 'That's a laugh, isn't it, Shirl? When this war's over we'll come back here together, and I'll show off.'

She sensed that his injuries were far worse than he was prepared to say, and she hoped he was getting proper medical attention for them. She supposed it would be too dangerous to produce a wounded British airman for treatment in occupied France. He was being so brave that she had wept over that first letter until it was sodden with tears, while she tried to ignore the acute and unworthy spasm of jealousy running through her at the thought of this unknown Marie teaching her darling Bernard to speak French.

Now he was in a convalescent home near Brighton where he had been for weeks, following delicate operations on his fragile burned body, and Shirley wondered again if he was ever coming home. She would have visited Bernard, of course, even though the journey would have been arduous, but her fiancé had been adamant that he didn't want her to see him until he was completely well again. She sympathized with Carrie now, knowing how long it had taken for Archie to be fit enough to come home. In Bernard's case it was taking so much longer. His letters told her he was progressing gradually, that he loved her and missed her, and he was aiming to be home in good time for the big Welcome Home dance at the end of October, even if he could only sit and watch. Which set Shirley off on her guilty dreams again, remembering the warm, hazy nights when she had danced in Hank Delaney's arms.

The women's knitting circle used to meet at St Jude's church hall. Now that the war was over, it was no longer needed for such activities, though the knitting group had become a refreshing ritual for many, and some of the older ones continued to meet for the company and to knit for their grandchildren. Carrie, Velma, Shirley and Gwen also still met on Thursday evenings, sharing the close friendship they had formed during the war years.

Carrie had been uneasy after Gwen's remark that Archie may not allow his wife to meet her friends as usual, but he had been surprisingly agreeable. Then she discovered it was because he had every intention of going to the pub with his father for a game of darts and a glass or two. And not just on Thursday evenings either. He told her he needed a drink to forget his two years' ordeal, but it didn't meet with her parents' approval when he came stumbling home smelling of beer, and she wondered how long it would be before something erupted between them all.

To everybody's fury Archie had flatly refused to agree to the party they had been planning for the week after he came home, saying he wasn't going to be paraded like a trophy. Nothing that she, or either set of parents, could say would make him change his mind, and since he was in what her mother called one of his funny contrary moods, Carrie was no longer inclined to try, preferring to let things be rather than provoke another of his rages.

But tonight at the church hall with her friends she was going to forget their problems for a couple of hours. They had brought their cups of tea to their usual table in the corner of the church hall. There were important things to be discussed, and Gwen was the first to ask what they all wanted to know.

'So, Velma, was Stan very upset when you told him you wanted a divorce?'

'I still think you're mad,' Shirley said at once. 'Stan seems like such a charmer, and we wanted to get to know him properly instead of only seeing him now and then. I suppose he won't even be coming to the Welcome Home dance if you've given him his marching orders.'

She was still hoping desperately that Bernard would be there, but whether he would be able to dance with his wounded leg was another matter. Not that she gave a hoot about that! All she wanted was to have him home, and for everything to be as it was before. And not for a single moment was she going to think that he was certainly making a meal of his injuries.

Velma stirred her tea more vigorously than necessary, making a swirling vortex of it and pausing for a moment before she answered. Though what could she say? What was she *prepared* to say, even to these friends with whom she had shared so many confidences? For the first time she felt so much older than they were – older, but not so much wiser.

'It didn't quite happen like that,' she said at last. 'In fact, nothing has been decided at all yet.'

'I knew it!' Shirley said, triumphant. 'The minute you saw him again, you realized you really loved him after all, and you couldn't do it.'

Velma sighed. 'You are a romantic little ninny, aren't you, Shirley? Not everything happens the way the Hollywood flicks would have you believe. We're not all star-struck by the sight of a uniform.'

Shirley's face flamed at her tart remark, and they all knew exactly what she was thinking. How star-struck had *she* been by the glamorous GI Hank, who had been Clark Gable and Errol Flynn all rolled into one!

'That's not fair, Velma,' Carrie said. 'Shirley didn't mean anything of the sort. We just want you to be happy, that's all, and to do what's best for everybody. So how did it go?' she added, just as keen herself to know.

Wanting a divorce was such a daring thing to do, especially for a woman, and there was no knowing how the prim residents of Penhallow would accept the idea of Velma's rejecting a war hero. Glancing at the huddled grey-headed matrons at the far end of the room, their knitting needles clacking away like noisy crickets and the gossip almost tangible, Carrie knew there was no doubt that was how most would see it.

'You didn't tell him at all?' Gwen said. 'You mean you chickened out at the last minute! I knew you would, and I'm sure it's for the best, Velma.'

Velma glowered. 'You don't know anything about it, and I'm not saying any more until Stan and I have talked again. He only had a seventy-two hour pass and we stayed at the hotel the whole time, instead of coming home to the cottage. We both need time to think, but he's promised he'll be back for the dance, and by then we'll have decided what to do.'

Carrie was more perceptive than the other two, sensing that Velma was going through some kind of turmoil. Out of the four of them, she and Velma had been the only ones who had been faithful to their men during the empty war years. Shirley had had her fling with her GI, going completely overboard and being madly in love for those few short weeks; and Gwen . . . well, she conceded that Gwen could be forgiven for going off the rails when she thought she was a widow. The town gossips could think what they liked, but she and David were blissfully happy now, and it would be a disaster for anything to spoil it.

But Carrie thought she recognized something in Velma's eyes that the other two were missing. There was a certain glow, a sense of fulfilment, that you couldn't hide. And Velma had it.

As they both lived in the same direction, when they

left the village hall that evening, she and Velma walked home together. Penhallow didn't have the luxury of more than the occasional street light, but now that the blackout restrictions had long gone most houses' occupants left their windows uncurtained, and with the new electricity in the area lights beamed out from houses and cottages, just for the joy of it.

'What really happened on your weekend, Velma? Or would you rather not talk about it?'

'There's nothing much to tell, except that it wasn't exactly what I had expected. Stan had come down a day early to spend some time in St Ives, wanting to spend time alone for reasons best known to himself. He persuaded the hotel to give us a room with a double bed in it instead of the two singles I had asked for.'

'Well, that wasn't so unusual. You are married, after all.'

'It changed things.' She hesitated. 'I've been holding back all evening, wondering whether to say anything, but if you're not rushing home, come back to the cottage for a cup of cocoa. Archie won't mind if you're a bit late, will he?'

'It depends on when he gets back from the pub with his dad,' she said with a grin, and then she saw Velma's face, pale in the glow from someone's sitting-room light, and spoke quickly. 'No, he won't mind. He probably won't even notice.'

She wasn't too sure about that, though. Archie could be sweet and loving, sweeping her off her feet with kisses, and she still adored him with all her heart.

But he could change like a chameleon into someone she hardly knew anymore. It must be the same for all POWs, finding it so difficult to adapt to normal life again, she thought, and so she bit her tongue more often than she would normally have done.

In reality, she often felt like screaming that he should think himself lucky he had returned safe and sound, when they had just heard of several young men in the village who had been missing, and whom their relatives now knew would never come home. There were others who had lost limbs, and one man in the village who had lost an eye and whose face bore a livid scar. Every day when he walked to the newsagent to get his daily paper, he risked the curious stares of local children who were then shushed away by their mothers, which seemed to make the whole thing worse, and must make him feel like a leper.

War hadn't touched Cornwall in the same way as it had ravaged London in the Blitz. But although they hadn't known the relentless bombing raids that had rained down on Plymouth and Coventry and so many other cities, like the tentacles of an octopus the war had snaked out and touched them in the loss of so many sons and fathers, even here in this remote corner of Cornwall. They had sent their loved ones away in all good faith for King and country, and some of them had never come back.

Velma lived in Tinners' Row, in what had once been a miner's cottage. It had thick stone walls and a flagstone floor in the kitchen, which kept it cool in summer. Winters in the far south-west were mostly mild, and the interior of the cottage was warm and cosy and well-established. As a regular soldier for some years, Stan had wanted Velma to move to Norfolk nearer his army base and to live in a modern house, but she had stubbornly refused. She loved her cottage and she loved Cornwall, and she had no intention of ever moving away.

Besides which, she couldn't bear the thought of being just another Army wife, but it was only when the bus company was crying out for female volunteer bus conductresses to replace the men who had joined up that she knew why.

She had got a job on the buses, and with it had come independence, money of her own, and no need to conform to what the army expected of its lackeys.

Carrie watched her trim figure as she went into the kitchen and put the kettle on the gas stove. Velma was tall and elegant, and Carrie admired her tremendously. She had always thought Velma's marriage was rock solid, and when she had announced that she wanted a divorce, her friends had been stunned.

In the small sitting-room, Carrie picked up the framed wedding photo on the mantelpiece. Stan was also tall, handsome in a military sort of way, and with Velma smiling beside him in her slim white dress and veil they made a striking couple. How could all that happiness have gone so sour? How could you contemplate ending a marriage that had lasted for ten years? She admitted that Velma hadn't seen too much of Stan in all that time, but surely that made every reunion a sort of honeymoon.

You thought you knew people so well. Carrie was still holding the framed photo, wondering how Velma could break Stan's heart like this, and vowing that it would never happen to her and Archie, no matter what, when Velma came back into the room with two cups of cocoa. She put them down on the little lace doilies she had made to preserve the polished table, and then took the photo from Carrie's hand and replaced it on the mantelpiece.

'I know what you're thinking,' she said, 'and I know it's not what people would expect of me. I grew up here, and everybody knows me. They knew my parents and my brothers and what happened to them, and half the village turned out to watch me go to my wedding, glad and probably a bit relieved, if the truth were told, that the introverted Velma Dark had found happiness at last. And now this.'

She looked so bleak for a moment that Carrie's heart went out to her.

'It's your life, Velma. Nobody can live it for you, and only you and Stan know what goes on inside your marriage. You shouldn't worry too much about what other people think.'

'No? Tell that to Gwen, still desperate that David won't get to hear how she carried on when she thought he was drowned. And tell it to Shirley, still riddled with guilt over the affair with her GI, and wondering if she should tell Bernard or not.'

'Well, we all agreed that she shouldn't. Why load

69

her guilt on to his shoulders when he's got enough worries of his own?'

There was a big question mark in all of this, though. When Shirley and Bernard eventually got married, would the wedding night prove once and for all that Shirley had been unfaithful? You heard such tales of husbands denouncing their wives for infidelity, and Carrie had read certain medical books in the library which said sternly that it was always obvious if a female had been tampered with, and a doctor could always tell. It was such a cold and clinically condemning way of describing the act of love that Carrie hadn't read any more. But the implications were there. If a doctor could tell, so could a husband.

She realized that Velma was gazing unseeingly into the fireplace where logs blazed in winter, and which was hidden now by the beautiful firescreen Velma had embroidered on the many nights she spent alone. It was no way for a marriage to be, Carrie conceded. She'd have travelled to the ends of the earth to be with Archie.

'It wasn't like I had planned,' Velma said again. 'Not at all.'

'In what way?' Carrie took a gulp of steaming cocoa and burned her lips. But Velma was looking almost bemused now, caressing her own cup as if unaware of its heat, and Carrie felt faintly alarmed. And then Velma looked directly at her, and her voice was clipped to the point of abruptness.

'The reason Stan needed to be alone with his

thoughts before we met, was because he had had news of some army colleagues he was with in the desert. They were regular soldiers like himself, good friends that he had known for a long time. They were preparing to come home when their vehicles ran into a minefield, and they were all killed. You don't expect things like that to happen now the war is over. You think everything will go back to the way it was before, nice and tidy, but it never does. And it really cut Stan up. In all the years I've known him, I've never seen him cry. It's not what men do, is it? But I saw him cry then, great, agonizing weeping, I mean, and it nearly broke my heart.'

She rushed on, telling it quickly to get it over with, her eyes brimming with tears as she relived the shock and horror of those moments, and then the overwhelming feeling of love and pity she had felt for Stan. Perhaps she had never really understood the reason he was a soldier, or the unique male comradeship he valued so much.

But she had also never expected him to turn to her with such need, such overpowering need, as if to blot out the terrible images, that it would have been cruel to turn away from him. And she had never been a cruel person.

'It must have been dreadful for him,' Carrie said softly, seeing how Velma was still caught up in the memory of those fateful few days. 'But I can see this is distressing you, and if you'd rather not tell me any more, I'll understand.'

Her reply startled Carrie. 'I've never said much

about our relationship to any of you, have I? Our physical relationship, that is.'

'Well, it's none of our business.' Carrie began to feel uncomfortable, not sure she wanted to hear this. Some things should be kept private, unless you felt you had to talk to a family doctor or vicar. Even then it took nerve bordering on desperation to discuss such personal problems. Velma had always been a private person, and Carrie already felt slightly embarrassed to hear her mention her physical relationship with Stan. She couldn't imagine discussing what went on between herself and Archie.

'Stan was a wonderful lover when we first got married.' Velma continued as if Carrie hadn't spoken. 'So strong and masterful, and I was madly in love with him. But as the years went on, we seemed to drift further and further apart in that respect, until it simply never happened at all. When he came home on leave, we behaved more like brother and sister than husband and wife, companionable enough, but with no joy left between us. Do you understand what I'm saying, Carrie?'

'I think so.' It sounded so sad, when she and Archie couldn't wait to be alone and be as close as if they shared the same skin. She blushed at the thought. There was nothing wrong with them in that respect. There was nothing wrong with them at all, she amended hastily.

'We were like you at first,' Velma said, as if she could read her mind. 'And then our marriage became so sterile there seemed no point in it anymore. So I decided that this weekend was to sort things out, once and for all.'

'But it didn't.'

Velma spread her hands helplessly. 'How could I refuse him when he needed me so much? When I had needed *him* so much for all the years when it seemed he was so self-sufficient in his own world? Perhaps I had never realized how much I needed him, and I had built a wall around myself to shut out the fact that I wanted love as much as the next person. So we made love – though that's a poor word for what happened. We clung to each other as if we were drowning, and we made love as if it was the last night on earth, and it was so wonderful – *so* wonderful.'

She swallowed. 'I'm sorry, Carrie. I know this is embarrassing you.'

'Don't be silly, of course it isn't. I'm just so glad that this happened for you, and that everything is all right again.'

Velma shook her head. 'No. I know it won't last. Stan will be regretting it already and he'll retreat into that hard army shell of his. Before we parted, he apologized to me. Can you imagine how that made me feel? I had adored him, worshipped him. I had felt like a young bride again, sharing his passion, but when he seemed to be throwing it all back in my face I almost blurted out that it didn't matter, and that I knew we were long past the lovey-dovey stage and I didn't expect it to happen again. How low a trick would that have been, after learning that so many of his friends had been blown up in a minefield?'

She scooped up the empty cocoa cups and took them to the kitchen, as if to indicate that the discussion was over. Carrie didn't dare ask how Stan's leave had ended. She couldn't bear to hear any more, and it seemed to put her own problems, even those of Gwen and Shirley, into a different perspective. All she longed to do now was to get home and feel the warm comfort of Archie's arms.

She left the cottage, sure that Velma would want to be alone now. She was far later than she had intended, and Kellaway Terrace was in darkness as she approached it. Assuming that everyone had gone to bed, she slipped indoors quietly. The next moment a light was switched on, and she blinked like an owl as her eyes got accustomed to the brightness.

'Where the hell have you been until this time of night?' Archie roared.

Chapter 5

Carrie felt her nerves jump. This was Archie in his blackest mood. She tossed her handbag and jacket on a chair and refused to admit how her legs were shaking.

'You know where I've been,' she said. 'I told you I was meeting my friends at the church hall. I'm sorry if it's later than you expected, but Velma asked me back for some cocoa and we were talking so much I lost track of the time. Would you like me to make some for you?'

She tried to stay calm and to defuse the potential row that was signposted, but inside she was boiling with rage at his attitude.

'I don't want your bloody cocoa,' he yelled. 'I want to know what you and those floosies have to talk about that takes half the night!'

'Don't use that horrible word, Archie! They're my best friends, and I don't see any reason to desert them now, just because the war's over.'

'Just because the war's over,' he mimicked in a high-pitched, sneering voice. 'What the hell did any of you know about the war? You had it cushy!'

'What did you want me to do then? Go and live in Bristol or London and get bombed out? Would that have made me more worthy in your eyes? You might have been in a German prisoner of war camp, but at least you were housed and fed and clothed for the past two years. You weren't blown out of the sky like Shirley's young man, nor presumed drowned like David Trewint. Even now, when we should all sleep easy in our beds again, soldiers are dying and being blown up in minefields left behind by the enemy. We might not have had any of that in Cornwall, but we had to make do with having our food rationed and not being able to eat properly unless we knew anybody in the Black Market—'

She was stopped by a blow to her cheek that sent her reeling.

'Shut up, you silly bitch,' Archie shouted. 'You don't know what the hell you're talking about.'

For a moment Carrie could hardly breathe for the pain in her cheek and the shock of Archie's fist. He had never struck her before, and never in her whole life had she ever imagined he would. He frightened her. While she was still fighting for breath and trying to hold back the tears she was too proud to show, she heard her father call from upstairs, and saw the dull glow of the torch he still used at night, unable to get out of the wartime habit. His voice sounded suspicious.

'What's going on down there? Is everything all right?'

'It's all right, Dad,' she called back, praying that her

voice didn't wobble too much. 'We're just having a chat before we come up.'

'Do it quieter then,' Walter said, before closing his bedroom door again.

That was her father all over, never wanting to get involved, Carrie thought, with a rare flash of anger at him. That was why he was still Parks and Gardens with the council instead of anything more worthwhile.

She stood with her hands clenched at her sides, resisting the urge to press them to her burning cheek, when she heard a strange sound in the room.

She had briefly closed her eyes to blink back the threatening tears, and when she opened them again she realized the sound was coming from Archie, and that he was clearing his throat with what sounded suspiciously like a stifled sob. His voice was strangled, his eyes wild and shocked.

'You should have got him down here. I deserve a thrashing for what I just did to you. I never meant to hurt you, Carrie. I would never do that!'

She ignored the fact that he had just done exactly that, and that her cheek stung like the devil. All she could think was that this was Archie, whom she loved so much, and who had lived through the kind of hell that none of them could ever imagine. She rushed across the room and put her arms around him.

Tension had made his body as hard as iron, and heaven knew how long it had been like this, or how long these senseless accusations had been building up in him since he came home this evening, clearly expecting his loving, patient little wife to be back before him.

But the fact was that women had been doing all kinds of jobs during the war that they never would have dreamed about before, and that few of them were prepared to sit around being virtual serfs to their husbands anymore. Husbands were no longer the only capable breadwinners in a family, however much of a shock it might be to some of them to realize it.

But right now, Carrie ignored the smell of beer on his breath, and the stale odour of cigarettes in his clothes after being in the thick, smoky atmosphere of the pub. She ignored everything but the fact that this was the man she had promised to love, honour and obey. She had waited too long for them to be together again for this to mean the end of it all.

'Archie darling, it doesn't matter. It really doesn't matter. It was a bad moment, and it's over.'

She knew she was being weak. She should not only beg him never to do it again, she should insist on it, and not allow herself to be a victim. While he was looking so ashamed, she should make him promise. But she couldn't do it. It would only humiliate him more. Besides, extracting promises would mean nothing until he had got rid of his demons in his own way. She knew it instinctively, and for now she was prepared to forgive and forget. In doing so, she was strong.

He clung to her until she felt him begin to relax. She could hardly breathe for the way he held her so tightly, but she didn't dare to move away until he was ready.

'Are you still offering to make me some cocoa?' he said at last, his voice muffled against her hair.

'Of course I am,' Carrie said shakily. He finally released her and she went into the kitchen and put the kettle on with trembling hands. At the same time she pressed a cold cloth against her cheek, hoping it wouldn't look too awful in the morning. She still felt totally shocked at what had happened.

For all his size, Archie had never been violent to anyone before, as far as she knew, anyway. But he had never been a POW before, and that changed everything. He had lived in the kind of world she couldn't possibly know, and never wanted to, she thought with a shiver.

She only discovered just how badly shaken she had been when she went to put his cup of cocoa on the table and he reached out his hand for it. Instinct alerted her that he might be going to hit her again, and she flinched, spilling the cocoa before it reached the table, and without warning she burst into tears.

'Carrie, don't. *Please* don't,' he said, cradling her in his arms again. 'I was only reaching for the cup, sweetheart.'

'I know,' she wept. 'I know, I *know*.'

'Look, let's forget it, anyway. I don't really want a blasted drink. Let's just go to bed. I promise I won't even touch you unless you want me to.'

'Don't be daft. I want you to hold me and make me feel safe. I just don't want . . . anything else,' she added, praying that this wouldn't provoke him again.

He gave a strange sort of laugh. 'Don't worry. What

with all the beer I drank tonight, and what I did to you just now, any hope of that has long gone.'

Instead of pulling turnips and potatoes on a local farm for the war effort, Shirley was now working in the local haberdashery shop in the centre of the village. She was already dreaming of her wedding, which would hopefully be next spring. She and Bernard had been engaged for long enough, and although her parents had allowed the engagement, they had insisted that there would be no marriage until she was twenty-one years old and knew her own mind. She would reach that milestone in January, and her dad must give his permission for the wedding then – though he would have kept her wrapped up in cotton wool for ever, if he'd had his way.

As for knowing her own mind, well, of course she did. She had fallen for Bernard the moment she saw his blond, tanned good looks. Just like a film star, she thought dreamily. And so was Hank, in a different, darkly dramatic way.

She shivered, willing the seductive thoughts of the American out of her mind. He was in the past and that was where he had to stay. In the daytime, with work to keep her occupied, domesticity at home with her parents and sisters, and writing daily letters to Bernard to keep his spirits up, she could easily forget.

At night, it was different. She didn't want to dream of Hank, she truly didn't. She wanted to put those few months away for ever and never bring the memories out into the daylight again. But she couldn't stop her dreams, and that was something she panicked about. How awful it would be, when she was married to her darling Bernard, if her night-time dreams were still of Hank. It would be as bad a betrayal as the original one.

She knew why she had started thinking of him again. Several girls in the area had become GI brides, and by all accounts they would be going to America early next year, voyaging across the Atlantic on the liner Queen Mary to their fantastic new lives. And Shirley couldn't help the treacherous thought that it might have been her making the trip.

She squashed the images at once as the manageress of the haberdashery reprimanded her. 'Are you going to count those boxes of pins, Shirley, or are you going to stand there daydreaming all day?'

'I'm sorry, Miss Willis,' she gasped, and got back to her task.

Counting boxes of pins was a poor substitute for dreams, though. And last night she had had *the* dream again. The one about the last monthly dance before the GIs had gone overseas and never returned. The one where Hank had been more persuasive than usual, and she had been powerless to resist.

'You know I think the world of you, don't you, Shirley?' he had said in his wonderfully rich American drawl, which he had told her was from the mid-west.

They were slowly dancing to the plaintive melody of 'I'll Be Seeing You', which she was always going to think of as Their Song from now on, she thought fervently. He was so handsome, and she was completely besotted by him.

'I know.' She caught her breath, thinking that this was truly like something out of a movie. 'And I'm going to miss you so much when you leave Cornwall.'

They didn't know, then, how soon that was going to be.

'It's getting very hot in here, honey,' Hank went on, smoothing her soft blond hair. 'Do you want to go outside for a spell?'

'All right,' she said huskily, knowing that this would mean a walk along the shoreline, and stolen kisses, her imagination soaring ahead to one of those romantic movies where the lovers walked off into the sunset.

The fairy-tale island of St Michael's Mount loomed up in the soft velvet night like a benevolent crouching lion as they walked along the sands, their arms entwined. And when Hank had begged her so hesitantly, almost reverently, for a little bit more than she was really ready to give, she had found it impossible to resist. She was Scarlett O'Hara to his Rhett Butler, Guinevere to his Lancelot, and it was all so much more magical than she had ever dreamed it would be.

Unfortunately, dreams had a habit of switching from one scene to another with cruel disregard for the way you wanted them to be. In the circumstances, perhaps it was better that they never reached that part where their two bodies merged together, leaving one loving silhouette in the darkness, with waves rippling on the shore and reaching a crescendo, the way they did in the movies at the implied climax of their love.

That was the Hollywood way. In Shirley's dream,

the next scene was the one where she was lost and alone and very frightened, facing a reality that she had never considered, for when Hank and the GIs had disappeared from the scene overnight, he had left more than memories behind. That was the moment she always awoke, her heart pounding and tears streaming down her face.

And because she was essentially a good girl, a clean-minded girl, she always stumbled out of bed and kneeled by the side of it, hands clasped, begging God to forgive her and to let her forget.

How could she let any of that happen when she was married to Bernard? And how could she stop it?

She was jolted out of it all by Miss Willis's sharp voice for the second time that morning.

'*Shirley*. Would you please attend to Mrs Tremayne and get that silly look off your face?' Shirley turned to the customer and apologized as Miss Willis muttered. 'Young girls these days have always got their heads in the clouds.'

The customer was more generous. 'Oh well, you can understand any little lapse, Miss Willis. I'm sure Shirley's thinking about young Bernard coming home any day now. Have you heard from him lately, love?'

'I write to him every day and he writes back nearly as often. He hopes to be home in a few weeks now,' she added, crossing her fingers as Mrs Tremayne did so.

'Make the most of him when he does, my dear,' the woman said with a tight smile, and Shirley remembered that one of her sons had died in France.

If there was ever an example that you just had to go on, no matter what, Mrs Tremayne was it.

After the shock of Archie's unprovoked attack, Carrie had spent a difficult night, lying stiff and taut beside him, while he thrashed about in his sleep as usual. She wondered if she could find an excuse not to go to work tomorrow, sure that her tender cheek would be bruised and swollen, and not wanting to answer curious questions. By morning, she had found the answer. She would say that she had tripped and knocked her face on a gatepost on her way home from Velma's cottage. Tinners' Row was dark and unlit, and that was going to be her solution.

Her face didn't look as bad as she had expected when she examined it in the mirror, just slightly darker on one side than the other, but she made the explanation at breakfast after her mother commented on it at once, looking accusingly at Archie. He was saying nothing, eating his toast savagely, and letting Carrie get on with it. She hoped he was smarting inside, too, just as she was.

'You'll need to put some witch hazel on that cheek, Carrie, if you don't want your workmates wondering what on earth you've been doing,' Edna went on.

'It's time you gave up going out to work,' Archie put in at once. 'I'm back now, and I told you there's no need for it.'

'I like working,' she said steadily. 'It wouldn't hurt to put a few more pennies in the pot when we'll be thinking about a home of our own sometime, either.'

'A man still needs to be the breadwinner, Carrie,' Walter put in, before Archie chose to reply to that. 'There's plenty enough to keep a woman occupied at home, and your mother never went out to work in all the years of our marriage.'

'I know, but things are different now, Dad. Women did all kinds of jobs during the war and families never came to any harm because of it.'

'That's not the point,' he said. 'You did it when the men went away to fight, but they have a right to expect to have their jobs back, and women should be content to stay at home now and look after their menfolk as nature intended.'

'What, cooking and cleaning and generally being skivvies, you mean?' Carrie said before she could stop herself.

'Is that what you think I've been doing for the last thirty years of marriage, my girl?' Edna said indignantly.

'No, of course not, Mum. I didn't mean that at all.'

Out of the corner of her eye she could see Archie, still quiet, drinking his morning cup of tea with a complacent look in his eyes. She could tell he was happy enough to let her wrangle with her parents over this, knowing he had their backing for his own feelings for once. Amazing. It wasn't all that often that her mother agreed with Archie over anything.

'Anyway, I've decided to stay at home today,' she said, startling them all. 'Perhaps you'd let my department know, Dad. Just say I had a bit of a fall but I'm all right and I'll be back on Monday.'

She and her father usually travelled to work together on the bus to Penzance, and, being a stickler for the truth, she knew Walter wouldn't want to lie for her. But her eyes didn't flicker as she made the announcement, and she saw him nod.

And despite the fact that Archie might think he had gained a small victory by having her at home all day, what she intended to do was to call at Penhallow library and see about getting her old job back. Men didn't care to be librarians, and she hoped that would satisfy them both. She had no intention of staying at home all day twiddling her thumbs, especially with her mother watching and criticizing every little thing she did. Until she and Archie had a home of their own, and the babies started coming along, she meant to carry on working.

For a brief, dreaming moment she imagined what those babies would be like. Small and delicate like her, with smooth brown hair and wide blue eyes, or robust like Archie . . . that was the boy, of course. Of one thing she was certain. She wouldn't want any son of hers to follow in his father's footsteps and be a butcher's boy. She couldn't bear the thought of her spanking new prefab smelling of butcher's blood from two of them!

She brought such disloyal thoughts up short. She didn't despise what Archie did. His father's shop in the village had the proud sign above the door of Pollard and Son, Family Butchers. Continuity like that was something to be proud of. It was just that Carrie would prefer it to stop right there.

Uneasily, she wondered if she was becoming a snob. She met all sorts of people in her job, and some of the snotty nosed and badly behaved evacuees they had dealt with during the war years had certainly made her appreciate her own home, and the way Edna waged war on the slightest speck of dust. And no matter what job Archie did, she would always love him. Last night might have disillusioned her a bit, but in the end it made no difference to her love for him. Married people didn't fall apart because of one little problem. They muddled through.

At that moment she felt his arms slide around her and she realized she had been sitting silently at the breakfast table for the past few minutes.

'Take an aspirin for that knock and do as your mum says and put some witch hazel on your cheek, love,' he advised, just as if her poor ravaged face had nothing to do with him. He was obviously finding it perfectly easy to adopt the fiction she had provided. 'If you feel like taking a stroll down to the village later, call in the shop and say hello to Dad and me. You take it easy and see how you enjoy being a lady of leisure, and I'll see you at dinner time.'

He planted a kiss on her lips, tender and loving, ignoring the fact that her parents were watching, even though it was rare for any of them to show physical affection in public. But this was clearly Archie's way of trying to make amends. He didn't have the words, but he could show it in other ways, and she could see that he fancied the thought of his lady-wife who didn't need to work anymore calling at his shop.

'I'll see,' Carrie said.

The house was quiet after both men had gone. Carrie helped her mother clear away the breakfast things and do the washing-up. Then there were the beds to be made, the floors to be swept, the rugs vigorously shaken in the backyard, the furniture to be dusted and polished. Nothing must interfere with the morning rituals, and only then, halfway through the morning once all the chores were finished, Edna made them both a cup of tea, and asked Carrie in a no-nonsense voice what had really happened.

'I told you. I tripped and knocked myself on a gatepost.'

'I wasn't born yesterday, Carrie. That young man has got a temper, and your father may be easily pacified by your explanation, but I'm not.'

Walter Penney was a gentle man who preferred to see the good in people, rather than the bad, but that didn't make him a weak person. Carrie had never thought that.

'Dad doesn't have your suspicious mind, either.'

'Mind your manners, young lady. You might be a married woman, but while you're living in this house, you'll keep a civil tongue in your head.'

And while her mother spoke to her like that, it made Carrie feel less like a married woman and more like a badly behaved child. It was one more reason why she and Archie needed to get away to a home of their own. You didn't get married to remain tied to your mother's apron strings. But there seemed no point in provoking Edna any further, especially since the small colony of prefabs seemed to be getting no nearer to completion.

'I'm sorry. But honestly, Mum, it's just as I said. I tripped and hit my face, and I'm ashamed that you can think of suggesting that Archie did this to me.'

And if she went on saying it long enough, she would start to believe it herself.

Her mother sniffed. The girl was loyal, but Edna's hearing was more acute than Walter's, and she was pretty sure there was more to this than Carrie was telling her. However, she had also been brought up to believe that whatever happened between husband and wife was their own affair, and since Carrie didn't seem unduly upset she was prepared to leave it at that. But she was going to keep a watchful eye on that son-in-law of hers in future. There was no knowing what kind of brutes he'd had to mix with in that prison camp, and they always said that violence rubbed off.

'I think I'll do as Archie suggested and take a stroll to the village,' Carrie said, feeling that the more distance between her and her mother, the quicker the tension between them would fade. 'Is there anything you want from the shops?'

'Just some sewing thread. I need to turn a couple of worn sheets, sides to middle. I sometimes think your father puts his foot through them on purpose.'

'I doubt that,' Carrie said with a smile. Walter wouldn't dare.

She wasn't going to worry about any of it anymore. It was a beautiful day, and the sooner last night was put behind her the better. Her spirits lifted as soon as she left the house and made for the village. They still referred to the centre of Penhallow as the village, even though it had begun sprawling outwards with the clusters of new council houses that had been built prior to the war, and now the half-built prefabs. Once the bus link between Penzance and St Ives had been firmly established, more and more people from both places had discovered the quaintness of the village, and so it had grown.

But the hub of it was still the same, and the village green was pleasantly shaded by the centuries-old oak trees and the usual sprinkling of old men lazing and yarning on its benches. A number of acquaintances stopped to chat or to say hello and ask after Archie, but although Carrie thought it was a very pleasant way to spend an hour, she decided she wouldn't want to do it every day.

She wore her straw hat to keep the fiercest rays of the sun off her fair skin, and the bonus was that it shaded her sore cheek sufficiently that either no one noticed it or they were discreet enough not to mention it. By the time she reached the haberdashery for Edna's sewing thread, she had almost forgotten it was there.

'Good Lord, what's happened to you?' Shirley exclaimed, keeping her voice down so that Miss Willis didn't come rushing out from the back room for a nose.

'Nothing much. I just tripped.'

Not even to her good friends would she admit the

shame of having Archie strike her, and her eyes dared Shirley to question it.

'Well, as long as that's all it was. It looks a bit sore. Did it hurt much?'

'Only a bit, but it's all right now. Have you got some white thread? Mum's got a big sewing job to do,' she said, not wanting to discuss her face and the memories it produced.

'So if it isn't that bad, why aren't you at work?' Shirley persisted, fetching the box of threads and selecting what Carrie needed. 'I thought it would have taken more than a little fall to keep you at home.'

Carrie forced a laugh, putting as much enthusiasm into her voice as possible, though it wasn't easy with Shirley's scrutiny.

'I'm playing truant for once, and taking the chance to practise being a proper housewife. It's nice not to have to rush into Penzance and work in a stuffy office, so I'm enjoying the sunshine. I'm going to call at Archie's shop to say hello.'

She knew she was prattling, and she mentioned Archie's name deliberately, to reassure Shirley that there was nothing wrong between them.

'You'll be pushing a pram next,' Shirley said.

From the look in her eyes Carrie knew Shirley immediately wished she hadn't said it, but every now and then it seemed as if she had to punish herself by referring to what she and Hank had done, however obliquely.

'I doubt it. Archie's not keen on starting a family

yet, and we've got a lot of time to make up before we even think about it.'

Shirley gave a bitter laugh. 'That's all very well, but things don't always happen just the way we want them to, do they?'

Carrie wasn't sure who was most relieved to hear the shop door bell tinkling. She paid for the sewing thread and left Shirley to her new customers, glad that she hadn't retorted that there wasn't much chance of her starting a family just yet anyway, since Archie had made it clear that he wasn't ready for fatherhood, and that ever since that one homecoming night of complete abandoment, she knew he had taken pains to be careful.

Remembering how excited she had been at his homecoming, and then the way he had said it so clinically, putting a damper on the spontaneity of their lovemaking, she somehow didn't feel like making small talk with him and his father after all. She decided to give Pollard and Son, Family Butcher a miss, and walked to the library instead, where she was instantly immersed in the familiar smell of old books, and was assured that she could have her old job back whenever she was ready.

Chapter 6

Gwen had cheerfully given up work when David came home, thrilled beyond words to have him safe when she'd thought she would never see him again. It was no hardship for her to stay at home and look after him, since all she wanted to do was to cherish the fact that he was alive. In any case, the job she had had during the war no longer existed when the Services canteen was closed down, and she certainly had no wish to work in Penzance anymore, nor to meet any old acquaintances with whom she had shared such wild times.

Looking back, she hardly recognised the person she had become then. It was like seeing a mirror image of someone who looked like her, who talked like her, but who certainly didn't behave like her. Someone who was her alter ego that she no longer wanted to know. That other woman had become cheap, taking reckless pleasures where she could, flirting with men she didn't even like, in order to forget the real, hurting woman inside.

It had never really worked. David was in her heart

and in her soul, the other half of her, and she could never be complete without him. Realizing only too well now how she had so often tarted herself up for a few hours of dubious forgetfulness made her even more determined to be the best wife she could for him.

Now that life was normal again, she got up every day before it was light, sending David off in the early hours with his lunch box to meet his fellow fishermen before they set off into the cold dawn waters of St Ives. He cycled the few miles, determined to keep fit and to exercise as much as possible. There was still a weakness in the leg where he had been shot twice, and sometimes Gwen heard him wince when he turned over in bed, but he never complained, nor told her any details.

Carrie said that Archie never told her anything, either. It seemed to be the accepted way among ex-servicemen. There were scars, and not only physical ones, that went too deep to be spoken about. Gwen knew that to her cost.

She looked out of the kitchen window of her cottage in Frog Lane to see a familiar figure in a yellow frock and a ribbon-trimmed straw hat walking along the lane. She leaned out of the window at once.

'Carrie! What are you doing at home today?'

Carrie had been deep in thought when she heard Gwen's voice. She had started walking towards the moors on this glorious day, but it was past midday now and the sun was beating down and becoming uncomfortable on her back. She had turned back towards the village, taking a short cut home through Frog Lane.

At her friend's call, she paused at Gwen's gate and then walked up her front path. 'I'm having a day off for once. But the sun's so hot and I didn't mean to walk so far. I have to get back for dinner or Mum will skin me.'

'Oh, come in and have some lemonade first before you collapse. You look really flushed – or am I missing something? Did Archie do that to you?'

Carrie was ready to deny it, and then her shoulders went limp. Why bother, when the heat of the day and the reaction to all that had happened last night was taking all the stuffing out of her?

'It's nothing,' she muttered. 'We had a bit of an argument, and it was over in a minute.'

'You shouldn't let him get away with it. If you do, he'll only do it again, and it's so mean, when you were looking forward to having him home so much.'

'I know. But I don't want to talk about it, Gwen, and I think I'll skip the lemonade after all. It really is later than I thought.'

She couldn't be bothered to continue with the unlikely tale of tripping and hitting her face. Her parents and friends knew about Archie's nightmares, though he wouldn't be too pleased if he knew she had confided in them. So it would have been so much simpler to say he had been thrashing about in the night and caught her an accidental blow. Why hadn't she thought of that? Why did she have to complicate things, when the other explanation would have satisfied Edna?

She hurried on home, unaccountably angry. But

whose anger she resented most, her mother's or Archie's, she couldn't have said.

Dinner would be on the table at five minutes past one o'clock, to give Archie time to get home and wash, and they had better be there on time. Normally, Carrie and her father ate their sandwiches near the sea-front in Penzance, but today she would be eating rabbit pie at home, and Walter's plate would be warmed up in the evening.

She was in a restless, unsettled mood by the time she reached home. Edna asked at once if she had bought the sewing thread or if she had just been idling the morning away all this time.

'I didn't know there was a curfew on me,' she snapped. 'I've bought your thread and I've been to see Gwen. She offered me some lemonade because I was so hot, but I didn't dare stop any longer in case I was locked out.'

She set the table with three knives and forks almost viciously, and Edna eyed her daughter silently for a minute before tipping out the potato water into the sink and then banging the lid of the saucepan back on and giving it a shake.

'I don't know what's got into you, girl. I thought you were counting the days until Archie came home, but sometimes I swear that you were in a better frame of mind while he was away. We all have to get along together in this house, and I don't want your father upset by any more nonsense like we had last night.'

Nonsense! Edna was fond of that word. It covered all eventualities. Nonsense was what she thought they got up to when they went to bed at night. Nonsense was what happened when there were ructions downstairs. Maybe nonsense was what happened to Archie while he was a POW . . .

He came indoors a few moments later, just before Carrie had the chance to erupt. He walked jauntily, smiling at them both, his hands stuck in his pockets as if he didn't have a care in the world.

'Mm, something smells good, so what have you girls been doing today?'

Carrie looked at him mutely. He was acting the breadwinner, the indulgent man of the house – except that this wasn't his house – and she was the little wife, doing nothing except keep house and make herself nice for when he came home. Beds made themselves, floors swept themselves, washing was scrubbed all by itself and miraculously ironed and aired by unseen hands – or the fairies. She was full of an unreasonable resentment she didn't want to acknowledge, but couldn't seem to shake off.

The rabbit pie was filling the house with a delicious smell, which was more than she could say for Archie, despite his good spirits. He couldn't help it. You couldn't chop fresh meat and slap minuscule ration portions on to the scales without getting blood on your hands and your clothes, even though both Pollard men prided themselves on wearing their crisp, blue-striped butcher's aprons, and kept their heads covered with smart straw hats while they were serving customers.

Just because they lived in a small village, Archie's

dad was often heard to say, it didn't mean you had to let your standards drop. Since they were the only butcher's shop for miles, they had the monopoly on it, anyway.

'Lordie, what a whiff,' Edna said, bringing the pie to the table. 'Get upstairs and wash, Archie, and make sure your nails are clean before you come to the table.'

Carrie inwardly groaned. Treating Archie like a child wasn't the way forward for any of them, but to her surprise he merely laughed and blew her a kiss before retreating upstairs at a gallop.

'Will-co, mein Fuhrer,' he called back, and at the sight of her mother's outraged face, Carrie also burst out laughing.

'Well, you did ask for it, Mum,' she said with a giggle. 'Archie knows perfectly well how to behave inside the house, and I've got a bit of news that will make him smile even more.'

She hoped it would. She didn't plan to give up work altogether, but working at the local library within sight of Pollard's shop, and going home in the middle of the day together every day too, must surely restore his good humour. For now, she decided that any mention of the prefabs must be put to one side. In any case, she knew it would be months before they were fitted out properly, and as long as their names were still on the list they stood as good a chance as any other couple of getting one. She wasn't changing her mind about that.

He came downstairs a few minutes later, smelling of Pears soap and rubbing his hands together, before wafting them under Edna's nose as she put the three plates of food on the table.

'Does that suit your honourable ladyship?' he said cheekily.

Carrie felt a sudden thrill of excitement in her veins. For that one moment it was if they were seeing a glimpse of the old, wonderful Archie she had known all her life. Even if it only came and went in moments, it was proof that his good nature was still there beneath all the hard veneer. It made her certain that they would eventually get through whatever it was that bedevilled him, and life would be all honey and roses again.

All the same, she crossed her fingers at the thought, because there was no sense in tempting fate.

'You didn't call in the shop this morning,' he said, sprinkling salt lavishly over his vegetables. 'Did you go out, or just put your feet up with a magazine like all you housewives do? I swear I don't know what you find to do all day.'

Carrie almost choked over her dinner as he winked at her. He was in great form now, and Edna was falling for it, hook, line and sinker. Her face was a picture, and Carrie wished she could have had a photo of it at that moment.

'I suppose you think this dinner cooked itself, young man?'

He put his head on one side. 'Well, perhaps it did, unless you went out and trapped the rabbit at the crack of dawn, and then came home and skinned it before stuffing it into a pie. For a minute I thought you might be doing me out of a job, dear mother-in-law. But, oh no, I forgot! I supplied the rabbit, didn't I?'

Edna finally saw that he was teasing, and managed a wry smile.

'All right, you've had your fun, and I'd forgotten what a joker you could be when you're not scowling. I suppose we should be grateful for it.'

Please don't comment on how refreshing it was compared with his black moods, Carrie begged her silently, but thankfully, for once, Edna restrained herself from stating the obvious.

'So what have you got to tell me, Carrie?' he said, when he had finished eating and pushed his plate away without even a hint of a belch. 'I heard you tell your mother you had a bit of news.'

Instinct told her to tread carefully. She didn't want to spoil the good mood he was in today, and if this determination to be tolerant was his own reaction to what he had done last night, then that hateful slap might have been worth it after all.

'I've decided to give up my job at the council,' she began. Before she could say any more he had put his arm around her shoulders and squeezed.

'That's my girl! I knew you'd see sense now you've got me to look after you.'

'Wait a minute. I've only just decided, and I haven't even told them yet. I'll probably have to work a week's notice. But before you get too excited about it, I've been offered my old job back at the library, and I really want to take it, Archie. We'll be able to wave to one another across the green when trade is slack, and walk to work there and back as well. We'll see more of one another than if I was at home all day!'

The more she said, the more convincing she hoped she sounded, and the more nervous she felt. She desperately hoped he wouldn't go all grouchy on her now. She had practised this little speech all the way home from Frog Lane, getting the best in first, and then the anti-climax – if that was how he chose to see it.

He didn't say anything for a minute, and then he shrugged in an offhand way.

'I suppose if you must pander to the old biddies and their book-reading habits, then that's not a bad solution,' he said, and she could have whooped for joy.

She knew it shouldn't really be like this. It wasn't what Emily Pankhurst and all those suffragettes had fought for thirty years ago – not that they had fought for jobs for women, exactly, it was more for them to be recognized as people, and not just to be slaves to masculine whims. It was so they could have a voice in things. They didn't have to be strident and march all over the place to achieve their aims, nor should they have to get them by bedroom tactics, either.

There were more subtle ways. A bit of careful thinking, and tact, could still produce the end result. And if it meant harmony within the household, who cared if it seemed as if she was making a compromise? The joy of it was that Carrie really loved working among the books in the library, but if Archie thought she was doing it just to please him, she wasn't going to tell him otherwise.

*

When they went to bed that night he put his arm around her tentatively. He had got home from the pub much earlier than usual, and they had all played a game of whist before bedtime, her mum and dad playing against herself and Archie. The honours had been even, and there had been a feeling of well-being among them all. It was how family life was meant to be, before the war came and interrupted it.

'We should probably have been playing Happy Families tonight, shouldn't we?' he said, echoing her thoughts in a delightfully harmonious way. He chuckled against her cheek, careful not to press too hard.

'Well, that's what we are, isn't it?' she whispered. 'Oh, Archie, I do love you, and it's so lovely not to be in bed alone every night with only my dreams of you to keep me company.'

'Is that what you used to do? Dream of me?'

'Of course I did. All the time.'

'Tell me about your dreams. What were we doing in them?'

Carrie felt her face grow hot. 'Oh, all kinds of things. Lovely things. Cycling to St Ives and throwing pebbles into the sea, then stopping at a tea room for scones and jam and cream, or walking over the moors in the rain, or looking for mushrooms before the sun was up. You know, all the things we used to do.'

She became aware that his hand was gently moving up and down her back where she was curving into him now. It was making her tingle deliciously. They were warm beneath the blankets, facing one another with not an inch to spare between them, their bodies pressed tight, and she could feel him hardening against her through her thin nightdress. At her intake of breath, he knew perfectly well that she was aware of that too.

'And this, Carrie?' he whispered seductively against her mouth. 'Did you ever dream of this?'

'I don't know if it's proper for me to say,' she said tremulously. She had been brought up to be modest at all times, and even now . . .

'Anything between us is right and proper, but I also know that I have to earn your trust again after—'

She put her fingers to his lips before he could mention last night. She didn't want the ugliness of it to intrude, and she brushed aside all feelings of immodesty, feeling the excitement building as his fingers inched up her nightdress.

'I did dream of it, Archie,' she said, her voice no stronger than a sigh. 'I dreamed of you holding me like this, and loving me, and sometimes I wanted you so much I didn't know how to bear it without you.'

'Do you want me now?'

Although his voice was still soft, his breath caressing her face, she wasn't sure if this was a new Archie, asking her permission, or if he was subtly demanding her submission. Whatever it was, the moment was so infinitely sweet that it only heightened her desire for him.

'Oh yes. Oh yes, yes, *yes*!'

She slid beneath him as he rolled over her in one fluid movement, pushing her into the mattress, his kisses hot on her mouth. Her arms were around him and she was pulling him into her, inflamed with a matching desire. Oh yes, she had dreamed of this. Yes, she had wanted him, needed him, and ached for him . . . in the lonely hours of the endless nights, she had rocked herself into his pillow, trying to imagine it was Archie that she held, and failing miserably to capture his spirit.

But there was no failure now. His body was warm and heavy on her, loving her as she had dreamed of being loved for all those lonely months, saying uninhibited words of love that he didn't normally use, and she cherished every moment . . . until he moved away from her and slid out of the bed.

That was when she knew it was unfinished, and was never likely to be while he held this crazy notion of not wanting to bring children into the world.

She watched him leave the bedroom to go to the bathroom, and felt the slow trickle of tears on her cheeks. It stung where she was bruised, but not as much as the realization that they still had a long way to go before they achieved the kind of marriage she wanted.

It wasn't that she had thought they would start having babies right away. They needed to get to know one another all over again before that happened. But it should happen naturally.

If the good Lord had willed it, she would have been carrying very soon. Now it seemed that if Archie willed it, she would not.

There was also something else tucked away in a corner of her mind. This house wouldn't be big enough for them all once she started having babies. They would have to find somewhere of their own then.

But since she knew that was the worst reason for wanting to start a family, she quickly smothered the guilty thought, and as Archie got back into bed and folded his arms around her with loving kisses instead of having his ritual cigarette, she thanked God instead for sending him safely home to her.

Shirley got the letter she had been waiting for a few days later. By the time she met her friends at the church hall on Thursday evening, she was ecstatic.

'No need to ask what's put that soppy look on your face,' Velma said dryly. 'So when's the hero coming home?'

'A week on Saturday,' Shirley said joyously, the words like a mantra now that she had said them so often and bored Miss Willis half to death. 'They're sending him all the way by ambulance, can you believe it? It's not just for Bernard, mind. They have a small convoy of ambulances coming our way with stretcher cases, so he's been lucky to cadge a lift. I don't think it would have been too comfortable for him to travel all that way by train.'

It was almost the first time she had acknowledged that Bernard was still going to be far from fit, or admitted that there had probably never been any suggestion of him being able to travel hundreds of miles by train. She still wouldn't believe it, though in her mind he was going to be exactly the same as he had been when he went away.

She knew things were very different for other people. Some of the men in the village had come back with terrible injuries, and some had never come back at all. You didn't know whether to avoid the women who went around looking so sad and bereft, or to try to say something to them. You didn't know how to behave, because nothing really prepared you for it. It wasn't like someone very old who had lived their life and was expected to die; it was often young men, as young as Bernard. Even Carrie's husband wasn't the same as he used to be, though it was only nightmares, apparently. Not that Carrie ever said much about it, but they all guessed that he still had problems.

Shirley shivered. Normally, she could happily skim along on the surface of life, a bit flighty, a bit fluffy, but she had feelings too. She had had them for Hank, and for the baby she had lost, though nobody ever asked her about that, and if they had she wouldn't have told them. It had been a terrifying time, but sometimes she still let herself imagine what it would have been like, whether it would have been a boy or a girl, who it would have looked like . . . and that was when her fantasies stopped abruptly, because it would have been disastrous if it had looked exactly like Hank.

In spite of all that, she loved Bernard with all her heart, and she was going to spend the rest of her life showing him just how much. The bubbling excitement came to the surface again.

'We're going to hang out the flags at our house and at Bernard's, like you did for Archie, Carrie. His mum and dad and his kid brothers will be making such a fuss of him that he'll probably soon get fed up with it, especially his mum.'

Her son the hero, Shirley thought with a flash of jealousy. He might be his mother's son, but he was *her* fiancé, and she intended to spend as much time as possible with him from now on. After all, they had a wedding to plan.

At the thought, her smile froze a little. They hadn't been able to talk about the wedding for ages, nor to make any plans. Old Hitler had seen to that. But now Bernard was coming home, and the war and everything it involved was all in the past. Everyone could make plans for the future now, and being married to Bernard and starting a life of their own, away from both their crowded family homes, was Shirley's goal.

She could see herself in a white dress with a filmy white veil and her two younger sisters as bridesmaids. She dreamed of the silky white dress, even though she knew she wasn't exactly virginal white herself.

That was the one thing to mar her thoughts of the wedding. Because after the excitement of the ceremony and the little get-together her parents had promised her with as many rations as they could muster for a decent spread there would be the wedding night.

It was naturally assumed that a bride was pure until her wedding night, and it was the husband's privilege to be the first and only one to be intimate with her. She didn't know how or where she had gleaned the information, but it was said that a husband could always tell if he wasn't the first. She still didn't know how, but it was the only thing that frightened her about their magical first night together.

'Shirley's got that glazed look on her face again,' she heard Gwen say laughingly. 'Thinking wicked thoughts, are you, lambkin?'

Her eyes flickered. 'Of course not! I'm just wondering what to wear to welcome Bernard home.'

Velma felt momentarily envious, wishing she had felt that glow of anticipation about Stan, and still amazed at the passion he had shown her that night in St Ives. But when she thought about it later, at home alone as usual, she began to think it was no more than a gigantic need for release, following his traumatic news, and not love at all.

Well, of course it wasn't love. Not young love, like Shirley's and Carrie's and Gwen's. Velma was annoyed with herself for feeling like Methuselah too often these days, especially compared with her friends. In the war years, it hadn't seemed so marked. The hall had been a sociable place then, all the wives, sweethearts and mothers doing a job of work for the men overseas, knitting their gloves and socks and balaclavas. Now, there were only sparse groups meeting for friendship, and she often felt the odd one out, even among their foursome.

'Whatever you wear, Bernard won't care,' Carrie told Shirley. 'All he'll want is to see your smiling face again.'

'He wouldn't care if you met him at the door in your birthday suit,' Gwen teased. 'He might even prefer it.'

Shirley went bright red. Despite what they all knew about Gwen, Shirley always felt that she was the one who had strayed the most, but she didn't like that kind of talk, and her chapel-going mother definitely wouldn't like it. Just like Carrie's mum, Mrs Loe disapproved of her daughter's friendship with Gwen Trewint.

'Stop it, Gwen,' Carrie said. 'You're embarrassing the poor girl.'

'Well, she'll have to get used to it when they're married, won't she?'Gwen said tartly. 'Even if she only gives him a glimpse of her upper half now and then when she takes a bath. Or is she planning to spend her married life as a nun?'

'Hardly,' Shirley muttered, and they were all aware that the temperature in their corner had gone down a few degrees.

Velma patted her hand. 'Don't let anything spoil Bernard's homecoming, sweetie. You've got the rest of your lives to look forward to, and we should all put the past behind us now. That's the only place for it really, isn't it?' she said, attempting to make a joke, and glaring at Gwen for stirring up the bad memories for Shirley. They all wanted to forget those times.

'Don't worry, nothing's going to spoil it,' Shirley said, perking up quickly.

She had always had the ability to do that; nothing depressed her for long. There was only one thing that had done that, and they had all helped her through it. It had bonded them in a way that nothing else could have done, Velma reflected, and it made nonsense of her own ancient feelings. They were good friends, and would always remain so.

Chapter 7

Carrie was delighted to find Archie waiting for her outside the church hall that evening, saying he had decided to leave the pub early to escort her safely home. Not even Gwen's teasing aside that he was checking up on her could dampen the moment. He looked so strong and upright now. These few weeks of her mum's nourishing cooking had done him good, despite the meagre rations they still had to contend with, and the juggling with food coupons. He tucked Carrie's arm inside his as he called out cheerily to the others.

'Good-night, girls. Sleep tight and don't let the bed bugs bite.'

Carrie giggled. He was obviously still in a good mood, and she was the lucky one, she thought. Gwen's David never came to meet her; Shirley's Bernard wasn't home yet; and Velma – well, they weren't sure whether Velma would want Stan meeting her from anywhere. She had been in such an odd mood lately.

'So what did you girls find to talk about tonight?' Archie said chattily.

'Oh, same as usual. The price of fish, and when Shirley's going to get married, and what we're going to wear for the Welcome Home dance.'

'Do you really want to go to that?'

Carrie stared at him indignantly. 'Of course I do! We all do. It would be a terrible slight to the organizers if we didn't turn up, wouldn't it? Besides, I want to show you off.'

He squeezed her arm affectionately. 'So I'm a prize trophy, am I?'

'You're *my* prize trophy. And I'm yours. There's one thing I'm glad about too. You never had the chance to look at any other girls while you were in that horrible prison camp, did you?'

She said it without thinking. It was just a sunny observation, no more, but she should have known that Archie wouldn't see it that way.

'That didn't make it any better. Most of the blokes would have given anything to see a friendly female face, and a hell of a lot more than that, too, if they weren't so starved of food and energy that they couldn't have done much about it.'

'That's coarse talk, Archie.'

'It's the way it was. If you don't want to hear it, don't listen.'

She didn't reply. It was rare enough for him to say anything about what went on in the camp, or about the conditions in which they lived, or their captors, but to think of those men aching for a bit of female company in the way Archie implied just made her feel uncomfortable.

111

It was even worse to think that Archie himself had felt like that. Of course she wanted him to miss her and want her, but she supposed she was still keeping their love on a kind of ethereal plane, instead of acknowledging the desperate need a man could feel for a woman. And such flowery language probably came from too much book-reading, she told herself.

'I do understand, Archie,' she said at length, when the silence had gone on too long. His steps had quickened and she had a job to keep up with him. 'But if you don't slow down I'll have run out of breath before we get home.'

'All right,' he said abruptly. 'But you shouldn't remind me of those times, Carrie. That's one reason why I don't care about this dance you keep on about. Too many of them will be reminiscing over old times as if it was no more than a bloody picnic, talking about how brave some of them were, and the medals they got, and the poor bastards who didn't make it. Anybody with any sense would just want to forget the whole bloody thing.'

At least you came back. You have your health and strength and your job. And me, she added silently. But she didn't dare say it, aloud.

'It's still weeks away,' she said instead. 'You'll feel differently by then.'

She fervently hoped so, anyway, and she took his grunt as an agreement.

'Did you know Bernard Bosinney's coming home on Saturday week?' she went on, still pleased at

Shirley's news. 'They're sending him home by ambulance, can you believe?'

'Poor devil must still be in a bad way then.'

'Why do you think that? Shirley says there's a whole convoy coming this way, most of them stretcher cases, and he's been lucky enough to get a lift instead of coming by train.'

'If you believe that you'll believe anything.'

'What do you mean?' She didn't like the way this conversation was going, and she wished she'd never mentioned Bernard at all.

Archie sounded impatient. 'I mean, my dear innocent girl, that they don't send perfectly able-bodied men all that way by ambulance unless there's a very good reason for it.'

'I know he's not exactly able-bodied in the way you mean—'

'Didn't you say the poor bugger had got shot down over France and had some serious burns that didn't get properly attended to at the time?'

'Well, that was what Shirley told us. It was his thigh and his side.' She tried to ignore the fact that Archie swore far more than he used to, and just hoped he wouldn't forget himself in front of her mother or she'd never hear the end of it.

'Then it stands to reason he needed far more treatment than just a kiss on the backside and a ride home in an ambulance. Your friend Shirley's in for a shock if she expects him to be hopping around at this dance you all seem so keen on.'

They were nearly home now, and it hadn't been a

comfortable walk. If she was honest, it had been more depressing than pleasant, and now that Archie's good humour seemed to have vanished, Carrie found herself hoping he wouldn't make a habit of meeting her at the church hall on Thursday evenings.

'Did you play darts tonight?' she asked quickly, to put him in a better frame of mind before they went indoors.

When he scowled, she knew she shouldn't have bothered.

'I did, and I lost ten bob, since you're asking.'

'You *gambled*?'

All their money should be being put aside for when they moved out of Kellaway Terrace. They had never discussed it as such, but it was what Carrie had expected. It was what she thought he would understand.

'Good God, woman, are you going to block that bit of fun now? It's not a crime, and it makes a change to have money to bet on anything, instead of betting matchsticks on whose cockroach will win the race across the cell floor, so don't start thinking you can deny me that pleasure.'

'I won't,' she snapped. 'Just don't let my mother know you're in the habit of gambling, that's all, because I'll have to take her tongue-lashing, not you.'

And then she realized what he had said, and her face went white.

Shirley didn't know what she was expecting to see when the ambulance rolled up outside the Bosinneys' front door. On the Saturday afternoon he was coming home, she was there with Bernard's mum and dad and his two young brothers, both growing so fast their long trousers looked more like short ones now, having been let down so many times they resembled concertina bottoms. But nobody was concerned with the years of make-do-and-mend anymore. The world had turned the corner, if that wasn't an impossibility, as her clever friend Carrie would have told her, and they had everything to look forward to now. The house was bedecked with bunting, and flags hung from every window, and Bernard's mum had put his photo in their front-room window just to show how proud she was of him.

Shirley's heart was thumping with excitement by late afternoon. She knew exactly how her friends must have felt now. It was one thing to know their men were safe, which brought the most enormous feeling of relief and thankfulness that all their prayers had been answered. It was something else to be actually waiting for the moment when she would clasp Bernard in her arms again. And no matter what his mum and dad thought, she aimed to be the first to do that.

'It's here,' Frank Bosinney shouted, his twelve-year-old legs coiled so tightly together Shirley was sure he'd wet himself with excitement at any moment – if he hadn't done so already. 'The ambulance is here, Mum! Come on, Sam.'

He hurtled past his brother, two years his junior, to reach the front door first. But Shirley was already there, her hands clammy, hardly able to breathe, having dreamed of this moment for so long. She had even practised saying a couple of words in French that Bernard's dad had taught her, and then decided it would be daft to say them. She was sure Bernard would prefer to forget that awful time, anyway, and every time the thought entered her head, she had glossed over the thought of someone called Marie, who had helped him on his way to recovery from his injuries.

The ambulance door was being opened now, and the driver and his mate were helping someone out of the back of it. Or rather, they were lifting someone out of it on some kind of chair. Someone who looked like Bernard, spoke like Bernard, but who wasn't the Bernard she knew. Shirley swallowed in disbelief. All his recent letters had been loving and cheerful, and in her mind she was still picturing him as she had last seen him, so dashing in his air-force blue uniform, his hair bleached even blonder than usual by the sun, his face tanned with health. Now, all she saw was a broken man being aided by strangers as they lifted the chair carefully out of the vehicle – and then he caught sight of her and waved, his face lighting up.

'Don't worry about this contraption. I can walk perfectly well, but these warders insisted on keeping me in it until I reached dry land.'

He was as cheeky as ever, and Shirley breathed a huge sigh of relief as he got out of the chair and shook his helpers' hands. He wasn't crippled, and a sense of shame quickly followed the relief, because for a moment, a tiny moment, she had wondered how she would ever have coped if he was.

She was still standing, transfixed, when his mother rushed past her and enveloped Bernard in her arms, weeping copious tears over him, while his dad cleared his throat and tried not to show any emotion at all. The boys were shrieking and leaping up and down, and neighbours all along the street were emerging from their houses now, and cheering Bernard as if he'd just won the George Cross.

It was a wonderful homecoming, but for Shirley it wasn't quite as she had imagined it in her dreams. Then, she had been the only one greeting Bernard, and she had floated into his welcoming arms, his strong, loving arms, and they had somehow drifted off into the sunset together, Hollywood style.

Instead of which . . . her heart jolted as the ambulance trundled away, and Bernard slowly walked towards the front door with his kit over his shoulder, his leg dragging, his body twisted, and she knew that life was never going to be the same.

'Why was I so naive?' she wept to her friend Carrie the next day, feeling that of all people she would be the one who would understand the most. 'I knew he'd been through a terrible time, but somehow I didn't expect to see him like that. It was a shock, Carrie, and I'm afraid I showed it. His mum and dad must have known how I felt and when Bernard said he needed to stretch out on the bed and rest they couldn't get me out of the house quickly enough. I feel such a wicked person.'

Shirley had met Carrie after morning service at St

Jude's, unable to face her own chapel service that day, and they walked away from the church together.

Carrie tried to reassure her. 'Don't be silly. You're not wicked. You're just human, and Bernard should have had the sense to warn you. He's as much to blame as anybody.'

Shirley shook her head. 'That's just it! He probably told me long ago in his letters, but as usual I only read the bits I wanted to read. Like how he loved me and missed me. You know, all the sweet things. I didn't read the bits about his treatment and all that medical stuff because it upset me too much.' She took a shuddering breath. 'I'm paying for it now, though, aren't I? I'm expecting any moment that he'll tell me the engagement is off.'

'He's not likely to do that, is he? He'll be had up for breach of promise,' Carrie said dryly, but she was increasingly alarmed at Shirley's plunging depression. The only other time she had seen her like this was when the awful truth had dawned on her that she was expecting Hank Delaney's baby. The next moment she heard what she had feared.

'You know what this is, don't you?' Shirley said melodramatically. 'It's my penance. God's punishing me for what happened. He's making me pay by testing whether I can cope with Bernard being . . . like he is. But I probably won't have to, because I'm sure Bernard will have seen it in my eyes, and he won't want me now.'

'I think you're being absolutely ridiculous, Shirley. Look, why don't we go and see Velma this afternoon?

She'll tell you the same, and she never minds a visit on a Sunday afternoon. Unless you've got other plans.'

Archie would be having his now customary Sunday afternoon snooze, and Gwen and David always spent Sunday afternoons cycling over the moors or into St Ives. Velma was often at a loose end, and wouldn't mind the company.

'I'm going to Bernard's for tea later. Nobody's said anything different, though I half expected Frank and Sam to come racing round to our house to tell me not to bother. Anyway, they didn't, so all right, we'll see Velma this afternoon.'

Shirley gave a wan smile. 'I'm doing it again, aren't I? Relying on you all to tell me what to do.'

'That's what friends are for, isn't it?'

'I know, but nobody ever had such good friends as I do.'

'So go home and think sensibly. Bernard has never stopped writing to you, and he's never stopped loving you. Dry your tears and put on your prettiest dress and when you see Bernard at tea-time be sure to let him know that you love him.'

When they parted company, Carrie asked herself mockingly when she had turned into such a wise old owl. She wasn't at all, but it was always easier to see someone else's problems from a different perspective. Shirley would always be the weakest one of the group, the one least able to cope with illness or disability. But none of them had expected Bernard to come home apparently so disabled. She wondered if his parents had even been aware of the extent of his injuries, or if his letters to them had been bland enough to stop them worrying unduly too. It was a big mistake to keep the truth hidden, thought Carrie, but you could hardly tell that to someone who had wanted to keep the extent and effects of his wounds to himself, as if they were something to be ashamed of.

But with Shirley's new anxieties, it made her more thankful than ever that at least Archie had no physical injuries. She could just imagine how demoralised that would have made him feel. David Trewint still had problems with his leg after the bullets had struck him, but he was determined to exercise as much as possible to strengthen it, and to get the most out of the life that had been handed back to him. And Stan Gould obviously dealt with his problems in his own tight-lipped way, except for that one time when he had broken down before Velma about what had happened to his mates.

By the time Carrie got home, having left her mum outside St Jude's while she talked to Shirley, the pots and pans were already being banged about, and she gave a sigh, thinking that somebody being home a little late to help get dinner ready was such a tiny fuss, compared to the problems that other people had.

Despite Edna's obvious annoyance that Carrie had gone off with her friend instead of coming straight home as usual, the house was filled with warmth and homely activity and the enticing smell of the small piece of beef Archie had brought home for Sunday dinner and the simmering vegetables her dad grew in the back garden and on his allotment.

Through the kitchen window she could see her father and Archie now, leaning on their spades and debating something or other, probably putting the world to rights in their own way. It was all so ordinary and yet so wonderfully satisfying.

Impulsively, Carrie did something she rarely did. She put her arms around her mother and kissed her flushed cheek.

'Goodness me, what on earth was that for?' Edna said, too flustered to make the tart comment that was on the tip of her tongue.

'To show that I love you and appreciate all that you do for me and all of us,' Carrie said simply, even though she had never said such a thing in her life before, and she was blushing deeply at saying it now. But sometimes you just had to seize the moment.

'Go on, you daft 'a'p'orth, you're getting all sloppy. What have you done?' Edna added suspiciously.

'Nothing!' Carrie said, turning away with an embarrassed laugh. 'I just think we should tell people the way we feel about them a bit more than we do, that's all.'

'Well, if we don't hurry up and get this dinner on the table, we'll have two hungry men telling us in no uncertain terms how they feel.'

But she had a suspiciously moist look in her eyes when she said it.

Carrie met Shirley on the corner of her road that afternoon, and they walked to Tinners' Row together, their arms linked. Shirley was pale, but she looked decidedly better now, her eyes were steadier, and her hair was a soft golden cloud around her pretty face.

'I've been thinking,' she said, 'and before you say that's a bit of a miracle, the way you always do, I intend to tell Bernard I'm sorry.'

'Is that such a good idea? Perhaps he has no idea of the shock you were feeling when you saw him.'

'He knows. I could see it in his eyes, and I have to make it up to him.'

She was so determined to make caring for Bernard her life's work that Carrie hoped she wouldn't smother him with sympathy and make him feel even worse.

Velma greeted them gladly. The cottage that she loved so dearly had sometimes felt claustrophobic lately, and she had no idea why that was. She kept it sparkling, just the way her parents had kept it. She scrubbed and dusted and polished until the whole place shone, and yet it had begun to feel less like a home than a prison. She had become morbid, and it had all started that night when Stan had broken down so completely, and she had discovered that he was human after all.

All her carefully built-up reserve, and her plans for asking so calmly for a divorce so that they could both get on with their lives, had vanished at the knowledge that he had needed her so badly. Just once. But now there was nothing, just the sterile emptiness of a cottage that had no warmth of human contact about it, merely the fanatic cleanliness of a frustrated woman.

122

She was furious with herself for even thinking such stupid thoughts, denying that she was any such thing. But the thoughts still lingered, long after she tried to put them out of her mind, so she was pleased to see two of her friends turning up so unexpectedly that Sunday afternoon.

'I'll put the kettle on,' she said at once, 'unless you'd rather have lemonade?'

They opted for lemonade, which saved the bother of making tea, and they chose to sit on the wooden bench in Velma's neat back garden, with the fragrance of late-summer roses still heavy on the air.

'So to what do I owe this honour?' she said formally. 'I thought you'd be cosy with Bernard by now, Shirley, not wanting to visit an old fogey like me.'

Now why on earth had she said that? Velma was thirty-five, she reminded herself, not an ancient monument. Thirty-five . . . childless . . . husband-less, for all that she saw of Stan . . . and miserable.

'Bernard doesn't look as well as I expected. He looks a bit sort of grey, and he seems to be all twisted and he drags his leg, and I was so upset when I saw him that I behaved really badly,' Shirley said in a rush.

'She's overreacting as usual,' Carrie said. 'I knew this would happen.'

Shirley turned on her 'Oh, you're always so right, aren't you? Just because you and Archie are so lovey-dovey now—'

'Not always,' Carrie murmured, remembering that vicious slap on her cheek – an uncomfortable reminder of his black moods.

'And Gwen and David are like two peas in a pod, and I suppose Velma's going to get what she wants, and I don't know how things are going to turn out for me and Bernard now, I just don't.'

Velma sucked in her breath. If they only knew . . .

'Don't you think it's time you stopped acting like a drama queen, Shirley? If you expected everyone to come home from the war without a single problem, you're even more simple than I took you for. So Bernard's dragging his leg and he's a bit twisted. He's not exactly Richard the Third, is he?'

When Shirley looked blank, Velma sighed.

'I'm sure all this will pass in time. As for him looking grey and all the rest of it, well, for heaven's sake, he'd just spent hours squeezed up in a wretched ambulance, alongside stretcher cases who were undoubtedly ten times worse than he was. Count your blessings, darling, and show him how happy you are that he's come home to you.'

'That was quite a speech, Velma,' Carrie said, when Shirley sat there chewing her lip and saying nothing.

'It wasn't meant to be. But Shirley and Bernard were obviously meant to be together, and to let all that be affected by a little injury is ridiculous.'

'I *am* here, you know,' Shirley said, nettled. 'You don't have to talk over me. And I'd say it was more than a little injury to be shot down in a plane and go through all that Bernard has. It's a miracle he's come back at all. He could have been captured by the Germans instead of finding his way to that French farmhouse. He could have been surrendered to them even then. He could have been blinded, or killed. So don't belittle him!'

She stopped abruptly, aware that she was rambling on.

'I'd say you were the one doing that, by running away at the first sight of somebody who wasn't quite as perfect as when he went away,' Velma said.

'I didn't run away. And Bernard will always be perfect to me, no matter what his injuries!'

'Why don't you go and tell him so then?' Carrie put in. 'I would imagine it's what he needs to hear.'

Shirley allowed a small smile to touch her lips.'I know what you're doing. You're ganging up on me, aren't you? Forcing me to see the right thing to do. That was your idea in coming here, wasn't it, Carrie?'

'Well, it worked, didn't it?'

The way it had worked before, she thought silently. When they had persuaded Shirley that no good would come of confessing to Bernard all about Hank and the baby that had never been. It would be even more disastrous to confess it now, with Bernard still in a fragile state, by the sound of it.

Shirley stood up and brushed down her skirt.

'I'm going to see him right now,' she announced. 'I'm going to prove that I'm not in the least afraid of his injuries, and that we've still got a wedding to plan.'

'I wouldn't be in too much of a hurry to talk about the wedding right away, though,' Velma advised. 'You're only twenty, Shirley, and Bernard's only a few years older. Let him get his breath back after his ordeal – and his strength too. He'll need it to cope with Miss Sarah Bernhardt!'

Even though she had no idea who Velma was talking about, Shirley gave them a theatrical wave as she left them at the cottage and made her way back through the village to Bernard's house.

She felt considerably better now, finally admitting to herself that she *had* been afraid yesterday; afraid of hugging Bernard too tightly in case she hurt him; afraid that she wouldn't find the right words to say; afraid that when they were married and she saw the full extent of his wounds she would recoil in horror and ruin everything; afraid that after all the joyous anticipation of his return home they were two different people after all.

But as usual her friends had put her on the right track. Above everything else, she was madly in love with Bernard, and if her new role was to be a kind of nursemaid as well as a loving wife, she would play it to perfection.

'Do you think we achieved anything?' Carrie asked Velma.

'I'm sure we did, but in the end it's up to her, isn't it? Time has a habit of sorting things out, and, whatever we say, only the two people involved in any relationship really know what goes on and how to solve their own problems.'

'As long as Shirley remembers to keep her mouth shut about the other business, you mean.'

'Yes. That too.'

'Was there something else, Velma?'

'No. Do you want another glass of lemonade?'

Carrie shook her head. 'I don't think so, thank you. I need some fresh air after all this emotional upheaval, so I'm going to take a walk before I go home, and I'll see you on Thursday as usual at the church hall.'

When she had gone, Velma went back to the garden with a book, but she couldn't concentrate on the words. They seemed to jumble in front of her eyes, and she had the strange feeling in her stomach that had been there for the past week. It was a gnawing sensation that made her feel vaguely sick, and a couple of times, during her morning stint on the buses, she had felt dizzy.

She had put it down to the lurching movement of the bus through the narrow lanes towards Penzance, but if it continued she knew she might have to visit the doctor. She wasn't keen on doctors; she had seen too much of them during the weary and distressing months before her parents died. The more she could keep away from them, the better she liked it.

But she had never been afraid to face up to the truth, and if by the middle of the week the feelings of nausea still hadn't gone away, she knew that eventually she would have to seek the doctor's opinion. She also knew that the symptoms were not unlike the ones her mother had had, and if it was a growth like the one that had killed her mother, she would face that just as stoically too.

Chapter 8

Shirley went straight to Bernard's house and found him in the garden, joking with Frank and Sam. He wore an ordinary shirt and flannel trousers, the wind was ruffling his fair hair, and he looked so revived after yesterday, and so much like he always had done, that she caught her breath. He held out his hands to her at once.

'At last!' he said. 'I thought you were never going to get here.'

She wondered if he really hadn't noticed how badly she had behaved yesterday, or if he was simply choosing to ignore it.

'Carrie wanted to go and see Velma, and I said I'd go with her. Besides, I thought you'd want to spend some time with your family before I turned up.'

He put his arm around her. 'I'd rather spend time with you. It's been far too long, and I'd forgotten how pretty you are.'

'Had you? I didn't forget a single thing about you!'

She had, though. She had forgotten he even existed when her wonderful GI had told her she was beautiful enough to star in Hollywood movies. And she had been gullible enough to believe him, had even fantasized about being 'discovered' drinking a cup of coffee, the way some of them were – according to Hank.

He had such stories to tell . . . but in the end she had to accept that they were only stories, because when the GIs vanished from the scene so dramatically, she had never heard from him again. She had just had the little reminder . . .

Bernard had both his arms around her now, and she realized how tightly she was hugging him back as he whispered wickedly in her ear.

'We'd better stop this, or we'll be exciting the neighbours. We can have the front room to ourselves after tea, though, and I can't wait to get you on my own.'

That's what she wanted too, she told herself fervently. Once they were alone together they could pick up where they had left off, all those months ago. It was the best way to forget the past, to blot it out of her memory – and Bernard must have similar thoughts. He had suffered so much, and she wanted to make it up to him. It was going to be all right, and there would be no ghosts to haunt either of them. Then she felt him wince as she hugged his wounded side a little too tightly, and she remembered that he still wasn't completely restored to her.

Archie was in the kitchen when Carrie returned home, searching for aspirins for a raging headache, his eyes still blurred from sleeping too heavily in the daytime.

'Why did you have to go out on a Sunday after-noon?' he complained. 'Don't you females have enough to gossip about on Thursday evenings?'

Carrie spoke lightly, sensing a 'handle with care' label.

'We don't gossip. We discuss. Shirley wanted to see Velma and I went with her, that's all.'

'Is the honeymoon over already then? I suppose she couldn't take it when she saw the cripple.'

'That's a horrible thing to say, and he's not a cripple. He can walk perfectly well. Bernard's parents and brothers were just as anxious to see him as Shirley, and she wanted to give them some time together. She's gone there for tea, anyway.'

He scowled, and she knew that nothing she said was going to please him.

'I wonder what she got up to while he was away,' he said next, jolting her. 'A good-looking piece like her would have had those GIs sniffing around when they were based near Penzance. Even in the prison camps we knew how you girls went to dances and fraternized with the poor boys far from home.'

It was so near the mark that Carrie had to turn away from him before he saw the truth of it in her face. He didn't know. He *couldn't* know. But it just proved how a casual remark like that could catch anyone off guard. It could catch Shirley out.

'We hardly saw the GIs around here, and anyway it was almost our duty to be nice to them. They *were* far from home, Archie, and if you had been in a similar situation, you would have appreciated a friendly smile and the chance to do normal things, and to have a bit of relief from the war now and then,' she said.

But for all its expanding size, Penhallow was still what the GIs had called a one-horse town, which they rarely visited more than once. For any kind of entertainment, you had to go to Penzance. You went by bus or bicycle, or by car if you were lucky enough to have a father with a car, and enough petrol to drive you there.

'I bet you saw plenty of Yanks, working in Penzance.'

'You couldn't help seeing them, unless you went around with your eyes closed. You couldn't help seeing the people you worked with every day, either, or the people on the bus, or the people at church, or my mum and dad,' she added sarcastically, starting to get annoyed with his insinuations. 'Are you trying to say you think *I* had my head turned by a chap in an American uniform now? Do you have such little trust in me, Archie?'

'You wouldn't be the first,' he snapped. 'And stop talking so much. You make my head rock even worse than before.'

'Well, stop making such stupid suggestions, or you won't be the only one with a headache.'

She was slightly shaken, all the same. Where did all this talk of GIs come from? He didn't normally deign to mention them, and the GIs had been gone from the area for over a year now. Then he went on, and it all became clear.

'We had a customer in the shop the other day whose

daughter married one of them. She's going to America next year to live in some flash house with a big car. Must be a bit different from living around here. It's no wonder they could get the girls, with all their money and their chocolates and their nylons.'

Carrie put her arms around him. There was a strange vulnerability about him now, and everyone knew the Yanks' reputation of being 'overpaid, over-sexed, and over here'.

'Well, they didn't get me. And they didn't get any of my friends, either, so stop looking so black, can't you? What you need is some fresh air to get rid of that headache, so let's go for a walk.'

And hopefully it would also put any speculation about the Yanks out of his mind. But for all those endless hours in a prison camp, when the POWs had little else to do but think about what was going on back home, it was obvious that those imaginings could fester into nightmares. It must have been the same for all of them so far from home, including Archie Pollard.

Gwen propped her bicycle against David's and sat down on the grass verge beside him as they took a breather on their ride back from St Ives that afternoon. She caught sight of Carrie and Archie walking towards them across the moors, their hands held loosely.

'Look at them,' she said, waving. 'They look happy enough, don't they? He was lucky to come home as well as he did, after all that time locked up.'

'He'll be well enough on the surface,' David told her. 'But you can't go through that kind of hell for two years without it leaving some scars. He should have taken more time to adjust to civvy life again when he came home, instead of going straight back to the shop. Though he probably enjoys hacking through a carcass, and imagining it's some Jerry bastard's neck.'

'David! You don't really think that, do you?'

If so, knowing about the way Archie had struck Carrie that night, she didn't feel too comfortable. She hadn't told David anything about that. He'd never cared much for Archie Pollard, and she didn't want to give him any more ammunition to sneer about.

He laughed at her indignant face. 'Probably not. Though there were a hell of a lot of chaps who would have welcomed the chance to do a damn sight more than wring their necks.'

'I suppose they were only obeying orders, same as you were,' Gwen said, not really knowing why she was defending the Germans, but knowing that it must be true.

'Yes, well, some found it easier to obey orders than others. And some took a sadistic pleasure in brutality. Not everybody joined up just for the good of the country, Gwen.'

'You did, and so did Bernard Bosinney. And Stan Gould was a regular soldier before the war began.'

'More fool him,' he retorted. 'Bosinney didn't even need to go. He had a cushy number as a schoolteacher in Penzance, and I'm damn sure he could have swung his ticket. War's a mug's game, and if the damn government ever got us into another one, I'd think twice before I signed up again, I can tell you.'

She was shocked at his vehemence. He had always loved the sea, so the navy was his natural home when the war began, but if he hated it that much why go back to being a fisherman? There were other jobs where you didn't risk your life regularly in one of the treacherous storms for which the Cornish coast was notorious.

'Did you ever think of taking a shore job?' she asked him abruptly. 'After being torpedoed, I mean. Didn't that make you want to stay safely on dry land?'

They had had this conversation many times, and it always produced the same result. He looked at her as if she was mad. 'What the hell for? The sea's in my blood, same as it was in my father's blood. Being torpedoed didn't put me off, and no bloody Jerry U-boat was going to scare me off.'

'Sorry I asked,' Gwen said with a grin, because it wasn't worth getting in a stew about. They had too much to be thankful for, anyway.

Carrie and Archie had reached them now, and flopped down on the grass beside them, both flushed from the walk, and probably another heated argument, Gwen thought shrewdly, despite the way they had been holding hands. Hers and David's tiffs were pinpricks compared with what she suspected went on when Archie's temper was roused.

'Where have you two been today?' Carrie said.

'St Ives as usual,' Gwen told her, 'and then along to Hayle and back.'

'Gluttons for punishment, aren't you?' Archie said. 'It wears me out just looking at you. Don't you ever go the other way? Penzance is no further than St Ives, and I'd have thought David would have seen enough of the place.'

Carrie glanced at Gwen, knowing very well why she wouldn't want to cycle to Penzance, where there were too many old acquaintances who knew her from her wild times.

'We like St Ives best,' Gwen said quickly, 'don't we, David?'

He agreed readily enough, but Carrie detected the glint of resentment in his eyes as he glanced at Archie. There had always been rivalry between these two, even as schoolboys, then again latterly when one became a butcher and other a fisherman, as if meat or fish was any more important in the food chain. Somehow it just seemed to emphasize their differences. Now, David would almost certainly think that his war had been won fairly and squarely, while Archie's had been spent doing nothing, if that was how you saw being incarcerated for two years behind prison wire with sadistic captors.

'I'd have thought you'd had enough of the sea,' Archie went on, lying flat on his back, his hands behind his head as he squinted up at the sun. 'Why don't you get a proper job like the rest of us?'

'You mean standing behind a shop counter all day like a woman, I suppose. Why don't you mind your own damn business, Pollard?'

'Time to go, I think,' Gwen said, standing up so fast

that David, who had been leaning against her, fell sideways. 'Come on, David, let's have another half-hour's ride before we go home.'

'Do as the little wife tells you now,' Archie called out, as they cycled away.

They couldn't quite hear the reply, but it sounded very much like *Bastard*.

Carrie turned on him at once.

'Why did you goad him like that? He's always perfectly polite to you until you get him going, and Gwen doesn't like it.'

'Who the hell cares what Gwen thinks?'

'I do. She's my friend.'

'And everybody else's, by all accounts. Does the husband know about her little jaunts while he was away being a hero, I wonder?'

Carrie went very still. Had her mother been saying something she shouldn't? As far as Penhallow was concerned, it was only hearsay, because nobody here had actually seen Gwen doing anything she shouldn't. She had been very careful about that. And Carrie was prepared to defend her to the death, if need be, she thought, as melodramatic as Shirley now.

'What's that supposed to mean?' she snapped. 'First you hint about girls making up to the Yanks, and now you're picking on Gwen, just because you don't care for David. It's petty, Archie, and it's childish.'

'Call it what you like. People in the shop gossip, and your precious friend's name has cropped up more than once, so I'm only putting two and two together.'

'And making five.' She put her hand on his arm. 'Archie, don't let's spoil this lovely day by bickering over things that don't even concern us. Has your headache gone yet?'

She was prepared to put his bad grace down to the headache. She was becoming too bloody forgiving altogether, she thought, suddenly angry, but it was still early days since he had come home, and you couldn't get over two years of hell in a few short weeks. She smoothed her hand across his forehead, and he grunted.

'That feels good. It's not so bad now, and I'm sure it'll be right by bed-time.'

She couldn't mistake his meaning,

'That's good,' she said with a smile.

She hoped it would be. The last time had been a disaster. Archie had been as loving as always, and she was feeling warm and cherished, but when it came to the point, nothing happened. He failed miserably and went off in a rage at himself and at her, and at the whole bloody German army for emasculating him. Before Carrie knew what was happening, he had got out of bed and into his clothes again, banged out of the house at midnight, and didn't return until the early hours, leaving her bewildered and upset.

When he finally slid back into the bed beside her, she lay rigidly, as quiet as a mouse, not wanting him to know she was awake, and knowing he had to get over this in his own way. But as soon as he was asleep the nightmare had returned and she had to suffer the rest of that awful night clinging to the edge of the bed as he thrashed about, for fear he really would lash out at her in his sleep.

She prayed that the failure wouldn't happen again, but there were no guarantees on that. And how would it affect him if it did? By now, she knew what a fragile hold he had on his temper, and she knew only too well that he was just as likely to turn against her as to want her understanding. In fact, she was sure he *wouldn't* want any hint of understanding. He would only see it as being patronizing. *As if a bloody woman could possibly know what it meant to a man.* She could almost hear him say it.

At least he needn't worry about her falling pregnant if they didn't do it. There was no chance of that at all.

She found herself wondering why they called it *falling* for a baby. It was a strange way of looking at it. You didn't fall anywhere, and nobody pushed you. You made love and a baby was the proof of that love.

'What are you looking so soppy about now?' she heard Archie's irritated voice say. 'If I've upset you about your friend, I'm sorry, but there's no smoke without fire.'

'Well, I'm just as sure that there is, but I wasn't thinking about anything important, just that it's time we went home for tea,' she said, putting dreams to the back of her mind for the present, where they belonged.

Shirley snuggled up to Bernard on his mum's old sofa in the front room. As an engaged couple they were allowed to spend time alone, and Frank and Sam had been warned not to disturb them. Sam had howled his objections at once, demanding to know why they couldn't go in the front room as well.

'Because they want to canoodle, you idiot,' Frank said loftily.

Shirley giggled. 'Where did you hear such talk, Frank Bossiney?'

'At the pictures,' he told her obligingly. 'I'm not sure what it means, but it's what older people do.'

Bernard grinned. 'You'd better get out of here then, and let me and Shirley get on with our canoodling before Mum gives you a whack for snooping.'

She loved hearing the to and fro of their chatter. It was the way it had always been. It was the way her younger sisters ganged up on her sometimes, wanting to do the things she did, wanting their hair curled the way she did hers, wanting to experiment with her lipstick and face powder, and trying on her clothes. It was being part of a family, and she didn't mind the boys grumbling a bit before Bernard shooed them out of the room. They had all the time in the world now to be together.

'At last I've got you all to myself,' Bernard said, slipping his arm around her and pulling her close. 'I'd forgotten how good that could be. I'd forgotten the softness of your hair and the blue of your eyes, even though I'd pictured it all a thousand times, but nothing could compare with the real thing.'

'Am I the real thing?'

'Real, and wonderful,' he said solemnly. He caressed her hand, then lifted her fingers to his mouth and kissed the modest engagement ring she wore. 'And mine.'

How could she have forgotten, for a single moment, how romantic he could be? Shirley marvelled. He could have been a poet, and he had the looks too, sort of dreamy and gentle. You could keep Hollywood and all the tinsel stuff on the screen. *This* was real. She leaned into him but he immediately eased back from her and grunted, and she saw the flash of pain twist his face for a moment.

'Sorry about that. I sometimes forget that my skin is not as elastic as it once was, after all the treatments I had.'

'Was it very awful, Bernard, being burned, I mean? I can't imagine it. I don't *want* to imagine it either. It just sounds so terrible.'

The minute she said it she knew how clumsy and tactless she was being. He had told her so little, and she knew she shouldn't ask him when he would obviously prefer to forget. She felt her face go hot, hoping he wouldn't think she was just probing, as morbidly curious as some of those people who revelled in hearing all the gory details.

'It certainly wasn't a picnic,' Bernard said, leaning back against the sofa, with his arm still loosely around her. It seemed a touch symbolic that they had been so close a moment ago, and now they were not. As if he had gone away to somewhere she couldn't reach, reliving a time she couldn't know and never wanted to.

She remembered Carrie saying something of the same after Archie came home. They had all gone through experiences that separated them, however much they would wish it to be different. She didn't know how much David Trewint had confided in Gwen about his near-drowning, nor if the rather stiff Stan Gould ever revealed what went on in his regular army life. They didn't know Stan very well, and Shirley was a bit in awe of him anyway, being twice her age.

She wasn't at all sure how they would all get on together at the dance in Penzance in October, since the four friends from the knitting group had been so determined to make it a mini-reunion of their own: Carrie and Archie; Shirley and Bernard; Gwen and David; Velma and Stan. For them it was to be a triumph and a joy too, since their men had all survived, and she just hoped it would all be as wonderful as they had planned. Apart from Velma wanting a divorce, of course.

And now she was the one retreating into her own little dream world, she realized, while Bernard was oddly silent, leaning back on the old sofa with his eyes closed. It gave her a chance to study him. There were lines around his eyes that hadn't been there before, and a new tension around his mouth. His face was thinner than before, but he was still as good looking as ever, his fair hair flopping over his forehead now, the way it had when he was a small boy.

It was more often slick with grease in the RAF way these days, of course. They were called the 'Brylcreem boys', but Shirley had always preferred Bernard's hair soft and newly washed.

It occurred to her that she didn't think she had ever seen him sleeping before – although she was sure he wasn't asleep now – and she had never realized quite how long his eyelashes were. All these years of knowing him, yet you could still discover new things about someone you thought you knew as well as yourself.

'What are you thinking?' she heard his voice say lazily.

'You're not asleep!' she accused him.

'Did you think I was?'

'Not really.'

'So what were you thinking?'

She laughed. 'If you really want to know, I was thinking how good looking you are, but I didn't want to give you a swollen head by telling you so.'

'You wouldn't think I'm so good looking if you could see certain other parts of me,' he said, suddenly grim, his face changing so fast it took her by surprise. Until then, there had been little hint of anxiety, but now the lines of tension around his mouth were intensified.

'Stop that kind of talk, or you'll make me blush,' she teased him.

'You'll have to get used to it if we're going to get married.'

'Well, there's no doubt about that, is there? *Is* there?' she added in alarm. She loved him so much, but suddenly he seemed so distant, and, as always, it took very little to fill her with guilt, as if a black hole was opening up in front of her and she was about to be punished for all her wrongdoings.

'I don't think we should rush into it, Shirley. We've all had a rotten time of it in the past five years, and it takes time for life to get back to normal again. I'll still have to visit the hospital in Penzance for regular check-ups for a while, and I'm sure you didn't have a pleasant war, either. It couldn't have been all fun and games digging for victory or all those other jobs you had, mucking out on the farm in the cold and wet.'

She looked away from him mutely. For a horrible moment she wondered why he had used those words 'fun and games'. The affair with Hank had been over and done with long ago, and so had the trauma of the miscarriage, but she hadn't realized how near the surface of her emotions the strain of that time still was. She knew that she needed to be constantly on her guard from now on, if she wasn't to misinterpret every little phrase or nuance in Bernard's voice. It wasn't what she had wanted, or expected.

He came back into her focus properly, and she saw that he was looking troubled now.

'Oh God, Shirley, I didn't mean I don't want us to get married. Of course I do. I've been thinking of little else but being together again. I just don't want us to rush into it before we're ready, that's all.'

It seemed pointless to remind him that she had been ready for two years now.

But there was something else bothering her, such a delicate thought that she hardly knew how to say it, or even if she should. But it was probably better to say it than to have it mouldering in the background.

'Bernard, there's nothing wrong, is there? I mean –

oh Lord, I've simply got to say it. You're not bothered about the, well, the *other* side of marriage, are you? I mean, with your injuries and all . . .' her voice petered out as she floundered.

He gave a short laugh. 'Good God, Shirley, you're not supposed to ask a chap such things. I never met a girl who could be as bold as you! Anyway, it's the girl who's meant to have qualms about her first time and all that.'

Shirley blinked back the sudden, threatening tears, because her first time was lost for ever, and not to this man whom she truly adored.

'How many girls have you met lately then? Except for the nurses at the hospital, and French Marie, of course.' She couldn't stop the brief, searing jealousy at even saying the name. She thought she had got over it, but apparently she hadn't.

'Not many,' Bernard replied, humouring her until he saw how serious she had become. 'The nurses were doing their rotten job on me, and I was half delirious most of the time I was at the French farmhouse. I didn't notice Marie as a person at first, though I badly needed her at the time. She gave me what basic medical treatment she could in very dangerous circumstances. She reminded me that I was still alive despite my wretched stinking body and I owe her a lot – probably my life.'

Shirley shivered. 'I'm sorry. I didn't mean to remind you, Bernard. It must have been awful.' And her jealousy was so shameful when she owed this French girl her gratitude for sending Bernard back to her.

'It was, and I didn't mean to stir up all this stuff either. All I meant earlier is that we need to make up for all that lost time and do our courting properly.'

'Don't you mean our canoodling?' she said, blinking again.

'That too, so come here, my Cornish wench,' he said with a laugh, and the next minute he was kissing her as passionately as ever, and virtual stars were exploding overhead, and waves were rushing on the shore . . .

But a long while later, alone in her bed, Shirley finally admitted what a disappointment the whole afternoon had been. What a let-down. All this talk of doing their courting properly made Bernard sound like an old man instead of only twenty-three. She was twenty, and they had already been engaged for two years.

How much longer did he need to know that they loved each other and wanted to be together! She had wanted him to come home and sweep her off her feet, sure that together they could blot out the past and look forward to the rosy future ahead of them. Now, without even knowing it, he had put doubts in her mind that she didn't want. She wanted the old Bernard back, but she wasn't even sure he existed anymore. And what she *didn't* want was to have reminded him of that other girl. How foolish that was!

She knew very well you could never turn back the clock and have things exactly as they were before, especially after such terrible times as they had all gone through in the war years. But the war had separated them as nothing else in the world could have done, in body and in spirit, and she had never realized until now just how much distance had to be covered. She felt totally confused, and just thinking such disloyal thoughts about Bernard was making her feel as guilty as sin again, and she turned her face into her pillow and wept.

Chapter 9

August had merged into September and early October, and Carrie was limping with a bruised foot. If anyone asked, she would say she had stubbed her toe on the dressing-table, which wasn't so far wrong, since it had happened in the bedroom. But it wasn't the dressing-table she had bumped into. It was Archie.

She had reached out to cuddle up to him in the middle of the night and found his side of the bed empty. Alarmed for a minute, she then decided he had probably gone downstairs for a drink of water as he sometimes did. And now she needed the lavatory. She got out of bed and tiptoed towards the door without bothering to put on a light. The next moment she fell headlong over a solid object on the floor, stubbing her toe badly.

She smothered a scream, frightened of waking her parents and starting a panic, but the next second she almost died from fright as she was grabbed and held tight and someone's hand was clamped over her mouth.

'Archie!' she gasped, when she could struggle free. 'What on earth are you doing on the floor!'

As he pulled her down beside him, she tried to ignore the throbbing pain in her toe. He was still half asleep as he mumbled in her ear.

'Bloody bed's too soft. Felt as if I was drowning in it after the hard bed at the camp. Often dreamed of you sharing it, and now you're here.'

By the time he was properly awake he had become very aroused. Before Carrie knew what was happening, he was on top of her and his hands were fumbling beneath her nightdress, clearly reliving his fantasy.

She didn't try to stop him. Didn't want to . . . because despite the circumstances he was so much like the old Archie, passionate and wanting her, and saying the words of love she had ached to hear for so long. He was her lover, and the circumstances no longer mattered. Only the closeness mattered, and the feeling that they were still the sweethearts they had always been.

They remained locked together for a long while afterwards, until she was sure he was sleeping, and she could no longer bear the hardness of the floor. Her toe was hurting so much, but only then did she slide out of his embrace and do what she had intended and visit the lavatory before getting back into bed. But she felt warmer inside than she had of late, sure that Archie was slowly coming back to her. She had expected it to happen instantly, but you couldn't rebuild a lifetime in days. Even so, the self-imposed armour surrounding him was slowly being chiselled away, and beneath it she knew he was still the same. There was still the ten-year-old boy she had solemnly declared she was going to marry when she was six.

She might have known the euphoria wouldn't last, but Carrie was determined to cash in on it while it did. Archie remained in a reasonably good mood, partly because she was now working at the library, across the green from Pollard's butcher's shop.

'Why don't we take our old gramophone and some records up to the moors like we used to? What do you say, Archie? We could ask Shirley and Bernard to come with us too if you like.'

It was no good asking Gwen because Archie would react at once to having to spend an afternoon being sociable to David Trewint. And Velma wouldn't want to come and play gooseberry. Velma was still in rather a strange mood. She was usually such a calm person, but lately she seemed touchier than usual, and Carrie supposed it was the reaction to having finally made up her mind to ask Stan for the divorce on his next leave.

'Why the devil would I want to spend time with those two fairies?' Archie said in answer to her suggestion.

'I wish you wouldn't be so nasty about my friends, and why do you call them by that silly name, anyway?' she said hotly.

'Well, Shirley looks as if a strong wind would blow her away, and the cripple's always been a bit of a fairy in my opinion. If you don't know what that means, look it up in one of your library books.'

'I do know what it means, and you're totally wrong,' Carrie snapped. 'Honestly, Archie, I don't know why you're picking on Bernard like this. You never used to be so bitter.'

'No? Well, maybe it comes from being a prisoner of war for two bloody years and seeing a side of life I didn't particularly care for. We had the bastards there, too, you know, toadying up to the Jerries.'

'Who?' Carrie said, not sure where this conversation was going, or how it had begun.

'Fairies. Shirt-lifters. Call them what you like, they make me sick.'

Carrie sighed. She knew very well what the terms meant, but to accuse Bernard Bosinney of being that way was just plain stupid. He'd taught art and music at a school in Penzance, which to Archie would no doubt be cause for suspicion, but he was as red-blooded as the next man, and he'd nearly died for his country too.

Maybe that was what really nagged away at Archie. Through no fault of his own, he'd done nothing heroic in the war, and he couldn't boast about the exciting or dangerous experiences that the others did. POWs had everybody's sympathy, but the heroes got all the accolades. It had never occurred to Carrie until now. She was proud of Archie, and always would be, but she could see how he might be feeling.

'Well, for your information, Shirley assures me that Bernard is perfectly normal in that respect,' she said delicately, although Shirley had never said any such thing. 'So I don't want to hear any more daft talk about him, all right?'

He stared at her for a moment, and then grinned. 'Oh well, if he's already had his leg over, that's different.'

She kept the smile on her face through gritted teeth. Archie had always been a plain-speaking man, but sometimes she wished he'd curb his tongue a little. It was hardly romantic to talk about a chap getting his leg over, but she knew that men used the sort of words that women never would. In any case, he was well off the right track now, even though she had put the idea in his mind.

'I didn't say that. I just said that Shirley knows him better than we do, and they'll be getting married next year, so don't you dare say anything out of place.'

He was grinning now. 'All right! You can be quite forceful when you want to, can't you, Mrs Pollard?' he said lazily. 'I'd rather have you defending me in an argument than accusing me.'

'I'll always defend you. You're my husband, aren't you? So what about this outing next weekend?'

He agreed to the plan, though he said they'd better not be out after dark with the music or they might be accused of starting a witch's coven on the moors. Which got her laughing again at such a daft idea. It may have been true a couple of centuries ago, but not now. But she revised any idea of asking Shirley and Bernard to come with them. It would be just like Archie to start making remarks that would upset everything. She hadn't seen Shirley much since Bernard came home, but they would all be getting together on Thursday evening as usual, and she expected her friend to be twittering with excitement by now.

Archie was right in one way, she reflected. Shirley *was* like a fairy, but in the nicest sense. She was bright and pretty and dainty, and it was no wonder that the dashing Hank Delaney had taken such a shine to her. It was just so awful that it had ended the way it did. But it could have been worse. They had all agreed on that. It could have been so very, very much worse.

'So how did the reunion go?' they asked Shirley eagerly, and more than a little anxiously, on Thursday evening.

She could be a real blabbermouth sometimes, and it would have been terrible if she had blurted out everything to Bernard in the hope of easing her wretched conscience. Gwen, whose conscience was far more adaptable, had been the most adamant in saying it would be an absolute disaster to load her guilt on to Bernard. It wasn't fair, and it wasn't necessary. And they all knew that Gwen herself had enough guilt of her own to put Shirley's in the shade. Except for the miscarriage.

'It was fine. Bernard's fine, considering. He still has to have regular check-ups at the hospital in Penzance, but apart from that, yes, it's all fine.'

If she said it often enough, she was sure she would believe it, too, Shirley thought. Well, she *did* believe it.

'So did you bombard him with plans for the wedding, or did you manage to hold your tongue?' Velma said.

'We both agreed that it's best to wait a while,' Shirley said airily. 'In any case, you know my parents wouldn't agree before I'm twenty-one in January, but I wouldn't want a winter wedding. I'd like a June wedding, but we're not even going to think about it yet. We're just going to enjoy being together again.'

'Good for you,' Gwen told her. 'So what's he going to do now he's home? Is he going after his old job?'

Shirley looked bleak. 'I don't know. He won't talk about work. He says he's got to get properly well first before he tackles anything. I'm not sure he wants to go back to teaching, not in Penzance, anyway. He wouldn't want to travel there and back every day, but if there was an opening in the infants school here, I suppose he might think about that. Nobody's pushing him to do anything yet.'

It would have been really good to report that Bernard was going to do something spectacular with his life now, after being a war pilot. Going back to teaching children seemed a bit tame, though she was too loyal to say so, or even think it for more than a second.

She was more uneasy about the way Bernard was obsessed with his medical problems, almost to the extent of ignoring the need to get back to a normal working life. She hadn't expected there to be any real problems after all his time in hospital, but now she knew how wrong she had been. There hadn't been a mutual agreement on postponing the wedding plans, either. It had been his idea, not hers. But short of begging him to marry her at the earliest opportunity, she had had to agree that it made sense. Even if it didn't.

'So what of your plans, Velma?' Carrie asked. 'Are you definitely going to give Stan his marching orders while he's home at the end of the month?'

'It's not quite as simple as that, is it? And I wouldn't be so brutal.'

'I never thought you would. But you've been saying for long enough that you want a divorce, and when you make up your mind about something you don't let anything stop you, do you?'

'That's your opinion of me, is it?'

Carrie was startled by the tension in her voice. It hadn't been an accusation, and it was actually Carrie's opinion of herself, too!

'Good Lord, I'm not criticizing. I think it's wonderful to know exactly what you want, and be fearless enough to go through with it. It won't be all that easy to be a divorced woman in a small village like this.'

She realized she was making things worse, when she had only meant to support Velma. There was no doubt, though, that no matter who was the guilty party divorce was still disapproved of in most circles, and they were all aware of it. In a close-knit village tittle-tattle was even worse, and there would be plenty of gossip as to why a marriage of ten years had ended in divorce and who was to shoulder most of the blame.

Velma was a strong person, who could always weather any storms, but she looked less than her usual confident self right now.

'There's nothing wrong, is there, Velma? Don't say you're having second thoughts after all,' Shirley put in.

'I might be. But probably not. Perhaps I've only just realized what a final step it is, and it needs thinking about.'

Gwen wasn't so tolerant. 'I thought you'd been doing that for umpteen years. The poor chap deserves to know what you've got in store for him. Besides, once the deed is done, have you ever thought that he might want to find a new wife? And he's no spring chicken, is he?'

'He's only forty, for God's sake,' Velma said angrily. 'Although I realize that might seem old to the rest of you, especially Shirley, being just out of the nursery.'

'Well, pardon me for breathing, but he *is* old enough to be my father.'

Carrie could see that they were all getting heated, and it wasn't what they came here for on Thursday evenings. It was none of their business what Velma and Stan decided, and who ever knew what went on behind closed doors in a marriage?

'Why don't we all have a cup of tea and simmer down a bit?' Carrie asked, though she wasn't keen on taking the role of peacemaker right now. If anything, that was always down to Velma, but she seemed to be the unwitting cause of dissent among them tonight, and she was decidedly put out over something. It was better not to ask and not to know. But that was hardly being a true friend.

She half hoped Archie wouldn't turn up to meet her later, then she might get the chance to walk home with Velma and find out what was wrong. It was a futile hope, of course. He was outside the church hall a couple of hours later, arms folded, swaying only slightly after an evening at the pub, and smiling fatuously.

'How's the flying hero, Shirley?' he called out at once. 'Glad to be home?'

'He's doing all right, thanks, Archie.'

'Good.'

Carrie held her breath, but to her relief he didn't say anything more. They parted from the others and went off together, arm in arm.

'Thank you,' she said.

'What for?'

She knew it had to be said. 'For not being a pig to Shirley and embarrassing me by saying anything funny about Bernard.'

'Would I ever embarrass you?' he said, with a grin and a squeeze of her arm.

She knew very well that he would, but as he was so cheerful she wasn't going to say any more. Why spoil things, when the evening was just turning to dusk, there were stars appearing in the sky, and a lovers' moon was riding high? The scent of night stocks and honeysuckle from village gardens was filling the air, and the joyous realization that the world was at peace at last could still sometimes be overwhelming.

'So have you asked any of them if they want to come with us next weekend and have a dance on the moors? It's all right by me, but I've got no objection if it's just us, either.'

'I think it'll be much nicer to be just us,' she said softly, knowing he was making a gesture. He didn't often say sorry, but he usually made things right in other ways. Not that he had anything to say sorry for at the moment. She crossed her fingers as she thought it, though, just to be on the safe side.

Velma had intended to say something to her friends, but at the last minute she decided to keep it to herself for the time being. Sometimes things happened in your life that were too momentous to share, until you had come to terms with them yourself. She wasn't sure that she believed in fate, and she certainly scoffed at coincidences ruling your life. But they happened, and now she knew it.

She had continued to feel unwell of late, but she had been putting off the day when she visited Dr Tozer as long as possible. In any case, she knew and recognized all the early signs of the illness that had killed her mother. The one that nobody put a name to, until a doctor detailed it sombrely and regretfully. The illness that was inexorable and fatal.

She had had the nausea, the dizziness, the feeling that her body was already swelling and that something was taking it over, something that was out of her control. She knew the doctor could give her pills to deaden the pain when it became too bad for her to

157

cope anymore. She had seen it all with her mother, and knew how quickly she could go downhill once it got a real hold.

She hadn't had any pain yet, just the certainty that she was going the way her mother had gone. That was her fate after all. Inevitably, as the suspicion of what ailed her became a certainty in her mind, she wondered how she would cope all alone. She had lived much of her married life without Stan, both in wartime and peacetime. It was what the wives of regular soldiers did, and she had never balked at that – nor known in the beginning how it would eventually drive them so far apart until they no longer really cared about one another, or needed one another.

But now this *thing* that was invading her body was making her vulnerable in a way she hadn't known before. She became upset far more easily, even to the point of tearfulness over idiotic things like mislaying a book or a shoe. She became impatient with passengers on her bus, instead of exchanging cheery words with them. Now that the world was at peace again, and the men and women were coming home to their loved ones, she realized how much she was missing Stan, his quiet companionship, his tenderness when she was hurt, his solidity. She realized how she would need him in the days ahead, and that was another torment in her mind, because how fair would it be to ask for his support now?

She had finally gone to see Dr Tozer the evening before, and the coincidence had occurred that morning. A letter arrived from Stan, and she had opened it quickly, reluctantly, knowing she had news of her own to tell him, because it was his right to know, whatever happened.

'My dear Velma,' it began, as it always did.

'I have some news, and I want you to think things over very carefully before you give me an answer. I've been offered a post as training instructor at a base near Salisbury, and I mean to take it. There is living accommodation for both of us if you would agree to give up the cottage in Cornwall and share my life fully.

We need to get some things resolved between us, Velma. Apart from that night in St Ives, for which I have deeply apologized, I have felt for a long while that our marriage has become stale, and I have even wondered if we would be better apart permanently. It is no marriage for either of us to be living like this, and we are still young enough to make different lives for ourselves.

I want you to think seriously about this. I shall have a week's leave soon, and we must discuss it more thoroughly when I come home.

I don't think you will be too upset by this letter, and I sincerely hope not. I have the feeling that this will not be a shock to you, so let's both think about where we are going with our lives and where our future lies.

Your loving Stan.'

She had wept over the letter. She had read it a hundred times and wept over it every time. It was too cruel, especially coming right now at such a vulnerable time for her. He was dignified as always, stating things calmly, putting into his own words the words she had intended to say herself. The shock of it had hit her like a slap in the face. It made her ask so many questions. Was he implying that he had met somebody else and *wanted* them to part? Was that what he meant by discussing where they were going with their lives, and thinking where their future lay?

Her first thought was to talk it over with her friends. They had all supported one another through every moment of the war years, and she knew she could rely on them to give her honest answers.

But then she backed away from that idea. The others were all so happy now. Carrie had Archie back home, even if the situation at her parents' house couldn't be ideal, and Velma was sure Archie could be physically violent given enough provocation.

Gwen and David behaved almost sickeningly like two lovebirds, but she couldn't blame them for that; and if only Shirley could restrain her bubbly nature and be patient with Bernard, it surely wouldn't be long before she saw herself as the heroine in a Hollywood movie, welcoming her wounded hero back home with tender loving care.

No, she could tell them her news. For the moment the conflict in her mind was hers alone, and she would deal with her double shock in her own way. The shock of knowing that Stan was also questioning their marriage – and the other one.

*

On Friday morning Carrie glanced out of the library window and saw Velma hurrying across the green, her head down as if she was deep in thought. There were no customers at that moment, and Carrie asked her boss if she could take her ten minutes' break. A few minutes later she had caught up with Velma.

Aren't you working today?'

'Not until this afternoon.'

'Good. Let's go to Lawson's Tearoom and have a chat over a cup of tea. I'm worried about you, Velma.'

'Are you? There's no need!'

Carrie linked arms with her as they walked to the tearoom with the chintz curtains at the windows and the matching tablecloths inside. 'You may fool the others, but you can't fool me. I think there's something bothering you, but you don't have to tell me if you don't want to. I know we usually all turn to you, but—'

'As the elder statesman, you mean, or the all-knowing wise woman?'

'I didn't mean anything of the sort, but you can't deny that you've become very touchy lately, so what's up?'

They pushed open the tearoom door and the bell tinkled overhead. It was busier than Carrie would have liked, for if there was really anything to tell, Velma wouldn't like her business broadcast to all and sundry. She was a private and sensible person, which was why she had been so good for Shirley when she was in trouble, and managed to put the brakes on her inclination to confess everything to Bernard.

They found a corner table and Mrs Lawson brought them their tea and a plate of her homemade Cornish biscuits. Velma knew that if there was anyone she felt able to confide in, it was Carrie. Fate – which she didn't altogether believe in – had arranged for them to meet like this on this glorious October morning.

'I had a letter from Stan,' she said abruptly. 'And I think – in fact, I *know* – he's been feeling the same way about our marriage as I have. He says that when he comes home on leave, we should discuss our future.'

Carrie sensed how brittle she was now. She spoke carefully.

'But doesn't that make it easier for you, Velma? Isn't that what you've been planning all this time? If it means there won't be any big scene with Stan, I'd have thought you'd be glad to know he won't make a fuss.'

She gave a short laugh. 'It doesn't do my self-esteem a lot of good, to know that my husband has probably been planning to ask me for a divorce for heaven knows how long!'

'You don't know that!'

'I don't have to be a genius to read between the lines, and he could hardly have made it plainer. And now I don't know what to do.'

'But it's what you *wanted*. Why does it make so much difference who makes the first move?'

'Darling, it makes all the difference in the world now.'

Carrie became slightly alarmed. Her friend really did look white and drawn.

'You're not ill, are you, Velma?'

She didn't answer for a minute. 'You probably don't remember my parents very well, do you, Carrie? You would have been very young when they died, but my mother was ill for several years, a horribly long, lingering illness that eventually killed her. When she died my father simply gave up the will to live, and he went soon after her.'

'Go on,' Carrie said, when she seemed lost in painful memories. Dear God, Velma wasn't about to tell her she had the same illness, was she?

'I've always had a sneaking worry at the back of my mind that I would catch it, even though you say you can't catch it, nor can it be passed on. But they don't know everything, do they? Doctors, I mean. They didn't know that both my brothers would be killed early in the war and that if I hadn't had Stan I don't know what I'd have done. I needed him then, and . . .' she paused, and took a shuddering breath. 'I'm going to need him now. But it's not fair to expect his support, when, until I knew for certain, I was all ready to ask for a divorce and for us to go our separate ways. But everything's changed now.'

'For God's sake, Velma, you're frightening me,' Carrie said in a low, urgent voice, glancing around and feeling thankful that the tearoom was virtually empty now except for themselves. 'I'm sure you're mistaken about all this – whatever it is. Have you been to the doctor to ask his opinion?'

'Oh yes.'

'And? You do know that if you need anybody, we'll

always be here for you, don't you? Me and Gwen and Shirley. We'll always stand by you, just as you always stood by us when we were feeling low and miserable.'

Velma gave the first real smile that morning as she squeezed Carrie's hand.

'You're a lovely girl, Carrie, and so are the others, but I'm going to need more than any of you can give me. I know I should tell Stan, and by the time he comes home I shall have decided how to go about it.'

'Tell him now! He has a right to know, Velma, and he'd be very hurt to think you were going through this all alone. Write a letter if it's too difficult to put it into words. He's still your husband, after all.'

'Oh yes, he's still my husband.' And she hadn't mentioned the fact that Stan had asked her to go and live with him in Salisbury when he took up his new post.

'Well?' Carrie felt she just wasn't able to get through to her anymore. Velma had gone through enough traumas in her life, yet she was always so elegant and dignified, able to sort out everyone's problems, with a clear-cut vision of what she wanted to do with her own life. But right now she looked as helpless as a kitten.

She touched Velma's hand. 'Has Dr Tozer said anything definite, like, uh, how long it would be . . . before anything happened?'

She tried to put it as delicately as she could without actually asking bluntly how long it would be before Velma became bedridden, and worse. She couldn't bear to think of her friend ill and dying. They had just come through a terrible war, and now to be faced with this. It was tragic.

Velma had a wry smile on her face. 'Well, of course he's given me a time limit. Nine months, actually.'

Carrie drew in her breath. So soon . . . she felt the tears start to her eyes.

'My God, Velma, you're being so brave! I know I couldn't face a death sentence the way you are.'

Velma finally saw the way her friend's mind was working, and couldn't blame her. She was being pretty dim herself today, or else it was because she still hadn't been able to put it into words. She was simply putting off the moment, and she was reluctant to do it even now. Once it was said, it made it real. But you couldn't hide it for ever. She gave a shaky laugh.

'I'm not *dying*, Carrie.'

'Aren't you? Well, thank goodness for that. But if you're not ill, what's this all about? Why have you been leading me up the garden path all this time?'

Carrie felt massively relieved and also very foolish for getting it all so wrong. But Velma had certainly led her to believe something was the matter, and although she had looked so pale before, her face was now flushed with colour. Her angular features looked beautiful – almost radiant.

'Haven't you guessed yet? I'm not ill, Carrie, I'm expecting a baby.'

Chapter 10

Carrie was stunned to hear Velma's news. It wasn't that she thought she was too old to have a baby, because of course she wasn't. But the circumstances were so unlikely. She had already been married for ten years, and no baby had materialized; she was on the brink of separating from Stan, professing that she no longer loved him; and now this.

She wasn't the only one to be stunned. It had been obvious from Velma's manner than the news had come as a complete shock to her. She admitted to Carrie that she really had believed she was ill and that she had her mother's complaint. Before they parted, Velma swore her to secrecy for the present, since she wasn't prepared to share the news with Gwen and Shirley yet – nor anyone else, not even Stan.

'But you have to tell him!' Carrie said. 'Surely this changes everything.'

'It changes nothing. We're still as distant as ever with each other – well, except for that brief time at St Ives,' she added with a flush to her cheeks, 'and now he's made it clear that he doesn't see a future for us.'

'He's already made the future for you, hasn't he?' Carrie said bluntly. 'You can't leave things like that, and you don't just have yourselves to think about, Velma. There's a child involved.'

She felt as if she was taking on the role of mentor now, the role that Velma had always played in the past. But right now Velma looked as if she'd been knocked sideways, as if all her carefully built-up plans were crumbling down about her.

'I wanted children once,' she said, 'and I think Stan did too, but over the years I accepted the fact that it was never going to happen. I wouldn't let myself think that I'd missed a vital part of my life. And now he's made it perfectly obvious in his letter that we've both reached a turning-point in our lives, so how can I tell him? He'll think I'm blackmailing him to stay together.'

'How can you *not* tell him?'

Velma looked down at her square, capable hands, and Carrie could see that they were trembling.

'I feel so mixed up. One moment I'm in despair, thinking that this is the worst possible thing. The next minute I'm filled with awe that the miracle has happened, and then I almost feel like screaming with joy.'

'Doesn't that tell you everything, then?' Carrie said huskily, because she had rarely seen Velma reveal such emotional upheaval. 'You want this baby.'

'Of course I *want* it. Did I ever say anything different?'

Carrie began to laugh. 'I'm not quite sure what

you've been saying for the last ten minutes, but I think you need time to get used to the idea that you're not dying, thank goodness, and that there's a new life beginning. You've got it all, haven't you, Velma?'

'Except a husband.'

Carrie's head was still full of it while she helped her mother prepare the vegetables for the evening meal. Of course Velma had a husband, she thought savagely. She knew she was seeing her friend's situation through rose-coloured glasses, but once Stan heard the news everything would come right. Stan was hardly going to desert her when they were about to become a real family. He was a decent, upright man – probably a bit dull too, she admitted, but he had been Velma's choice, and they must have had a pretty passionate interlude in St Ives for this to result.

Who would have thought it, though? Velma was the least likely one of the four friends to be in this pickle now. Shirley . . . well, she had learned her lesson well and good after the Yanks left town. Gwen seemed to have a charmed life, and had once declared that she probably wasn't capable of having babies if it hadn't happened already, and that it didn't bother her at all.

That left Carrie. She paused over the bowl of cold water into which she was peeling potatoes, her eyes momentarily unfocused as she gazed through the kitchen window. Would Archie ever get rid of this ridiculous idea that they shouldn't bring children into the world to provide more army fodder for the next lot, as he put it, and decide that the time was right for them?

'Are you going to stand there dreaming all day, Carrie?' her mother said sharply. 'Since you've been back at that library your head seems to be full of rubbish lately. Book-learning rubbish too, I daresay.'

'That's all you know,' Carrie muttered beneath her breath, but she should have remembered that Edna had good hearing.

'That's enough of that sort of talk, miss. Just because you're a married woman, you shouldn't forget your manners. Have some respect for your parents while you're living in this house—'

Carrie flung the knife into the potato bowl, splashing water everywhere, and marched out of the kitchen.

'Come back here this minute, Carrie!' Edna called after her furiously.

'Make me!' Carrie yelled back, as defiant as if she was ten years old and still discovering her place in the family. She dashed upstairs and slammed her bedroom door behind her, her fingers trembling for the bolt that Archie had insisted on fitting to ensure their privacy.

It had seemed insensitive at the time, and a bit of a cheek, too, since this *was* her parents' house, but now she shot that bolt across in triumph, and leaned back against the door, her eyes closed, her hands clenched. She would have to apologize later, though. She knew that. She had been unnecessarily rude, and her mum would never let it go until she said sorry, and even then there would be an atmosphere in the house all evening.

She moved slowly across the bedroom and flopped down on the bed, staring at the ceiling. What the dickens was she getting so het up about, anyway? Velma was the one with the problem, not her. Velma had to sort things out with her marriage, while hers was doing just fine – give or take a few details, which she was prepared to gloss over for now, compared with Velma's momentous news.

She almost wished she didn't know Velma's secret, and especially wished that she hadn't been the only one that Velma had confided in. It was obvious that she wouldn't have done so to Shirley, nor Gwen, who was often brittle and sarcastic and may have made some so-called teasing comment that would have bruised Velma's fragile feelings right now. Like what a shock the village was going to get to see an old married lady like her finally falling for a baby. It would, too.

'Carrie, open this door!' She heard Archie's furious voice, and she realized he had probably been banging on it for the last few minutes while she had been lost in her own thoughts. 'What the hell are you doing in there?'

'Nothing. I'm coming,' she said, and hurried to slide back the bolt.

He looked at her suspiciously. 'What's going on? Your mother's downstairs looking as black as thunder, and you're locking me out of my own bedroom.'

'I'm *not* locking you out,' Carrie said, starting to smile at the absurdity of it all. Her mother was upset because she had dared to slam out of the kitchen in a pet, and Archie looked as accusing as if he thought she was in here packing her suitcase – or having a liaison upstairs in her mum's house with a secret lover!

She drew in her breath at the thought, and her smile grew wider. Chance would be a fine thing, even if she ever wanted it, which she didn't.

'Have I said something funny?' he snapped. 'I thought you realized that I've had enough of being behind locked doors for the past two years.'

Carrie's patience snapped, along with her sympathy.

'Oh, for heaven's sake, Archie, you've been out of that prison camp for months now, and it's time you put it behind you. As for being behind locked doors, it was you who fixed the bolt to the bedroom door, remember?'

'Yes, to keep other people out, not your own husband! And when you've been holed up for all that time, you'll have cause to talk. But you never will be, will you? You didn't even volunteer for proper war work. Even that dopey Shirley got stuck in and did her bit, and from what I hear Gwen did her bit as well, though not in the way her precious David might imagine.'

She wasn't going to show by a flicker of an eyelid that she had any idea what he was talking about. But she wasn't prepared to leave it there, either.

'I really don't know what you've got against my friends. None of them has ever said a word against you, and you're being really hateful, Archie. If you knew how much I missed you and longed to have you back home, you wouldn't keep on like this. All I wanted was for the war to be over and for us to be together again, and you keep on spoiling it.'

He crossed the room and pulled her into his arms. He had come straight upstairs and hadn't yet washed after work, and he smelled of blood and fresh meat. Trying not to wrinkle her nose, she closed her eyes and nestled into him.

'I know I'm a prize bastard sometimes, but God, if you knew how much I've missed you too, Carrie. It was only the thought of you that kept me going, especially when they slung me into the pit for a day or a week, depending on how they felt at the time.'

'What pit?' she mumbled.

'Solitary confinement, to put it politely. A rats' hole would be more like it, and if you'd ever felt the filthy little bastards running over your feet and pissing on you, and trying not to breathe for the stench, you'd know what I mean. So don't go thinking I can forget it that easily.'

As his voice grew grimmer, Carrie held him tighter. 'I'm sorry, Archie. I didn't know.'

'Nor should you. It's not a fit subject for women to hear, and I'm not talking about it anymore. I'm going to get washed and changed, and then we'd better report to the dragon lady for supper.'

When he had left the bedroom, Carrie knew she would have to wash and change her clothes too. The smell of Archie's working day was on her, and not only that. For a few brief moments she felt she had glimpsed the kind of hell none of them ever spoke about, and she wanted to erase it from her mind as much as he did.

For the first time, she wondered if anything was ever going to be the same for any of them again. Some scars went too deep to talk about. There were secrets to be kept hidden, not to mention her own secret longing for a normal life, a home and children of her own. It wasn't a huge ambition by some people's standards, but it was hers, and she was as passionate about getting it as she was about Archie.

She thought about that for a moment, but it was true. He may not have been in the front line and classified as a proper hero, but her love for him had never wavered all the time he was away fighting his own personal battles, and it wasn't wavering now. And by the time she went downstairs again, her hair brushed and gleaming, her face fresh and her skin fragrant, wearing a clean patterned frock, she felt curiously uplifted.

'Do you have anything to say to me, miss?' her mother said with a sniff, while Archie stood hovering in the background with a grin on his face.

Her father wasn't home from work yet, and Carrie was prepared to eat any amount of humble pie to restore harmony to the house before he arrived.

'Yes. I'm sorry for being so rude.'

Archie pretended to smother an exaggerated belch.

'It was not me, it was my food,' he rhymed, at which Carrie burst out laughing at his cheek, and even Edna forced a wry smile to her lips.

'All right, you've had your fun, so help me dish up

this food before your dad gets in. You know he likes it to be ready and waiting on the table for him.'

It was her way of accepting the apology.

But the whole episode upstairs had evidently roused Archie. He was on good form all evening, chivvying Walter into playing cards with him, even though Walter looked very tired that night.

As an incentive Archie promised to buy him a pint of beer at the pub next time he felt like joining him and his father for a game of darts.

'You should get out more, Walt,' Archie observed. 'You're looking quite pasty. I reckon working in an office all day is bad for your health.'

'You're a cheeky young devil, aren't you? No, when I get home at night I like to put my feet up and relax, not go gallivanting about.'

Archie guffawed. 'You can hardly call going to a pub in Penhallow gallivanting about! I've been told the Yanks called it deader than a graveyard.'

'Who told you that?' Edna said indignantly, looking up from her sewing.

Archie shrugged. 'Oh, I hear things. You do, when you're serving customers and trying to juggle their meat ration. You get to hear quite a bit of gossip when you're chatting up the local ladies,' he added with a wink at Carrie.

She smiled back, though her heart seemed to be doing a nice jig in somersaults right now. He couldn't mean anything really. It was just idle talk to brighten up her dad's rather gloomy mood. All that hinting about Gwen, for instance. He couldn't *know*. Nobody in Penhallow did, because she'd been careful to have her flings in Penzance and not here.

A guilty thought swirled around her mind. For no more than a moment, Carrie wondered what it must be like, having known a number of men. Really known them, in the biblical sense. Wouldn't you feel embarrassed, stupid even, having to undress and be exposed in front of a stranger? Or perhaps undressing didn't come into it. Perhaps it had sometimes been no more than a hasty connection in the dark, a pretence of love, to make Gwen forget, for that short while, the tragic news that David was missing, presumed drowned . . .

'Carrie, are you star-gazing again?' Edna asked. 'I swear I don't know what's got into you lately.'

Well, Archie had, for a start . . . she blushed furiously as the deliciously wicked thought flashed into her head, and she was thankful her mum wasn't a mind-reader. But Archie must have been at that moment, judging by the look he gave her.

She knew it even more when they went to bed that night. The minute she got between the sheets she felt his hands reaching for her.

'I've been waiting for this all evening,' he whispered into her neck. 'Ever since we had that little spat earlier and you got all defensive about your friends, I couldn't wait to get you alone.'

'And, instead, you had to listen to Dad telling you his boring stories of Town Hall politics!' Carrie said teasingly.

He laughed softly. 'It's called taking the rough with

the smooth. I have to put up with your old dad's yarns and your eagle-eyed mum for the privilege of having my wife to myself.'

'Is it a privilege then?'

'What do you think?' he said, and then the teasing was over as he rolled over her and pinned her beneath him. 'You can't imagine how often I thought about this while we were apart. Having you here like this, touching you, tasting you, dreaming of you, and knowing that nothing was ever going to separate us again.'

'Archie, that's almost poetic,' Carrie said, a catch in her breath as she cherished the words he didn't always say.

'Well, it's hardly Wordsworth or one of those chaps you probably read about in the library, but it's not bad for an old soldier, is it?'

'Not bad at all,' she murmured, as his fingers found her, and then she was pulling him into her hungrily, revelling in the fact, minutes later, that this time he didn't pull away. This time, she had it all.

Velma examined her profile in the long mirror in her wardrobe door, standing this way and that, trying to detect whether or not anybody would be able to tell yet. Though who was likely to guess? She had been childless for so long that friends and neighbours in the village would probably have assumed long ago that she was unable to have children. It was going to be a shock to them, as much as it had been to her. And she was still totally undecided as to what she should tell

Stan. When his letter had arrived on that fateful day, she had had the darkest suspicion that he might be breaking the news gently that he had found someone else.

Her reaction to that had taken her totally by surprise. Unreasonable jealousy had flooded through her, as sharp as a physical pain. She hadn't even told Carrie about that feeling. It seemed almost shameful after her constant declaration of her intention to ask Stan for a divorce once the war was over.

And how did she feel now? Betrayed, hurt, weepy, angry . . . sometimes with the extraordinary urge to beg him to stay, to start all over again . . . all things that her own common sense told her were more to do with the changes that were taking place in her body than a change of heart. It wasn't that she loved him any more now than before she knew about the baby. She had always faced facts, and she knew it was because she couldn't bear to think of him wanting someone else and not her.

'You're such a dog in the manger,' she muttered to her reflection in the mirror. 'Why shouldn't he have a new life, with a woman who would be perfectly happy to be an army wife? What difference would it make to me? I'd still be here in the cottage that I love, in the Cornish village that I love, and with a baby of my own to love.'

She turned away from the mirror, sighing impatiently, knowing she seemed to be repeating the words like a mantra, as if the more she said them, the more she would believe them.

But she had always been a sensible woman, and she didn't believe in looking back and mourning over what couldn't be changed. She hadn't actually said the words to Stan about a divorce, but she still knew in her heart that they had to be said. Baby or not, it wasn't fair to hold on to him for purely practical reasons.

A sudden noise in the street below made her glance out of the bedroom window. There was a small group of neighbourhood boys of about five years old running about and kicking a ball, whooping with laughter and chattering like magpies, then racing along Tinners' Row as their mothers called them in for their tea.

Without thinking, Velma's hand went to her stomach. Would he – or she – be playing in the street like that, one day? She had never even thought about what he – or she – might look like. He would be a tall child like them both, of course, handsome like Stan, and pencil-thin like her. She drew in her breath painfully. There was no point in speculating. After all this time she had never expected to have a child, but now that it was here, a living part of her, her days and nights were filled with thoughts of nothing else.

With a feeling almost amounting to a Greek tragedy, she echoed her friend Carrie's words. *How could she not tell Stan?*

'What's wrong with you lately, Velma?' Gwen asked on Thursday evening. 'You look really washed out tonight.'

'It's probably nothing that a good night's sleep won't cure,' Velma said coolly. 'I haven't been sleeping too well lately.'

'My mother said she saw you coming out of Dr Tozer's surgery the other day,' Shirley said. 'You're not ill, are you?'

Velma deliberately avoided Carrie's eyes. 'I think I'm a bit run down, that's all. But it's nice of you to ask.'

She knew she was behaving oddly, making a mystery out of a perfectly normal situation. It wasn't as if she wasn't married and had anything to be ashamed of in being pregnant. These were her friends and it was ridiculous that she just couldn't get the words out and tell them. But she couldn't.

'You know your trouble, don't you?' Gwen went on. 'You've decided to get Stan out of your system, so you need to go ahead and do it and then find some other bloke to warm your bed.'

'Thanks for the advice, Gwen. It'll be good to have somebody's worldly experience to fall back on when I need it.'

Gwen's mouth fell open and Shirley looked startled. Gwen's lapse from grace had been forgiven by all of them, knowing the circumstances that had led her to it. But it was never mentioned now, especially in such sarcastic terms. And it was so unlike Velma to lash out in such a way.

'Well, I didn't mean anything, just that you have to move forward, don't you?' Gwen went on angrily. 'You're not exactly an ancient monument, Velma, and I'm sure you could find another bloke to marry you.'

Carrie knew it was time to intervene before things began to get heated.

'Why don't you shut up, Gwen? You're only making things worse. You and David are such lovebirds now, and good for you, but I'm sure that if Velma goes through with this divorce idea, she won't want to rush into marriage with somebody else. I know I wouldn't if anything happened between Archie and me.'

She gave a small shiver. Archie may not be everybody's dream-boat, but he was hers, she thought fiercely, and she couldn't ever imagine wanting to be with anybody else. None of them could, except Velma, and she wasn't too sure about that now.

As far as Carrie was concerned, there could surely be no possibility of Velma asking for a divorce now that she was expecting a baby. But it wasn't her business, and until Velma told the rest of them what she was going to do, Carrie would respect her secret.

There was one sure thing about expecting babies, though. You couldn't keep it a secret for ever, and in a few months from now the whole village would know about it.

Shirley made an attempt to cut through the tension that had crept between them. 'Let's talk about something else, for heaven's sake. The reunion dance is less than two weeks away, and I don't think Bernard's too keen on going after all. He thinks he'll show himself up because he drags his leg a bit, but I told him that's silly. There's going to be many more people there with far worse problems than his. We've all got to be there, haven't we?'

'Of course we have,' Carrie said, seeing her face pucker. 'I'm sure you can persuade Bernard to come round in the end. Work a bit of magic on him,' she added, trying to cajole her friend out of her sudden gloom.

'I don't seem able to do that any more,' Shirley muttered.

The others instantly picked up on her mood.

'Don't tell me there's trouble in paradise already,' Gwen said with a teasing laugh, at which Shirley glared at her.

'You're so darned smug, aren't you, Gwen? Just because everything's turned out so well for you, despite, well, you know what! David turned up safe and well and you just picked up where you left off.'

Gwen looked enraged at another pointed hint about her wartime indiscretions. Once that evening was bad enough, but twice was infuriating.

'David did have a couple of bullet wounds, you little idiot, and he was torpedoed and spent hours in the freezing cold Atlantic not knowing if he was ever going to be rescued or not. But since we're not all living in the past like some people, we don't keep on about it for ever more.'

Carrie was alarmed. Thursday evenings were when they all forgot about the war years and had a few laughs, but this one was turning into something of a nightmare. First Velma had got all huffy, and Shirley clearly had something on her mind, and Gwen was always more inclined to stir things up rather than help.

Maybe it was because they had nothing to bind them together anymore. It had just been the four of them during the bad times, all anxious about their menfolk and longing for them to come home, but now they had all returned and nothing was the same anymore. It should have been better. It should have been wonderful. It was what they had all hoped for and expected. But somehow it wasn't. Apart from Gwen, that is.

Carrie reluctantly admitted it. She had confidently believed that Archie would be as keen as she was to move out of her parents' house and get a place of their own, preferably the prefab she had set her heart on. But he didn't even seem remotely inclined to move. Gwen had remarked that he had it so cushy now, with Carrie's mum's cooking and all, so why would he ever want to rock the boat? Sometimes Carrie wondered uneasily why she had ever liked Gwen at all.

'You don't understand,' Shirley was saying baldly. 'None of you do.'

'Why don't you tell us what's wrong then?' Velma said. 'We can't help you if we don't know what's happened.'

'Nothing's happened, at least I don't think so. How can I tell? All I know is that if I hear the name Marie one more blessed time, I shall go mad!'

'Who's Marie?'

'I told you before, but I don't expect any of you to remember. She's the farmer's daughter in France where Bernard was rescued, and they looked after him for months. She tended his wounds and was a blooming saint by all accounts, and he never stops telling me that he wouldn't be here if it wasn't for her. I heard somewhere that if somebody saves your life, then that life always belongs to them.'

'That's plain stupid, Shirley,' Carrie told her. 'Think how many people's lives were saved during the war. They can't all belong to somebody else! I'm sure Bernard is grateful to her, and so should you be.'

'I know, and I am, but I thought she'd be in the past.'

'She is, you ninny,' Velma told her.

'Oh yes? That's all you know, then. Bernard's got her photo in his wallet, and his mum let it slip the other day that he's had a letter from her. That's not keeping her in the past, is it?'

Chapter 11

By the time she got home that night, Carrie decided there was no point in worrying about other people's problems. They all had something to look forward to, and she was quite sure Shirley could wheedle Bernard around her little finger and get him to come to the reunion dance. Gwen had no problems there. If anything, she might even prefer it if David didn't want to come, in case any of her old flames happened to turn up. What a disaster that would be.

As for Velma, well, who knew what Velma thought anymore? Stan was due home a few days before the dance, and for a mischievous moment Carrie thought it might be interesting to be a fly on the wall in the cottage in Tinners' Row for that particular reunion. But perhaps not. She was enormously fond of Velma, and she admitted that she herself was certainly like Shirley in one respect. She wanted everybody to have a happy ending.

'Do we have to go to this bloody dance?' Archie complained, jerking her out of her thoughts. 'I've never been much for dancing, nor for prancing around with a whole lot of folk I don't know.'

'Oh, for heaven's sake, Archie! You'll know a lot of people, and it's not as if we're going to turn up on our own, is it? We'll have Velma and Gwen and Shirley, and their chaps as well.'

'That's just what I mean. What the hell do I have in common with any of them? Bernard's just bloody sorry for himself, and Stan Gould always looks as if he's got a bad smell under his nose. I hated David Trewint's guts at school, and I can't think of anything to change the feeling – and it's mutual. I suppose all the heroes will be wearing their medals, too.'

My God, he was impossible today – but Carrie was instantly alert. There it was again, that sense that Archie was feeling less of a hero than any of them. He never put it into words, and Carrie guessed that he never would, but she knew he felt it. Despite her irritation, she felt a wave of sympathy for him, but it would be disastrous to his pride to even hint that she understood.

'Of course they won't be wearing medals. Nobody's likely to turn up in uniform, are they? They'll all be too thankful to be back in civvies.'

She hoped she was right. Such a thought hadn't occurred to her before, but on her way to work the next morning she called in at the haberdashery to ask Shirley what she thought about it.

'Bernard certainly wouldn't want to wear his uniform, even if it was still all in one piece,' Shirley said. 'I daresay Stan might, being a regular and all, but

I'm sure David Trewint won't. Gwen said he couldn't wait to be rid of the thing.'

'That's all right then,' Carrie said, relieved. 'I'm walking around on eggshells half the time, wondering what Archie's going to complain about next.'

'Are you?' Shirley said. 'You never said so before. I thought you and Archie were getting along fine.'

'Oh well, so we are, but you can't expect him to have forgotten all the other stuff so quickly, can you?'

'I suppose not. No, of course not.'

Carrie didn't want to refer to him being in a POW camp, nor even think about it, especially after that little revelation the other night about being stuck in the pit. He had revealed later that it was cold and pitch black too. She shivered, trying not to imagine the horror of it, and the rats . . . She was suddenly aware of the dark shadows beneath Shirley's eyes, and remembered her outburst the previous night.

'Are you feeling all right, Shirley? You look a bit peaky. You should be getting your beauty sleep in time for the dance.'

'How can I sleep with all this hanging over me? I thought that once Bernard came home everything would be wonderful, and it's not.'

Carrie didn't think she had all that much hanging over her, and she had to agree with Velma that Shirley could be a proper tragic actress when she chose. They might all find it amusing, but the reality of it was she really suffered.

'I think you're making too much of this Marie business,' Carrie told her. 'He's home now, and he's got you, hasn't he? You've got plenty to think about with your wedding coming up next year, and you'll soon forget all about this other girl.'

'Yes, but will he?'

Carrie squeezed her arm as Shirley's first customer of the morning came into the shop. 'I reckon you're just the one to make him, Shirley.'

'I shall wear my blue dress with the white daisies on it,' she told Archie on Saturday afternoon, a week before the dance. 'You always liked that one, didn't you? It would have been nice to get something new, but it'll be a waste of coupons, and we don't need to squander our money.' *Apart from you going to the pub most nights*, she added silently.

'In what way?' he said idly, only half listening. They were watching a village cricket match, and the October sun was still warm in a blissfully blue sky. Carrie was only mildly interested in the cricket scores, being far more excited at the prospect of their going to a big social event together. But she had already decided that she couldn't really afford to splash out on a new dress for it.

'We need to save up, don't we?' Carrie went on.

'Do we?'

'Oh, for goodness' sake, Archie, of course we do. How are we ever going to have a home of our own if we don't save up for it? We'll need new furniture and curtains, and I want a nice garden where we can grow plants and flowers as well as vegetables, and your gratuity won't go far enough for all that.'

He finally took in what she was saying.

'Are you still thinking about this bloody prefab?' he said, loudly enough for people near them to look their way and tut. He wasn't really angry, just annoyed at having his concentration disturbed.

'I'm thinking about our future. One of us has to.'

'I'm more interested in the present, thanks very much. When you've been in a situation where you don't even know if you're going to have a future, you're thankful enough to let it take care of itself.'

'I know all that, Archie, but don't you think it's fun to plan ahead?'

'Fun? It sounds more like bloody hard work to be counting every penny to buy furniture and curtains, and I don't intend to kill myself with gardening.'

'I'd do that. I always liked working with my dad on his allotment. You'd be surprised what I learned about growing vegetables while you were away.'

'I daresay, but right now I'd rather watch the cricket.'

He folded his arms and rammed his hat more firmly on his head to shade his eyes from the sun, ignoring her. Carrie was tempted to do the same and just sit and sulk. Married women weren't meant to do that, but she was so resentful of his offhand manner she could have screamed. Instead, she said she would go inside the small pavilion and help make the tea and sandwiches for when the game ended.

As she stood up, brushing the grass from her skirt, he caught her hand.

'We'll talk about it some other time, Carrie.'

She looked down at him, his face tanned and healthy now after those awful years in captivity, his body filled out from her mum's good cooking, and instantly forgave him everything. Maybe she was weak, but compared with other people's problems, she knew she had everything she had ever wanted.

In contrast with the brilliance outside, the interior of the pavilion was dim, and she had to blink a few times to accustom her eyes to the change. She knew Velma would be among the helpers here, since she always offered to do the teas for the cricketers. She saw her at once, buttering slices of bread with a scrape and a promise, and a slightly more lavish helping of fish paste.

'Have you come to help or hinder?' Velma greeted her.

Carrie laughed. 'Mostly to get out of the sun. But give me a job and I'll do it.'

'You're looking cheerful today, but then you usually do.'

'She's always been a proper little ray of sunshine, our Carrie,' one of the older women helpers said. 'Especially now that Archie's back, eh, my dear?'

'Oh, of course, Mrs Endersby!'

'Well, you just sit there and look pretty, while we get on with the task.'

'I'd much rather be useful.'

'There's not much left to do now,' Velma said. 'In fact, when I've covered these sandwiches, let's go for a stroll. I could do with some fresh air.'

Mrs Endersby nodded. 'She's been looking a mite

flushed, so fresh air's the best medicine for her. Go on now, both of you. The rest of us will finish up here.'

She shooed them out of the pavilion like a mother hen, and Velma smiled gratefully at Carrie.

'I'm glad you turned up. Much more of her fussing and I'd have been a nervous wreck by the time they came in for tea.'

'You do look hot.'

'So do you. It's something to do with the weather, don't you think?'

'And the other thing.'

'Ah yes, the other thing.'

Carrie looked at her anxiously. 'Oh Lord, Velma, I hope that didn't sound disrespectful. I know what it is. I'm just trying to be discreet.'

Velma laughed, hugging her arm. 'It's all right. I hardly know what to call it myself. It's probably no bigger than a speck, and it's still an *it* as far as its gender is concerned, but it's still a little person, for all that.'

'But are you really all right? Mrs Endersby said you looked flushed.'

'You know what a fusspot she is. I'm perfectly well, apart from first thing in the morning. Dr Tozer advised me to eat a dry biscuit and sip hot water instead of tea. It does the trick, but he forgot to say it might happen in the evenings too.'

As she grimaced, to Carrie it sounded like entering a different world, and she supposed that it was. It was a world that none of them had entered yet – except Shirley, and that had ended almost before it began.

She smothered the twist of envy and thought instead how awful it must be to feel sick every single morning.

'Have you decided on anything yet?'

'Such as am I going to wear my best navy blue dress or my beige two-piece to the dance?'

'You know exactly what I mean. Have you told Stan?'

'No. Not yet. And I don't want to talk about it either.'

But Carrie noted that she didn't say 'not ever'.

'I thought Gwen and David might have been here today. He was always a bit sporty and he used to like playing cricket.'

Velma shrugged. 'I daresay he doesn't consider watching other men chase about after a ball exciting enough after life in the navy and being torpedoed. Archie doesn't seem to mind it, though.'

'He likes the lazy life after working all the week in the shop.'

Carrie sometimes wondered whether the others considered chopping up carcasses of dead meat all week an entirely savoury thing to do, compared with Stan being a regular soldier and on call for any national emergency, Bernard being a teacher and therefore something of an intellectual, and David braving his life against the elements every single day. Chopping meat was hardly the most dynamic thing a man could do. But such thoughts were disloyal, she thought fiercely, and where would the village be without a butcher to serve their needs?

'Has Bernard decided what he's going to do yet?'

she asked Velma, diverting her thoughts quickly. 'Shirley said he might apply for a teaching job in Penhallow.'

'I'm sure she'll be relieved if he does. There'll be less chance of running into anybody who remembers the time the Yanks were in Penzance.'

'Let's just hope they don't run into anybody like that at the dance then, for Shirley's sake – and Gwen's.'

It could be an evening fraught with tension for some, as well as the general excitement and a huge and belated welcome for their returning heroes. At least she and Archie had no such fears on that score, Carrie thought. Nor Velma, although she had anxieties of a different sort.

Velma was thinking the same when she went home from the cricket match late that afternoon. The reunion dance was only a week away, and Stan would be home a few days earlier.

Although she hadn't told the girls yet, she had done her final journey on the buses on the previous day. Ostensibly she had resigned because the jobs belonged to the men who had done them before they went away to war, and who rightly deserved to have them back. More truthfully, it was because every lurch of the bus around the winding and narrow Cornish lanes sent her stomach heaving.

So she would have all the time in the world to be with Stan and to tell him her news – if she chose to do so. She had been adamant that she wouldn't, but as the moment approached she changed her mind as often as a perverse wind. One minute she longed to tell him, to see the delight and awe on his face, and the next she was too afraid that she would see the expression of an animal being trapped.

She was too proud to hold on to a man who no longer loved her. She had firmly believed she no longer loved him, but that night in St Ives she had seen a vulnerable side to him that she hadn't seen in years, if ever. It had reminded her of why she had fallen in love with him all those years ago, the tall, handsome stranger who wasn't a Cornishman and therefore had all the colour and glamour of a foreigner to someone born and bred in a remote village in the tailpiece of England.

She knew she was being silly. Because of the war, all sorts of people met and mingled now. Those who had never moved more than a few miles from their homes were seasoned travellers, if you could call being sent to foreign parts to fight being seasoned travellers. But Cornish men and women had always been an insular race, suspicious of strangers, and you couldn't help the way you were born.

So she would wait until after the dance to decide whether or not to tell Stan about the baby. She would give them these few days together to see if there was anything there to recapture. If there was . . . her heart gave an unusual flutter and then raced on . . . if there was, she couldn't deny that she would welcome it with open arms and an eager heart. If not, she would let him go.

Meanwhile, she thought, pushing that surprisingly

stomach-turning possibility out of her mind, she would clean and polish the cottage so that it looked like a palace for Stan to come home to. It would gleam and shine and be filled with the fragrance of fresh flowers from their own garden. It would be a home fit for a hero.

Shirley desperately wanted Bernard to apply for the teaching post in Penhallow, and prayed that he wouldn't think it would be wasting his abilities to be teaching infants. Tongues wagged everywhere, and the days when the GIs had arrived in their midst in preparation for D-Day had been a time of great excitement for the community. The farm where she had worked was near Penzance, and she and her fellow land girls had enjoyed the company of the glamorous Yanks in the evenings, along with half the female population of the area.

But it wasn't only the girls. Whole families welcomed these friendly young men from across the ocean into their own homes, and got to know them well. She was darned sure there were other girls who had known them as well as she had known Hank Delaney.

She shivered, feeling her heart give that peculiar little leap every time his name came into her mind. And not only his name. If she closed her eyes for a moment she could still picture every line of his face; the shape of it; the way the laughter lines around his eyes creased up when he smiled at her; the way his dark hair was so springy and wavy; his sensitive, magical hands that could send her almost delirious with pleasure; the way their bodies had fitted together on that one perfect night before he left, as if they were always meant to be together.

'All right, I've made up my mind,' Bernard said abruptly, bringing her out of her reverie so crashingly that she gasped. 'Sorry. Did I startle you? I didn't think you were actually asleep, even with your eyes closed. Though how anybody could sleep with my kid brothers kicking a ball against the wall of the house, I'll never know.'

'I wasn't asleep.' She snuggled closer to him on his mum's front room sofa. 'So what have you made up your mind about?'

Hopefully to get married the minute I've had my twenty-first birthday so that I can get this other madness out of my head for ever.

'I'm taking the job offered at the school here. It's just as important to train young minds as older ones.'

And when did you become so pompous? Or was it always there and I never saw it before?

'That's wonderful, Bernard. We'll be able to see far more of one another than if you had to go to Penzance every day.'

He laughed. 'Oh, come on. Penzance isn't exactly on the other side of the world, is it?'

Neither is France.

'I'll leave it a few weeks until the middle of term, and then take up the post,' he went on. 'I'm quite looking forward to it now I've made up my mind.'

'No regrets then? About anything?'

He finally sensed that she was in what his mother would call a funny mood today. It wasn't funny ha-ha, either. And she wasn't as bubbly as usual.

'What's that supposed to mean? I've got quite a few, if you must know. I regret that I got shot down over France and didn't come home in one piece. I regret the fact that we ever had to go to war, and that our lives were disrupted, and even more so that so many shattered lives were the result of it. I know I can't take the whole burden of the war on my shoulders, but sometimes it feels like that. I'm sure it must be the same for everyone who was involved.'

'And those of us who weren't can have no idea, can we?'

He gave her arm a squeeze. 'Don't be daft, Shirley. I wasn't implying anything of the sort. You all did your bit at home, I'm sure.'

'Why did you have to add that bit?'

'Which bit?'

Shirley had a wild urge to giggle at this absurd conversation, tempered by the realization that Bernard might be here in body, but in spirit he still hadn't come back to her. Not completely.

'I'm not even sure which bit we're talking about now,' she said. 'But it doesn't matter. Nothing does, except that you're home, and we can pick up our lives where we left off. We are doing that, aren't we, Bernard?'

'Of course we are,' he said, pulling her close and giving her the most satisfactory kiss.

But he still hadn't mentioned the letter he had

received from Marie, nor shown her the photo he carried in his wallet.

Carrie had guessed correctly about Gwen's feelings. By now she was secretly hoping that David wouldn't want to go to the dance. The nearer it got, the more nervous she became. She bitterly regretted the flings she had had when she thought he was never coming home again. She had truly thought he was dead, and although that might be a perfectly valid excuse, it was not the sort of confession you wanted to make to a husband who was very much alive. And after that brush with death, David was determined to make the most of that life.

They had cycled to St Ives again that Sunday afternoon, even though she'd have thought he would have seen enough of the place. They never tired of it, though. The maze of winding little streets tumbled down to the sea, and the little white-washed houses made it an enchanting picture-postcard of a town.

St Ives was an artists' paradise, and there were always folk sketching the ever-changing scenes on the quay. Gwen and David sat there now, enjoying the sunshine alongside the trickle of tourists who had begun to discover the place. It was probably good for local businesses, and there were a number of bed-and-breakfast establishments and quaint little tea rooms which had recently sprung up, but she felt it would ruin it completely if it became a regular tourist spot.

David flexed his leg a few times, stretching and relaxing the muscles, as he had been advised to do.

'Are you sure you'll be up to dancing next week?' Gwen asked, noting the movements. 'We don't have to go if you'd rather not. I really don't mind, David.'

'Of course we're going. Do you think I'd miss the chance to show off my dancing skills to two-left-feet Pollard?'

Gwen sighed. 'Why do you always think ill of Archie? He's not so bad.'

'He's an oaf, and always has been, ever since we were at school,' David said. 'But I can still do a twirl or two, so of course we're going to the dance. You've been looking forward to it, and if the town's putting on a big show like you say, it would be wrong to snub them, wouldn't it?'

'You're right, and I want to show you off too, so that's settled then,' Gwen said brightly, ignoring the sinking feeling in her stomach.

She hoped they could all stick together, despite the way David and Archie felt about one another, and the fact that Stan Gould always seemed a bit aloof. She wasn't sure about Bernard. But she and Carrie, Shirley and Velma intended to remain a complete unit, the way they had during the war. Whenever any one of them needed help or advice, the other three were always there.

Velma had been the luckiest, she thought. Nothing bad had happened to Stan, even though he might have expected it, being a regular soldier and all, and was presumably in the front line from the beginning. But since war wasn't a regular occurrence, thank the

Lord, she supposed you never knew what would be expected of you, nor how you would react.

'A penny for them,' David said lazily, watching her. 'Or even more, depending on what you think they're worth.'

Gwen flushed. Privately she knew she had been a bit bitchy lately, sniping and snapping at the three best friends she had ever had, but only because she was so nervous about her past coming out.

'Oh, I was just thinking how glad I was to have three such good friends while you were away, and especially when—'

He put his fingers over her mouth. 'We don't talk about that, do we? It's a closed chapter, and the future is the only thing that matters, my love. Just be thankful that nothing's going to separate us again.'

'I am thankful, more than you know,' Gwen said, hugging his arm, and wishing the little knot of anxiety in her stomach would go away once and for all.

She was just as thankful to get her mind away from the sheer horror of imagining David beneath the waves after his ship had been torpedoed, being sucked down in the inky blackness and fighting for his breath. It had been her own personal nightmare that she had never revealed to David, and it had gone on for months, before she had found her own form of release.

Carrie had also had her share of worry until she learned that Archie was a POW. Until the news came through there had been such a long silence from him that she, too, had feared the worst. People said that no news was good news, but in Gwen's opinion it was the daftest thing anybody ever said. No news was just no news. At least Archie was fed and housed while he was a POW, however awful the conditions were, and from what they heard later about some of those terrible concentration camps, conditions could be likened to purgatory. But Archie hadn't been in one of those. He had survived, and he was still alive.

They had all had a bad time with Shirley when she realized that GI Hank had left a little package behind. Shirley was such a sweet and utter dumbo, Gwen thought, with a surge of affection, and she had got totally carried away by her sweet-talking Yank. Not that Gwen could really blame her, she conceded. Hank the Yank was a real charmer. And Shirley wasn't the only girl to have her head turned by the slick GIs in their smart uniforms.

But like the three musketeers they had all rallied around Shirley when she needed it, and the others had all rallied around Gwen. From that moment on, she vowed to be nicer to them all the next time they met – providing mealy-mouthed Archie Pollard didn't have too many digs at her darling David.

'Do you want to go for another ride?' David broke into her thoughts.

'You know what I'd really like to do?'

'What's that?'

'Go home and have a cuddle.'

He laughed. 'Gwen Trewint! When did you become so forward? Are you trying to make a dishonest man of me in the middle of the afternoon and in broad daylight?'

'Yes please,' she said with a grin. 'We *are* married, so there's no law against it, is there?'

But she hardly needed to tease, because David was already disentangling their bicycles from the wall he had propped them against, and from the gleam in his eyes she knew he wasn't going to object to an hour or two between the sheets!

Chapter 12

Velma was as nervous as a new bride as she waited for Stan to arrive home. She wasn't sure that was the right comparison, though, because they were far from being newlyweds, and after the shock of his letter she had no idea whether Stan would want to, well, to be a proper husband. That time in St Ives seemed like a dream now, an idyllic, sensual dream, in which they had been transformed into the lovers they had once been.

If it wasn't for the evidence in her belly now, she might still believe she had imagined it all. She pressed her hand lightly against herself, knowing it would become evident to everybody soon. And because she was basically an honest person, she knew she couldn't hide it from Stan any longer. Carrie had been right about that. It was his right to know he was to become a father.

He arrived home in the late evening on Tuesday, driving slowly down Tinners' Row in a large black automobile that had the street children running after it and cheering. Velma gasped when she saw it, and had the front door of the cottage open before he had got out of the car.

'Have you come into a fortune?' she greeted him, thankful to have something to say to cover the awkward moment.

Stan smiled. 'I've borrowed it for the week. I thought we should go to the ball in style, and it's big enough for a couple of your friends to come with us if you like.'

And it would save them the bother of having to make too much conversation.

As she thought it, she wondered just how soon they would get on to the subject that must be uppermost in both their minds. Stan's letter. There was something else on her mind as well, but that was going to wait.

He had put down his travelling bags now and he looked around the cottage slowly. Since she had no work to go to anymore Velma had plenty of time on her hands, and she had put every effort into giving the place a spring clean, despite its being autumn. The vehemence with which she had tackled every sparkling surface was evident, and Stan gave a small whistle.

'Good God. Have the fairies been in to give the place a once-over?'

It was such a harmless remark, and one that she would normally have laughed off, if she hadn't been in such a sensitive frame of mind. She'd worked hard to welcome him, filling all her vases with late-blooming roses from the garden, and their sweet and over-powering scent was everywhere.

In an instant she saw his words as sarcastic, as if implying that she never did much housework, when she had always been so proud of this cottage where she had been born.

Unbidden, smarting tears brimmed on her lashes, and then her innards suddenly erupted. Before she could say anything she had to make a dash for the outside lavatory in the backyard, retching all the way.

She didn't even know that Stan was right behind her. The wooden door was swinging open, and she felt his cool hands on her forehead, holding her as the paroxysm subsided and she slowly straightened up.

'What brought all that on, my love?' he said quietly.

It was those few words that did it. She could have held on to her secret until she felt the time was right. She could somehow have got around the fact that she was sick most mornings, and often in the evenings too, and was likely to be so until these first months were over. But it was those two words, those tender words that she hadn't heard from him in a long time, that did it.

'I'm not ill,' she wept, tears streaming down her face as he held her close now. 'Oh, botheration and all that! Can't you guess what's wrong with me? I thought it would be obvious! I'm having a baby.'

She felt his arms go rigid against her, and she leaned against him, knowing she had done the worst thing a woman could do. The thing she had vowed *not* to do, when he had been the one to hint that their marriage might be over. He was an honourable man, and she had given him the one thing that would bind him to her. But it didn't please her in the way such moments between a man and a woman should. If anything it shamed her, because she felt she was as good as blackmailing him to stay with her now. She broke free of his embrace.

'I'm sorry,' she mumbled. 'I didn't mean to blurt it out like that. I didn't mean to tell you at all—'

'Not tell me? What the devil do you mean?' he said angrily.

'Well, I was probably going to tell you after the dance, when I saw how things stood between us. After your letter, I didn't want to feel you were beholden to me in any way, if you feel that's best.'

'For God's sake, Velma, let's go inside and discuss this. I don't deny that it's a shock, but I can't understand what you're saying now.'

She walked stiffly ahead of him, knowing she was doing this all wrong. Any one of her friends would have handled this situation better than she had. She was the eldest of the four of them, the one Shirley sometimes teased about being a wise old owl, but right now she felt as young and gauche as a child.

Yes, it would have been a shock to him. It had been a shock to her. She had gone to the doctor, expecting to hear that she had her mother's complaint, and that she was going to die. She had assumed they were never going to have children. Now that they were – she caught her breath on a lingering sob – now that they were, she had got used to the idea, and she knew how much she wanted this child, and that she would move heaven and earth to protect it, even if she had to do it alone.

'Sit down,' Stan ordered. 'I'd offer to make some tea, but I think a tot of brandy would be preferable. Medicinal for you, and a shock remedy for me.'

She closed her eyes, hearing his decisive movements as he went to the sideboard and got out the bottle of brandy that was rarely opened. He poured them each a small glass and put one of them in her shaking hand. She opened her eyes and took a sip, feeling the stinging liquid course down her throat, while hoping distractedly that it wouldn't harm the baby.

'I know it was a shock, and I'm sorry I blurted it out like that,' she muttered again, since she couldn't think of anything else to say.

'So how long have you known?'

Velma bit her lip to stop it trembling. She was normally a strong person, and a capable one, but right now she felt near to dissolving into jelly. He was so distant, so aloof and polite, a stranger she had been married to for ten years, whom she hardly knew at all. She blamed the army for that. And herself, too, the honest part of her insisted, because there had been countless times when he had asked her to join him wherever he was posted, and become a proper army wife. And she had always refused, always insisting on keeping her own private space in the little corner of Cornwall that she loved. She smothered a sob.

'Since St Ives,' she mumbled. 'Well, that was when – when—'

'It is mine then.'

The shock of that statement nearly knocked her sideways. She couldn't believe she had heard him say those words.

As if there had ever been anyone else, or ever would be . . . a furious retort shook her lips. And then she saw that Stan's mouth was twitching with *laughter*.

'Velma, your face is a picture. Of course I know it's mine. I never doubted it for a minute, but I must say it takes a bit of getting used to. A child is not something we've really considered before and it certainly gives us something to think about.'

'Like where our future lies,' she said, repeating the words of his letter.

'Well, exactly. Look, I'm going to make that tea after all, and then we'll talk. Incidentally, I suppose your knitting circle friends know all about this. They'd naturally have been in the know before I was.'

He was in the kitchen before Velma realized that he had sounded almost petulant at that moment. He was forty years old, and he had sounded like a small boy who was jealous because she had confided in her friends before him. She had to put him straight, and she followed him as he put the kettle on the stove.

'I haven't told anyone except Carrie. I knew she would be the one who would understand the most.'

'Was there such a lot to understand? The act of making a baby is all too easy for some people. It just took us a little longer, that's all.'

It had been all too easy for Shirley . . . She put her hand on his arm.

'Stan, you're not terribly angry, are you?'

'Why should I be? It takes two, doesn't it?'

Dear God, this was awful. All her plans of asking him for a divorce when the war was over, her calm, calculated plan, which she was sure they would think was the most sensible solution for them, had fizzled out in her mind now. She wanted this baby, and she wanted *him*, and his letter had thrown her into total confusion. She felt her head droop, and then, unbelievably, his arms had closed around her, and he was holding her tight.

'Look, I know I'm being a brute, and it's only because I'm so overwhelmed by all this that I hardly know how to react. So what does your friend Carrie say?'

'Carrie is a romantic, but she also has a very sensible head on her shoulders. She obviously thinks I should do what my heart dictates.'

'What the devil does that mean? There's no medical reason why you shouldn't have this baby, is there? And you would never think of giving it up for adoption, would you? Not under any circumstances. I wouldn't allow it.'

Not even if you were to leave me . . . ?

'Of course not. I think I'm just discovering how much I wanted children, but I thought it was too late for us. And then your letter came, and it seemed to me that you felt our marriage was over, and I didn't know how to tell you—'

'Well, you certainly found a way,' he said, starting to smile again. 'Throwing up the minute I came home was a pretty good giveaway, my love.'

There it was again, those two precious words that meant the world to her. They had never been a very demonstrative couple with actions or words, so when he said those particular words they became all the more precious.

'So where do we go from here?' she said quietly.

'That's what we have to talk about. We've got a week to do it in, so let's just have a cup of tea and a piece of your special homecoming chocolate cake, which I'm sure you've made, and just relax.'

She was more than thankful to do that, even if it was putting off the moment, and any decision about their future. She was never going to ask for a divorce now, but she had no idea what he had in mind.

She also knew he was too upright a man to desert her, and she was determined not to feel guilty any longer that things might have been so very different if she hadn't become pregnant. In any event, none of it mattered. Now that Stan knew the truth, and the shock of it was subsiding, everything else could wait.

'Oh, I meant to tell you, Archie. We've been invited to go to the dance with Velma and Stan in the posh car Stan has borrowed for his leave,' Carrie said.

He groaned, as she knew he would. She had carefully waited until they were cosy in bed together, and by now he had had his cigarette and he was in a jolly good mood because she had been extra responsive to his lovemaking – even if it had been over almost before she'd known it was happening . . .

'They're organizing a bus to take folk from the

district, aren't they? Why can't we go in that? I don't know that I fancy his poncey company there and back. Squaddies and regulars never did get on that well, and I suppose they'll expect us to stay with them all evening.'

'Well, with them and our other friends,' she said, deliberately making it sound as if they were his friends too, when she was fast beginning to realize that he didn't really care for any of them. 'Anyway, if you promise not to tell, I'll let you into a little secret.'

'Oh yes?'

He was diverted at once, never averse to a bit of local gossip. Whoever said it was only women who gossiped!

'You've got to promise me first. It's not my secret, and until it becomes common knowledge, I'm telling you privately.'

'All right, I promise,' Archie said, humouring her.

Carrie supposed it was all right. Velma had said she was going to tell the others tomorrow evening at the church hall, and then everybody would know!

'Velma's expecting a baby.'

For a moment she thought Archie hadn't heard, and then he gave a loud outburst of laughter that got him spluttering and coughing, and had her mum banging on the bedroom wall next door.

'Shut up,' Carrie giggled. 'Mum will wonder what's going on in here.'

'She probably knew that earlier. But how the hell did it happen? I didn't think old Stan was home often enough to get his leg over.'

'Don't you remember they spent those few days in St Ives a couple of months ago?' she said, ignoring his choice expression.

'So that's when he cracked it, the sly old bugger.'

'Archie, honestly!' she protested, not letting this go. 'There's nothing sly about a married couple having a baby. It's normal. It's what most married couples do. It's what every woman wants when she gets married, and it's what the wedding service says – that marriage is for the procreation of children.'

She was starting to get upset, though he didn't cotton on to it.

He gave a chuckle. 'And don't forget the mutual comfort, old girl. We do our share of that, don't we? And old Stan scored a goal this time.'

She noted that Stan was now 'old Stan' and apparently more acceptable now it was proven that he was a red-blooded man who did the normal thing that married couples did.

'You know I want a baby sometime, don't you, Archie?'

She said it without thinking. He still had his tunnel vision that the world wasn't a fit place to bring babies into, but that was nonsense. Babies had been born throughout the war years, and even in the middle of the Blitz in London and Plymouth and many other places, and he was just being stubborn. She felt him turn away from her.

'Maybe. When the time's right.'

She banged her pillow into shape and turned her

back on him, refusing to snuggle up to him in their familiar spoons-in-a-box style.

'Just don't make me wait until I'm too old to enjoy it,' she said.

'You won't be. Your friend's nearly forty, isn't she?'

'She's thirty-five, and I'm not going to wait that long!' she snapped.

'Better find a lover then,' Archie said, obviously finding this conversation about Velma, whom he considered practically middle-aged, a big hoot.

'I just might!' Carrie said loudly, which got her mum banging on the wall again, followed by the sound of her dad grumbling about all the noise going on.

Then, of course, she couldn't sleep. Archie always fell asleep almost instantly after they had made love, and he was snoring in seconds. She wished desperately that he didn't have this aversion to having babies. It was apparently all right for other people, but not for them. It was so unfair. And despite that flippant remark about her finding a lover, she knew she never would. For all his faults, and his uncertain temper these days, she loved Archie as much as she had ever done. Loved and adored him, and knew that there would never be anyone else for her.

She instinctively knew that Velma felt the same about Stan. The divorce plan was simply because they were so often apart that it hardly seemed like a real marriage. Being married meant being together always, understanding each other, learning about each other, forgiving each other. It took a lifetime to do that. It was what she had vowed to do when she had fulfilled her childhood dream and married Archie.

For Shirley and Gwen it had been different. Both of them had had lovers – Gwen more than one. She had her own reasons for what she had done, and Shirley had simply been carried away by the excitement and glamour of the GIs. But Carrie couldn't imagine what it would be like to love anyone but Archie. She couldn't imagine feeling relaxed and comfortable enough with any other man to abandon all the morals she had been brought up with, to have an affair.

But presumably being relaxed and comfortable wasn't the way you wanted to feel at such times. If you were passionate enough about someone to fall in love with them, the thrill of it all would have nothing to do with the mutual comfort of the marriage vows, and more to do with a sensual, sexual need . . .

The words slid into Carrie's mind. Words she didn't normally use. Words that weren't familiar in her everyday world, but which hinted at something darker, forbidden and more thrilling, words to make her blood tingle and surge and make her bury her face in her pillow, sure that she shouldn't even be thinking about such clandestine emotions here in the bed she shared with Archie. Unless they were applied to the love she shared with him, of course.

That was all right then. Because he did thrill her, excite her, make her blood tingle and surge . . . On an impulse she twisted around in the bed again, put her arms around him and held him tight, pushing those other thoughts completely out of her mind. She needed nothing to do with lovers, because she had

Archie, and God had been compassionate and sent him back to her when so many others had never come back. He was still young and strong and alive . . .

'Again?' she heard him say teasingly, and then he had turned to her too, and even though she knew it wouldn't happen, not so soon after the last time, she was more than happy to lie in his arms and feel cherished until he was ready.

'Are you serious, Velma?' Shirley squeaked on Thursday evening. 'You're having us on, aren't you? And if I may say so, it's in pretty poor taste,' she added, her face drooping for a moment, which indicated that she still wasn't fully over what had happened to her. Any mention of babies brought it all back.

'Of course she's not making it up,' Gwen said, looking closely at Velma's flushed face. 'You don't make up something like that. You've certainly knocked us for six, though, Velma. What's going to happen about the divorce now?'

'I'm not thinking about that for the time being.'

'But you can't go through with it now,' Shirley said. 'You wouldn't want to bring up a baby on your own. What does Stan say? You have told him, I suppose? Did you get this out before you blew it all by asking for the divorce?'

Velma looked from one to the other and knew exactly why she had chosen to tell Carrie before either of these two. Shirley was an airhead and Gwen was just too cynical. She was fond of them all, but if there had to be a choice Carrie was the one she'd really choose for a friend.

'Stan knows, and we're considering what we're going to do after the dance,' she said shortly. 'We're just enjoying his leave for the moment, and he's pleased that I've given up work so we can spend more time together.'

'You'd have had to give it up eventually, anyway,' Gwen put in. 'You could hardly carry on working on the buses when you got fat and forty.'

'I won't be forty when the baby's born. I shall be nearly thirty-six, and that's not old at all.'

She was uneasy about that, though. Plenty of women had babies into their late thirties and forties, but she had never thought she would be one of them.

'You'll be a wonderful mother, Velma,' Carrie told her. 'Much more sensible than somebody too young to know what she's doing.'

'I hope that isn't a dig at me,' Shirley said, more upset than she expected to be at this talk of mother-hood.

It had been a total disaster when she had discovered what was happening to her, and a terrific and guilty relief when the miscarriage had happened, but afterwards she had felt more bereft than she ever let on to her friends. They were the only ones she had been able to confide in at the time, but even they didn't know how she had mourned the child that never was, how she had truly felt that someone very close to her had died. And if he was in heaven now, she truly hoped that God was taking good care of him, and not punishing him for being a bastard.

'I'm not digging at anybody. Are you all right, Shirley?'

'I'm fine. So you're still going to the dance, Velma?'

'The world doesn't stop just because I'm having a baby, darling. We've offered to take Carrie and Archie in the car Stan has borrowed, but I'm afraid there won't be room for any more, so we shall see you all at the dance hall.'

Velma was glad it was out in the open now. Her stomach was already getting rounded, her bosoms were fuller, and people were sure to notice soon, so the sooner it got around the village, the fewer explanations she would have to make.

'Do we have to keep it a secret?' Gwen asked, as if reading her mind.

'Not any more,' Velma said quietly.

She wondered if they were all thinking the same thing at that moment. They had supported one another all through the war years. They had been a team, sharing tears, anxieties, secrets and traumas, and now it seemed as if the tight little unit that they had been was gently splintering. This was a secret that didn't need to be kept, and somehow it was like breaking the thread that had bound them together.

'Everyone in the village will be pleased for you, Velma, and we'll all be there when it's born, just as we'll all be there when Shirley and Bernard get married,' Carrie said, and Velma knew that she, at least, understood.

She had planned to walk part of the way home with Carrie, as she often did, but when they left the church hall it was to find Stan waiting outside. She felt a little rush of something totally unexpected. Gladness. Warmth. Love.

'Congratulations, Stan,' Carrie said at once, when the others seemed to be tongue-tied. He really was a handsome man, tall and distinguished, with just enough grey in his hair to add authority. As he offered his arm to Velma, Carrie wondered why her friend had ever thought of divorcing him, but you never knew what went on in other people's marriages, she reminded herself. Which was just as well.

'Thank you,' he said with a smile. 'Are we seeing you all on Saturday night?'

'Don't worry, we'll be there,' Shirley said, before scuttling off home to spread the news to her mum and dad and sisters the amazing news that Velma Gould was having a baby. Perhaps if she said it often enough, and told enough people, she might not feel such an ache in her own heart at the telling.

'You already knew, didn't you?' Gwen asked Carrie almost accusingly, when the others had gone.

Carrie sighed. 'Only recently. I think she had to tell somebody or burst. She thought she was ill at first, Gwen, like her mother. It must have been quite a shock.'

'It didn't do Shirley much good to hear it. We'll have to watch her before she goes all noble and decides to confess everything to Bernard after all.'

'I'm sure she won't,' Carrie said, though she wasn't sure at all. Shirley had had such a strange look on her face when Velma told them her news.

Gwen was right. They would have to watch her. You had to look forward, not back over what might have been. There was no sense in wasting your emotions on past regrets either. By the time she and Gwen parted, Carrie found herself being glad that in comparison with the others she had such an uncomplicated life.

'Your dad's not feeling well,' her mum announced the minute she got in the door. 'I don't like the look of him. He's sort of grey around the gills, but he won't see the doctor, of course. He was always a stubborn man.'

It was her way of saying she was worried about him.

'I'm all right, woman,' Walter said from the depths of his armchair. 'Your mother fusses too much, Carrie, so take no notice and make us all a nice cup of cocoa, there's a good girl.'

'All right, if you're sure you're not ill, Dad. Where's Archie, by the way? Isn't he home yet?'

Her heart sank. She hated to see either of her parents unwell, and she hated it when Archie stayed out so late at the pub. It inevitably meant he would come home smelling of beer, probably tipsy and talking too loudly, and then he would be fumbling for her and cursing with frustration when nothing happened, due to what he charmingly called brewer's droop. Sometimes it was all right, though, and Carrie found herself hoping guiltily that tonight he would manage it and that he would forget about not wanting a baby and go all the way.

218

All this baby talk was going to her head, she thought savagely, as she put the pan on the stove to heat the milk. It wasn't the end of the world if it didn't happen for a year or two. They were young and had their lives ahead of them. And how would it be for Shirley if another of her friends became pregnant?

Carrie slammed the cups and saucers on to a tray, wondering why she had even thought of such a thing. She clenched her hands involuntarily. It was time to be selfish and think of herself, not silly Shirley's problems!

'I'm all right, you know,' she heard her father's quiet voice behind her. 'You shouldn't take any notice of your mother's fussing. I'm as tough as couch grass.'

'I know,' Carrie mumbled, aware that she hadn't been thinking of him at all at that moment, but rather her own needs.

He put his arms around her. He had always been more demonstrative than her mother, and she leaned her head briefly against his shoulder.

'You're a good girl, Carrie, but you and Archie should be looking for a place of your own. A married couple need their privacy.'

'Are you trying to get rid of me?' she asked, a shine of tears in her eyes.

'Of course not, but I hope when those prefabs are ready he's not going to be difficult about you renting one.'

'I hope so too,' she said, turning away just in time to catch the pan of milk on the stove before it boiled over.

Chapter 13

'You look smashing, and you're making me feel fruity just looking at you. Are you sure we have to go to this bloody reunion dance? I'd much rather lock the bedroom door and stay here instead. What do you say?'

Carrie laughed. Archie was nothing if not blatant. She twirled around in her blue dress with the white daisies on it, knowing she looked her best. Her brown hair was loose and softly curled, and Archie caught and held it as he pulled her towards him.

'Archie, stop it,' she giggled. 'You know we're going, so don't mess me about after I've taken all this time to get ready.'

It was a heady feeling, though, to know she could put that special gleam in his eyes without even trying. She wouldn't have been averse to staying home, either, if it hadn't been that she had been so looking forward to this day. In a way it would put a seal on all that had gone before. The war was well and truly over, their heroes had come safely home, and good friends were all together again.

She felt his kiss burrowing into her neck, sending

warm shivers of delight running through her.

'Archie, please,' she said faintly.

He laughed, and let her go. 'All right, I can wait. I'll be on my best behaviour tonight, knowing that among all those other poor sods I'm the one you'll be coming home with later.'

'Oh, you can be so romantic!' Carrie teased him.

But it was romantic. *He* was romantic, in his own sweet, brash way, even if her mum would definitely disapprove of some of the earthy things he said to her. It didn't matter. Some wise person had once said that nothing that went on between a man and a woman was wrong, providing they both approved and enjoyed it. And she did approve. And she definitely enjoyed it. Whenever he held her, caressed her, adored her, she felt as if there was no one else in the whole world but the two of them. It was the way he made her feel, so wanted, so loved. They shared a history of their own, memories of their own that were private, intimate, secret. It didn't matter what other people thought. It was just the two of them who mattered. She hugged his arm and stood on tiptoe to press a tiny kiss on his lips, knowing she had better calm down before she started feeling too amorous for her own good.

'That'll have to do for now, then, so let's go and wait for Stan and Velma. We don't want to keep them waiting. You will be nice to him, won't you, Archie?'

'I'll even kiss the bugger if it makes you happy,' he said.

'I don't think you need to go that far!' she replied,

still laughing, her eyes glowing as they went downstairs.

Carrie sat in the back of the big black automobile with Velma, while Archie sat in front with Stan. That hadn't seemed such a good idea to Carrie, but once the two men began talking about army days and cars and tanks they got along surprisingly well. She breathed a sigh of relief. It was going to be a marvellous evening.

'Are you feeling all right?' she whispered to Velma.

'Absolutely fine. And you?'

'Of course.' Carrie felt the colour steal into her cheeks, and hoped Velma couldn't guess that if Archie had had his way, they had been a hair's-breadth away from staying home after all. She was sure he hadn't really meant to deprive her of this evening, but she knew she would only have had to say the word. And oh yes, it was a glorious feeling to know she was so loved and so desired.

It was dusk by the time they reached the dance hall in Penzance, and it was reassuring and welcoming to see a flood of light blazing out, so different from the days when no street lighting was allowed, and never a chink of light to be seen through blackout curtains, under threat of being bawled at by the air-raid wardens. The night the lights had all been switched on again had been something magical.

The banner across the front of the dance hall said 'Welcome Home to all our Heroes'. They had all earned the right to be here, and Carrie's heart swelled with pride to know that Archie was one of them. Her hero.

The bus from Penhallow and surroundings had arrived at almost the same time, and they found the rest of their friends immediately. It was a relief to them all. In a crowd you didn't have to make so much small talk, but you didn't feel isolated either. Stan took command and found them a table at once, which they quickly established as their own for the evening. They all expected to do their share of dancing, but there would also be a few speeches and toasts as befitted the occasion.

'It's good to see you, Bernard,' Carrie said, as he and Shirley sat close together. 'Are you looking forward to getting back to work?'

'As much as any teacher looks forward to dealing with the dear little brats,' he said, his tolerant tone belying the words.

'Why do it then? I wouldn't do your job for all the tea in China,' Archie said.

'I don't suppose he'd do yours,' David put in, grimacing.

'Why don't you chaps go and get us some lemonade?' Carrie said quickly, as the two men started glaring at one another.

By tacit agreement, she and Gwen had sat on opposite sides of the table, which unfortunately meant that Archie and David were going to remain in full eye contact with one another.

'Yes, come on, before it gets too crowded,' Stan said at once.

'Well done, Carrie,' Gwen commented when they had gone. 'We don't want to start World War Three just yet, do we?'

'Not ever,' Velma said with a shudder. 'Don't even hint at such a thing.'

Gwen shrugged. 'They said the first one was the war to end all wars, didn't they? But it didn't, so why should we be so lucky?'

Carrie felt a frisson of alarm. Such talk was guaranteed to start Archie off on his topic of not bringing babies into an unstable world. It would hardly be tactful in front of Velma, and would only start Shirley fretting again.

'We're here to enjoy ourselves tonight, Gwen, and to put it all out of our minds, so don't go saying such things when the boys come back.'

Velma laughed, and as they all looked at her in surprise, she said: 'Thanks for calling Stan a boy. If he'd heard you, you'd have made his day.'

Carrie looked across to the four men, at the other end of the hall now, so different and yet oddly united as they waited to be served, and smiled.

'He's very distinguished, and I bet he always was, even when he was a boy. I can imagine him taking charge of all the young recruits.'

'He'll take charge of Velma too,' Shirley said. 'You've got to give him that chance, Velma. You can't push him out now.'

'I'm thinking about it,' she said shortly. 'There's more than just the thrill of having a baby to think about, Shirley. There's the rest of our lives.'

If anyone should be aware of that, it should be Shirley, thought Carrie. Imagine what life would have been like for her if she hadn't had the miscarriage. Imagine how she would have explained it to her parents, to Bernard, to narrow-minded, insular Penhallow.

'You'd think they'd have a bar in this place,' Archie complained, dumping a tray of drinks on the table, while Stan placed a second one more carefully.

'Well, for one thing, they probably don't have a licence,' Gwen pointed out, 'and for another, they wouldn't want to risk any trouble.'

'Oh really? Surely any simpleton can work out that late-comers are just as likely to arrive with their bellies full of beer,' he retorted.

Carrie saw Gwen's face go red. She was no simpleton, and her opinion of Archie Pollard's big mouth was not much different from her husband's.

'That was uncalled for, Archie,' David snapped.

'If the cap fits,' he said carelessly.

Carrie squeezed Archie's hand as David muttered angrily. They all thought Archie was behaving badly as usual, but she recognized the tension in his jaw and his body, and sensed his feeling that this place was already becoming too crowded. Soon it would be jam-packed, and it was all closing in on him, the way the prison walls had enclosed him, making it hard for him to breathe, stifling him.

'Don't be difficult, Archie,' she breathed in his ear. 'Let's just enjoy ourselves, and as soon as the music starts we'll have a dance.'

'You know I'm not much good at dancing.'

'Waste of time coming then, wasn't it, Pollard?' David jeered.

Just as Carrie thought the trouble was going to start right there, Bernard put in his two-penn'orth.

'Why don't you two call a truce for the evening and let the rest of us enjoy ourselves? We've come for a night out, so don't spoil it for everybody.'

'Quite right,' Shirley said adoringly.

She looked radiant tonight, Carrie thought, she really did. She could quite understand how Shirley's GI had fallen for her, right here in this very hall, and how easily Shirley had had her head turned. Catching Velma's glance, she wondered if she was thinking the same thing. If Shirley had had qualms about tonight, she certainly wasn't showing them now.

The sound of a drum roll stopped all conversation, and a Town Hall bigwig stepped on to the platform where the band sat in readiness.

Full of pomposity and self-importance, he unfolded several sheets of paper and cleared his throat.

'Welcome, one and all,' he greeted them. 'This is a very special evening for all of us, and especially our brave heroes. But in saying that, I don't discount our brave Cornish heroines who kept the home fires burning, and kept a welcome in their hearts for their men – and women – who went to war. I know you'll want to get on with the dancing, so I don't intend to make a long speech.'

'Thank God for that,' said Archie. 'What a load of tripe.'

'*Shush*!' came voices all around him.

'What I do want to say, from the bottom of my heart, and everyone else's, I'm sure, is how grateful we are, for your patriotism, your dedication to duty, your love of country. You may not all have medals, or have come home honourably wounded, and we thank God for that, but you all served your country fearlessly, and so we salute you, my friends, and wish you a wonderful evening and a wonderful life in our free and beautiful land.'

This was followed by cheers and foot-stamping and a few cat-calls, and then the speaker held up his hand once more. The groans were audible.

'Just one more thing. We must not forget the Americans who were based here, and whom we took to our hearts, just as they took us to theirs. I can announce that they are hoping to arrange a reunion visit sometime next year, possibly around the anniversary of D-Day. I hope we will all welcome them in the same spirit as we did in our time of trouble. Thank you very much. Now let the dancing begin!'

As the band struck up a deafening few chords by way of introduction, for a few mind-spinning moments Carrie felt as if everything was crowding in on her too. She could identify totally with Archie's feelings. Maybe it was because her heart had skipped a beat and then raced on so erratically that she found it hard to draw breath. Not that she herself had anything to fear from the Americans coming back for a reunion, nor Gwen – as far as she knew – nor Velma. But Shirley did.

She looked at her friend quickly. The blood had drained out of her face, and she looked as white and sick as Velma sometimes did.

'I have to find the ladies' cloakroom,' Shirley gasped in a strangled voice, and fled from the room.

Without a second thought, the other three women rose with one accord and went after her, followed by Archie's laughing remark in their ears that this was the way women always acted. When one wanted to go, they all wanted to go.

There were other people in the cloakroom. It would have been impossible for it to be otherwise. Women were chattering excitedly to one another, old friends and strangers. Others were applying make-up or straightening their stockings. Chains were being pulled in the row of lavatories and hands being washed.

And Shirley was shrinking back against the wall of the cloakroom, looking as hunted as if Old Nick himself had found her.

'You see?' she stuttered, as Velma caught hold of her trembling hands. 'It's all coming back to haunt me, just as I knew it would.'

'Don't be ridiculous,' Gwen snapped. 'For one thing, you don't even know if GI Hank is going to come back, or if he even survived D-Day! He's never bothered to get in touch with you, has he?'

'That's not helping, Gwen,' Carrie said, sure that Shirley would interpret this as meaning Hank had had his way with her and then forgotten her. He'd only wanted her for one thing, and he'd had it.

Velma was being practical, rinsing a clean hanky under the cold tap and pressing it on Shirley's forehead. Her voice was firm.

'You've got to forget it, Shirley. We all agreed at the time that it would ruin everything for you and Bernard if you gave in to your guilt and confessed. There's nothing to show that it ever happened.'

Shirley sucked in her breath, and a flash of something like sorrow passed over her face. 'Oh well, it's all right for you, isn't it? You'll have your baby, and you'll have your husband if you want him. No problems for you, are there?'

Carrie gave her arm a little shake, aware that several people were glancing their way. 'There are no problems for *you*, Shirley. Not if you remember our pact, and don't do anything silly. We're all in this together, remember?'

She didn't want to make it sound like some secret society, but it was the most vital secret any of them had ever had to keep, and if it was to come out now it would be disastrous for all of them. She was quite sure Shirley would be a real blabbermouth once she got started, and Bernard would end up hating them all. Archie might think it a scream, Bernard would put on his stuffy schoolmaster's hat, and she had no idea what David or upright Stan would think.

She heard Shirley give a prolonged shudder before nodding shakily.

'I know you're right, and that I've got to keep my head. But it was a shock, hearing what that chap said about the Yanks. I'll be all right now.'

'You'd better be,' Gwen muttered. 'Let's go back or they'll wonder what we're doing in here all this time.'

As they returned to their table, they could see that Archie and David were wrangling over something, and Bernard was looking morose. Carrie sighed, hoping this evening was not going to turn out a severe disappointment. Or even a disaster. She realized Stan was holding out his hand to Velma, and that he had been the only one who stood up when they returned to the table, being the gentleman that he was.

'Would you do me the honour of this dance, my lady?' he said, in a pseudo-genteel voice. Velma's giggle was almost schoolgirlish, as she put her hand in his before Stan swept her out on to the dance floor.

'Prat,' Archie muttered.

'I think that was sweet,' Carrie said swiftly. 'I hope they'll be all right now.'

'Why wouldn't they be?'

'Well, with the baby coming. It changes everything, doesn't it? They've got a lot to think about, that's all.' She was floundering, knowing she had almost let the cat out of the bag about Velma and the divorce. But it was surely never going to happen now.

'Are we going to dance?' Gwen asked David.

'If we must.' But he gave her a wink as he said it, because they had always enjoyed dancing in the past, and he had told Gwen earlier that he'd be damned if he'd let Archie Pollard think he wasn't up to it.

'Come on, girl, let's show them how it's done,' Archie said at once, just as Carrie knew he would.

The two men's rivalry went back a long way. Sometimes it was just friendly banter, more often downright antagonism. She prayed it wouldn't go too far tonight.

'How about you two?' she asked Shirley and Bernard.

'We're waiting for a slower one,' Shirley said at once. 'We like the romantic tunes, not all this fast stuff.'

Which was in total opposition to the way she had flung herself around at the GI dances, and she avoided looking at Carrie as she said it.

'Told you he wouldn't be capable,' Archie said, as he and Carrie were quickly enveloped in the crush on the dance floor.

'It's not that. It's to save him having his injured parts knocked about by other people in these faster tunes. Show some consideration, Archie.'

His arms tightened around her.

'Injured parts, eh? Well, I'm glad I don't have any injured parts, aren't you? Everything present and correct and in working order, wouldn't you say?'

She giggled. 'Shut up, you're embarrassing me.'

She could have added *mostly in working order*, but she didn't dare, especially now that he was in such a good mood. His humour might be at the expense of his contemporaries – though she could hardly count Stan Gould as one of those – but at least it made for a reasonably harmonious atmosphere.

The harmony continued as the evening wore on. It was surprisingly easy to be part of a crowd yet to be separated from them when they chose, courtesy of the dancing and the necessary refreshment and other breaks.

It was only towards the end, when the lights were lowered considerably and the band struck up a favourite nostalgic song that had meant a lot to so many people during the war, that Carrie heard Shirley draw in her breath. By then Velma and Stan were already on their feet again, as if determined to savour every moment of this evening before whatever decisions they were going to make. Gwen and David were giggling together like a couple of idiots over some remark David had made, and Archie had gone off to the gents.

A girl singer had come on to the stage, and the plaintive words of 'I'll Be Seeing You' reverberated around the hall. Bernard had got rather clumsily to his feet and held out his hand to Shirley, but Carrie could see that the very last thing she wanted to do was to float around the dance floor in Bernard's arms, when in her heart and soul she was sharing this tune and this dance with Hank. She had told her friends that this was Their Song. But Bernard had been willing to dance so infrequently this evening that Shirley had no option but to join him.

With a look of something like desperation on her face she leaned into Bernard's shoulder as they danced slowly around the room. She tried not to let the words flow into her head, tried not to think of Hank, but as the singer reached the end of the song, she could hardly bear it.

'I'll be looking at the moon . . . but I'll be seeing . . . *you*!'

She gave a shuddering sigh and involuntarily clung on to Bernard a little more tightly as he stumbled.

'Sorry,' he murmured. 'I'm a silly twit for getting emotional, but this song was a great favourite of us chaps during the war. We all thought of our sweet-hearts whenever we heard it and got a bit moony. I suppose it was the same for you, waiting at home.'

'Yes, it was.' She was almost numb as the music ended and he led her back to their table, his arm still loosely around her.

If only he hadn't said those words. Making the guilt rush over her like a tidal wave. Imagining Bernard feeling sad and lonely far from home, and then the terrible ordeal of having to bail out from a burning plane and crawl to safety somewhere unknown, unaware of what dangers might be awaiting him . . . and then to suffer the ravages of his burns, and the nightmare of not knowing who or where he was . . . save for the tender compassion of a French family who had taken him in and tended his wounds as best they could.

She sat close beside him when they reached their table, holding his hand tightly. The lights were still low when without warning he leaned forward and kissed her. It was so spontaneous and so sweet that her love for him overcame all else at that moment, and she refused to let anything else blur the feeling. She did love him, she honestly and truly did, and she wanted nothing more in all the world than to be his wife.

'Shirley, there's something I have to tell you,' he said quietly, suddenly serious. 'But not now. Not here,' he added, as the others came back to the table. Then the lights went up again as the master of ceremonies announced that there would be another short pause in proceedings while the band took a welcome break.

'He means while they go off and have a leak,' Archie whispered wickedly in Carrie's ear. 'They must be desperate. The evening's nearly over.'

She wasn't listening. She was looking at Shirley, who looked as if she had had all the stuffing knocked out of her. She guessed how Shirley must have felt when she'd heard that song, but it was over now, it wouldn't be played again that evening, and she had to pull herself together. On an impulse she caught hold of Shirley's hand.

'Come to the ladies' with me.'

'Again?' Archie echoed. 'Blimey, it must be catching.'

This time it was only the two of them, apart from the other women milling around trying to freshen their lipstick, or queuing up for the lavs. Why was there always a queue in the ladies'?

'What's happened, Shirley?'

'Nothing. Not yet. I don't know. I just have this horrible feeling.'

'What feeling?'

'Bernard says he has something to tell me.'

'What's wrong with that?'

Shirley looked at her as if she had only just come into focus, and Carrie knew she had been off

234

somewhere in a nightmare of her own. They all knew what that nightmare was. They all thought she had finally got over it. Perhaps coming here tonight was not such a good idea after all. It should have lain ghosts, not resurrected them.

'I know what he's going to tell me. It's about the French girl. Marie. He's going to tell me he had something going with her, probably that he realizes he loves her after all, more than me, I mean. And I can't bear it, Carrie. It's all because of me and . . . because of what happened. It's my punishment, just when I know how much I really do love Bernard.'

'For pity's sake, you don't know if he's going to say anything like that at all!

As for it being your punishment, do you think you're the only girl here tonight who doesn't have nostalgic memories of those other dances? Of course you're not!'

'I bet you don't, Miss Whiter-than-white.'

Carrie glared at her. 'I didn't let myself get seduced by a Yank, if that's what you mean, but I didn't object to dancing with a serviceman if he asked me. It was almost our duty to do so, to make them feel happy and secure for what lay ahead.'

'We did that all right,' Shirley muttered. 'But I know I'm right about Bernard. I've got a Cornish sixth sense in these things. My grandmother was the seventh daughter of a seventh daughter, and she could see things too.'

Carrie tried not to laugh out loud at her friend's suddenly mysterious tone.

'Well, if she could see things she's probably seeing right now what a twerp you are. Come on, let's go back and have another dance, or they'll think we're spending all our time in here. Put a smile on your face, and remember what we told you. Nobody knows anything without being told outright. That goes for you too.'

'You're a good friend, Carrie,' Shirley said, allowing herself to be dragged out of the ladies' cloakroom.

'I'm a practical one, anyway.'

'At least Velma's looking more cheerful, isn't she?' Shirley added, in an attempt to be generous and think of somebody else besides herself. 'I reckon things will turn out all right for her and Stan after all.'

Carrie nodded, but all her attention was drawn now by a scuffle taking place at the far end of the dance hall. It was far from unknown for fights to break out at dances. In fact, when the Yanks had been here it was almost a regular occurrence when the local squaddies objected to Cornish girls dancing with GIs. But they hadn't expected anything of the sort to be happening tonight.

'Something's going on down there,' Archie said excitedly as they returned to their table. 'It looks as if David Trewint's involved, but these perishing dancers get in the way so you can't get a good look. It seems like a good scrap, and he was in the middle of it, flexing his muscles as usual, and thinking he's God's gift to women.'

Carrie felt a chill run through her. David had

always fancied himself as a bit of an amateur boxer in his schooldays, which was why he was so keen on keeping fit now, and he was just as handy with his fists as Archie when it was needed. It also explained some of the competitive problems between them. But if David was involved in a fight here, it could only mean one thing. Some chap must have made a snide remark about Gwen being more than friendly during the war, when David was missing, presumed dead. Or worse, one of Gwen's lovers had turned up.

Without answering Archie, Carrie moved swiftly away from the table.

'Where the hell are you going?' he bellowed.

She ignored him. If Gwen needed rescuing, she was the one to do it. Velma and Stan were dancing; Shirley would be ready to keel over in a moment if a whiff of Gwen's scandal came out, fully expecting hers to be next; and after only a couple of dances, Bernard looked pale with exhaustion.

'Carrie, come back here!'

Archie was furious now, and she knew he'd be outraged that she wasn't heeding him, but she managed to weave in and out of the dancers until she had reached the far end of the hall. Gwen looked red-faced and close to tears, and a chap in a scruffy civvy suit was holding David by the throat. The chap was muttering about having the right to ask a lady to dance, and from the way he was swaying about he'd obviously had too much to drink. He had also underestimated David's strength. As Carrie neared them, followed closely by Archie now, David twisted out of the man's grasp and punched him in the groin with his fist, winding him and sending him flying. At the same time, two hefty bouncers pushed through the small excited crowd who had witnessed the whole thing. They separated the two men, gripping David's arm and hauling the other chap off the ground.

'Any more trouble from you two and you'll be slung out,' one of them shouted. 'I'm warning you. Keep well clear of each other from now on or you'll find yourselves thrown in the cells for the night.'

'Don't worry. The bastard can keep his tart,' the drunk mumbled, holding his nether regions tenderly. 'She's had more blokes than I've had hot dinners, anyway.'

Carrie saw Gwen draw in her breath, unsure whether or not David had got the gist of what he was slurring.

'Come on, you mad-head,' Archie said, grabbing David, clearly tickled to death that David Trewint had got caught up in such an embarrassing situation. 'It's time you got back to the table and cooled off.'

Carrie caught Gwen's arm, seeing that she was near to passing out, and steered her quickly back through the dancers to the ladies' cloakroom. At this rate she'd be spending half the evening in there, she thought wildly.

'I knew it was a mistake to come here tonight,' Gwen said, choked. 'I was afraid this would happen. Terry Vane was always stupid when he had too much to drink, and he must have had a skinful at the pub before he got here.'

Carrie was alarmed. It was obvious that this Terry Vane was one of Gwen's past encounters, and right now she looked as vulnerable and near to confessing as Shirley ever had. They had all made a pact that none of them ever told anything. If one thing came out, there was a fear that it all would, and it wouldn't be only the two who had strayed who would be condemned. In this tight-knit little community, they all would.

Carrie desperately hoped that David hadn't actually heard what the drunk had been saying. But Archie had.

Chapter 14

As far as the organizers were concerned the Welcome Home reunion dance had been a rousing success, but there were those for whom it had been more of an ordeal than a celebration. And others for whom it had been something of an intriguing experience.

'That bloke had a lot to say for himself, didn't he?' Archie said later in the darkness of their bedroom.

Carrie started. They had been in bed for half an hour and she had been on the verge of falling asleep, exhausted after the various stresses of the evening and the drive home in Stan's hired automobile, and all she wanted to do was sleep.

'What bloke?'

Archie snapped on the bedside lamp, leaning up on his elbow and gazing down at her as she squinted against the sudden burst of light.

'You know very well what bloke. The one who said Gwen had had more blokes than he'd had hot dinners. *That* bloke.'

'Archie, go to sleep, for pity's sake. I'm tired.'

'Don't come over all innocent with me. I reckon you

know more about it than you're letting on. You and those other floosies too. You're probably all in it together. And I didn't miss the little ripple of excitement among the females when that Town Hall chap mentioned that the Yanks might be coming over here next year for a reunion.'

He wasn't being aggressive or accusing, just ruminating, almost finding a perverse humour in the fact of four women having their little secret. If he only knew! But it struck such a sensitive nerve in Carrie that she didn't see it that way.

'Honestly, Archie, you're making mountains out of molehills,' she snapped.

'I swear that sometimes you're more of a gossip than the old codgers on the village green. I've no doubt there were plenty of girls at the dance who remembered the Yanks fondly, and perfectly harmlessly too. I didn't happen to be one of them, so can we please go to sleep now?'

'I wasn't pointing the finger at you. But you can't deny that dear old Gwen looked more than put out when that chap started taunting her.'

'So would I be! So would anybody be. It's not a very nice thing when you are out for an evening with your husband and somebody starts making stupid allegations that aren't true. You could see how drunk he was, and I'm sure he didn't know what he was saying half the time.'

'Maybe not, but the real truth often comes out when a bloke's drunk.'

'Well, I wouldn't know about that, never having

been drunk myself, and I would imagine it's just as easy to throw wild accusations about as well.'

She was becoming alarmed now, aware that her heart was racing. Archie had mistakenly decided that Gwen was the one who had been consorting with Yanks, and not Shirley, which was one good thing. The *only* good thing. And knowing their history, Archie would also find a lascivious enjoyment in the fact that David Trewint's wife might have been having a good time on the side while he was out of sight and out of mind. Maybe it was no more than that, just a bit of crowing over David, and hopefully he would have forgotten it in the morning. Maybe.

'I wasn't pointing a finger at you, Carrie. And I'm not accusing anybody, I'm just thinking out loud.'

'Well, don't. You know what they say. Too much thinking's bad for you, especially at this time of night.'

She tried to make a joke of it to take his mind off the incident with the drunk, which had evidently stuck in his mind far too thoroughly for comfort.

Unfortunately it turned his mind to other things.

'You're right, so let's forget the lot of them, sweetheart. You know I never doubted you for a minute, and we've still got a lot of time to make up for.'

Although his hands were already roaming beneath her nightie, Carrie didn't think he'd be capable. Not that he'd had any beer to dampen his ardour, but it was very late and there had been enough excitement all round for one evening. But not as far as Archie was concerned, and almost to her surprise he made love to her with a mixture of tenderness and enthusiasm that left her gasping with pleasure.

She had to admit, too, that she welcomed it, and not only to get his mind off Gwen. She was fully awake now, her own feelings aroused by the argument in a way she hadn't expected to be. She had never used lovemaking as a diversion tactic before, but he had generated a piquant excitement in her, too.

The unexpected conversation had been fraught with danger, the risk of a slip on her part betraying the secrets the four friends had vowed to keep. She knew she was being overly dramatic. Theirs might not be the kind of secrets the brave folk in the Resistance movement in France had been forced to keep – her thoughts moving briefly to some of the emerging newspaper reports outlining the horrors of that time – but it was risky on a personal level.

But tonight's lovemaking had been so good, so loving . . . and at times like these, he was her old Archie, she thought, still wrapped in his arms. The one she had promised to love, honour and obey, and would do always. Providing honouring him also meant being loyal to her friends, she added silently.

The incidents at the dance had left their mark. Gwen didn't turn up at the village hall on the following Thursday evening, and no one had seen her all week. As Carrie went off to fetch them all some tea, the other two were still discussing it.

'Probably keeping her head down,' Velma said. 'That was a horrible experience for her.'

'It wasn't too good for me, either, hearing that the

GIs might be coming back next year for a reunion,' Shirley muttered.

'That doesn't need to involve you.'

'No? What if he comes looking for me?' She didn't need to say his name.

'Why would he? Life goes on, Shirley. You shouldn't flatter yourself that he's thought of nothing but you all this time. How do you know he wasn't already married? Some of them were, you know.'

'That's a beastly thing to say!'

'It's being logical. How do you know he even came back from D-Day? You've had no news of him from that day to this, have you?'

Carrie came back with a tray to find them glowering at each other, Velma tight-lipped and Shirley flushed and looking as if she was about to burst into tears.

'What's going on?'

'Velma thinks Hank was either married all the time or got killed on D-Day,' she said brutally.

Carrie sighed. 'Look, I know you thought the sun shone out of his eyes at the time, and you wouldn't want to think the worst of him, but Velma's not saying anything we haven't all thought at some time or other, is she?'

Velma hadn't finished with her yet. 'Put it another way. Do you *want* him to come looking for you?'

'God, *no*! How would I explain him to Bernard?' she said nervously.

'There you are then.' Velma sat back with a satisfied smile, which to Shirley was simply smug. 'So forget it ever happened, like we've told you a hundred times.

Carrie said Bernard was going to tell you something. What was it?'

She flinched. 'I don't know. Whatever it was, he's keeping it to himself for now, and I'm getting more twitchy by the day.'

Carrie patted her hand. 'As long as you're wearing his ring on your finger it can't be anything bad. It's you he loves, and he's the one for you, isn't he?'

'Of course. Oh yes. Yes, of course he is.'

'Methinks the lady doth protest too much,' Velma murmured.

Shirley scrambled to her feet. 'I don't think I want that tea after all, Carrie. In fact, I don't think I want to be here at all. I'll see you all next week probably.'

'*Shirley*, don't be silly.' Carrie called after her, but it was too late.

'Let her go. We're reminding her too much of Hank the Yank tonight.'

'Well, you didn't help, did you? What's up, Velma?'

'Nothing. Everything. I don't know.'

'Good Lord, I'm beginning to think everyone's gone mad tonight, and I'm the only sane one here. Did Stan get off all right yesterday?'

The minute she said it, she guessed what was wrong, and why Velma was extra sharp tonight. She had no idea how far the discussions had gone with regard to Velma and Stan's future, but from the shadows beneath her friend's eyes, which she hadn't noticed until now, she guessed that nothing was completely resolved.

'He did, and I don't want to talk about it. We're still

thinking about things. About whether or not I'm prepared to leave Cornwall, if you must know,' she added.

Carrie could have said that for someone who didn't want to talk about it, she had volunteered that bit of information quickly enough.

'Then I won't ask. It's your business, Velma, and you're the ones who have got to make the decisions.'

But the thought of Velma leaving Cornwall was something Carrie didn't want to contemplate. She had known Velma all her life and she would miss her enormously. Carrie didn't know how she could bear to even consider it. She herself would never want to leave this far corner of England that she adored. But then she had never been anywhere else, she thought with sudden annoyance.

But wherever Velma went she would be with Stan and their baby, which must make all the difference. If she didn't go she and the baby would be alone, and from what Carrie had gleaned, seeing how Velma and Stan had danced so compatibly only days ago, she didn't think Stan would be satisfied with a part-time marriage any longer.

'Why are you staring at me like that?'

'Sorry. I didn't think I was.'

Velma gave a sigh now. 'Oh God, I'm sorry too. I'm being a real grouch tonight, and I know I was a pig to Shirley. I'd say put it down to my pregnant emotions if I didn't know it was far more than that. And you might as well know it as well.'

'Are you sure you want to tell me?'

'Yes, but not here. Look, this tea is like cricket's wee, as usual, so let's go to my cottage and have a proper cuppa. You did say that Archie's not meeting you tonight.'

It was obvious now that Velma did want to talk, and when they got to the cottage in Tinners' Row she sat down heavily in an armchair, without any attempt at making tea or cocoa or anything else.

'I think Stan has met someone else,' she said abruptly.

'*What?*'

Carrie sat up straight, her mind whirling. It was the last thing she had expected to hear. She supposed Shirley had a point in thinking about Bernard and the French girl who had nursed him back to health. Didn't they say that patients often fell for their nurses? But *Stan?* Upright, rather dull and stolid Stan?

Velma gave a short laugh at the sight of her face.

'Darling, don't look so aghast. I shouldn't have come out with it like that, and it's not as dire as I made it sound. I don't mean that he's on the point of leaving me, or anything like that. He wouldn't do anything so rash.'

Was there the tiniest note of bitterness in her voice? Was she remembering the night they had made love so passionately in St Ives, which was apparently rash for Stan, and very unlike him?

'Well, has he said he's found someone else, or is it all in your imagination?'

Velma went off at a tangent. 'When I think of the times I stopped myself writing him a Dear John letter,

247

knowing how awful that must be for servicemen who received them, and how I never, ever wanted to hurt him—'

'What, like asking for a divorce? Didn't you think that would hurt him?'

Velma seemed to sink further into the chair, and without warning she was weeping. Deep, body-racking sobs, as if the end of the world had come.

'Oh God, I'm so sorry, Velma. I didn't mean to say such a cruel thing. Please stop and tell me what I can do.'

'Leave me alone for a few minutes and go and make that cocoa,' the muffled voice came out. 'You can lace mine with brandy, too. It's in the sideboard.'

Carrie crept out to the kitchen, thinking she didn't know this woman at all. This was a different Velma, one who was vulnerable and afraid, and her heart went out to her. But she did as she was asked, and when she returned with the two mugs of cocoa the paroxysm had stopped, and Velma had already got the bottle of brandy beside her.

'Don't worry, this isn't a habitual thing, only when I'm depressed,' she said with a half-smile, noticing Carrie's look as she tipped the alcohol liberally into her mug. 'I'm not that keen on the stuff.'

'I'm not criticizing, just concerned, that's all.' And it probably wasn't doing the baby any good. 'So are you going to tell me what's wrong or not?'

'I just don't understand Stan anymore. He said in his letter that we should decide what we want to do with our future lives, and at the time I took it to mean he had met someone. If I hadn't just learned about the baby it might even have been a big relief – well, in a way – and sort of relieved my conscience. But I did know about the baby by then, and I was bubbling over to tell him one minute, and scared to death the next. God, I'm worse than Shirley, aren't I? And I'm supposed to be the sensible one.'

'You are the sensible one, otherwise you wouldn't be questioning it like this. But what did he actually *say* when he was home?'

Velma spread her capable hands. 'Nothing. Absolutely nothing. I just felt he was watching me all the time, waiting for me to make the first move. It made me so tense I could have screamed.'

'But at the dance . . .'

Her face softened. 'Oh yes, at the dance I felt as if everything was going to be all right. We used to love dancing, and our steps matched so perfectly, the way they always had. I had great hopes that it was going to be all right. But just before he left, he told me that I still had to make up my mind whether or not to leave Cornwall to live in these wretched married quarters with him. And it couldn't wait for ever. I know it was an ultimatum. Go with him, or our marriage is over.'

'Honestly, Velma, aren't you forgetting the baby? It can't be over, and how do you know that married quarters would be wretched? He's a regular soldier, so it would hardly be living in a tent, would it? Even if it was, it sounds very exotic to me. You know, sheikhs in the desert and all that.'

Carrie tried to jolly her along, although she looked

so tragic that too much teasing would be awful. But then Velma gave a weak smile.

'God, I'm pathetic, aren't I? You do me good, Carrie, you really do. Look, do you want a proper drink? We've got some port somewhere. We could get tiddly and forget our sorrows.'

'I don't think that would be a good idea,' Carrie said, laughing now. 'And neither do you. Think of Junior Gould.'

Velma caught her breath, and pressed her hand lightly to her stomach.

'I do, all the time. So promise me you'll forget this conversation and put it down to my unpredictable moods.'

'What moods?'

She couldn't forget, of course. She wanted Velma to have a happy life, and how she could have it without Stan now, Carrie couldn't think. A baby needed two parents in its life, and Stan and Velma would be such perfect ones. But it wasn't her problem. What was a problem was how the four women who had shared secrets and traumas, good times and bad during the war years now seemed to be losing touch with one another. Thursday nights were no longer the same. It was rare for all four of them to be there together. Sometimes there were three, sometimes just two. Carrie dreaded the time when she – or one of the others – would turn up and they would be the only one. That would surely mean the end of something wonderful. Men had their old comrades, their army mates, their workmates, their drinking pals, their sports pals; women who had such close friendships as the four of them had had during the war had something to cherish, something too important to throw away, and yet it seemed to be happening, and there wasn't a thing they could do to stop it. It was a bit like magic: once you brought it out in the open and tried to examine it and analyse it, the wonder of it was lost for ever.

But by the beginning of December, on a damp and dismal morning, she had something far more personal to worry about. The lingering Cornish summer they relished every year had finally gone, having merged as languidly as ever into a Indian summer and mellow and fruitful autumn, as if reluctant to let the bright skies and sunshine fade from this glorious place. But now it seemed as if the first hint of winter had sneaked in, with swirling winds denuding the trees of their kaleidoscope of autumn leaves, and rain that cut into the skin like vicious little gnat bites.

By mid-morning Carrie was looking out of the library window, wondering whether it had even been worth anybody coming to work today, since so few people were out and about. She saw the postmistress scurrying across the village green, a mac over her head, her galoshes splashing in a couple of puddles in her haste to get out of the rain.

'Just look at Mrs Peake,' she said to her boss, laughing at the woman's attempts to hang on to the mac, which was suddenly ballooning away from her in a gust of wind. 'There must be something pretty important happening to get her out from her cubby-hole.'

Everyone knew that the post office was the hub of Mrs Peake's life, and that she fancied herself as the pivot of the community behind her glass-fronted counter. It wasn't an unreasonable assumption, since hers was the place that brought good news and bad.

'She's coming here.'

Carrie looked up again, and something like a premonition swept through her like a shivering wave. She put down the books she had been tidying, and waited, her heart thudding, almost with a dreadful presentiment of what she was going to hear.

'Carrie my lamb, there's been a telephone message for you from Penzance.

It's your dad. He's been taken ill and he's in the hospital. They say your mother should go there right away. It's something to do with his heart.'

Mrs Peake was holding her own chest now, her eyes a mixture of excitement at being the one to impart the news, and sympathy at the message. Her breath was wheezing, as if she was the next one who would be needing hospital treatment.

Carrie didn't wait to hear any more. She grabbed her coat and bag and flew out of the library, straight across the green to Archie's shop. She rushed inside, pushing past the two women customers haggling over the price of day-old sausages.

'Archie, Dad's in the hospital in Penzance. His heart. We have to go there,' she gasped, almost inarticulate for once.

Afterwards, she remembered how calm he had been. How masterful in an instant, taking control, taking over . . .

In a daze she saw him throwing off his straw hat and his overall, shouting to his father than he was taking the van . . . and then bundling her into the waiting vehicle with its nauseating smells of raw meat enveloping her . . . then driving straight to Kellaway Terrace and telling Carrie to stay put while he fetched her mum. Her knees were like jelly, knowing she should be the one to do this, to calm her mother down and reassure her with the useless platitudes that everyone repeated. He would be all right. He was in the best place, having the best treatment, and all that rot. Words that meant nothing, and wouldn't come, anyway.

In any case, she couldn't seem to move, and minutes later her mum was outside the house, her coat slung over her shoulders, her hat crazily askew on her head, and Archie was shoving Carrie to the middle of the seat while Edna sat beside her. The three of them were wedged together in the front of the totally unsuitable vehicle as they careered through the wet lanes to Penzance, saying nothing, the women with their hands clasped tightly together, and fear in their hearts.

They were too late, as Carrie had known they would be. It wasn't only Shirley who fancied herself as blessed with a sixth sense, she thought wildly. Her dad had had a massive heart attack minutes after they had got him to the hospital, and there was nothing they could do to save him. They were very sorry. But it all happened so quickly, they assured them, and Walter had felt no lingering pain. Were there people they could contact? Would they like a cup of tea? Time to themselves before they saw the deceased?

That was the moment Edna cracked. So much kindness, so much consideration, and then that awful word. Deceased. Carrie saw her face, the colour of parchment as her clenched hands tightened even more, and then she collapsed.

The nurse flew out of the room, calling for assistance. She was young, and probably didn't know how to handle this. But Archie did.

'Come on, old lady, let's get you comfortable,' he said gently, easing her back on to her chair and rubbing her cold hands between his. He looked at Carrie. 'Go and see if you can find that tea, love. Tell them to make it strong and sweet, and to put a tot of brandy in it. I'll see to her here.'

She fled. Most men would have taken fright, as Carrie herself was doing, she thought in swift shame, but Archie seemed to know instinctively what to do. In the corridor, she blundered into an orderly.

'We need tea,' she gasped. 'And a tot of brandy in it for my mother. My father – my father – has just died.'

There. She had said the word. The heartbreaking, unbelievable word to apply to the father she had always adored. Sobs wrenched her throat, but she knew she had to be strong, the way Archie was strong, for her mother's sake. Edna had always seemed so tough, so caustic, compared with her gentle dad, but without him . . .

'Go back to your family and I'll see to it,' she heard the orderly say, and then she seemed to be surrounded by people, as the nurse who had left them earlier appeared with an older woman in a darker uniform, and she was ushered back to where Edna was now weeping quietly in Archie's arms. The sight of her like that, more vulnerable than she had ever known her, tore at Carrie's heart.

'Let me talk to your mother, dear,' the sister said quietly. 'You and your husband go with the orderly to fetch the tea.'

'I shouldn't leave her –' Carrie began, knowing that she desperately wanted to. Guiltily, she wanted to be anywhere but this place, with its overpowering anti-septic smells, and the swish of uniforms and the squeak of rubber-soled shoes on polished lino floors. She wanted to be anywhere where these people wouldn't expect her to eventually look at the *deceased*, who had once been her beloved dad.

'Take slow, deep breaths, sweetheart,' she heard Archie instruct her, his arm tightly around her now as if afraid she would fall over at any minute. She did as she was told, feeling like an automaton as she went with him and the orderly to a small room where a kettle was boiling merrily on a stove, and a teapot and cups, milk jug and sugar bowl were standing ready on a tray. It all looked so homely, so ordinary, as if this wasn't a place where pain and heartbreak lived, and where lives drained away. She tried to remember that this was a place of healing, too, but the thought did nothing to comfort her. It hadn't saved her father.

*

Dazed and confused, somehow they got through the next days. People came to the house and went away again, bringing offers of help that were kind if futile, and sometimes a dish of stew or a baked pie as if knowing that the family wouldn't be up to anything as mundane as preparing food. Archie's parents arrived at intervals, armed with homemade scones and cuts of cold meat.

The few relatives on Walter's side were informed of the date of the funeral, as was Edna's sister; neighbours and acquaintances sent awkward notes of sympathy, and people who were real friends rallied round, as always.

Velma sent a huge bunch of flowers from her garden with a message that Carrie wasn't to feel alone, and to call on her any time she needed someone to talk to. Shirley and Gwen both turned up at the house and hugged her with tears in their eyes, and in some strange way Carrie felt as if her father's death had repaired the slight estrangement with her closest friends. It was the only glimmer of warmth she felt in that strange, sad week.

She had never been close to her mum's sister. Her aunt Phyllis had been widowed for years and lived in Falmouth, but she and Edna fell on one another, embraced by the ties of childhood and now widowhood. And it seemed as if the whole of Penhallow and half of Penzance, too, had turned out to support the family as Walter Penney was laid to rest in St Jude's churchyard.

But it was a relief when all the mourners who had come back to the house for a bite and a cuppa to pay their respects to Edna and Carrie and Archie finally left them alone. Phyllis was the last to leave, hugging them all tightly, and vowing to come and see them again when Edna was feeling better, just as if she was suffering an illness. Carrie realized they were all treating her that way. Far from being the strong and sharp-tongued woman she normally was, she seemed to have faded visibly since Walter's death.

'You sit down, Mum, and I'll see to all this,' Carrie said, when they had taken the mounds of dirty cups and plates out to the kitchen. 'Put your feet up and have another cup of tea with Archie.'

Truth was, she needed something to do with her hands. She couldn't bear for the three of them to be sitting around looking at one another and not knowing what to say. Did you carry on as before? Did you turn the wireless on to hear the news of the day, when none of them cared a jot what was happening in the world, compared to the enormity of what had happened here, in their own small world? Did you mention going back to work, which Carrie dearly wanted to do, just to feel that there was some normality in her life? Archie had already done so, of course. People needed provisions, and he and his father supplied them.

She paused for a moment, her hands deep in washing-up water, her head hanging low as a wave of sadness for her dad swept over her. Never again to see him in his beloved garden or allotment, or to hear him making the peace between her and her mum. If she tried very hard, she could almost see him now, through the kitchen window, leaning on his spade for a breather, and smiling back at her . . .

From the front room, Archie's voice seemed to float into her consciousness, clumsy and reassuring at the same time, placating the bereaved.

'You don't need to worry about being alone in the house, Edna. Me and Carrie will always be here with you. We'll look after you and see that everything goes on as before.'

Carrie's hands froze, as if she had plunged them into a bowl of ice instead of hot washing-up water. Her eyes smarted, and whether or not she had seen a vision of her dad, or if it was all in her imagination, the image vanished abruptly. Her heart was thumping, and at that moment she hated Archie as she took in what he was saying. She didn't *want* to be here always. While she lived here, in the house where she was born, she would always be the child. She cared for her mother, but she and Archie should have a home of their own. It was what married people did. Her dad had wanted that for her too. Now, in an instant, she knew she would never get it.

Chapter 15

Shirley felt as though she had been walking on eggshells ever since the night of the dance. She knew Bernard was still bursting to tell her something, and she didn't want to hear it. He hadn't said it yet, and in a strange way she knew he was finding it just as difficult to get the words out. She knew what it was going to be, anyway. Bernard was going to tell her he had fallen in love with French Marie, and she just couldn't bear it. In her head, she had to keep giving her that silly name, as if to ward off the seriousness of it all. But this was her come-uppance, and she knew it. It was God's way of paying her back for her wickedness with Hank.

But now there was this terrible thing that had happened to Carrie. Poor Carrie. She had always been so fond of her dad, especially compared with her awful nagging mother, and in the few weeks since it happened everyone had put their own troubles aside and done their best to support her and cheer her up. It was the old wartime spirit, Shirley thought, but it couldn't last. Eventually, each of them had their own problems to deal with in their own way. They couldn't be a unit of four for ever, the way they had always expected to be. That had begun to change from the minute all their men came home. Shirley wasn't often given to deep thinking, but it was a serious thought, which depressed her while she counted buttons and wound ribbons neatly on to their cardboard bases in the haberdashery shop.

'A penny for them,' Miss Willis said with a smile. 'You'll ruin your pretty face if you keep frowning like that, my dear. And with Christmas nearly on us, and your young man home to share it with you this year, I'd have thought you'd be full of your usual madcap excitement.'

Shirley forced a smile. 'I am, of course, but I was thinking of Carrie.'

'Ah yes, the poor lamb. Such a tragedy. Her father must only have been in his fifties, hardly any age at all.'

It seemed more like approaching Methuselah to Shirley, but she refrained from saying so, since Miss Willis must be around the same age as Carrie's dad.

'And you'll have your birthday to look forward to in January, too, won't you?' the woman went on encouragingly. 'I suppose you and Bernard will be thinking about wedding bells next year.'

'I expect so,' Shirley said, momentarily choked. 'But it hardly seems right to be thinking of celebrations like that when my best friend's so miserable, does it?'

'That's very thoughtful of you, my dear. Look, you're obviously a bit upset, so why don't you go and make us both a nice cup of tea while I see to these customers?'

As Shirley fled to the tiny back room to put the kettle on, she overheard Miss Willis remark in a stage whisper to the customers that there was more sense in young Shirley Loe's head than many people gave her credit for. It was a backhanded compliment if she ever heard one, she thought indignantly, but it put a small smile back on her face all the same.

Gwen was also fearful that there had to be a reckoning one of these days. She wondered just how long it was going to be before David asked the question that must be going round and round in his mind.

Was there any truth in what that drunken lout had said at the dance?

He hadn't mentioned it again, but it could only be a matter of time. How could he ignore it? No sane man would. Unless he desperately wanted to believe that it couldn't be true, and feared that he might see in his wife's eyes that it was.

Gwen shivered. It seemed so long in the past now, and although she wasn't as dumb as Shirley, nearly wetting herself over whether or not to confess to Bernard, she too had had her moments of doubt. But in the end, she had concluded that it was far better to forget it ever happened. She and David were blissfully happy now, each of them blessing this second chance after the miracle of his rescue, and not wanting to do anything to harm it. Perhaps he was feeling like that about the damaging remark that oaf had made too.

Two weeks after most of Penhallow had rallied around Carrie and her family, and attended Walter's funeral, Gwen and David were putting up a few Christmas decorations, wondering if it was actually decent to do so in the circumstances. But they reasoned that it wasn't *their* family who was bereaved, and life had to go on.

David had just put the small tree he'd got from a local farmer into a bucket in the living room, when he said the words she had been dreading to hear. He wasn't looking at her, and she stared numbly at his back as he tied a few baubles and fir cones on the tree. As he spoke, in a so-calm voice that was oddly threatening, her heart thudded so fast she thought she was going to faint.

'So is there any truth in it, Gwen?'

'Any truth in what?' she stuttered, knowing exactly what he meant.

'Oh, come on, you're not stupid. We've both managed to ignore it ever since the night of the reunion dance, but we can't ignore it for ever, can we?'

He turned around then, and she knew her face must look stricken, revealing everything he wanted to know. And yet, miraculously, she presumed that her expression hadn't given the game away, for with two short strides he was across the living room and had caught her in his arms. If he hadn't, she would probably have fallen down.

'Christ, I'm sorry, darling, but I had to ask. It's been burning away inside me all this time, and it's like something festering that won't go away. The chap was obviously out of his mind with drink, and he'd probably been fancying you all evening. I couldn't blame him for that, but it was hardly a tactful way to ask you to dance, was it?'

'Is that what you think he was doing then?'

God, this was awful. Either David was being incredibly stupid, which she knew he wasn't, or he was taking the easy way out, and giving her the chance to deny everything. He would take it on trust that whatever she told him was the truth, and, once she grasped the straw he was offering and said what he wanted to hear, that would be the end of it.

'Who could blame him?' he repeated. 'You were the best-looking woman in the place. It was all a lot of drunken rubbish, but all the same, it was a rotten thing for the bastard to say, attacking your reputation like that, and if I ever get my hands on the bugger again—'

After he had been so calm, the sudden vicious expletives took her unawares.

'We-ell—'

Why didn't she just agree? Why did she have to hesitate? Why sully their second chance at happiness?

He released her and stood back a pace, his arms rigid by his sides now.

'Well what? Is there something you want to tell me?'

Her lips were shaking so much she could hardly speak, but she knew she had to say something, because of the sudden suspicion in his eyes. His voice had hardened, and she remembered how tough and wiry he was, pitting his wits against the sea every day, having survived being torpedoed and almost drowned. She prayed they would survive this now.

'David darling, it's nothing like you think.'

'I don't know what the hell to think! Was the bastard telling the truth then? Were you having it off with every Tom, Dick and Harry all those months when I was away?'

'Of course not!' Her nerves jumped, because he wasn't normally so crude. He left that to people like Archie Pollard.

The next minute he was excruciatingly sarcastic.'Just the select few then, was it? Just enough to make you forget that your husband was doing battle with the Atlantic as well as the whole of the bloody German fleet.'

'I thought you were dead!' With the release of the torment her mind had suffered ever since the dance, Gwen heard herself screaming now, and could do nothing to stop it. 'Do you know what that was like for me, never knowing what had happened to you, with just a cold and clinical telegram from the War Office telling me you were missing, believed drowned? Can you imagine what that was like?'

His reply was a stinging blow to her cheek that sent her staggering backwards.

She couldn't believe what he had just done. He had never hit her before in her life, and he was shouting back at her now.

'Can you imagine what it was like for *me*, with freezing black waters closing over my head, and the life being choked out of me with every second that passed, being dragged down and down until I thought I would reach the bottom of the world before I was suffocated by the crushing pain in my chest, and all the time praying for oblivion to put an end to it? Imagine that if you can, while you were behaving like an alley cat!'

Before she could guess what he was about to do, he had snatched their framed wedding photo from the mantelpiece and hurled it across the room, where the glass splintered into pieces. Without a second thought, Gwen slapped him back so hard that he lurched backwards, and their precious Christmas tree toppled and fell with a screech of shattered baubles. It was like the shattering of their marriage.

'You *bastard*!' Gwen screamed at him. 'When I thought you were dead, I was more distraught than I have ever been in my life – until right this minute. I thought I was going insane, and if it hadn't been for my good friends—'

'Oh yes, your precious friends. I suppose they were all in on it too, egging you on, no doubt, and laughing at me behind my back all this time.'

'Of course they weren't!'

'And what about that bastard Pollard? I'm sure your dear friend Carrie couldn't resist giving him a bit more ammunition to fire at me.'

Gwen momentarily calmed down. The feud between the two men that had lasted since childhood had obviously gone deeper than she realized. To her and Carrie it was just a nonsense thing, an overblown schoolboy tit-for-tat slanging match. Now she saw how much such a revelation to Archie would hurt him. She had to go carefully, speak delicately, before she made things even worse.

She put her hand on his arm, and he shook it away at once. She stepped back a pace, as if afraid that he was going to strike her again, and for a brief moment he had the grace to look shamefaced. Her voice shook uncontrollably.

'David, please listen to me. You're getting this all out of proportion. I know Carrie hasn't told Archie anything that would compromise me. My friends were wonderful to me when I thought I would never see you again, and I don't know how I would have managed without them. We all supported one another in ways you couldn't imagine. Archie was a POW for two years, remember, and Bernard Bosinney was badly wounded after he baled out in France; Shirley went through agonies worrying about him. Velma – well, she had her own problems, but through it all, we listened to one another, and we cared for one another.'

'And promised to keep one another's tacky little secrets.'

It was so near the mark, so bloody, heartbreakingly near the mark, that Gwen drew in her breath on a sob. Her shoulders drooped, and her hands fluttered resignedly.

'If that's what you think, then I can't say anything more,' she said dully, 'but I pity you for never knowing what true friendship means, and for taking a completely unsavoury view of it.'

She turned and fled upstairs, throwing herself on the bed. The day was ruined, and their marriage with it. She had truly thought they were the lucky ones. After what had seemed a tragedy at sea, David had come home safely, and they had blessed their good luck a thousand times. Now, it seemed as if that luck had only been borrowed, and it had all been snatched away by one drunken remark.

After a few moments, Gwen lifted her head, aware of a strange sound coming from downstairs. She went to the bedroom door, her heart pounding as she realized David was sobbing. She crept back downstairs to find him holding the broken wedding photo in his hands, and she took it gently away from him, replacing it on the mantelpiece with shaking fingers. She put her arms around him.

'David darling,' she whispered, knowing that the next few minutes could be vitally important to them both, 'it's only a photo frame, and it can be mended. The photo inside it is still intact, and so are we. Everything else can be mended.'

When he didn't answer, she wondered if he had understood what she was saying. And then his arms reached around her too. She was enfolded inside them as their tears mingled, and she breathed a long, shuddering sigh of relief.

Carrie was finding it difficult to come to terms with her father's death, and not only because she missed him so much. She had always known he was the buffer between herself and her mum's sharp tongue, but even though Edna had been more subdued than usual these past few weeks, she hadn't expected Archie to turn into the man of the house, and, in doing so, almost shut her out.

If it didn't make her so angry it would be almost ludicrous, she raged. She knew she should be glad that he was shouldering so much of the necessary business of death, and she was, of course. But now he obviously considered himself the breadwinner of the family, which in truth he was, and she knew she should be grateful for that, too. But Walter had always been a thrifty and careful man, and had ensured that his family was provided for after his death. Strictly speaking, Archie didn't *need* to do all this, and in particular he hadn't needed to make that remark on the day of the funeral that had turned her knees to jelly.

She didn't *want* to live in this house for ever, turning their marriage into a threesome. She didn't *want* to be the dutiful daughter, caring for an older parent. Edna wasn't old, anyway, and had more spirit in her little finger than many women half her age. It wouldn't be long before that spirit returned, and she would be ruling the roost again. Or rather, Edna and Archie would be doing so between them.

Carrie knew she couldn't keep quiet about her feelings for long. When there was something that needed saying, it wasn't in her nature to keep it bottled up and festering. She had her mother to thank for that, she thought savagely. So once she and Archie were in bed on the night of the funeral, she had let rip.

'Are you completely mad, Archie?'

'Don't think so,' he said good-humouredly, clearly not understanding – yet. 'Not the last time I looked, anyway. What's got your goat, sweetie-pie?'

'Don't sweetie-pie me,' Carrie snapped, brushing off the hand that invariably reached for her breast, 'and I'd have thought that even an insensitive twerp like you could see that this isn't the time and place for any fun and games.'

'I doubt that old Walter would have minded us having a bit of a cuddle,' he chuckled, still more amused at her anger than anything else.

Carrie slapped his hand away. 'For God's sake, Archie, my dad's just been buried, and a cuddle's one thing, but not what you're thinking of.'

'Reading my mind now then, are you?' he said, an edge coming into his voice for the first time. 'So like I said, what's got your goat?'

'*You* have. Saying what you did to my mother.'

'And which bit of conversation was that? I swear, you're getting more like her every day with your whining.'

She gasped, furious at such an accusation. It wasn't that she didn't love her mother, but she knew all her faults, having lived with them all her life, and she didn't particularly want to emulate them.

'I never whine,' she said tightly.

Archie turned his back on her and switched off the bedside light.

'Well, if you're not going to tell me what's biting you, and if you can't be bothered to give your husband a bit of nightly comfort, I'm going to sleep.'

Carrie sat bolt upright in the bed, glaring down at the shape of him in the darkness. Sometimes she thought she actively *hated* him. Of all the men she knew, he must surely be the most aggravating and insensitive. And the one that she had loved all her life, of course – and she certainly couldn't imagine being married to anyone else. Against her will, her thoughts wandered for a second.

Bernard Bosinney didn't appeal to her in the slightest and Shirley was welcome to him. Stan Gould was far too aloof, and David Trewint was pleasant enough, except where Archie was concerned, but he wasn't her type. She didn't have a type. She had only ever loved Archie, and had never looked at anyone else.

'What the hell are you huffing and puffing for now?' she heard him say from the other side of the bed, and she realized she had been sighing heavily.

'Archie, I have to talk to you. I can't leave it like this.'

'Leave what, for Christ's sake? It's late, and if you're not in the mood for anything else, at least let's get some sleep. It's been a long day.'

'Do you think I don't know that?' Her voice suddenly broke. 'I feel as if I've done enough crying to sink a battleship all this past week.'

He turned around instantly, his arms pulling her back beneath the bedclothes.

'What the hell is wrong, sweetheart? I can't help if I don't know!'

She snuffled into his shoulder. If she had any sense

she would leave it, and just relish being safe and warm in his arms, but if she did that, the resentment was never going to go away.

'You told my mother we would always be here to look after her now that Dad's gone,' she said, feeling as forlorn as a lost kitten.

'So what's wrong with that? Don't you want her to feel as reassured as possible? I'm only the son-in-law, but any fool can see she needs people around her right now.'

'You said we would always be here to look after her. You said she needn't ever feel that she was going to be left alone.'

He moved slightly away from her, and the moonlight shining through the curtained window allowed her to see him looking down at her.

'For God's sake, Carrie, what else would I have said? The poor old duck was feeling pretty sorry for herself, and this is where we live, isn't it?'

Her impatience with him boiled over. 'Oh, Archie, you don't see it, do you? This is where we live for now, but not for *always*. Mum wouldn't expect that, and Dad certainly wouldn't. This is only a temporary thing, remember.'

'If you're still thinking of those damn prefabs, you can forget it. There's been a hold-up in the building, anyway, and a bloody good thing too. You wouldn't catch me in one of them, and I'm telling you that right now.'

'Well, I want one!' She tried to keep her voice down, but it all came out in a strangled stage whisper. 'Dad and me looked over the plans in the council offices and they're lovely little places, so I don't know what you've got against them.'

'They're rubbish. They say they're only meant to last ten years, and then where would anybody be? You can't compare them to a solid cottage made from Cornish stone that's been standing for ever.'

'And probably full of damp and dry rot, and needing proper wiring for the electricity, and a decent bathroom with an indoor lav,' Carrie almost sobbed.

'Been reading it all up, have you?' he said sarcastically. 'Well, you don't have your daddy here to fawn all over you and back you up anymore, and your mother needs you here, so that's the end of it.'

She gasped at his crass words, but before she could lash out at him again, they heard the banging on the bedroom wall, and Carrie's heart nearly stopped. For a bittersweet moment it was just as if her dad was banging on the wall to tell them to be quiet and that he needed his sleep. For that one exquisite, split-second moment she forgot that he was dead, and she almost called back to him. Then as she remembered, all the fight went out of her, and she was weeping in Archie's arms.

'It's far from being resolved, and Archie refuses to talk about it anymore,' she said resentfully, when she met her three friends on the Thursday evening, two weeks after Christmas. 'I know Archie thinks he's doing the noble thing, but it's not what my dad would have wanted, and now that we've got Christmas over,

Mum's back to her old tricks again. I knew the peace wouldn't last long.'

'Couldn't you get somebody to move in with her, like that sister of hers who was at the funeral? They seemed like two of a kind to me,' Shirley suggested.

'Exactly. You all met her. Would you be brave enough to suggest it to either of them?' Carrie said.

'It's an idea though, Carrie,' Velma said. 'She's been here for a visit before, hasn't she? So does your mum keep in touch with her regularly?'

'Not really. Christmas and birthdays, of course, though before she left after Dad's funeral they were promising to write to one another more often.'

'You should make sure they do then. It could be the answer to all your problems. What do you think, Gwen?'

'Probably. I don't know. You can't make people do things they don't want to, can you?'

They all looked at her. She was paler than usual, but as she had never said a word about any outcome of the dance, they assumed it had passed off peaceably.

'What I mean is,' she went on, 'I'd like to make David give up his job and do something safer on land, especially in bad weather, but he never will, not even for me. In fact, *especially* not for me.'

'What's that supposed to mean?' Velma asked in the small silence that followed. 'You two are all right, aren't you? Didn't you have a good Christmas?'

'We're fine. What about you? Is Junior making his presence felt yet?'

She turned the questioning so neatly no one really noticed it.

'Oh yes. He was kicking so much one night that Stan swore he was pushing him out of bed.'

'That's probably because he knows he's not really wanted,' Gwen said sourly. 'He's making sure Stan knows about it too.'

'Gwen, that's a rotten thing to say,' Carrie said, her own troubles forgotten in an instant.

Gwen flushed deeply. 'Well, it *was* a mistake, wasn't it? Same as Shirley's. Don't you think kids sense that kind of thing, even before they're born?'

'Crikey, who's getting all philosophical now?' Carrie said quickly, seeing Shirley's mouth about to wobble, and her eyes blur. 'Anyway, so you had a good Christmas, and it sounds as if Velma did. We had a very subdued one in the circumstances, so how about you, Shirley? Now we're into the new year, I suppose you're counting the days until your twenty-first at the end of the month, and thinking about setting the date. Is it still on for June?'

She knew she was gabbling to cover the awkward little atmosphere that had arisen between them. But she groaned as soon as she mentioned June, knowing it was hardly the best reminder for Shirley. There was a wedding to plan, but the thought of the GIs coming back for their own D-Day reunion in the same month might be a coincidence too much for her to take.

'It will definitely be in June,' Shirley said defiantly, surprising them all. 'There's no reason why it shouldn't be, is there? Bernard always knew I wanted a June wedding, and that's not really rushing into things. He hasn't said anything to the contrary, and that's all that matters to me. We might even try for one of those prefabs you've been on about for ages, Carrie.'

'That's right, rub salt in it, why don't you?' she muttered.

Shirley clapped her hand over her mouth. 'Oh Lord, I'm sorry. I know Archie's got a thing about them. Everyone seems to be saying the wrong thing tonight, don't they? I was just thinking what fun it would be if we were neighbours. But I'm sure it will all work out all right in the end for you and your mum, Carrie. I can't really imagine Archie wanting to live with her for very long. They wouldn't get on for ever, and they'd soon be at each other's throats – and I've done it again, haven't I?'

But she realized the others were starting to laugh at her now as she blundered on, making matters worse.

'So come on, Velma. What's the latest with you and Stan?' She turned her attention quickly away from Carrie. 'Have you decided to leave Penhallow or not?'

'Not yet. I can't think straight until the baby's born. Then I'll decide.'

'Stan must be pretty patient if he's agreed to that.'

'He doesn't have much choice, does he? I'm determined that the baby will be born in the cottage where I was born, and he's promised to be here when the time comes. After that, well, we'll see.'

Carrie hoped Velma was as confident as she sounded. She hoped Shirley was as happy about her proposed wedding date as she seemed. She hoped Gwen's occasional sniping, and the odd little twitch at the corner of her mouth, didn't signify any problems at home. And as for herself and Archie, she hoped that pigs would grow wings, and that her Aunt Phyllis really would get a sudden inspiration to leave Falmouth and come and live with her sister. It would solve everything.

Chapter 16

Cornish winters were never as fierce as those upcountry. The beginning of 1946 had its usual share of sunshine and squalls, dips in temperature, and the morning sea mists that clothed the moors with an ethereal beauty. Despite the peninsula tailing down to the Atlantic, with coasts surrounding it on three sides, winters could be mild and pleasant. It was often said that if there was rain on the north coast, it was usually sunny in the south. But if the weather did deteriorate, the one thing the coasts had in abundance was lashing winds and spectactulary raging seas.

None of it bothered Shirley Loe; what did bother her was the Christmas card that had arrived for Bernard from France. His mother had put it in a prominent place on the mantelpiece, and seeing the strange foreign words on it, Shirley immediately identified it.

'Is that from her?' she asked him bluntly.

'You mean Marie, I suppose,' he said.

'Well, is it?'

'It might be,' he teased. 'Or it might be from some

other French mam'selle. It might even be from one of
the little darlings I'm trying to teach the rudiments of
French to at school!'

'Not to the infants, you're not.'

He finally acknowledged her annoyance, and
handed the card to her.

'Here, read it for yourself and then you'll know, my
suspicious little pet.'

'You know very well I can't read French.'

'I've offered to teach you enough times, haven't I?'

The fact that he sounded so superior at that
moment annoyed her even more.

'Well, since I'm never likely to go there, nor have
any use for the language, I don't see the point.'

She glared at the inside of the Christmas card,
seeing a mass of writing, and unable to understand a
word. The only thing she recognized was the name
Marie at the bottom. She flung the card at him, oozing
jealousy.

'Did you send her one as well?'

Bernard sighed. 'Shirley, grow up. This family
saved my life, and the card is from all of them, not just
Marie. I knew this would happen, which is why I
didn't want Mum to put it on the mantelpiece.'

'No, you'd rather put it in your wallet along with
her photo, and the letter you got from her in the
summer, and I bet that wasn't the only one, either.'

The minute she said it she knew she'd made a
mistake, since she wasn't supposed to know about
that. If he'd told her in the beginning it wouldn't have
come to this, but he hadn't. He'd treated her as a child

as always, the way everyone did, Shirley thought petulantly.

'How do you know about that?'

'I don't know. Your mother probably told me. I don't remember.'

She expected him to be furious with her, but she must have looked so guilty and dejected that he wasn't. Being a teacher, he was a master of patience, and, instead, he put his arms around her.

'Shirley, when two people love each other, they have to trust each other. I don't have any secrets from you, and I'm sure you don't have any from me. Without trust, what kind of a future will we have?'

Her heart gave an uneasy leap. If he only knew the worst secret of all . . .

'Do you mean to tell me that all the time Marie was looking after you, you never once thought of her as a woman instead of just a nurse?' she said, choked, almost wanting him to say that he had, if only to ease her own conscience.

To her horror, he didn't answer for a moment, and she wondered if she had insulted him now. He was always so honourable . . .

'Since we're being so honest with one another, Shirley darling, it's what I've been trying to tell you for some time, but I could never seem to find the words. I can't deny that I felt a great affection for Marie.'

'*What*?'

'Now don't go off the deep end,' he went on quickly. 'Marie and I became close out of necessity, and I owe her my life, but we weren't close in the way you mean, any more than you would ever have become close to someone else. Not that I expected you to behave like a nun while I was away, and I'm sure some of those farming types thought you were a little smasher in your Land Army uniform. But faithfulness means as much to me as it does to you, and I never forgot that I had you to come home to. The thought of you was what kept me sane when I thought I was going mad with pain and delirium.'

'Oh, Bernard.' Her soft lips trembled, and as shame swept through her, it was on the tip of her tongue to confess everything. To get it all off her chest once and for all, and beg his forgiveness. It was so very tempting.

'So you see, darling, you have nothing to fear from Marie. If she wants to keep in touch, then you should think of her as an old friend, or a distant relative, who just wants to make sure that her patient survived.' He hesitated. 'I've been wondering about inviting her and her parents to the wedding, then you'd see that your fears are all for nothing, but I wasn't sure how you'd feel about it.'

Her feelings changed at once, but she choked back her instant refusal and tried her darnedest to be as reasonable as possible.

'Well, I'm not sure how I feel about that! I want to say no – unless you really, *really* want her to come. I know you owe her your life, and I'm so grateful for that, but I still can't help feeling jealous for all the time you spent together. But if it means that much to you, Bernard, then, well, I suppose I'd have to agree, because I know how mean and selfish I sound, and I know I'm being awfully young and silly and thoughtless as usual, and I don't mean to be, truly I don't.'

He gave a soft laugh as she rambled on, getting more tied in knots with every word. Then he gave her a huge hug and kissed her shaking lips.

'Don't you know that's one of the things I love about you? My beautiful butterfly sweetheart, as scatty as they come!'

'Thank you!' she said indignantly, but the dangerous moment had passed, and she thought she had coped with it fairly well, even if it did mean inviting the French family to her wedding. But they probably wouldn't come, she thought hopefully. They hadn't sounded like a family with money, and why would foreigners travel all that way to be with people they hardly knew?

That sort of thing was left to a group of Americans who were willing to travel halfway around the world to be in England on the anniversary of D-Day. And soon, hundreds of excited GI brides would be thinking about making the voyage across the Atlantic to be with their husbands and start their glamorous new lives. She shivered, and Bernard held her more tightly, caressing her cheek with his lips.

'Let's go in the front room,' he whispered in her ear. 'It's turned so chilly that Mum's lit a fire in there for once. Everybody else is out, so me and my best girl can get as cosy as we like without interruption.'

As she hugged him back, there were times, Shirley

thought gladly, when he could be every bit as romantic as a sophisticated GI, or any handsome film star on the silver screen.

When she popped into the library to look for a book on wedding etiquette and a chat, Carrie told Shirley she had made exactly the right decision. Not that the wedding was going to be a grand affair. The money didn't stretch to that, and they still had to be careful with rations for the small reception her mum was planning to arrange at the village hall, but they wanted everything to be right.

Finding Carrie on her own in the library that morning, though, Shirley couldn't resist repeating the gist of the recent conversation to her.

'There's absolutely no need to upset things,' Carrie soothed. 'We've told you often enough that you've got to put it right out of your mind, Shirley. It happened and now it's over, and you have to look forward, not back.'

'I know,' Shirley said, fidgeting with her collar and going bright red. 'The thing is, Carrie – well, I don't know how to say it, really – but, well, supposing Bernard can tell – on our wedding night, I mean?'

Carrie hid a smile, knowing at once what she meant. 'I can guarantee that you'll be so tense with nerves that he won't be able to guess a thing!'

'Is that how it was for you?'

'Well, not exactly. I mean, we hadn't actually done it before the wedding night, but even now, if I'm not really in the mood, it's not always as comfortable as it could be. And I'm not saying anything else, because it's far too personal to discuss such things with an unmarried girl,' she added, teasing to cover her embarrassment at revealing too much about herself and Archie, even to a friend.

Shirley's eyes were wide. 'You mean you tell him when you're not in the mood? Is that all right then? I mean, isn't it a wife's duty—'

'I'm not his slave,' Carrie said smartly. 'Those days went out with the Victorians, Shirley. Women have a right to say what they want nowadays, although you have to be tactful and I wouldn't go as far as to deny him completely. Fair's fair, and he's still the man, isn't he?'

She giggled suddenly, and Shirley looked a little annoyed, as if realizing Carrie was visualizing something unique to her – and to every other married woman, come to that. Married women and single girls . . . there was a world of difference between them. Apart from that one time with Hank, Shirley was still chaste . . . though that couldn't be true, either. Once *it* happened, that was it. You could never go back to what you were before. You were no longer pure, and if it became known, the church would condemn you for ever. She sucked in her breath between her neat little teeth.

Carrie squeezed her arm. 'Cheer up, Shirley, Bernard is so besotted with you, he's hardly going to notice anything on his wedding night except that his beautiful bride belongs to him at last.'

Shirley perked up at once. 'I hope you're right. And

he *is* besotted with me, isn't he?' she said happily, clutching the book on wedding etiquette to her chest and scampering out of the library in a sudden downpour to go back to work.

Carrie watched her go, and prayed that she would keep her nerve. She caught sight of Archie in the rain-streaked window of his shop and waved to him across the green. There were no old men sitting and yarning on wooden benches there today, for the January weather was threatening to turn stormy, and a gusty wind had whipped the remaining leaves from the trees long ago.

It was true what she had said, though. She wasn't always in the mood the way Archie was, and since their last row she was even less inclined to pander to his needs any time he wanted to make love. She was full of resentment that he and her mother seemed to have formed such a pact between them now. Sometimes she felt more like an interloper than the daughter of the house. And she missed her dad so much. She missed his calm manner, and the way he could always pour oil on troubled waters without really seeming to do so. She was realizing more and more that his apparent passiveness had never been weakness. It was the much-needed buffer between herself and her mum.

She swallowed hard as several ladies came into the library, more to shelter from the rain than to browse among the books, and told herself this wasn't the time or place to get maudlin. She wondered what they would think, these buxom Cornish ladies with their down-to-earth chatter, if they knew how she talked to her dad every time she went to the churchyard. It was as natural to her as breathing, and she always came away in a calmer frame of mind, as if he had somehow given her the answers she sought.

It was more than Shirley's so-called sixth sense, it was a special kind of perception between her and Walter. They had always had it, and she knew it hadn't died with him. She had never explained any of it to Archie, and wouldn't even try, sure that he would either scoff or think she was crazy.

'Are you all right, Carrie dear?' she heard one of the ladies say. 'We were just saying how well your mother seems to be coping, having you and Archie there to keep things going.'

'Oh. Oh yes, she's doing very well, thank you.'

Why wouldn't she, Carrie thought savagely, with Archie forever pandering to her and calling her 'my old girl' and chivvying her out of her black moods.

'But you'll still be feeling the loss of your dad,' the woman went on kindly. 'You were always like two peas in a pod, and I'm sure he's somewhere up in the Great Beyond looking after you.'

She nodded vaguely skywards, and Carrie had a job not to laugh, when she was obviously doing her best to be tactful. It wasn't quite the way she thought of the special connection between herself and her dad, but it was a kind of comfort all the same. Her dad had always tried to ease the friction between her and her mum, and she made a mental note to be extra nice to her mother when she got home.

*

The minute she stepped through the front door, brushing off the rain that had persisted all day, she heard the blazing row. Probably the whole of Kellaway Terrace had heard it, she thought drily, since it had obviously being going on for quite a while, and Edna was in full flow now.

'I don't want to hear any more about it, Archie. I know you mean well, and I appreciate all that you do, but this is my home, and I'll not have you smoking in it. Walter hated the smell of cigarette smoke, and with all that Parks and Gardens stuff he was so keen on, he was very strict about not letting it pollute the air we breathe. Just because he's gone, God rest his soul, there's no reason for us to drop our standards.'

Archie snorted derisively, and Carrie held her breath, knowing her mother wouldn't like this one bit – even though she knew full well, as they all did, that it wasn't Walter who had put the ban on smoking in the house, but Edna herself.

'What standards are these then, old girl? Have we gone up in the world now? Perhaps me and Carrie should start calling ourselves Lord and Lady Pollard, and you can be the dowager duchess. How does that suit you, your ladyship? Just as long as you don't expect us to bow and curtsey to you, mind.'

Carrie groaned. Sometimes he went too far. A sense of humour was sadly lacking in Edna, and there was no knowing how she was going to take this. To her surprise, there was no more than an answering sniff.

'You're cracked in the head, that's what you are,

Archie Pollard, but just remember to do as I say and do your smoking in the garden and we'll get along fine. And just because it's raining –' she forestalled him – 'there's no reason why you can't go and do it in the shed, providing you don't burn it down. I've no doubt Walter was in the habit of having a sneaky puff in there.'

Carrie felt her eyes water. So her mother had known all the time. People could still surprise you when you least expected them to. She pushed open the living-room door and let them know she was home.

'We're invited to a small do at Shirley's house for her twenty-first,' she said to Archie by way of greeting. 'It's only for a few friends, and they're not making too much of it, with rations being what they are, and they'll be making a bigger splash for the wedding later in the year.'

'She's still set on marrying the Bosinney boy, then,' Edna said with a sniff.

'Well, of course she is. Why shouldn't she be?' Carrie replied, suddenly nervous. Her mother not only had a suspicious mind, but also a canny way of putting two and two together and coming out with the right answer.

'No reason,' Edna said. 'I just sometimes thought that of all of your friends, she'd be the one to go off the rails while young Bernard was out of the picture.'

'Changed your mind from Gwen now then, have you?' Carrie said, nettled. 'I wonder you haven't pointed the finger at Velma or me before now.'

'There's no need for that kind of talk, my girl, but now that you've added to the headache Archie's given me, I'm having an early night and taking to my bed.'

Carrie watched her go, seething as she realized she had fallen into the trap of causing the stiff departure after all.

'Why am I always the bad guy?' she said to Archie.

He laughed. 'You're not. But I reckon she's missing your dad more than she lets on, and she has to take it out on someone. She only keeps on about me smoking so she can mention his name and have something to say about him.'

'Do you think so?'

'I know so. I spent a long time studying human nature while I was a POW, and people react to things in strange ways. This is your mum's way.'

'Crikey, Archie, I didn't know you could be such a deep thinker!'

'There's a lot of things you don't know about me, my girl, but all you need to know right now is that when we've had a bite to eat we should have an early night too, if you get my meaning. All this argy bargy has got me excited.'

A long time later, lying in his arms, and hoping Edna had been keeping her head well below the bedcovers and not noticed the creaking of the bed-springs in the room next door, Carrie thought back over what Archie had said earlier.

'Is she really missing Dad that much? She never says so to me.'

'Well, she wouldn't. You're her daughter. She needs someone of her own age to talk to, and she's not one for making close friends, is she?'

'Only Aunt Phyllis, and she's her sister.'

Archie shifted a little way away from her. 'That's it then. We should pack her off to Aunt Phyllis for a week or two. We'd have the house to ourselves and kill two birds with one stone. Think about that!'

'Don't be daft. You don't pack my mother off anywhere.'

It was a glorious idea though, and Archie topped it off.

'So we need to be devious about it. You write to Aunt Phyllis, saying your mother's looking peaky, which she is, and ask if she could invite her to stay – without letting on that it was your idea, of course.'

'Archie, you're brilliant.' She was being sarky, but he chose not to see it.

'I know. So come here and let me show you just how brilliant I can be.'

'Again?' Carrie said, marvelling, and abandoning the words that were already forming in her mind for her letter to Aunt Phyllis. Some things were more important.

A couple of weeks later Carrie arrived home from work one rainy afternoon to find her mother staring out of the kitchen window.

'You won't make it stop by glaring at it,' she said with a grin.

'I've had this letter,' Edna said abruptly. 'I think your aunt Phyllis is going mad in her old age.'

Carrie's heart jumped. 'Why? What does she say?'

'She thinks I should go and stay with her for a few days, or a week if I like. She thinks it would do me good, after your dad, and since we're all we've got left now, daft old thing, we should see more of each other. Why on earth would I want to go to Falmouth in February? I never cared for the place all that much.'

'You care for her though, don't you, Mum? She is your only sister, and it's good of her to think of you in that way. She's right too. Families are important.'

'Well, I've got you and Archie, haven't I?'

'Yes, but we don't share the same kind of memories that you and Aunt Phyllis do, having grown up together.'

For a minute Edna looked at her oddly, and Carrie caught her breath. The last thing she wanted was for Edna to think she and Archie had put Aunt Phyllis up to this. She saw her clamp her lips and start to bang pots about, which was always a bad sign.

'I'll have to think about it. I suppose you and Archie could manage here if I did decide to go.'

'Of course we could.'

When he came home that night, Archie put the finishing touch to her doubts.

'Me and Carrie will take you there on the bus and come and fetch you when you're ready to come home. So you just write back and say you're coming, old girl. Do you a world of good to gossip over old times with your sister.'

She gave in, and it was arranged that she would go during the second week of February.

Before then, they had the excitement of Shirley's birthday to think about. Being twenty-one was an important milestone in a girl's life, and it also meant that her dad could have no more objection to Shirley and Bernard's wedding in June. It wasn't that he didn't approve of Bernard, of course, for a steadier chap he couldn't imagine. It was more Shirley's scatty nature that her father often wondered about.

But anybody with half an eye could see that she was madly in love with her young man, and when Bernard arrived early at her house on the day of her birthday they shooed Shirley's excited sisters away and went into the temporary privacy of the front room.

Bernard handed her a small box wrapped in shiny paper that she opened eagerly. Inside was a heart-shaped locket, and she smiled with delight as he fastened it around her neck. She leaned back against him as his lips nuzzled into her neck for a moment, and then she twisted around and into his arms.

'It's beautiful, Bernard, and I shall wear it always,' she breathed.

'Good. And you do realize its significance, don't you?'

'Well, it's a heart—' she began.

'It's *my* heart, all of it,' he said solemnly. 'It's from me to you, with all my love, for ever. You're the guardian of my heart, Shirley.'

She was momentarily humbled, knowing this was

his way of saying that whatever had happened in faraway France – or right here in Penzance, for that matter – was behind them now.

'I do love you, Bernard,' she said, knowing that she truly meant it.

It was their last emotional moment before the small sisters burst in, shrieking that other people were arriving, and that Shirley's mum was setting out the scones and plum jam, and the birthday cake she had made, and Shirley's dad was pouring glasses of his elderberry wine and saying they were all to drink a toast to the birthday girl.

Bernard gave Shirley's hand a last squeeze, and then the room was full of people, and there were kisses and hugs, and birthday gifts for Shirley. And the sweet moments were assigned to memory.

Later, they all played charades, and the day seemed to pass in a dream for Shirley. She had waited for it for so long, and now it was almost over, and they could move on. She fingered the locket around her neck, and caught Bernard's tender glance as she did so. This was so right, she thought tremulously, the way it was always meant to be. Nothing could separate them now.

All their friends and family had come to join in the celebrations. Archie and David had called a silent truce, to Carrie and Gwen's relief. When Velma arrived, she had caused a few laughs, pretending that she couldn't get through the door of Shirley's house with her bump now, and praying that Stan's leave would coincide with the birth of their baby next month.

'I can hardly believe it's almost here,' she confided to Carrie, under cover of the noise of Shirley's sisters racing around the place and screaming with excitement that they were going to be bridesmaids next summer.

'That's because you denied it so much in the beginning. You were already a couple of months gone before you realized it was a baby and not something worse.'

'That's right, Nurse Pollard!'

Carrie laughed. 'I'm no nurse. Just able to count.'

'Actually, I wanted to ask you something,' Velma said, easing herself into a more comfortable position, glad of a few moments in comparative privacy while the rest of the party chattered around them. 'The doctor thinks the baby may come a bit early, and there's always a chance Stan may not get home in time if that happens. Can I call on you if I'm in need of company when the time comes?'

'Good Lord, Velma, I'd be no good at anything like that. I don't know anything about delivering babies,' she said in a panic.

Velma laughed. 'I don't want you delivering him, you ninny. The midwife and the doctor will do all that. I just want a friendly face beside me, and a hand I can cling on to, that's all. I may look confident, but don't let it fool you.'

Carrie was about to tease her until she saw the look in her eyes, and realized that she really was scared of this momentous thing that was happening to her. She squeezed her hand.

'Of course I'll be there. You can call on me, day or night. We've always been there to hold one another's hands, haven't we?'

Edna was safely deposited in her sister's small, cramped flat in Falmouth, after deciding she might as well stay for a week after all. Carrie and Archie went back home on the bus, feeling as jubilant as two infants let out of school.

'Just imagine, the whole house to ourselves,' Archie chortled. 'I can smoke myself to death if I want to, and there'll be no black looks or snappy remarks.'

'Oh yes there will, because I promised Mum I'd keep you in line,' she told him. 'We have to prove to her that everything will carry on as if she's still here.'

'Well, not everything. We can spend Sunday afternoon in bed and there's nobody to say anything different.'

'We could do that every Sunday if we had a place of our own.'

'So we could, and as long as it's not one of those bloody prefabs I'd agree to it in time. But we couldn't leave your mum now, could we?'

'Couldn't we?' she said, her happy mood quickly fading as the bus dropped them back in Penhallow.

'It'll happen one day, Carrie, but let's just make the most of this week. You go on home and make the tea and I'll go to the shop and get a newspaper. We'll be like a proper Darby and Joan tonight.'

Hell's bells, she thought indignantly, she was only twenty-two, and she wasn't ready for that category yet! But she wouldn't let anything dampen her pleasure at having the house to themselves for a whole week. She would put on a special dab of her favourite ashes of roses perfume before they went to bed tonight. By then, Archie must see how wonderful it could be.

He was reading his newspaper when she put the cold ham and potatoes on the table for their tea, and he didn't look any too pleased.

'What's up?' she said.

'Bloody Yanks, that's what up! All these pictures of our Cornish girls getting ready to sail off to America to live with their GI blokes, and half of them with kids in their arms and all. You don't need three guesses as to what they got up to while we were away winning the war.'

It was hardly the time to point out that he didn't exactly win it single-handed, stuck in a German POW camp.

'The Yanks were winning the war too, Archie.'

'Oh yes, and they're coming back here to a big reunion in June, and now Penzance is putting on a bit of a show for them as well. The paper's printed a letter from the American organizer saying how much they appreciated the friendship shown to their boys, and there's a piece from the town council inviting anyone with an interest to be present at some reception or other. *My God*! It even prints a list of the GIs who won't be coming over because they never made it past the D-Day landings, just for local information. They'll be wanting a bloody plaque or a special monument next, and with such stupid names too. Who in their right mind would saddle a kid with a name like Chuck or Leroy or Clint or Hank or Fitzroy, and too many other daft ones to mention?'

'Can I have a look?' Carrie said, her heart thumping.

'What for?'

'Well, I may know some of the girls in the pictures.'

She hardly looked at them. All she wanted to see was the list of names Archie was so scathing about, but for a very different reason. It wasn't just the Christian names of the dead that were mentioned, but their full names and ranks as well. And there it was. Lieutenant Hank Delaney. Hank the Yank. Shirley's Hank. Shirley's lover.

Chapter 17

'You won't mind if I see the girls as usual tonight, will you, Archie?' she said, when she could trust herself to speak normally. 'Didn't you say there was a skittles match on at the pub?'

She held her breath, praying he hadn't changed his mind. She *had* to see Shirley, to warn her, if she hadn't already seen the newspaper.

'I was thinking of giving it a miss, but I did tell Dad I'd see him there.'

'That's what we'll do then,' she said with relief.

She raced around to Shirley's house, ignoring the fact that she was a married woman, as she so often did when the need arose, and forgetting that she should behave with more decorum. If ever there was a time for haste, tonight was it.

'She's already gone to the village hall, my dear,' Shirley's mum told her. 'She was in a bit of a fluster as usual, and I reckon 'tis all this excitement now her dad's told Bernard they can get wed in the summer.'

'I'm sure it is, Mrs Loe,' Carrie said, already turning on her heels and racing back the way she had come.

She was pretty sure that Shirley's fluster was due to something else entirely, but she could hardly ask her mother if she had seen the newspaper without inviting questions.

She had a stitch in her side by the time she reached the village hall, to find Gwen and Velma already there, their heads together. There was no sign of Shirley.

'Have you seen it?' Gwen asked at once, not needing to explain further.

Carrie nodded. 'I went round to call for Shirley, but she'd already left. She should have been here ages ago.'

'So where is she?' Velma asked.

They looked at each other. Shirley's temperament was often unpredictable, and there was no knowing what effect the newspaper article might have had on her.

'We should go and look for her,' Gwen said.

'Well, Velma can't, not in her state, and besides, it's dark and starting to rain again. She could be anywhere, so how would we know where to look?'

'We can't just sit here, pretending nothing's happened!'

'She wouldn't have done anything silly,' Carrie said uneasily. 'D-Day was getting on for two years ago now, so it's not as if he died yesterday.'

'It is to Shirley,' Velma said. 'That's exactly how it will feel to her.'

'Gwen, what did you do when you thought David was missing? I don't mean *later*, I mean what did you do immediately the telegram came? Think about it.'

Gwen looked at Carrie resentfully for a minute, and then she nodded slowly.

'I cried like a mad thing, and I prayed my hardest for him to be safe. There was nothing else I could do.'

'And when my dad had his heart attack, I prayed too, and ever since then I've often gone to the churchyard to talk to him. Stop looking at me as if I'm crazy, Gwen, I just know it helps.'

'Well, Shirley won't have gone to the churchyard because she knows her Yank's not there.'

'No, but she'll have gone to the church,' Carrie said, scrambling up. 'I'm going to find her and bring her back here.'

It might be a long shot, but she had the strongest instinct that it was where she would find Shirley, making her peace with God. For all her flirty ways, she was a staunch believer, which had made the whole shame of the illegitimate baby so much harder for her to bear.

The rain was falling steadily now, chilling her to the bone, and she clutched her coat around her tightly. Her hair was hanging in rats' tails by the time she reached Shirley's church, and she offered up her own prayer that her friend would be inside. The interior was dimly lit, and she didn't see her at first. Then she caught sight of the small, forlorn figure, her head bowed as she leaned against the front of the pew, her tumbling blond curls making her look vulnerable, and so very young.

Carrie slid into the pew beside her, and put her arm

around her. It was as if Shirley didn't even know she was there, and then Carrie felt her move imperceptibly towards her, taking comfort from her presence.

'It's over, Shirley darling,' she said softly.

'I know,' she mumbled. 'And I feel so guilty. All this time, ever since the dance, I've dreaded him coming back, wondering how I would feel if he came to find me. And now I know he never will, and all I can think of is how much I loved him for that short time, and how he might have had a son or a daughter, and I feel so wicked.'

Carrie began to feel alarmed at this self-punishment. 'You're getting it all out of proportion, Shirley. It was a shock to see Hank's name in the paper, but his family will have come to terms with it a long time ago.'

'But can't you see that I feel as if it happened yesterday,' she choked, echoing Velma's words. 'I have to grieve for him, Carrie, otherwise it was all for nothing. You see that, don't you?'

'Yes, of course I do. But you can't let it take over your life. You've got a wedding to look forward to. Bernard's a good man, and he deserves more than this.'

She spoke as delicately as she could, knowing that Bernard had now got into the habit of meeting Shirley from the village hall on Thursday nights, and if she was still in this state by the end of the evening, who knew what she might blurt out?

Shirley didn't say anything for a while, and Carrie

could feel her sobbing quietly beside her. After what seemed an age, she drew a shuddering breath, and mopped her eyes with her sodden handkerchief.

'You're a good friend, Carrie, but the first awful shock is over, and you needn't worry that I'm going to fall apart and confess everything to Bernard, because I never will. I've made my peace with God and promised Him that I'll be a good wife to Bernard. Any more tears for Hank will be in my heart.'

Dramatic as always, Carrie thought, but she felt a huge affection for this girl who had done no more than many other girls had done before her.

'Are you ready to see the others now then? You don't want to go straight home, do you?

Shirley shook her head. 'I can't do that. Mum will wonder what's wrong, and I can't let Bernard turn up later and not find me there, can I?'

'Attagirl,' Carrie said softly.

Next morning she woke up sneezing and spluttering, and knew that running around in the rain last night had done her no good at all.

'Well, this is a fine thing,' Archie complained. 'We've got rid of your mother for a week and you're under the weather. Are you taking the day off? You look as if you should stay in bed, and I'd join you if you didn't look like a dog's dinner.'

'Thanks,' Carrie said crossly. 'And of course I'm not taking a day off. It's only a little cold, for goodness' sake. I'll take an aspirin, and I'll live!'

He chuckled. 'I knew that would get you going,

though I reckon it's time you stayed home for good and looked after me like a proper wife should. They make women too tough in Cornwall.'

She resisted throwing something at him, and agreed that they did. Besides, once she was up and dressed and had eaten some breakfast, she didn't feel so bad. She had no intention of staying at home today, if only because she wanted to check on Shirley, and she called in at the haberdashery on her way to work.

'I'm feeling better now,' Shirley said, amazingly bright eyed, and not just from crying. 'Me and Bernard have decided to go into Penzance at the weekend to put our names down for one of the prefabs. Just to show our intentions to the world,' she added meaningfully.

Oh yes, she would be all right, thought Carrie later. Shirley was a survivor, no matter what happened. She would have the big white wedding, and probably the prefab too. At the thought, her lips unexpectedly trembled, her eyes watered and her nose began to run.

'For heaven's sake, Carrie, go home,' her boss told her. 'There's no point in being here if you're not feeling well. Go home, have a drink of hot lemon and put a tot of brandy in it if you have any. Take a couple of aspirins and a hot water bottle to bed with you, and indulge yourself for once.'

'I think perhaps I will,' she croaked, knowing it wasn't just her cold that was depressing her. Despite everything, Shirley would get what she wanted, even the prefab that Carrie coveted so much. She didn't begrudge her anything, but suddenly it all overwhelmed her. It just seemed so unfair. So bloody unfair. ·

She didn't think of anything much for the next couple of days. She was aware of Archie coming in and out of the bedroom, refilling her hot water bottle, holding her head while she drank the soup his mother sent round, sponging her down with a warm flannel, and being more wonderful and considerate than she'd believed possible.

On Sunday morning she awoke clear headed, and turned to look at him sleeping beside her. His hair was ruffled with sleep, his chin stubbly and in need of a shave. And he was so dear, so very much a man's man . . . and *her* man. Doing women's work while she had been poorly hadn't diminished him one iota.

'You're awake then,' he murmured, aware of her without opening his eyes. 'Do you want something?'

'Only you,' she whispered.

He turned towards her at once. 'That's the best thing I've heard for days, and it must mean you're feeling better.'

'I am, and I'm hungry. Could you make me some toast, Archie?'

He gave a rueful smile. 'Well, if that's all I can do for you, I suppose it'll have to do for now.'

She pulled him close and nuzzled into his neck. The feel of his roughened chin against her smooth skin sent a *frisson* of desire through her, but no more than that. Not yet.

'Just for now.' She was unconsciously seductive.

'But I'm sure I'll be fully recovered by tonight. Oh, and Archie.'

'What?' he said, as she hesitated.

'I do love you,' she said fervently.

He squeezed her tightly for a moment. 'I love you too, Mrs Pollard, and when I've made the toast and tea I'm bringing it back to bed to share it with you. Something else we can do without risking your mother's disapproval, isn't it?'

She stretched luxuriously in the bed after he had gone downstairs, feeling a sense of well-being now that the worst symptoms of the cold had gone. They still had a few more days before Edna came back from Falmouth, and she was determined to make the most of them. They hadn't had a real chance to play at keeping house until now. After Walter died, it had been very much Edna's house, and they were merely the lodgers. Archie must see how good it could be to have a place all to themselves. Her face puckered for a moment, knowing there was something she was supposed to remember, but whatever it was, it would have to wait.

Shirley and Bernard called round that afternoon to see how she was feeling, and she could see at once that something was up.

'Don't be grumpy, Archie,' Carrie murmured. 'Be a good host and show Bernard round the garden while me and Shirley talk about women's stuff.'

The minute the men went outside, with none too good a grace on Archie's part, she turned to Shirley.

'What's happened? You haven't had second

thoughts about anything since Thursday night, have you?' She wouldn't make it any plainer than that.

She thought Shirley was about to burst into tears, but she managed to make do with a loud swallow.

'No. But we went to the housing department in Penzance on Saturday morning to put our names down for one of the prefabs, and we were too late. They've all been allocated already, and I'd really set my heart on one of them, Carrie, just like you.'

'Good Lord, is that all? I thought something disastrous had happened,' Carrie said, unable to hide her annoyance. 'You can always find a cottage to rent, can't you?'

'I don't remember hearing you settling for second best! Anyway, you don't understand why I wanted it so much.'

'So why don't you tell me?'

Shirley looked down at her hands, twisting the handkerchief in her lap.

'I wanted us to start married life with a clean slate, with everything perfect, and those prefabs are so white and clean and new, and it seemed like a good omen for us to have one. You know how I believe in omens.'

Carrie gave a small smile. It was so very much the way she had thought of it before Archie came home from the war. Now, to her own surprise, which she didn't want to analyse right now, she knew it wasn't so important.

'It really doesn't matter where you live. What matters is that you're together, and I bet Bernard wasn't so bothered, was he?'

'No, but he doesn't have my reasons either. He doesn't know why it's so important to me, and I can never tell him.'

Carrie sighed. 'If you're going to let a little thing like this upset your plans, then you're more of an idiot than I took you for, Shirley, and that's saying something. For goodness' sake, cheer up before they come back inside – and I thought you were supposed to be cheering *me* up.'

'Sorry, but you look all right, anyway,' she said sullenly, 'and it's just that I want everything to be good for us.'

'It will be. So is your mum going to make your wedding dress?'

Shirley brightened up. 'Yes, and she's going to make my sisters' dresses too. I didn't know she's been saving her clothing coupons for ages, knowing that Dad was going to agree to the wedding once I'd turned twenty-one. Did I tell you Bernard went down on one knee and proposed again, once he'd asked Dad formally for his permission? I thought he was going to do himself an injury, but I managed not to laugh. I said yes, of course, even though I'd already said it once!'

Oh yes, Shirley was a survivor all right.

That night, cuddled up close in Archie's arms, and feeling blissfully relaxed after being invited to his parents' for supper and being ordered not to do a thing, she said what had been simmering in her mind all day.

'Archie, about those prefabs.'

'I told you, I wouldn't be seen dead in one of them.'

'Will you just listen to me for a minute? Shirley desperately wants to live in one of them when she's married.'

He snorted. 'That doesn't surprise me. She's just the sort to go for one of those rabbit hutches. I'm surprised you even considered the idea. We'd be far better off in an old traditional place, like our parents' houses, solid and long-lasting, like this one. There's history here, not something that'll probably fall down in ten years' time.'

'I know. So I'm going to write to the housing department and ask if they'll take us off the list and put Shirley and Bernard on it instead. What do you think?'

He didn't say anything for a minute, and then he switched on the light and leaned up on one elbow, looking down at her. Fleetingly, she thought that you could keep your Hollywood heroes. He was Adonis and Hercules all rolled into one . . .

'I think you're bloody wonderful, and I don't know what I've done to deserve you. But are you sure? You were so set on it, and if you're just sacrificing your dream on account of your friend, I'm not sure that she deserves it either.'

She pulled him down to her, feeling his arms go around her at once. She was the lucky one, she thought, her heart singing, and he was all she needed.

'I'm quite sure,' she said huskily, 'and it's like you said. We'll be happy with something solid and long-lasting, like our future. And if you don't stop staring at me as if I'm a mirage, and make mad, passionate love to me, I'll—'

She couldn't say anything more, because his mouth was crushing hers, and his arms were lifting her into him, and he was everything she ever wanted him to be.

'You're mad,' Gwen told her a couple of weeks later when it was all official. 'All this time it's what you dreamed about, and you're giving it up for Shirley.'

'She needs it more than I do,' Carrie said. 'Anyway, the housing department has agreed, and it's settled. Why should you be so bothered, anyway?'

'I'm not. But I think it's a shame, that's all. How much longer are you going to live with your mother? And how did she get on with her sister?'

'They got along just fine, and they're planning to do it again sometime. So what else is bothering you, Gwen?'

They had bumped into one another that afternoon, and were having tea and scones in the village tea-shop. March winds were whipping across the Green and they were glad of a sit down. Gwen stirred her tea viciously.

'David still can't forget what happened with that drunk at the dance. I know it's smouldering inside him, and I don't know what to do about it.'

'There's nothing much you can do, except give it time, Gwen, and be as loving as you can to him.'

'Oh, I do that all right, when he lets me. But how long does he need? It's been months now – and things aren't quite what they were in that department either, if you know what I mean.'

'I'm sorry.'

Gwen drained her tea. 'So am I, but it's my problem, not yours. You'll have one of your own pretty soon, won't you? Velma, I mean. I don't envy you, offering to be in at the birth, and she's about to pop, by all accounts.'

Carrie laughed uneasily. 'That's a charming way to put it, I must say. As long as the midwife and doctor are there, I'll only be there to hold her hand.'

'You hope.'

The night had closed in, and the wind was roaring around the village now. Tin cans were scudding along the streets and the rain was sheeting down. Fires burned extra brightly, fuelled up the chimneys by the increasing wind, and as lightning slashed through the sky Edna complained that it was one of the worst nights for years.

'You're right there, Edna. They say there's a ship from Swansea listing badly near Godrevy Point too,' Archie said. 'Who'd be a sailor in such weather? They'll be calling out the lifeboat soon, along with anybody with a knowledge of the coast around there. There'll be plenty of looters out and about, salvaging what they can if the ship breaks up and discharges its cargo.'

'They're no better than thieves, and if there's drink aboard it'll be worse,' Edna said disapprovingly. 'But never mind that. Is there somebody shouting outside?'

There was a loud banging on the door. Archie opened it and hauled a bedraggled urchin inside. He looked around, wild eyed, wiping his sleeve across his nose until he caught sight of Carrie, busily knitting a matinée coat for Velma's baby.

'It's one of the boys from Tinners' Row, isn't it?' Edna said sharply. 'What's your mother doing, letting you out on such a night?'

'I've a message for you, missus,' the boy gasped, looking straight at Carrie. 'Mrs Gould says can you come quick, because her time's come.'

'Typical!' Archie said.

Carrie was already pushing her arms into her coat. 'You can't tell babies when to be born, and I promised I'd be there.'

'I'll walk with you then,' he said roughly. 'It's no night even for a cat to be out and about. Come on, young 'un.'

'Take your knitting with you, Carrie,' Edna called after them. 'It's likely to be a long night. And don't be long, Archie, please.'

'I just hope the midwife's there,' Carrie said, gasping through chattering teeth as she went out of the house and immediately bent double in the force of the gale.

'She is, missus,' the boy shouted. 'Me mother sent for her an hour ago.'

'Stan should be home at a time like this,' Archie bellowed. 'I don't know what Velma thinks you can do.'

'I'm going to be her friend,' Carrie said, but the

310

wind took her voice away, and nobody noticed the words.

Once they reached Tinners' Row, the boy ran into his own house, and Carrie hugged Archie's arm.

'Go home, love, and be with Mum. You know how she hates a storm. I'll be home when this is all over, so tell my boss where I am if I don't turn up for work tomorrow. There's no knowing how long this baby will take to be born.'

She pressed a kiss on his cold cheek and rushed into Velma's cottage, trying not to betray how very nervous she felt. If this was a new experience for Velma, it was for her, too, and she prayed that she wouldn't let her down.

Velma was leaning over the kitchen sink, furiously scrubbing at the already pristine draining board as if her life depended on it. She gave Carrie a weak smile.

'Don't worry, I'm not going daft in my old age. Mrs Drinkwater said it's best to keep busy as this could go on for hours yet.'

'Where is she? Young Eddie said she was here.'

'Gone to make her family's supper. She knows what she's doing, Carrie, and we just have to sit it out.'

'Shouldn't you be in bed? And where's the doctor?'

She didn't want to say so, but Velma was hardly in the first flush of youth to be having a baby. And if anything happened suddenly, she thought in panic, she certainly didn't want to be here alone with somebody giving birth.

'I doubt that the doctor will be here tonight. He'll

have gone to Godrevy Point in case of emergencies.' As she smiled, she was instantly the old Velma again, and Carrie breathed a sigh of relief. Nothing was going to happen for hours yet, and Mrs Drinkwater wouldn't take all night to prepare a meal for her family.

'It's coming early then, like the doctor said.'

Velma nodded, and there was an undeniable look of excitement in her eyes now. 'So when it does, I want you to send a telegram to Stan and let him know. He'll get his compassionate leave then and he'll be home for two weeks. There was no sense in asking him to come any earlier and just wait about, was there?'

'I suppose not.'

Her voice was cut off as Velma gave a sudden cry and leaned over the sink, breathing heavily.

'Phew,' she said, when she could talk again. 'That was a fierce one. Look, let's go and sit in the living room and talk, and I'll get out my knitting. I see you've brought yours too. Very sensible.'

'You're being so brave about this, Velma.'

'No I'm not. I don't have much choice now, do I? The baby's not going to stay where he is for ever, and the sooner he's born, the sooner I shall get a good night's sleep without him lying so awkwardly.'

Oh yes, she was brave, thought Carrie. She thought so even more as the night went on, and the increasing and more frequent pains Velma endured were matched by the roar and clatter of the storm and the lashing rain on the windows of the cottage. Mrs Drinkwater had popped back and examined her patient, then gone away again, saying she was doing nicely, and she would be back again in a couple of hours and be prepared to stay the night.

'Doing nicely, am I?' Velma said through clenched teeth. 'I just hope Master Gould is going to be worth it, that's all.'

'You're sure it'll be a boy then?' Carrie said from the chair in the bedroom where Velma was now prowling around. 'Have you got a name for him?'

'Jack, after my father. And Stanley, after Stan. In that order,' she ground out, as if anybody was going to argue with it.

Carrie tried to concentrate on her knitting, but by the time midnight had come and gone her hands were shaking so much she thought this matinée coat was going to be a mass of dropped stitches if she wasn't careful. Surely this couldn't go on much longer. She offered up a silent prayer as she heard the midwife bustling about downstairs again, and when she was asked to put the kettle on the stove she fled thankfully.

'Doctor won't get here tonight,' she heard Mrs Drinkwater say cheerfully to Velma, 'they say there's quite a to do over at Godrevy Point now, with the ship breaking up fast on the rocks, and hordes of local folk flocking down there to see what can be done, and help themselves, too, if you follow me. But don't you worry. Me and the other little maid will see you through, my dear.'

Oh God, oh God, Carrie thought. *I can't do this. I don't want to do this.* She spilled water from the kitchen tap into the kettle and lit the stove with trembling hands. And then she heard Velma give a piercing scream. Her blood froze for a minute, then she heard Velma calling for her as the scream gave way to sobs.

As she heard Mrs Drinkwater telling Velma to bite on a towel, Carrie's jitters seemed to drain away, and she became incredibly calm. This was her friend, and she had promised to help her in whatever way she could. She ran back upstairs to where the midwife was wiping Velma's brow with a damp cloth.

'I'll do that,' she said. She couldn't deny that her heart was pounding, but the look of gratitude on Velma's face as she gripped her hand while she pressed the damp cloth to her forehead with the other was worth it all.

'We've got some way to go yet,' Mrs Drinkwater said, after another examination. 'Baby was eager to be born before his time, but now he seems to have decided to make us all wait awhile.'

'There's nothing wrong, is there?' Velma said weakly.

'Bless you, no, my dear. 'Tis a dry labour, that's all, but once you hold the babe in your arms, you'll forget all about the trouble bringing him into the world. They don't call it labour for nothing, you know.'

She laughed at her own joke, and told Carrie she might as well use that kettle to make them all a nice cup of tea while they waited for Baby Gould to be born.

'I don't want anything,' Velma muttered.

'You say that now, but you'll be glad of it when your

mouth gets as dry as dust from biting on that towel,' Mrs Drinkwater said with a chuckle.

Carrie could have throttled her for her cheerfulness, but she supposed it was better than having her worrying that the baby wasn't making his appearance yet. She made the tea and brought up the three cups, to find Velma yelling again.

'Is all this normal?' she whispered to the midwife.

'Lordy, yes, my dear. The louder she yells the less she'll be aware of the pain. I always encourage my mothers to make as much noise as they like, especially when the fathers are downstairs. It does them good to know what we women go through for their pleasure.'

Carrie didn't dare look at Velma. Remembering how Velma had described that wonderful night at the hotel with Stan when she had rediscovered her love for him, and remembering her own sensual delight with Archie, she was glad she didn't have the old-fashioned idea that lovemaking was merely for a man's pleasure.

Around four o'clock in the morning Mrs Drinkwater gave Velma permission to start pushing. By then she looked totally exhausted, but with a strength Carrie didn't know her friend possessed, she did as she was told, and at last they were rewarded by the sounds of a baby's first cry as Jack Stanley Gould slid away from his mother, to be met with a resounding smack on his little backside by the midwife.

'You've got a fine and lusty boy, my dear,' she said, just as Velma had known she would.

As the baby was quickly wrapped in a towel and

handed to his mother, there was a look on Velma's face that Carrie would never forget. It was beautiful and mystical at the same time, and she felt the most acute sense of envy at the sight of the baby's wizened little face and the tiny fingers plucking at the air.

'That'll be the doctor,' Mrs Drinkwater said briskly, as they heard a rapping on the door. 'Late as usual, but I daresay he's had his work cut out tonight.'

Carrie ran to let him in, and he too looked exhausted and grey faced. Once he had examined mother and baby and pronounced them both well, he congratulated Velma and gratefully accepted a cup of tea from the second pot that night.

'Was it a bad do over at Godrevy?' Mrs Drinkwater asked him.

'As bad as it could be. It was too rough for the lifeboat to be launched, though several mad-headed fools in small boats set out to try to rescue the crew. But the ship broke up on the rocks and the entire cargo was lost. There were a number of fatalities among the crew, and several of our own chaps who tried to help went down in the briny as well. No hope for any of them in those seas, of course.'

They learned later that one of them was David Trewint.

Chapter 18

The news of the local drownings plunged the whole of Penhallow and St Ives into mourning. David's death also affected Archie Pollard in a way that stunned Carrie. There had been a strong antagonism between them from schooldays, but in her mother's opinion it had been more of a love/hate relationship than Carrie had ever imagined.

'There's a very fine line between love and hate,' she informed Carrie sagely. 'Not that I mean love in any funny way, mind. But sometimes people who go on the way those two always did, forever baiting and taunting, rely on one another for a peculiar kind of friendship, and Archie will be discovering that now.'

'I don't know about that! But he's certainly started having nightmares again since that night, and I thought we'd seen the last of them,' Carrie said.

'There you are then; that's how it's showing itself. But he'll get over it, I'm sure; it's that poor young widow I'm sorry for.'

Considering how Edna had rarely had a good word to say about Gwen, Carrie supposed all that could be

317

forgotten now that she was bereaved in the eyes of the community. But it was a tragic way to attain respectability, and Gwen's grief was overwhelming. Carrie and Shirley rallied round, as always, but there was little they could say or do to make her believe that David hadn't gone out on that awful night with a kind of death-wish.

Velma sent flowers and a long letter of sympathy. She was unable to visit her as she was confined for her lying-in for two weeks, so she had to hear all the news from the others. The new baby was small and needed regular feeding, and three days after his birth Stan came home on two weeks' compassionate leave.

By then, Velma was in the midst of what the midwife cheerfully called the three-day blues.

'I felt like strangling her,' Carrie reported to Archie. 'She said it's quite natural for mothers to feel that way three days after the birth, and poor Stan looked completely bewildered. He's surprisingly domesticated, though; I suppose you have to be in the army, so apart from Mrs Drinkwater going in to see them twice a day, and a girl from the village coming in to cook the meals, Stan is seeing to everything else.'

'She won't want to be letting him go then,' Archie said.

Carrie started. She didn't remember telling Archie about Velma's problems, but it seemed he wasn't referring to any impending divorce, which to Carrie was surely impossible now.

'She won't want him going back to barracks and leaving her alone with the kid, will she?' he went on.

'She'll get used to having him around, especially if he's a dab hand with a duster. You always said Velma was house-proud but she'll want to get things done her way, and she won't want to waste her time brooding.'

'I hope not.'

'What's that supposed to mean?'

'Nothing, really, but I've been doing a bit of reading, and sometimes these baby blues, as Mrs Drinkwater calls them, can go on for much longer than three days, even for weeks or months.'

'Too much book reading is bad for you,' Archie said, 'and she'd better buck up her ideas with a kid to look after. This business with David will have depressed her too. Going through what he did, and then to be drowned in your own patch of sea trying to save a crew of bloody foreigners, makes you wonder, doesn't it?'

Carrie knew where his mood was heading. Any minute now he'd start ranting about anything and everything, and especially about the futility of going to church, because there was obviously nobody listening.

'We are going to the funeral, aren't we, Archie? Gwen will want us there.'

He oozed sarcasm. 'Oh, we'll do things right. We'll sit among the relatives she hasn't seen for years. They'll all be turning up out of the woodwork, all there at the send-off. We'll have a bunfight afterwards, then go our separate ways, and he'll be forgotten quickly enough.'

Carrie's mouth dropped open as he raged on. Then, to her horror, she saw the angry tears on his lashes, tears that he would never shed because they were unmanly. But she saw them, all the same. She touched his arm.

'We won't forget him, will we, Archie? Not his old friends.'

'Nor his enemies,' he retorted, turning on his heel and banging every door behind him on his way down to the garden shed.

'Leave him, Carrie,' Edna advised from the kitchen. 'He has to deal with it in his own way. We all have to do that when we lose somebody.'

It was almost the first time she had referred, even obscurely, to whatever way she had dealt with losing Walter.

'I'm going to see Velma,' Carrie said. 'I promised I'd sit with her today to give Stan a break.'

And she dearly wanted to know what decision Velma had come to about moving, hoping that thinking about it might have cheered her up. But Velma was listless and pale. She was allowed to sit out in a chair for a few hours a day now, and Jack slept peacefully in his crib beside her bed. They discussed Gwen for a while and agreed that she would get over this in time. Like Shirley, she was a survivor.

'Stan and I are going to stay together,' Velma finally said, in answer to Carrie's delicate enquiry. 'I know that will please you all.'

'You're not doing this for us, Velma,' Carrie protested.

'Sorry, that came out wrong. It will, though, won't it? Especially you, Carrie. You like everyone to be happy, don't you? Everything neat and tidy, and couples marching into the sunset together, as if we were all in some gigantic Noah's Ark.'

'I think that sounds a little mixed up! But what's wrong with wanting people to be happy? I would have thought that, of all people, you'd be happy now you've got your darling little son, and you and Stan have decided to make a go of it.'

Velma swallowed. 'I am, believe me. Or I would be, if I didn't feel so wretched all the time.'

'It will pass, Velma. The books all say so—'

'Oh, you and your bloody books!' she said, startling Carrie. 'Books don't know about feelings, do they? They can't describe the awful hollow in my stomach every time I pick my baby up to feed him, and he cries and cries and rejects me with that angry red face. They can't know how bloody undesirable it makes me feel when Stan gives him a bottle of gripe water and he manages to soothe him when I can't. You all thought I was going to sail through this, and I *can't*. I'm a bloody hopeless mother, Carrie, and that's the end of it.'

'You're a very stupid one if you don't tell Dr Tozer how you're feeling. I'm sure he can give you something to calm your nerves.'

Velma snapped back. 'Perhaps he can. But he's also said that Jack's a little underweight because he doesn't want to feed, and that we shouldn't travel with him for at least a month, so any hope of us waltzing off into the sunset just yet is out of the question. Stan will have to go back without us until we get the all-clear.'

'Just be glad you've *got* a husband.'

Velma looked at her silently.

'What's got into you, Carrie? You never used to be so catty.'

'Perhaps I'm just catching on to the way everyone else is acting around here. I came to keep you company, but I'm not doing a very good job, am I?'

'You are, as a matter of fact. And if you must know, I'm feeling horribly guilty about Gwen, because Stan and I have got our baby now, and the very night that he was born her David was drowned, and she's left with nothing.'

'You can hardly blame yourself for that! You know it's pointless guilt.'

'Tell that to Shirley over the way she felt with her troubles, and tell it to Gwen after David came home when she thought he was dead during the war. You can't dictate when or why you're going to feel guilt, Carrie. It just hits you, and when you're already feeling low, it adds to the enormity of it all.'

Stan came back when Velma was still drying her eyes after another bout of crying. It alarmed Carrie more than she admitted. Velma had always been so strong, yet now she seemed to be wallowing in self-pity.

'It's good to see you, Carrie. She needs female company from time to time.'

'She can still hear,' Velma snapped. 'She's not deaf as well as stupid.'

'She's contrary, too,' he continued with a smile. 'But at least we agree on one thing. That boy of ours needs a family, so we'll be moving to Salisbury as soon as the doctor says he's able to travel.'

'Providing I don't change my mind.' Velma said at once.

'You won't,' Stan said pleasantly. 'If I have to take you kicking and screaming, you and Jack are coming to live with me, my girl, like a good wife and mother should.'

'I couldn't believe the way they were carrying on,' Carrie reported to Gwen, on her next mission. 'I mean, we've always thought Stan was a bit stiff and starchy, and they've always put on this great air of politeness, but I swear they were all set to go at it hammer and tongs after I left, more like Archie and me!'

'Is that good?' Gwen said tiredly, her tone of voice implying that she couldn't care less what other couples got up to, since she wasn't part of a couple anymore.

'Well, at least it's normal! And I've got a message for you, Gwen. The doctor has forbidden Velma to go to the funeral, but Stan says he'd be truly honoured if you would allow him to escort you. That was his posh self talking, of course, but I know he meant it sincerely.'

Gwen flushed. 'If he really means it, it would be nice of him,' she said finally. 'Neighbours and relatives are already smothering me, and I feel as if I've suddenly turned into Joan of Arc instead of the bad girl of the village. On the day, you'll have Archie, and Shirley will have Bernard, so I'll be very glad to accept Stan's offer.'

'Good. I'll pop back and tell him if you like.'

Gwen took a deep breath. 'No. I'll do it myself. I have to get out of this house sometime, Carrie, and I haven't even seen the baby yet. David – David and I had bought him a silver spoon in readiness for the christening. I'll take it now.'

'She was far more dignified than I expected her to be,' Carrie told her mother as they did the washing-up that evening. 'I did admire her when she accepted Stan Gould's offer so graciously.'

'I always did say that girl had a strong backbone,' Edna agreed, having never said anything of the sort. 'And what about Velma? How is she coping with being a new mother?'

'Slowly. She finds it hard to understand why the baby won't take his feed, and Mrs Drinkwater says she may have to resort to the bottle, which Velma thinks is a failure on her part.'

Edna snorted in a fair imitation of Archie. 'Would she rather the child starved? I think I should look in on her myself and give her a bit of advice.'

'Oh, I don't think that's a good idea!'

'Why not? She doesn't have a mother of her own to turn to, does she? Besides, I'd like to take a look at the baby too. I'll go this evening now the rain's cleared up. They say we're going to be in for an early spring after those awful storms. We all know those weather forecasters are a useless bunch and don't often get it right, but let's hope they do this time. A bit of sun will cheer us all up.'

Carrie felt limp after Edna left the house with her hat rammed firmly on her head and a determined look in her eyes. Archie had disappeared behind the pages of the newspaper all this time, but once the front door had closed behind Edna he looked up with a chuckle.

'Poor Velma. She doesn't know what she's in for when your mother gets her teeth into something.'

'She means well, though. I have to admit that about Mum. She always means well, even if she goes about it badly sometimes. But you never know, she might just say the right thing to Velma to shake her out of her black mood. I couldn't do it.'

'You haven't had kids of your own, that's why,' Archie said without expression. 'Edna will soon put her right.'

Carrie caught her breath. He so rarely spoke of the future these days, and he presumably still had the nonsensical idea that it wasn't a fit world to bring children into. Gwen never would now, not with David, anyway. But Velma had done it.

'I hope I will, one day,' she ventured. 'Even though it's not going to be in a prefab. Now that they're getting on with the building again, I'm beginning to agree with you that they do look a bit of an eyesore, and I'm glad I sacrificed our place to Shirley.'

'Bloody hell, it wasn't a religious offering, Carrie.'

'I know. It was just a dream that didn't come to anything, that's all.'

She turned away so that he wouldn't see the shine of tears in her eyes. She had truly abandoned that dream with few regrets now, but not the other one. From the moment she had seen that special look in Velma's eyes when she held her baby for the first time, and then experienced that other magical moment when she was allowed to hold him too, she knew what she wanted more than anything else.

'Did I tell you Stan is escorting Gwen to the funeral?' she said next, since Archie was still looking at her warily.

'Yes, and we'll be there as well,' he repeated.

'Of course. It's important for Gwen to have all her friends around her.'

Instinct told her it was important to Archie, too. Her mother had been right. There had been a strong bond between him and David, and even if it hadn't been the kind of closeness that friends or lovers shared, it was still a bond.

'And when the baby's stronger and Velma's feeling well again they're all moving to Salisbury,' she said. 'I'm glad it's not too soon, for Gwen's sake.'

'She'll get over it,' Archie said, reverting to type. 'And I'm not being callous. You have to get over things, don't you? She's lucky to have good friends like you, and Shirley too. Velma's not the only friend she's got.'

David had been her only husband though.

As if to underline Edna's prediction the weather turned warmer by the end of March, and the day of David Trewint's funeral was calm and fragrant, with early spring growth already bursting through on trees and hedgerows, and the scent of fresh young grass was sweet on the air.

Supported by Stan Gould, Gwen looked dignified, slim and beautiful in black, and managed to stem her tears until everyone gathered at the graveside. Back at her cottage, where neighbours opened the door to the mourners, friends and relations gathered for tea and biscuits, and Carrie was touched when Archie told Gwen how much he admired her that day.

She gave a small nod. 'I know David would want me to be strong,' she said simply. 'And you know, in some strange way I feel as if I've been here before. I mourned him so much when his ship was torpedoed, and I went slightly crazy then. So I keep telling myself that these last months we had were a bonus. God sent him back to me and gave us a second chance, and I cherish the memories we made when he came home again.'

'He's never going to send him back to her this time though, is He?' Archie muttered as he and Carrie moved around the crowded little cottage.

'Shush, Archie, please.'

She was full of admiration for Gwen too. If anything, it was Shirley who had disgraced herself by weeping copiously in the church, but then Shirley could always shed crocodile tears whenever they were needed. Carrie bit her lip, knowing that was unworthy. They were all upset over what had happened to David, and it was still difficult to think rationally, when both he and Gwen had gone through so much trauma during the war – and then to have this disaster happen.

She looked across at her friend, chatting quietly with one of David's cousins now, and thought how graceful she was, and how well she was holding up. Tears would come later when she was alone. There was no doubt in Carrie's mind that there would be no repetition of the way Gwen had behaved when David was missing during the war. There would be no wildness, no going almost insane with grief and turning to reckless affairs for some kind of comfort. Gwen would cope, and if at some future date she found someone else to fill her life, Carrie knew with certainty that it would be someone she could love for a lifetime, and not for the moment.

She caught Gwen's glance at that moment, and in the imperceptible smiles that passed between them she could almost believe that Gwen knew exactly what she was thinking, and accepted it.

'How soon can we get out of here?' she heard Archie say roughly. 'The atmosphere is stifling, and I can't abide all these photos of David everywhere.'

'It's Gwen's way of keeping him alive a little bit longer, and reminding everyone of the happy times they shared,' she said disapprovingly.

She conceded that it was a bit much, though. Every surface was covered with snapshots or framed photographs, some of David alone, smiling and full of life, some in his naval uniform of which he had been so proud, even a school photo in which Archie sat next to David, their arms folded as they glared at the camera. There were photos of him and Gwen together, and in pride of place was their wedding photo. Yes, Carrie admitted, it did add to the claustrophobic feeling in the small cottage.

'We can slip away soon, if you like,' she went on. 'I think Stan will stay for a while, so shall we go and see Velma and tell her how it went?'

He groaned, but the thought of getting out into the fresh air overcame his reluctance at being obliged to bill and coo over a new baby. Though that was the last thing anyone would expect him to do, Carrie told him with a giggle. Men weren't supposed to be interested in babies even if Stan had no objection to giving baby Jack his bottle in the middle of the night now that the doctor had advised Velma to give him some bottle feeds instead of continually trying to feed him herself. Just as Edna had said, too, Carrie thought. Sometimes her mother did have some bright ideas.

Velma was looking decidedly better than the last time Carrie had seen her. The baby was still tightly wrapped in a shawl in his crib in the living room, but he had begun to fill out now, and looked less like a wrinkled old man than on the day he was born.

'Nice little chap,' Archie said, keeping well away.

'He won't bite, Archie,' Velma said with a smile. 'You can pick him up if you like. He's about due for a feed.'

'God, no! I mean, no thanks. If you're busy we won't stay—'

Velma laughed, managing to look more animated than of late.

'Don't get embarrassed. He's on the bottle most

times now. I'll just go and heat it up and then we'll get him out and you can see him properly. Actually, Carrie, you can wake him up if you want to hold him.'

Carrie didn't need to be asked twice. As she released him from the confining shawl Jack stirred, stretched, yawned and blinked his blue eyes as he opaquely registered his surroundings.

'Isn't he gorgeous?' Carrie said, breathing in the sleepy scent of him.

'He's very nice,' Archie repeated.

Velma came back a few minutes later and handed the bottle to Carrie. 'Here you are, sweetie, you can get your hand in for when it's your turn.'

Then her face shadowed. 'I haven't been able to stop thinking of you all today, and I don't expect Stan home for ages, so tell me how it went.'

'Pretty much as you'd expect,' Archie said.

Carrie elaborated. 'It was very dignified, and there were lots of people you wouldn't have expected, like the lifeboatmen, and David's workmates, and a few of his naval pals, though I don't know how they got to hear of it. There was family from both sides, and village folk, and Shirley cried a lot, of course, but Gwen was a real brick, and Stan was so good with her, Velma.'

'I knew he would be,' she said softly, watching as the baby sucked and tugged at the teat on the bottle Carrie was holding for him. 'I wish he could stay home longer than two weeks, but that's the army for you. There might not be a war on, but regulars still have to do as they're told.'

'Don't you ever think of asking him to give it up?' Archie said.

Velma looked genuinely astonished. 'Of course not. It's his life.'

'Not much life for you, is it? Especially now, with a baby to look after. I suppose he bawls all night, and if he's not throwing up at one end, he's doing unmentionable things at the other.'

Velma gave a small laugh. 'Good Lord, Archie, you're so knowledgeable that if I didn't know you better I'd say you were starting to get broody! You'd better hold Jack for a minute when Carrie's finished feeding him, and see how it feels.'

'I don't think I'll go that far, thanks very much,' he said hastily. 'And we'd better be getting back soon, Carrie.'

There was no special reason why they should, but she relinquished Jack to his mother reluctantly, and they stepped out into the hazy spring sunshine. Threading her arm through Archie's, she thought again how lucky they were. They were both healthy and they had each other. Whatever happened to other people, they had the strongest ties to bind them.

'I suppose you'll be wanting one now,' he said suddenly.

'One what?' she said, diverted from her own thoughts.

'A kid. A sprog. I didn't miss the way you got all maternal over Velma's kid.'

She spoke carefully. Perhaps she wasn't the only one to have felt a tug of something quite primitive in that beautifully domestic little household, she thought. In her case, it wasn't so unexpected, but she had never thought Archie might experience the same sense of wonder that she had.

'Of course I want a baby, one day when the time is right. I thought we'd both agreed that it wasn't sensible to start a family straight away.'

She certainly hadn't agreed anything of the sort, but she was learning fast that there were more subtle ways of getting what you wanted. If Archie chose to believe it had been a joint decision, and now he was wavering, so much the better.

'Those two didn't wait for any right time, did they? And it would make you give up work and start looking after your old man properly. We wouldn't want a baby while we're living at your mother's, though. She'd smother it from the start, and it would end up being more her kid than ours.'

'Well, if you hadn't scuppered the idea of the prefab, we'd have been moving in there in June, wouldn't we?' she couldn't help saying. 'Shirley's been told they'll be ready then, and they can move in right after the wedding.'

And although she had truly changed her mind completely over the prefabs, she could still feel a pang at the thought of the two of them losing the chance to be on their own, without Edna forever at their shoulders and dictating what they should do. The hell of it was that she had a perfect right to. It was her house.

'I might have known you'd harp on about that eventually.'

She realized he had unlinked their arms and was striding ahead. In seconds, it seemed, his mood had changed as it so often did. She rushed up behind him and yanked his arm back.

'I am not harping on about it,' she snapped. 'I do not want a prefab and I now think they're hideous if you want to know. I think the council made a great mistake in building them here at all. Is that what you want to hear?'

'Yes, if you mean it.'

'When do I say anything I don't mean? I've always been honest with you, Archie. I don't keep secrets from you.'

Except for Gwen's secret past, and the fact that Velma had once been determined to ask Stan for a divorce, and the worst-of-all secret they had all shared, that even now made Shirley's stomach turn somersaults every time she read in the newspaper about the plans for the GIs reunion around D-Day. They were coming to England for two whole weeks, to take in the 6th of June – and Shirley and Bernard's wedding day was arranged for Saturday the 15th of June.

'I can be a right bastard sometimes, can't I, sweet-heart? Archie said contritely, 'and you don't deserve it.'

He put his arm around her and kissed her quickly, regardless of anyone watching them in the street, and she was thankful he couldn't read her thoughts.

'Stop it,' she giggled. 'I don't know which is worse, having you ranting at me, or coming over all soppy.'

But she did, of course. She knew which was best, too.

A few days later, Edna waved a letter at them.

'I've invited your aunt Phyllis to come and stay for Easter,' she told them. 'I think she gets a bit fed up with that shoe-box she calls her flat, and she's lonely too. Seeing us all after your dad's passing, and then having me to stay with her, has made her miss not having family of her own. Anyway, she says she's coming.'

Archie grinned. 'Blimey, duchess, where's she going to sleep? You won't want her sharing your bed, will you? I wouldn't dare to make any rude comments about Auntie's size, but I shouldn't think there'd be much room if you did—'

'Don't be coarse, Archie. We've already discussed that, and of course we don't want to share my bedroom. We only use the front room at Christmas – apart from giving it a good clean and polish once a week – and Phyllis says she'll be quite comfortable sleeping on a camp bed in there. So it's settled.'

'I think it's a lovely idea, and it'll be nice for the two of you to get together again. How long do you think she'll stay?' Carrie said.

Her voice was calm, but there were thoughts going topsy-turvy in her head as a great idea started simmering.

'A week, I hope, or even more. We plan to do some walking if the weather's fine. When we were girls we often used to cycle to St Ives or Penzance for the day, much like your poor friend Gwen and her hubby used to do.'

'We could always get you a couple of bikes then, old girl, or even a tandem,' Archie offered with a chuckle. 'I can just see the two of you now, wobbling your way into Penzance like on one of those seaside post-cards—'

He was still laughing, and Carrie had a job to hold her face together as Edna stalked out of the living room and into the kitchen, telling him stiffly that she'd speak to him again when he had something sensible to say and could manage not to be so insulting.

'You've gone too far this time, Archie,' Carrie told him.

'No I haven't. She enjoys it, really. But I'd like to know why you got all excited when she was going on about Aunt Phyllis coming to stay.'

She laughed. 'I think I was having one of those future moments.'

'Oh yes. Like I was, imagining the pair of them on a bicycle made for two, I suppose?' He was indulgent, still in a good humour at his own jokes.

She lowered her voice so that Edna wouldn't hear. 'No, silly. I was just thinking that if they like each other's company so much, wouldn't it be perfect if they decided to move in together permanently? Mum wouldn't be dependent on us for company, and there would be nothing to stop us finding a place of our own then. In fact, we'd have to, wouldn't we? We couldn't confine Aunt Phyllis to sleeping on a camp bed in the front room for ever more!'

It seemed such a perfect solution it was almost dazzling, and she realized that Archie was still laughing as he swung her around the room.

'Sometimes, Mrs Pollard,' he said, kissing the tip of her nose between every syllable, 'I think I've married a prize schemer.'

You don't know the half of it, thought Carrie.

Chapter 19

Thursday evenings had undergone a radical change as far as the cosy get-togethers of old were concerned. Velma was busy with Jack, Shirley was too wrapped up in her forthcoming wedding preparations and spending all her evenings with Bernard. And Gwen simply refused to go to the village hall, where the older ladies of the town offered her sympathy that she either didn't want or couldn't take, and where she felt totally removed from the lives of her friends.

'I've got to work through this in my own way,' she told Carrie when she called on her one Saturday afternoon. 'You coped when you heard that Archie had been taken prisoner. We know how Shirley went to pieces after Bernard was wounded in France, but she coped too, even after all the GI business—'

'Yes, with our help! You don't have to go through this alone, Gwen.'

'I *am* alone,' she said simply. 'Don't you see? The rest of you all had hope. Velma was in a different position from you and Shirley and me, but she had a purpose in mind, and things have turned out well for her now. I don't have any more hope. David's dead and he's never coming back. And don't give me that stuff about meeting him again in an afterlife, because I'm not sure I believe in it anymore.'

At the shocked look on Carrie's face, she shrugged her shoulders and wilted a little. 'Oh, all right, of course I still believe in it. I'm just talking rubbish because I'm angry at David for dying, and I'm grief-stricken too. Just don't expect me to be the same old Gwen I was before, that's all.'

'So you're definitely not coming out on Thursday night?'

'I can't. I'll let you know when – and if – I feel like it again. What I'd really like everybody to do is to leave me alone to deal with this in my own way.'

'It wasn't exactly a snub, though it felt like it,' Carrie told Velma.

She began to feel like a social visitor doing the rounds on Saturday afternoons. Next stop would be Shirley's, to hear her effervescing over the wedding dress her mother was making for her.

'You can understand her, though,' Velma said. 'We can't pretend that nothing's happened, and Gwen has to give herself time to get over this.'

'I know. But how are *you*? You're looking much better, and Jack's putting on weight. He's quite a little butterball now, isn't he?'

'He's fine, and I'm well enough, but Carrie, I've been meaning to tell you something. I know it will upset Shirley, but we're not going to be around for her wedding. We're moving to Salisbury at the end of May. Stan's got some leave then, so he'll be here to help us pack up everything, and get us settled in our new home.'

At her words, Carrie felt an enormous pang at the thought of losing the friendship they had shared for so long. She couldn't begrudge Velma the chance of a new life, but she would miss her terribly. Everything was changing . . .

'I hardly know what to say,' she murmured. 'I'm glad for you, of course—'

The vehement response shook her. 'Say you'll miss me! Say you don't want me to go! Say you know how much I'm going to miss you and all my friends, and my beloved Cornwall. Say you know how I'll miss this cottage where I've lived all my life, and how I can't bear the thought of strangers living here. And then be my very, *very* best friend, and say you know I've made absolutely the right decision.'

It was such an unexpected outburst that after they had stared at one another in astonishment for a few seconds, they both burst out laughing, and then they were hugging each other amid tears and laughter.

'How soppy we are! But we'll have to arrange a farewell evening for you, Velma,' Carrie managed to say at last. 'We're not letting you go without a proper send-off when the time comes.'

'Perhaps,' Velma choked, unable to think of any such thing right now, especially as Jack had started bellowing again as if in total accord with the wailing noises inside his little world.

The baby demanded all the attention then, and although there was something else very much on Carrie's mind, Velma was still in such a strange mood, veering between joy and uncertainty, that she knew this was not the best time to bring it up. There was no immediate hurry, anyway. Not until the end of May. If ever.

'Oh, Carrie, you must come up to my bedroom and see how Mum's getting on with my dress,' Shirley said excitedly, the minute she opened the door. 'She's such a wizard at dressmaking, and the material is gorgeous – and the bridesmaid dresses too. Bernard asked his brothers to be pages, but they said nobody was getting them to dress up like little Lord Fauntleroy – and they refuse to walk down the aisle with the bridesmaids, too – so they're going to be ushers, can you believe!'

Carrie hid a smile. That was Shirley, flitting from one topic to the next, and selfish to the last, but so artless at the same time that people always forgave her. No wonder Hank had adored her for that sweet, brief summer spell.

Her heart gave a lurch, wishing his name had never occurred to her, even subconsciously. Shirley was so caught up in wedding arrangements now, that Carrie had assumed, and hoped, that it was all truly in the past. She discovered a little while later how wrong she was.

She had duly admired the soft folds of the half-finished, figured satin wedding dress, and assured Shirley that she would look beautiful, and that her sisters would look pretty in their lilac-coloured dresses too. She had listened to the excited babble of how much she and Bernard were looking forward to moving into their prefab and how she felt able to say it now, knowing that it wasn't going to upset Carrie too much . . . when her face crumpled.

'You know why I'm going on like this, don't you?' she almost wept. 'I can hear myself, getting as wound up as a spring, and I can't seem to stop. I just want to keep busy, busy, busy. I don't *want* to stop, because if I do I'll start thinking again, and I don't want to think about you know what—'

'For God's sake, Shirley, stop it!' Carrie said, appalled at this tirade.

She was starting to feel quite limp after witnessing Gwen's distress and then hearing Velma's news, and now this. In the pages of women's magazines, troubled girls wrote to elderly agony aunts with their problems, didn't they? Carrie was beginning to feel like an agony aunt herself, and it wasn't a role that she wanted, thank you very much. On the other hand, you didn't turn your back on your friends.

'If you've read the papers properly you'll know that the Americans will be leaving Penzance three days before your wedding. And even if they weren't, they won't be coming here to Penhallow, and there's nothing to connect you with them, unless you go on like this and make it obvious! You've got to put it all behind you, Shirley.'

'I know, and I will – I *have*. But the thought of this reunion they're making so much of brought it all back again, and when things are going so well, you always look over your shoulder and wonder what can go wrong, don't you?'

'Do you?' Carrie said, starting to smile because her friend looked so forlorn, and all of twelve years old with no make-up and her hair scraped back in a ponytail.

'I know I'm being silly, but every girl wants her wedding day to be perfect.'

'Yours will be, and you'll be the prettiest bride of the year.'

And please don't mention the wedding night, Carrie thought. I really don't want to talk about any more personal problems right now.

'Oh, and I might as well tell you a bit of news, Shirley. Velma won't be able to come. She and Stan are moving to Salisbury at the end of May.'

Shirley screeched at once. 'Oh *no*! I know we decided not to have matrons of honour, but after all we've been through together I need you all to be there! And then there's Gwen – oh Lord, what about Gwen? Will she be all right without David, do you think? I *told* you something would go wrong, didn't I?'

Carrie's patience finally ran out.

'You're being completely ridiculous, Shirley, and I'm not going to stay here and listen to your selfishness a minute longer. Velma and Stan have got their own lives to lead, and it's up to Gwen to decide how she feels at the time. You don't *need* us, and we can't be your nursemaids for ever.'

'Is that what you all think of me, then? I suppose *you'll* be coming, will you?'

'I wouldn't miss it for the world,' Carrie said drily. 'The sooner you and Bernard walk down that aisle, the easier I shall breathe.'

By the time she left Shirley's house her nerves were in shreds and she was in a rage. She had seen each of her three best friends today, and had come away from them all feeling disquieted and out of sorts with herself, and now that disquiet had taken the form of fury.

There was only one place to be when she felt like this, otherwise she would end up taking it out on everyone around her, which meant Archie and her mother. And they didn't deserve it.

It was a fine and pleasantly balmy afternoon, and before she had time to change her mind, she struck out for the open moors, keeping her head down so that she didn't have to talk to anyone she met, and she didn't stop for a breather until she had left Penhallow far behind.

The grass still held the dampness of early spring, and she had no wish to sit on it in her cotton dress and risk a chill. But she needed to breathe deeply and think, and she perched on the crumbling wall of an old mine, feeling the warmth in the stones reflected from the tall chimney behind her. Away in the distance she could see the shimmering sea beyond the quaintly tumbling town of St Ives. The bracken whispered all around her, reminding her that this was her special place for unwinding, absorbing the history of all those who had worked, slaved and died here. Such ghosts held no terror for a born and bred Cornish woman, and she gradually began to feel the release of tension.

'What a fool I am,' she said out loud to the sighing breeze. 'None of these problems are mine, and I shouldn't take them all on my shoulders, should I?'

She felt no strangeness in asking questions of the breeze, any more than she felt strange talking to her father in the churchyard. There were no answering echoes there, nor here, no disembodied voices to startle her, and somehow she was calmed by the silence.

Shirley, of course, would say it was her Cornish sixth sense that was guiding her to the place where she felt the most tranquillity. And for once, Shirley was undoubtedly right, Carrie thought with a wry grin, admitting that she had probably been a bit hard on her after all.

Suddenly out of the corner of her eye she caught the flash of a pink dress and blond hair. Her heart lurched for the second time that day. If she had somehow conjured Shirley up out of her imagination, she wanted nothing more to do with a sixth sense!

'I knew I'd find you here,' Shirley said, puffing hard, and no apparition, but very real. She flopped down on the grass, damp or not, while she caught her breath. 'I know I've upset you in some way, and I wanted to say I'm sorry, Carrie. You're right, too. I am selfish, always thinking of myself, even putting a damper on Bernard's suggestion about inviting his French friends to the wedding. They're not coming, anyway, but they've written to wish us every happiness.'

She couldn't help the small hint of satisfaction in her voice when she said it, but she still looked so young and so anxious to make amends with her friend that Carrie smothered a small sigh and forgave her, just as they all did.

'We're all feeling pretty tense at the moment, but you've got plenty to look forward to, and that's what you should be doing.'

'I will, I promise. And there was something I was going to ask you. Bernard will ask Archie himself, of course, but I wanted to know what you think. I mean, they've never been the closest of friends, have they? I always thought Archie looked down on Bernard a bit, if you really want to know.'

'Of course he doesn't!' Archie's actual words were that he thought Bernard a bit of a fairy because he taught music and drama to the infants, but Carrie wasn't going to tell Shirley that. It wasn't true, anyway. He had a real skill with the children.

'Bernard's thinking of asking Archie to be his best man. What do you think?'

That took Carrie by surprise. Archie was the last person she'd have thought Bernard wanted for his best man. It would mean that Archie would have to give a speech at the reception, and she couldn't guarantee the propriety of his jokes.

'It's because we're all such friends, Carrie,' Shirley went on hastily, 'and it would be so nice for us all to have this between us as well, wouldn't it? We don't know Stan Gould very well, and anyway, he and Velma won't be around on the day now, will they? David's gone, and Bernard wouldn't have asked him, anyway. But you and Archie, well, we can always rely on you, and it would put the seal on our friendship somehow. Please sound him out. It's important to me.'

Carrie always felt much older when she was talking to Shirley. There wasn't even two years between them, but Shirley still had that little-girl-lost look that could aggravate at times, and be overwhelmingly sweet at others. She was appealing now.

'Of course I'll pre-warn him that Bernard's going to ask him, and I'm sure he'll be honoured, Shirley.'

And if he wasn't, she'd darned well see to it that he accepted graciously.

To her surprise, Archie took it as a solemn duty, saying it would give him a chance to give his best suit an airing again.

'You'd be wearing it anyway, and Archie, you will be careful what you say, won't you? No barrack-room jokes, mind.'

He laughed. 'I'll be on my best behaviour, don't worry. I'm no good at speeches, though, so you can write it for me, if you like, being more of a book-learning person than I am.'

He also seemed mildly flattered that a studious fellow like Bernard Bosinney would ask him to be his best man. But it was good that they were keeping up the ties of friendship that had begun during the war years, thought Carrie. In her mind, she had supposed that the expanded friendship she and her women friends had begun would go on for ever. Their menfolk had been sent to various parts of the world, and had thankfully come back reasonably unscathed. It hadn't seemed such a foolish or unlikely dream for the friendship to continue, and it seemed sad that in peacetime their numbers were diminishing.

So when Bernard put the question of being his best man to Archie, Carrie was relieved to hear her husband answer graciously enough, shaking Bernard's hand as if they were long-lost friends. They never had been close friends, even as children, so this was a generous gesture on Bernard's part. It would also let everyone know that the wartime friendship of the women had extended to their menfolk. A small village like Penhallow was always rife with gossip, sometimes good-natured, sometimes bad, and anything positive was to be encouraged, Carrie thought keenly – especially towards Gwen.

But that was something she didn't want to think about. Gwen wasn't exactly a heroine in the town now, but she was treated with sympathy and compassion after losing David in such a tragic way.

'He was a hero, of course,' Gwen had remarked without bitterness to Carrie. 'He didn't hesitate in going out to rescue those men on the stricken ship. Being a seaman himself, it would have been in his nature. He knew just how it felt to be at the mercy of the sea. He was definitely a hero that night.'

Her eyes dared anyone, even her closest friends, to make the slightest hint that there might have been another reason why David Trewint preferred to risk his life during that terrible storm than to believe any gossip about his beloved wife.

*

Carrie had more personal things to think about in the next few weeks. Her mother was turning the Easter visit of her sister into the event of the year. The house had to have a complete spring-clean: rugs were shaken to within an inch of their lives; pictures and ornaments taken down and dusted throughly; surfaces polished until they shone like glass; kitchen drawers relined with paper; the bathroom virtually given a major overhaul; every piece of china washed and carefully replaced on the dresser. The front room eventually resembled a shrine, with Phyllis's camp bed covered in a chintz bedcover as the altar and a small bedside table with a lamp at the ready.

'Anything more and you'd think we were welcoming the bloody king and queen,' Archie finally exploded, when he was ordered not to come indoors from the garden until he had changed his shoes, and to wash his hands thoroughly before he dared to touch anything.

'Language, Archie,' Edna said in a steely voice. 'I hope you're not going to let me down when Phyllis arrives.'

'For God's sake, woman, she's only your sister. Hasn't she seen you in your curlers and nightdress before this?'

'That's as may be. I want everything to be as nice as possible for her. Don't forget she's been living on her own for a long time since her hubby died, and it'll be a change for her to live in a proper family home, even for a week.'

'If you make it too nice for her, she'll want to stay longer,' Archie said slyly.

'She may even want to stay for good!' Carrie added.

Edna sniffed. 'I doubt that, but if she wants to stay longer than a week, I daresay we could manage. She'll bring her coupons, of course, and they do say that the bigger the family, the easier it is to stretch the rations.'

Carrie didn't dare look at Archie. How long this blessed rationing was going to go on nobody knew, but since the government had seen fit to cut rations even more in February, Edna had done her share of grumbling about making ends meet.

Carrie was really looking forward to this visit of her aunt. The two sisters were alike in many ways, except one. Phyllis was far more easygoing and placid than her sister, and Carrie had every hope that some of it would rub off on Edna. Having Phyllis in the house would make life easier for all of them, and if she could be persuaded to extend her visit, or to come more often, and even to consider moving in permanently . . .

But that was something that was only in hers and Archie's dreams for now, and she knew better than to try to push it into Edna's. The best way to handle her mother had always been to make her think the idea came from herself – or from Phyllis.

'What's that soppy grin on your face for?' Edna said crossly now. 'Sometimes, Carrie, I swear you spend more time daydreaming than anything else. There's still the garden to tidy up, so why don't you and Archie go and do it, instead of cluttering up the place?'

'I think we've been dismissed,' Carrie said with a

giggle to Archie as they were bundled outside. 'I'll be glad when Aunt Phyllis is finally here, then maybe we can all relax.'

'She'll be good for your mother,' he agreed, 'and once they go off on their walking jaunts, we can have the place to ourselves.'

He glanced back at the house, caught sight of Edna watching them through the kitchen window, and waved before pulling Carrie close and kissing her soundly.

'Stop it, for goodness' sake, you'll give her palpitations,' she said, laughing.

'Why shouldn't I kiss my wife? I've got a licence, haven't I?' he bragged, a wicked gleam in his eyes, but he let her go and gave Edna a theatrical bow.

He could be outrageous at times, thought Carrie, but he thrilled her all the same. And if things turned out the way they wanted, there would no longer be any need to feel awkward at snatched kisses, or joyously creaking bed-springs, because there would be nobody but themselves to relish them.

'I do love you, Archie.'

'I should just hope you do,' he said enthusiastically, and kissed her again, ignoring the accompanying tapping on the kitchen window.

Phyllis arrived without any ceremony, and slipped into the general routine of the house with her usual minimum of fuss. Compared with Edna's frantic activity of the last weeks, Carrie still marvelled that they were actually sisters at all. If opposites were supposed to attract, it was certainly true in the natures of the two women, who got along remarkably well. Edna even seemed to mellow a little with her sister's milder approach to everything, though she could be just as caustic when she chose.

They all attended church on Easter Sunday, including Archie. To Carrie's enormous surprise, Gwen put in an appearance as well, and she immediately invited her to sit with the family.

'It's really good to see you here, Gwen,' she said quietly.

'I didn't intend to come. I didn't even want to, but we always came to church at Easter, so it seemed wrong for me to turn my back on it now.'

She might have been speaking ambiguously, but for Carrie she didn't need to make it any plainer. Every couple had their own rituals. Christmas had been the beginning of the end as far as trust between Gwen and David was concerned, but Easter was a time of rebirth and renewal of faith, and Carrie could only hope that Gwen was seeing it that way now. It was as her mother said. Everyone had to come to terms with grief in their own way, and in their own time.

She squeezed her friend's hand, and was rewarded by a faint smile.

'Come home for Sunday dinner with us, Gwen,' she said impulsively. 'Archie brought us a nice piece of beef, and between them Mum and Aunt Phyllis have prepared enough vegetables to feed an army. Please say you will.'

The unspoken words were that it would be better

for Gwen than to go back to an empty house and eat alone, and to Carrie's relief she said yes. There was a limit to how long a young woman could brood alone and retain her sanity. And Gwen was not yet twenty-five years old; she had years of living ahead of her. Even grief must fade in time.

Thankfully, Edna had no objections at all. By now she was championing Gwen just as if she had never said a wrong word about her in her life, and Phyllis took to her at once. So it was a reasonably jolly party eating Sunday dinner that Easter day, and Carrie thought how good it was when everyone managed to enjoy each other's company.

'You know, I could really get to like it here,' Phyllis said with a smile, when they were all replete with food and drinking cups of tea.

'So you should, since you and Mum were born here! I always wondered why you never moved back to this part of Cornwall when you were on your own, Aunt Phyllis,' Carrie said casually.

'I've been telling her that for years,' Edna put in. 'Living all alone in that poky flat, when she could find a little place down here and be close to her family.'

'Even closer if we have our way,' Archie murmured in a stage whisper.

'What are you two muttering about now?' Edna said sharply. 'Don't you know it's rude to whisper in company?'

'Aunt Phyllis isn't company. She's family,' Carrie reminded her, and got another chuckle from Archie. 'And Gwen's one of my best friends.'

But enough was enough as far as Gwen was concerned. Her face was becoming strained after being in company for a couple of hours, and she thanked Edna for the dinner before going home.

'We need some fresh air, so we'll walk some of the way with you, and leave these two to talk over old times,' Carrie said.

Once outside, Gwen turned to her with a suspicious look.

'What are you two playing at? Don't think I don't know when you're up to something, Carrie. I know you too well, and Archie's winking wouldn't fool a cat.'

'I've never tried to fool a cat,' he said. 'How does it work, I wonder?'

'Shut up, Archie. Shall we tell her, do you think?'

'Well, we've got to now, haven't we?'

It was just teasing, but Carrie suddenly saw how their banter was upsetting Gwen. They were such a closely entwined couple, their thoughts matching so well, and it emphasized Gwen's loneliness and how lost she was without David. She spoke quickly.

'We're trying to put the idea into Mum's head – and Aunt Phyllis's too – that it would make sense for them to live together. Only we're trying not to make it too obvious. You know what my mum's like. If she thinks someone's trying to push her into doing something, she'll just get obstinate about it, even if it's what she really wants.'

'Is it what she really wants?'

'*We* think so,' said Archie.

'Or is it what you two really want? Wouldn't it be a bit crowded?'

'Not if we move out, which is what we dearly want to do,' Carrie said. 'But we don't want to make her think the suggestion is on our account, Gwen. She has to think it's her own idea – or Aunt Phyllis's.'

Gwen started to smile. 'You always were a bit of a devious one on the quiet, weren't you, Carrie? But you're not going to get your prefab now, are you? You gave up that little dream when you handed it over to Shirley – a bit foolishly, if you want to know what I think.'

'Not really,' Carrie said lightly. 'There are other places.'

Gwen stopped so suddenly that the others had to stop walking too.

'That's not the end of it, is it? You've got somewhere in mind, haven't you? Oh, please don't tell me you're thinking of moving away from Penhallow. I couldn't bear it if I lost you as well as' – she swallowed – 'as well as David – and Velma.'

'Of course we're not thinking of moving away! We belong here, just as you do, and we wouldn't want to live anywhere else.'

'Where then?' Gwen said, obviously relieved.

Carrie spoke quickly. 'We didn't intend to say anything, and it's no more than an idea as yet, so you're not to say a word to anyone, mind. But we did hear that there'll be a cottage going vacant in Tinners' Row at the end of May.'

Chapter 20

It was one thing knowing what you wanted. It was something else deciding how to go about getting it tactfully. There was also the worry, according to Archie's practical mind, that if you didn't put in your bid, somebody else might pip you to the post.

'It's not a race,' Carrie told him crossly. 'It's a sensitive matter, and there's no knowing how Velma's going to take it.'

'She's leaving the cottage, so why should she care who lives in it after she's gone? She won't be here to see it.'

'That's just it. She does care. She's lived in it all her life, and it belonged to her parents before her. There are a lot of memories there, Archie. I know she wouldn't want it taken over by strangers who wouldn't love it as much as she does.'

'So what's your problem? We're not strangers. I can't see why you don't just go and tell her we're interested. Or don't you think she and her snooty husband will consider us good enough to pay the rent?'

'Oh, *Archie*,' Carrie said impatiently, 'of course they'll think we're good enough. In my heart I'm sure she'd be glad we want to live there.'

'*But*? Good God, you look as if you've got the cares of the world on your shoulders, girl. It's a simple enough thing to do, and if you don't feel like asking her about it, I will.'

'You will not! Archie, promise me you won't go barging in until we're ready. Nothing's settled at home yet, is it? Aunt Phyllis has decided to stay for another week, but that doesn't mean she wants to stay for ever.'

She looked away. 'I've had another thought about that, though. We'll get out the old photo albums tonight, ready for when Mum and Aunt Phyllis come back from their day at Penzance. The ones when we were kids, I mean. School photos, and especially the ones on the village green on May Day. Remember how we used to dance around the maypole? Those things go back in history, and I bet they used to do the very same thing when they were girls.'

He grinned. 'You really think that will entice Phyllis to stay longer?'

'Well, it might make them both feel nostalgic. It'll be May Day in a couple of weeks now, and if I know Bernard Bosinney he'll have been training the infants to do their usual performances, dancing around the maypole and showing off to their parents and everyone else in the town. If Aunt Phyllis stays long enough for that, she might start to wonder what she has to go back to Falmouth for.'

Archie put his arms around her. 'I always knew I'd married a genius. I still think you should give Velma a hint about her cottage, though. For all you know, she's already had people interested in renting it.'

Carrie's heart jumped uneasily. There was always that possibility, of course, and she had no idea whether or not Velma had already approached an agent about arranging for the cottage to be rented – or even sold, which was an even more depressing thought. And the more she thought about it, the more she knew that the cottage in Tinners' Row was exactly where she wanted to live. The only place.

'Let's wait until after tonight and then think seriously about what to do.'

Sometimes, thought Carrie – crossing her fingers – when things seemed to be going your way, you felt you had to put the brakes on them, just in case you went hurtling headlong towards disappointment. Though, being an optimist to the last, and strongly believing in omens like a good Cornish woman should, what could possibly go wrong now, she thought?

The ambulance rolled up outside the house just before tea-time on Friday. The sight of it made Carrie feel slightly sick, with overtones of her dad's death and David Trewint's drowning surging into her mind. She rushed outside, in time to see her mother being lifted out on a stretcher, covered by a blanket and protesting all the way. Phyllis stepped out of the ambulance behind her, reasonably unflustered.

'What's happened?' Carrie gasped.

'Now, Carrie, don't make a fuss,' Edna said sharply. Whatever it was, it certainly hadn't robbed her of the power of speech. 'We got off the bus in Penzance, and before I knew what was happening, I tripped and fell awkwardly with my leg twisted beneath me. So much for our day out! I couldn't even get up, and Phyllis had to get someone to send for an ambulance. They carted me off to hospital and told me I'd broken my leg, so they've put it in plaster and said I've got to keep off it until I can learn to manage these blessed crutches. How do they expect me to get upstairs to my own bedroom, I'd like to know!'

When she paused for breath, Phyllis took over as the ambulancemen carried the stretcher indoors, while Edna glared angrily at the small group of children and neighbours who had gathered to see what was going on, and shooed them away.

'She'll be the worst patient ever,' Phyllis said cheerfully. 'She's always been the same, never admitting to pain, and making everyone else suffer by snapping their heads off. We'll all have our work cut out, Carrie.'

Without warning, Carrie burst into tears, instantly hating herself for being so feeble, and also for the myriad thoughts spinning around in her brain now, some of which were less than charitable to her mother's plight.

The dream was fading as quickly as a mirage. She would never be able to leave here now. Velma's cottage would be rented long before they had any chance of moving in. Phyllis wouldn't want to stay with a difficult invalid who was constantly snapping at her. Archie would go off the deep end if he was obliged to see to anything unsavoury. Thoughts of commodes and invalid-bathing loomed large in Carrie's mind right then.

'I shan't be going back home yet, of course,' Phyllis told her, looking keenly into her tear-filled eyes. 'Edna will need me here, and there are things a young girl can't be expected to do, and nor would your mother welcome it.'

'You'll stay?' Carrie said weakly, hardly aware of Archie taking control, sending off the ambulancemen and closing the door firmly behind them after assuring them he would alert Dr Tozer to visit Edna as soon as possible, and getting her settled into an armchair, the cumbersome crutches beside her.

'Of course! I'll stay for as long as necessary, you silly girl. Did you think I was going to desert you now?'

'But you can't stay indefinitely,' Carrie said stupidly, knowing she was saying exactly the opposite of what she really wanted, and unable to stop herself.

Now that the first shock of her mother's accident was over, she felt horribly guilty for her own selfish thoughts. Archie was being so gentle with Edna now, fussing over her and finding a footstool for the stiffly plastered leg that was stuck out in front of her like a reproach, and ordering Carrie to make her a strong cup of tea with half her sugar ration in it.

'Do as he says, love,' Phyllis told her with a little push. 'Keeping your hands busy is the best way to deal with shock. And remember your mum and me have had all day to get used to this!'

Carrie did as she was told, filling the kettle with trembling hands. A fat lot of use she'd be as a nurse! She felt Archie's arms on her shoulders.

'Don't let it get you down, sweetheart. She's a tough old bird,' he said.

'I heard that!' came Edna's voice from the parlour. 'And I'll thank you not to whisper because I shall hear that too! There's nothing wrong with my hearing.'

He chuckled. 'See what I mean?'

'But how are we going to manage? How will she get upstairs with a broken leg? And what about the middle of the night if she needs the lav? Oh, Archie!'

She didn't know her aunt had come into the kitchen until she heard her voice.

'I'll tell you just what we're going to do, Carrie. We had plenty of time to work it all out while we were at the hospital. You're right about it being difficult for Edna to get up and down stairs, and she's just being meddlesome by making such a fuss now. I won't be much use to her downstairs in the front room if she's upstairs, but it's quite big enough for two single beds, so until we can get mine sent down from Falmouth, I'll sleep on the sofa in there and she can have my camp bed.' She coughed delicately. 'We'll have to make do with a bucket for you-know-what for the time being, but we'll get that sorted out. How does that sound? Oh Lordy, now she's crying again, Archie. It's only a broken leg, love. It's not a terminal illness!'

'It sounds a wonderful arrangement if you're both happy about it, Aunt Phyllis,' Carrie almost sobbed.

'Well, happy isn't exactly the word for it,' her aunt

said drily, 'but it'll do. Anyway, your mum always did enjoy being the queen bee when we were girls, so she can enjoy being waited on now, can't she?'

As if to underline her words, there was a tap at the front door, and a neighbour appeared with a jug of steaming soup covered by a lace-edged cloth.

'Just something tasty for poor Mrs Penney's supper,' the neighbour said, eyeing past Carrie to see the state of the invalid.

'Thank you, Mrs Bond. Mum's broken her leg, and she'll be laid up for a while, but I'm sure it won't affect her appetite,' Carrie told her, refusing to invite her in, but giving her the information she needed, thus ensuring that it would be passed down Kellaway Terrace quicker than blinking.

'That was very kind of her,' Phyllis said, as the enticing smell of vegetable soup wafted through the house.

Edna snorted. 'Nosy old trout. Still, she got what she came for, and she's a fair soup-maker, I'll say that for her.'

It seemed to set the seal on the sisters' attitudes for the foreseeable future.

If there was one good thing to be said about Edna's accident, it was that it had happened on a Friday, so the entire weekend was taken up with organizing the change of scene in the house and bringing Phyllis's bed from her flat, along with a list of clothes and other things she wanted.

'It looks as if I'll be here far longer than I thought,

so I might as well settle in comfortably,' she told Carrie and Archie.

Phyllis had balked instantly at Archie's suggestion of bringing her possessions in the butcher's van, so he had managed to hire a small van from a local garage and he and Carrie spent an exhausting couple of days going back and forth between Penhallow and Falmouth, and arranging for the district nurse to call on Edna for a few days, since the doctor's regular visits weren't necessary.

The nurse arranged for a commode to be hired, though Edna declared loudly that she would only use it at night. By day, she would struggle down to the old garden closet they'd had before Walter had installed their bathroom. It was perfectly serviceable, and it would be good to exercise her legs, anyway.

'Perhaps I should think about giving up my job,' Carrie said uneasily, as she and Archie drove back from Falmouth with the single bed and her aunt's other belongings bumping about in the hired van. 'It's hardly fair to leave everything to Aunt Phyllis. Mum's likely to get more cantankerous than ever as the weeks go on.'

'I've told you often enough I don't want my wife working,' Archie said. 'There's no need, and besides, it's a man's place to provide for his wife and family.'

'We don't have a family,' she said crossly.

'I know that, but who's to say we won't have one when we move into Tinners' Row? You know the old wives' tale: new house, new baby!'

It was the nearest he had come to saying he had no

more objections to babies being brought into the world. But Carrie wasn't as elated by his words as she might have been.

'You mean, *if* we move into Tinners' Row, don't you? We've still got to talk to Velma about it, and all this business with Mum has put it right out of my mind.'

'Stop putting it off and go and see her then. For God's sake, Carrie, don't let this business with your mother stop you. It might be just the thing we need to persuade Phyllis to stay permanently.'

'If Mum's bad moods don't put her off completely, you mean.'

She had to admit, though, that Phyllis seemed completely unruffled by Edna's moods. The two sisters complemented one another in a way that could only come from a shared history. The ties of blood were strong enough to overcome any differences in temperament, and there were plenty of those.

On Monday, once the fracas of the weekend had calmed down, the house hummed with the industry of Phyllis's cleaning. And the welcome smell of supper awaiting Carrie when she got home from work lifted her spirits.

'I'd like to visit a friend tonight, Aunt Phyllis. You don't mind, do you?'

'Why on earth should I mind, love? What an odd thing to ask!'

'Well, you've been caring for Mum all day, and I don't want you to think we're imposing on your good nature.'

Edna appeared from the front room, leaning awkwardly on her crutches.

'I don't need watching every minute of the day, Carrie,' she snapped. 'I'm perfectly capable of doing some things for myself, as Phyllis knows very well.'

'She's been doing some knitting for the baby of that friend of yours, as a farewell present when she leaves the village,' Phyllis put in, smiling.

'Has she?' Carrie said blankly.

It was so very tempting at that moment to mention the cottage, and to make an obscure reference in wondering who would move into it, but Archie came home then and the moment passed. Besides, how unsubtle *that* would have been! Far better to leave it until she had talked it over with Velma. And Archie was right. The sooner the better, even though the situation here was far from certain.

'I can't help feeling guilty now,' she told Velma, when she had related the circumstances of Edna's accident and the hectic weekend that had just passed.

'Why would you feel guilty?' Velma said. The baby had just been put down after another struggle with a feed, and Velma looked exhausted, but very glad to have some adult company. 'It wasn't your fault your mother tripped, was it? Just be glad your auntie was there to help.'

'Yes but all this time Archie and I have been hoping she'd decide to give up her flat and move in with us so that Mum wouldn't feel we were abandoning her if we looked for a place of our own. Did I somehow wish this accident on her so that Aunt Phyllis would decide to stay longer?'

'That's just plain silly. Forgive the criticism, Carrie, but you definitely need to move out! From what I know of your mother, she's breathing down your necks all the time, and it's hardly what newlyweds want at the height of passion, is it?'

'We're not newlyweds, remember?'

'Don't be touchy, darling. You missed out on two years of marriage while Archie was in the POW camp, and you virtually had to get to know one another all over again, so that still makes you practically newlyweds. But I agree. What you need to do is persuade that lovely auntie of yours to live with your mum permanently, and then you and Archie can move in here.'

She said it so casually that Carrie knew she couldn't possibly have meant it seriously. She was just making small talk, jollying her out of her gloomy mood. And without warning, she had burst into tears again, and Velma was mopping her up with a hanky and telling her calmly she had better tell her exactly what was wrong.

'You're not expecting, are you?' she added. 'You're showing all the classic signs, Carrie, especially being over-emotional without good reason – although you're understandably upset about your mum, of course—'

'For pity's sake, I'm not expecting, and Mum's a tough old bird, just like Archie said! I'm just being an idiot – and it's something you said, if you must know.'

She was sounding as petulant as Shirley, and she knew she should shake herself out of it but she began to feel young and gauche and awkward and embarrassed, and to wish she had never come at all.

Velma looked genuinely astonished. She caught at Carrie's shaking hands.

'Well, whatever it was, you know I'd never knowingly hurt you, Carrie. So why don't you get it off your chest and then we can be friends again. Not that we ever stopped being friends, and never will, I hope.'

'Even when you're miles away,' Carrie sniffed. 'But I suppose you'll write to me now and then?'

'Of course. Now stop waffling and tell me what I said to upset you!'

Now it was truly embarrassing, but she couldn't put it off for ever, and it was what she had come here for, wasn't it?

'You said you thought it would be a good idea for Aunt Phyllis to move in permanently with Mum and for us to move in here.'

'Well?'

'Well, I know you said it as a joke, but it took me completely off-balance, because it's what we've been thinking about for weeks, Velma, ever since you finally decided to move away. We don't even know what Mum and Aunt Phyllis would have to say about it yet, though, and now I've embarrassed you, haven't I?' she finished in a rush.

She realized Velma was laughing softly. 'Oh, you goose, why on earth did you think I was joking? Don't you think I want more than anything to leave my beloved cottage in good hands? I can think of no one else I'd rather entrust it to, because I know you'll love it and care for it as much as I do. Besides, when Stan and I bring Jack back to Penhallow for a visit any time, I'll always know there's a warm welcome waiting for us here.'

They hugged one another wordlessly, and Carrie made herself believe that at least she was halfway towards her dream.

There was just the little matter of getting her mum and her aunt to feel the same way about it. And since Velma had no intention of offering the cottage to anyone else now, Carrie could afford to bide her time about that.

Village preparations for the May Day celebrations were going ahead with their usual fervour. If Shirley complained that it was taking up all of Bernard's spare time, she couldn't hide her pride in the way he was coaching all the infant children with two left feet to dance around the maypole. On Saturday afternoons they practised their intricate steps on the school playing field, and Shirley volunteered to go along and make sure Bernard's gramophone was kept fully wound up, because once the music wavered, so did the children's steps. It was great fun, and Shirley was surprised to find how much she was enjoying being part of Bernard's world.

The infants' mothers appreciated her being there too, and she couldn't help thinking how lovely it would be when she and Bernard had babies of their own. It would surely obliterate all that other madness once and for all. She would never even think about it now, despite the constant reminders in the newspapers about the Americans' visit to Penzance next month.

As they went home on the Saturday afternoon before the May Day events, Bernard commented on the excitement the GI visit was generating in the area.

'You must have met some of them while they were here,' he said casually.

'Why would you think that?' she asked, flustered at once.

'Well, the farm where you worked was near enough to Penzance to go there some evenings, and you always liked dancing, so I'm sure you went to some of the dances in the town. I'm not blaming you if you did, Shirley. Lord knows you had a hard enough time of it during the war. You had to have some excitement.'

'And you think the Americans provided it?'

'I'm damn sure they did for some girls,' he said with a short laugh. 'Why? Is this a sore subject? Did one of your Land Army girls have a fling with a GI? If she did, it's history now, unless he's coming back for the reunion.'

'He isn't,' Shirley said, before she could stop herself, and immediately wondered if she had trapped herself in this bizarre conversation.

'Oh?' Bernard said. 'How do you know that?'

'I recognized his name in the newspaper list of those who had died,' she said hurriedly. At least that was true. Heartbreakingly true, when she thought of that beautiful young man. She felt Bernard squeeze her arm sympathetically.

'I'm sure she recognized his name too, but she'd have been glad to know what really happened to him instead of always wondering. It makes it all final, you see. Like putting a full stop at the end of a sentence.'

Shirley gave the ghost of a smile. 'That's the schoolteacher in you coming out, I suppose.'

'Something like that,' he said steadily, not watching her.

In an instant, she knew that he knew. Not all of it, of course, never all of it, but some instinct had told him the bare bones of it, the way it did when you loved somebody very much, and when the two of you had grown up together. The way she, too, had always known that his feelings for Marie had gone deeper than he pretended, or was willing to admit, even to himself.

'Things happen in a war, don't they?' she said quietly, suddenly feeling more adult than she had ever done before. 'People change because of circumstances, but afterwards, the lucky ones discover that nothing's changed so very much after all. Or am I talking my usual nonsense?'

'Or perhaps a whole lot of sense, my darling,' Bernard said, pausing to pull her into his arms and kiss her, ignoring the giggles of the infants who were sure to tell their mothers that Sir was kissing his girlfriend in the street in broad daylight.

*

As usual, most of the village turned out for the May Day celebrations on the green. The children performed beautifully, give or take a few wrong moves around the maypole that got them tangled up in their ribbons and only added to the fun.

'Bernard's a clever young man to train them so well,' Edna Penney remarked to her family. 'And just look at Shirley in charge of the gramophone. She's a lucky girl to be marrying him. He's just the type to tame that wild young miss.'

Carrie ignored the barb. It had been a major decision for Edna to turn out. She'd had no intention of hopping there on crutches, and she couldn't walk, so in the end Dr Tozer had produced an ancient wheelchair for her to borrow. She had flatly refused to be seen in it at first, until Carrie and Archie and Phyllis had all told her she was being ridiculous, but she could stay at home on her own and sulk for the day if she wanted to, because they were all going, so there.

In the end she gave in, and was now thoroughly enjoying being a minor celebrity, with folk constantly asking her how she was. Archie had gone to talk with his mates, and Carrie found a moment to slip away from her family and join Velma on the far side of the green, where baby Jack was sleeping peacefully in his pram.

'Just look at him. You'd never think he could be such a little monster in the middle of the night, would you?' Velma said cheerfully.

'You wouldn't be without him, though,' Carrie said.

'Of course I wouldn't. I didn't know what I was missing until he arrived. So have you said anything yet?'

'Not yet, but I don't think Aunt Phyllis is in any hurry to leave. Do we have to make a decision before you go, Velma?'

She shook her head. 'No. Stan and I have talked about it on the telephone and we've both agreed that the cottage will stay empty until you and Archie are ready for it. We both want you to have it, darling. But we'd better not talk about it now. I do believe I can see Gwen over there. Oh, I'm glad. I didn't think she'd feel able to come to this. Let's go and find her.'

The maypole dancing was over, and the Morris dancers were performing to their own jingling accompaniment now. Shirley joined her friends too, and Carrie knew a moment of sheer bliss, because the four of them were together again, the way it had always been, the way they had somehow envisaged it would be for ever.

'It really is good to see you out and about, Gwen,' she said swiftly, before she got over-sentimental.

Gwen shrugged. 'I couldn't stay cooped up for ever, could I? It was David who died, not me. And before you all think I'm being brash and uncaring, I have to say it out loud now and then, to make myself believe it.'

Glossing over that, Carrie said, 'So you'll come to the little farewell supper at Velma's then? She's insisted on doing it herself now, since it would be too much of a bother finding a baby-sitter for Jack.'

'She means she couldn't bear to leave him with anyone else,' Shirley said, 'and I don't blame her. Bernard and I want to start a family once we're married. He obviously loves children, and we want one of our own as soon as possible.'

She avoided their eyes, continuing to gaze down at Jack, blowing bubbles in his sleep now. But the message was clear. A child that belonged to her and Bernard would put the final seal on the past.

Carrie wanted that for herself too. But that was a secret she was keeping to herself. Along with that other secret she and Velma shared.

The plan was that when Velma left for Salisbury she would leave one set of keys with the housing agent, who would take care of Carrie and Archie's future letting details. Carrie would have another set of keys, so that she could go to the cottage and check that all was well there, until such time as she and Archie had sorted things out with her mother, and they could move in. As far as Edna knew, the arrangement was merely for someone to keep an eye on the place while it was empty.

'It's a great idea,' Archie said with a familiar gleam in his eyes. 'It means we can go there whenever we feel like a little privacy.'

'I'm not sure that's what Velma had in mind, Archie. She's being very generous, leaving the cottage empty until we're ready.'

'Well, it's what *I've* got in mind, sweetheart, and I'm more than ready. I don't imagine you'll be making too many objections to having the place to ourselves for a couple of hours now and then, either.'

How could she, when the thought of it made her blood tingle with excitement? It would be their own private place . . . providing there weren't too many prying eyes from the neighbours in Tinners' Row to watch their comings and goings . . . and that was prospect enough to slow down the seductive thoughts.

All the same, it would be lovely to get away from the house for a while on their own since Edna had now taken to the idea of the wheelchair for outings, and Phyllis was happy to push her around the village. The problem was the amount of space the bulky object took up in the house, and skirting around it at times could fray the best of tempers. And there weren't too many of those.

That night Archie gave a yelp of pain when he stubbed his toe on it for the umpteenth time, hopping around the parlour and cursing the wheelchair with a choice string of expletives that he made no attempt to suppress.

'Jesus Christ, that bloody bastard stupid thing!' he yelled. 'The sooner you get back on your bloody pins, old girl, the better I shall effing well like it!'

'Well, that makes two of us,' Edna snapped furiously. 'You don't think I'm stuck here with my leg in a plaster cast for the fun of it, do you? And if you don't like it, you and Carrie can go and live somewhere else, because I won't have blasphemers in my house, nor should I have to listen to your bad language from morning till night. Thank heavens

Phyllis has gone to the shops so she didn't have to hear such disgraceful carryings-on.'

'You're not being fair, Mum,' Carrie said hotly. 'It's only because he hurt his foot that it came out like that. He didn't mean it.'

'Well, *I* meant it about you two finding a place of your own. Me and Phyllis are perfectly content when you young 'uns aren't around all the time. We enjoy one another's company, and we've been thinking a lot about it lately.'

'Have you?' Carrie said, her heart jumping, hardly daring to believe what she was hearing. *Slow down*, she told herself, but it wasn't that easy. 'Seriously, Mum, do you mean you and Aunt Phyllis have been talking about her living here permanently?'

Edna gave one of her eloquent snorts. 'Well, if you hadn't given up your idea of the prefab to that empty-headed Shirley we could have thought about it even more seriously. But thanks to you, we're so cramped here that I'm sure Phyllis will want to go back to her flat as soon as my leg's out of plaster, and I shall really miss having company of my own age in the house.'

'Oh *Mum*!'

She didn't know whether to laugh or cry as she looked wordlessly at Archie, because, in the end, it was all so simple after all.

Chapter 21

Once it was agreed, Edna and Phyllis began making their own plans, but despite the fact that they were pleased that 'the young 'uns' were planning to move out sometime in June, Phyllis couldn't get all her affairs in Falmouth settled instantly, and Edna became more cantankerous as her weeks of limited activity extended. But by then Carrie felt as if she could cope with everything – almost – now that their own hopes and plans were out in the open, and the more tolerant Phyllis merely laughed off her sister's bleating.

'She really is a marvel with Mum,' Carrie told Velma, glad to get things properly organized before her friend went away. 'I suppose it comes from all their childhood memories and knowing each other so well – the same way as I put up with Archie's moods sometimes; I know they don't mean anything.'

'What's this, trouble in Paradise?' Velma said with a smile, and then looked at Carrie more closely. 'It isn't, is it, darling? You and Archie aren't changing your minds about the cottage, are you?'

'No, definitely not! We're thrilled about it. But just when I thought everything was going our way and the future was looking wonderful, Archie's been having nightmares again, the way he did when he first came home from the POW camp. It upsets us both, and I can't understand why it should be happening now.'

'Shirley's usually the one who thinks that when things are going her way something's bound to go wrong, not you. But perhaps Archie feels the same, only in his case it comes out in the shape of nightmares.'

'Have you been reading up on psychology now?'

'No, but perhaps you should. I'm sure there's something in those worthy tomes in the library that might explain it.'

'As a matter of fact I've given in my notice,' Carrie went on, her thoughts diverting as quickly as Shirley's. Perhaps she was turning into Shirley, she thought uneasily . . . 'Archie's been on about it for ages, and as there'll be so much to do with getting Aunt Phyllis's stuff moved in at home, and then ours moved in here, it seemed to be the right time. Besides—'

'Besides which, I daresay you'll be hoping to get one of these little charmers to take up all your time and energy one of these days,' Velma put in when she paused, giving the baby an extra cuddle to show him she didn't mean it.

'Remember how we all dreamed about what would happen when the war ended?' Carrie went on, as if she hadn't spoken. 'We imagined us all pushing our babies out together – except that we didn't include you in that, because you were planning to ask Stan for a divorce. You were going to be the honorary auntie. And look at us now! You're the one with the baby and Gwen's never going to have one – not with David, anyway. Shirley nearly had a disaster, but now she can't wait to get started once she's married. And then there's me.'

Velma wasn't usually slow to pick up on things, but she was too busy tickling Jack beneath his chin to notice the sudden change in Carrie's voice. She noticed the silence, though, and she looked up sharply.

'Is there something you're not telling me, darling?'

Carrie laughed shakily. Without thinking, her hand went to her stomach, still as flat and taut as ever, but it was enough.

'My God, you *are*, aren't you!' Velma said excitedly. 'And I won't be here to see it. Oh, how bloody can life get!' she moaned in a very un-Velma-like way.

But if she thought her dramatics would produce more laughter, she was mistaken.

'I don't know. I just think I might be. I'm not sure. And if I am . . .' Carrie swallowed. 'I don't know how to tell Archie, nor what effect it might have on him. I always thought this moment would be wonderful, and he's even sort of implied that he wouldn't object to us having a baby, but with these nightmares coming back and upsetting him so much – I really don't know, Velma! And what about Gwen and Shirley? How are they going to feel – if it's true? Will it upset Gwen, and will Shirley think I'm upstaging her?'

Velma snapped at her. 'Carrie, I could slap you, I really could. I've always considered you to be the strongest person I know, but just listen to yourself! This is your life you're talking about, yours and Archie's. It's got nothing to do with anyone else, least of all Gwen. I don't think she ever wanted children, anyway. As for Shirley, well, knowing her, it'll only make her more determined to play catch-up and have one of her own, once she and Bernard have done the deed. You're getting this all out of proportion, darling, and it should be the happiest time of your life.'

'I know. It will be. It is. If it's true. And I'm only guessing at the moment. Oh, I really am being an idiot, aren't I?'

'That's putting it mildly. Look, I'm due to take Jack to the doctor for his check-up this afternoon. Come with me, then you can ask his opinion. Anyone else in the surgery will just assume you're there with me.'

Velma and Stan's farewell party was planned for two nights before they left for Salisbury, since the night before would have meant too much frantic activity the next day. Gwen said airily that she supposed Jack was to be her token male, since everyone else would have their partners with them. But she said it in a much calmer voice than might have been expected, and the cottage in Tinners' Row was a very joyful place that evening when they were all together.

'I hope you're taking a good look around and planning where to put our knick-knacks and suchlike,' Archie whispered in Carrie's ear.

'Shut up,' she hissed. 'They'll hear you.'

'Well, it's no secret now that everyone knows we're moving in. I'm glad the secret's out, anyway. My parents were wondering how much longer we could cope with living in your mother's pocket. Only joking, sweetheart!' he added with a chuckle, 'you know I'm fond of the old girl, really.'

She knew that, but Bernard caught Archie's attention then to talk about his best man duties, and she was aware that her heart had given an uneasy little lurch when he mentioned that word secret. Looking around this crowded cottage now, she couldn't help thinking how many secrets were contained here. They were all such close friends, and yet there were still so many things they didn't know about one another, and never would in some cases.

As the excited chatter went on all around her, for a weird, almost surreal moment, Carrie felt as if she was a silent observer looking in on a cameo scene of sheer happiness, and she fervently wished she could preserve the moment for ever.

Shirley was bubbling now, clinging to Bernard's arm, and busily discussing wedding plans with him and Archie. And Gwen, although not overly maternal, was carrying Jack around on her hip as if *she* had no problem with the role of honorary auntie. Velma was luminous, so happy to know that she and Stan had a real future ahead of them with their own little family.

It was Velma who effectively stopped her thoughts. 'Carrie, stop dreaming. This is a celebration of Shirley and Bernard's wedding as well, you know. Stan and I won't be here to see it, so we thought they had better have their present tonight.'

Predictably, Shirley squealed with excitement as Velma handed over the ribbon-wrapped parcel, and then everyone laughed as she unwrapped the set of saucepans and an egg-timer, and read out the note that said 'Instructions how to boil an egg included'.

There were presents for Velma and Stan from everyone too. And once the excitement had died down a little, Stan poured them all a glass of wine and proposed a toast to good friends: those who were present – and those who were absent, he added, with a special smile at Gwen – and to lasting friendship.

'I thought I was going to cry when he looked at Gwen like that,' Carrie said, when she and Archie were on their way home, the last to leave the party. 'It was such a difficult moment for her, but Stan did absolutely the right thing by including David in the toast, even if he didn't mention him by name.'

'He was in all our minds, though,' Archie agreed, but Carrie was no longer thinking about him. Tears were very near the surface, knowing what this evening had really meant.

'I'm going to miss Velma so much, Archie. We've been close friends for so long, and it won't be the same without her. I'm glad we're not moving into the cottage until after Shirley's wedding. It would have seemed like indecent haste otherwise.'

'Sometimes I think I've married a crazy woman,' he

said, but the way he squeezed her hand told her he understood.

Losing David on that terrible February night had been the first interruption to a friendship that had lasted so long, but it had a been a tragic accident that nobody could have foreseen. Velma and Stan were going through choice, and even though Salisbury was hardly the other side of the world Carrie wondered if she would ever see them again. People always said they would write, and so they did, for a while. But circumstances changed, images faded, people drifted apart. It was inevitable.

'You've gone very quiet. What are you thinking about now?' Archie said, as they reached the end of Kellaway Terrace.

'Just that I love you so much, and I can't imagine a life without you, and I never want us to be parted again,' she said in a rush of emotion.

'We won't be, and that's a solemn promise,' he smiled. 'If Hitler couldn't do it permanently, I'm damned sure nobody else is going to separate us, sweetheart. And now that you've given up your job, we can concentrate on making that cottage in Tinners' Row the best little love-nest in the village.'

Sometimes, Carrie thought with a smile, he was more than satisfactory . . . and, whether mysteriously or miraculously, there were no more nightmares.

There was too much to be done to brood over Velma's departure for very long. It was time for Edna to return to the hospital in Penzance to have the hated plaster cast removed from her leg, which she declared had been driving her mad with itching that she couldn't scratch. She came home on the bus with her sister, revelling in the fact that she could now walk properly again, even if she was a bit wobbly and had to be careful not to fall on her weakened leg.

Phyllis needed to spend some time in her flat to sort out her belongings, and nothing was going to happen until after Shirley's wedding. But once the removal van had taken Velma's furniture from the cottage, Carrie and Archie's bits and pieces could be moved in, and the plans for reorganizing the house in Kellaway Terrace could begin. Phyllis would have their old bedroom; the front room could be restored to its usual state; and Edna could sleep in her own room at night.

The wheelchair, the crutches and the despised commode had been scrubbed, disinfected and dispatched to where they came from, and life could return to normal.

Carrie had prepared a meal for when they got back to Penhallow from the hospital, and Edna, although elated to be rid of the plaster cast, was glad to sit down and continue being waited on.

'It won't last,' Phyllis told her niece, as they laid the table between them. 'She'll be taking charge by tomorrow, but it's good to have her smiling again. Oh, and you should have seen Penzance, Carrie. All the flags are out again, the Union Jack and the Stars and Stripes, and you can't imagine how many people were milling about now that the Americans have arrived for their reunion. I swear that half the town had turned out trying to catch a glimpse of those they remembered.'

'Good Lord, so much has been happening lately that I'd completely forgotten about it!' Carrie exclaimed. 'I've hardly had time to look at a newspaper or listen to the wireless.'

Shirley wouldn't have forgotten about it though. With her wedding only a week away, Shirley's nerves would be on edge for more than one reason. The prefabs were now being occupied, and Shirley and Bernard's was ready, which was where they spent most of their spare time now, making it personal with pictures and curtains, and they were already playing at keeping house.

Now that Archie was taking his best man duties seriously, he was going to see Bernard that evening, to discuss his speech among other things. They were also meeting the vicar at the church to agree on the final details.

'As Archie's out, I think I'll go and see how Shirley's getting on at the prefab this evening,' Carrie announced.

'Don't you have enough to do, thinking about the cottage?' her mother complained, never a great fan of Shirley's.

'We're almost ready for the removal day, and there's hardly anything else to do there. You've seen how immaculate Velma kept the cottage! You could eat off her floors, Aunt Phyllis.'

'Well, I suppose you could if you were a dog,' her

aunt replied drily. 'Have you ever thought about having a dog, Carrie?'

'I don't think so,' she said smartly. 'Look, I'm going out now so I'll leave you and Mum in peace to gossip about us to your hearts' content.'

She blew them a kiss to show she was teasing, and went out of the house, smiling. It wasn't a dog she wanted to take up all her time.

It was a beautiful evening, the kind at which Penhallow excelled. The air was heavy with the scents of summer roses and honeysuckle and delphiniums, and there was a profusion of blossoms in every garden, however small. Walking through the streets in the early evening, saying hello to friends and acquaintances that she had known all her life gave her a renewed sense of well-being. She wondered again how Velma could ever bear to leave the place, and knew that the reason could only be due to a stronger love. Penhallow, and Cornwall, had such a hold on Carrie that she knew she could never live anywhere else. And with Archie feeling the same, she knew there would never be that kind of tug on her heart.

The prefabs, which he had once so scathingly referred to as monstrosities, were still blatantly new in a village of old cottages and weathered houses. But trees had been planted all around them which in time would grow and allow the new little houses to be absorbed into the community. They would have their place, just as the old miners' cottages had had theirs in their heyday. Continuity didn't have to end just because something new was added.

As she reached the block of prefabs and saw the one that would have been hers and was now Shirley's, she noticed a bicycle propped up outside, and recognised it as Gwen's. She smiled. Perhaps, like herself, Gwen had felt the need to keep in contact with the friends she had now that one of their number had moved on. The door was ajar, probably to let out some of the new smell of the interior paintwork, and also to let the fragrant evening in, and Carrie pushed the door open.

'Hello! Where are you?'

She heard muffled sounds coming from the bedroom. She couldn't hear their voices distinctly, but, knowing Shirley, she guessed that she would be going over every detail of the wedding; how her hair was going to be done, how she hoped that her dress wouldn't crease, and that the bridesmaids would behave themselves, and that the flowers wouldn't wilt in the heat of the day . . .

'Can anybody join in this conversation?' she began cheerfully, and then her voice died away abruptly.

Shirley and Gwen were sitting on the bed, holding each other tightly, and sobbing their hearts out.

'Oh God, what's happened?' she said, her imagination running wild.

It was hardly the way a soon-to-be-married girl was expected to behave. Had something happened to Bernard? Surely life couldn't be so cruel. Had his French nurse written to him, or even turned up unexpectedly after all, causing a different kind of trauma?

Even at this late stage, was Shirley going to be jilted at the altar?

Without saying a word, the two girls on the bed released their hold on each other and opened out their arms to Carrie. It wasn't the easiest of manoeuvres for the three of them to sit there hugging one another, and even though she didn't have a clue what was going on, Carrie felt the tears well up in her own eyes.

It had to be something terrible. It had to be. Maybe, at the eleventh hour, Shirley had confessed everything to Bernard and the wedding was off.

Finally, she managed to choke out the question.

'Will somebody please tell me what's going on, and why we're behaving like the three witches of *Macbeth*?'

Even as the words left her lips she knew it wasn't the best comparison she could have made, and nor was this any time for levity. Shirley gave an enormous sniff, worthy of Carrie's mother. Imperceptibly, she pulled away from the others, and they did the same, looking at one another with tear-streaked faces.

'We're saying a final goodbye to the past,' Shirley said. 'We were making a solemn pact that nothing that happened before Bernard and David came back to us will ever be mentioned or thought about again. We decided to cry as much as we wanted to, and then be done with it for good and all.'

'And that's it?' At the dramatic, typically Shirley-like explanation, Carrie felt foolish for even asking – and ridiculously left out.

Not that she had ever wanted the kind of secrets between herself and Archie that she and Velma had shared with these two during the latter part of the war years. It would have been unthinkable on her part, and on Archie's too, she was sure, even if he'd had the opportunity.

'Don't you think that's enough?' Gwen said furiously. 'Sometimes, Carrie, you can be so *smug*, and so God-damned perfect!'

Carrie's mouth fell open. She had never felt smug about it, and she wasn't going to do so now. As for being perfect, she was anything but that. Just thinking about how guilty she had felt over virtually manipulating her mum and aunt into living together so that she and Archie could move out was enough to make any such thought laughable. She may not have done it deliberately, but the intention had been there, and that was just as bad.

But nobody here was laughing now, and the wonderful friendship they had all shared for so long seemed suddenly precarious. Somebody had to repair it before it was lost for ever, and however indignant she felt at Gwen's remark, it was better to eat humble pie than to let things crumble irrevocably.

'I'm sorry you feel like that, Gwen, but since we're parting with a few home truths, let me tell you that I don't feel smug, and never perfect, and I think that what you've done here today is a wonderful and decent decision, if you want to know, and I admire you both for it,' she said flatly.

Shirley began blubbing again at once.

'Do you really, Carrie? You know I always look up to your opinions.'

'Well, my opinion right now is that you should stop crying, or your face will stay like that and Bernard will wonder what kind of a sketch he's marrying.'

'You mean a witch, don't you?' Gwen muttered. 'And I'm sorry for what I said, Carrie, but you caught us at the worst moment.'

'Why don't we just forget it then? I came to see how Shirley's getting on here, and I'd quite like a tour of the place.'

'Oh well, that'll take about five minutes flat,' Gwen said, quickly back to normal. But before anybody moved, Shirley put a hand on both their arms.

'Listen you two, I just want to say one thing, because you'll probably never hear it again. You're the best friends a girl ever had – and Velma, too, if she was here. We've been through a lot in the last couple of years, but we've all come through it, haven't we? We're all still here.'

She looked anxiously at Gwen. They weren't all still here. David wasn't.

'Of course we are,' Gwen said steadily, 'and whatever else happens, we've still got each other. So are we giving Carrie a tour of this place or are we going to sit here like total idiots all day?'

By the time they left the prefab and parted company, the sober mood had passed and the excitement of the coming wedding was taking over. From the determined look in Shirley's eyes that day, Carrie knew she was going to put on the performance of her life, and good for her. Nobody was ever going to guess at the heartache that was behind her, nor Gwen's grief over David.

'Gwen and I are going to sit together in the church, as Archie will have to stand beside Bernard,' she told her mum and aunt when she returned home.

'That'll be a comfort for poor Gwen after her loss,' Edna said. 'It won't make her feel so isolated, knowing all you others have got good partners. I'm sure she'll find someone else in time, though. She's a nice-looking girl, and it would be a pity for her to go through life alone.'

'Well, don't ever say as much to her, for goodness' sake,' Carrie exclaimed. 'She was devoted to David, and I'm sure she won't be thinking of anything like that for years, if ever!'

'I'd never say anything of the sort to her face. I'm not that insensitive, Carrie! I've just got the poor girl's interests at heart, and she's far too young to let such an unhappy experience blight the rest of her life.'

If it hadn't been such an about-face on her mother's part, Carrie could almost feel jealous of her concern for 'poor Gwen', she told Archie with a grin. But the grin faded soon enough, as she remembered that she had nothing to be jealous of Gwen for. She was increasingly thankful that Archie was going to be best man at Shirley's wedding, so that Gwen could have her company for the duration of the ceremony. It was going to be quite an ordeal for her.

The morning was as warm and sunny as a June day should be. Once she had seen Archie set off in his best suit for Bernard's house, Carrie took her time dressing in a soft blue-flowered dress, matching hat and crocheted cotton gloves.

'You look a picture, Carrie,' Phyllis told her. 'She's pretty enough to rival the bride, isn't she, Edna?'

Not given to making too many compliments, Edna wouldn't go that far, but she conceded that Carrie looked very nice, and Phyllis's eyes twinkled, telling Carrie that that was as much as she would get from her mother.

Carrie laughed. 'I'm not trying to rival anyone! I just want this day to be as wonderful for Shirley as my wedding day was for me.'

'No reason why it shouldn't be, is there?' Edna said, eagle-eyed as ever.

'None at all. And I'm off now. I'm calling for Gwen and we're walking to the church together. We want to be there in good time.'

She didn't want to rush. She wanted to arrive looking serene and unflustered after the brisk activity of the last few weeks. So much had changed in so short a time. Velma had gone; Shirley and Bernard would be moving into their prefab right after the wedding; Aunt Phyllis would be spending time at her flat before moving in with Edna permanently, and then she and Archie would be moving into Tinners' Row. So many changes, so much to look forward to . . . and she had to be strong for Gwen today, and for Shirley too.

Pre-wedding nerves weren't the only things Shirley had to contend with, but Carrie was sure that, now the day was here, she would find an inner strength. And she truly loved Bernard, which was the most important thing of all.

'All right?' she whispered to Gwen when they were shown to their seats in the church by Bernard's brothers, an impressive-looking pair of young ushers.

'I'm fine,' Gwen whispered back, calm and pale and looking quite beautiful, thought Carrie, in her mauve dress and hat.

They had little time to say anything more then, because the organ notes rang out to announce the arrival of the bride, and they turned to see Shirley, more ethereal a bride than anything Hollywood could create, not looking to left or right until she came level with her two best friends. She gave them the slightest nod and a trembling smile, and then her chin lifted slightly, and they knew she would carry this through with her usual flair.

As the couple repeated their vows, the lovely old traditional service brought no more than a shuddering sigh from Gwen as they reached the words 'until death do us part'. Carrie gripped her hand, knowing that all her thoughts must be with David, and then the words of the service moved on, and the moment had passed.

All too quickly it was all over, and in time-honoured Penhallow tradition the bride and groom led the entire congregation in the walk back to the village hall for the celebrations, being applauded all the way by neighbours and well-wishers who had turned out to watch the spectacle as always.

After the meal had been eaten and the toasts to the happy couple had been drunk, Archie's speech brought laughter and applause, and Carrie breathed a sigh of relief that he hadn't said anything to offend anyone. You never knew with Archie . . . And then the bride and groom circulated to thank people, and Shirley finally reached the table where Carrie and Gwen were sitting. She clasped their hands.

'Did I do all right?' she said, giggling a little with wine and excitement.

'You were wonderful,' Carrie said. 'A star in the making if I ever saw one.'

'Gwen?'

'I was proud of you, Shirley,' Gwen said steadily.

'I'm proud of you too,' Shirley told her softly, and then Bernard whisked her away to talk to other guests.

'She'll be all right, and so will you,' Carrie said.

'I know. And you too, once you and Archie move into Velma's cottage. It's the best thing that could have happened, Carrie. Funny how things turn out, isn't it?'

Carrie was thinking the same thing two weeks later, when they finally closed the door of the cottage behind them and looked around them with immense joy, knowing that this was where they belonged, and they were home at last. Archie folded her in his arms, looking down into her face, and her spirit flooded with happiness, knowing his excitement was as palpable as her own.

Ever since she was six and he was ten, when she had first solemnly declared that she was going to marry him when she grew up, she had been aware of his every mood, good or bad. But her innate Cornish sixth sense told her that the bad times were now over, and a surge of sensual pleasure ran through her veins, knowing how much she was loved and desired.

'So how does it feel, Mrs Pollard, to be a lady of leisure in your own home at last, without the dragon lady looking over your shoulder all the time?' Archie said teasingly, interspersing each word with little kisses.

'Are you referring to my mother?' she said with a laugh.

'Who else? But she'll never be watching us again, nor checking on how early we go to bed, nor how late we get up on Sunday mornings. From now on, it'll be just the two of us in our own place, doing exactly what we like, whenever we like, and that sounds pretty damn good to me.'

'Does it?' Carrie twisted slightly in his arms so that she could look right up into his face. His dear, beloved face, that she had loved for all these years.

'Well, doesn't it?'

'Oh yes, yes *yes*! It sounds like everything I ever wanted. Except for one thing, Archie.' Her voice faltered, grew husky with emotion. 'Early next year there will be more than just the two of us here. I should have told you before, but I wanted to wait until I was sure, and I know I shouldn't have kept it a secret, but this seemed like the right time and the right place for sharing the best secret of all. You're not angry with me, are you?'

She held her breath. It was a secret that had been

bursting to be told, but until they were actually here it had seemed so right not to tell him, or anyone, about the baby she knew she carried now. She couldn't bear it if he wasn't as overjoyed about it as she was . . . and she would know instantly.

He didn't answer for a moment, and then a smile illuminated his face, and his arms enfolded her again, just as surely as the love and warmth of this weathered old cottage wrapped itself around them.